THE UNWANTED DEAD

Straight after graduating in Spanish and French, Chris Lloyd hopped on a bus from Cardiff to Catalonia and stayed there for over twenty years. He has also lived in Grenoble – researching the French Resistance movement – as well as in the Basque Country and Madrid, where he taught English and worked in educational publishing and as a travel writer. He now lives in South Wales and is a translator and novelist.

Lloyd is also the author of the Elisenda Domènech crime series, featuring a police officer with the newly-devolved Catalan police force. The result of his lifelong interest in World War Two and resistance and collaboration in Occupied France, *The Unwanted Dead* is his first novel set in Paris, featuring Detective Eddie Giral.

THE UNWANTED DEAD

Chris Lloyd

ORION

First published in Great Britain in 2020 by Orion Fiction,
an imprint of The Orion Publishing Group Ltd.,
Carmelite House, 50 Victoria Embankment
London EC4Y 0DZ

An Hachette UK Company

1 3 5 7 9 10 8 6 4 2

A CIP catalogue record for this book
is available from the British Library.

ISBN (Hardback) 978 1 4091 9025 7
ISBN (Trade Paperback) 978 1 4091 9026 4
ISBN (eBook) 978 1 4091 9028 8

Typeset by Deltatype Ltd, Birkenhead, Merseyside

Printed in Great Britain by Clays Ltd, Elcograf S.p.A.

www.orionbooks.co.uk

For Liz. For everything.

Friday 14th June 1940

I

Two things happened on June the fourteenth, 1940.

Four men no one knew died in a railway yard and a fifth man stepped off a balcony.

There were other things that happened on June the fourteenth, 1940.

The soldiers of the 187th tank destroyers wanted to look their best as they invaded Paris, so they took a wash in the muddy waters of the Ourcq Canal, six kilometres outside the city. In a race to grab the best beds, General Bogislav von Studnitz set up shop in the Crillon Hotel, while all around him, German officers spread their dusty uniforms on the city's finest bed linen. And in the summer sun, Wehrmacht bands honked endlessly up and down a deserted Champs-Élysées until finally a giant swastika was unfurled over the tomb of the unknown soldier just in case there was anyone left in Paris who didn't yet know we'd lost.

But in my world, four men no one knew died in a railway yard and a fifth man stepped off a balcony.

'Christ, what a stink,' Auban cursed.

'Show some respect, Detective,' I told him. A bruiser in the right-wing leagues who'd brawled his way through the thirties, Auban was tough and muscular. Even in the growing heat of a summer morning, he dressed in a way that wouldn't let you

3

forget that, a heavy leather jacket over a white shirt so tight as to show off his chest. He glared at me and turned away.

'This way, Inspector Giral,' he said through gritted teeth. His usual cocksure insolence was now suffused with a fear he couldn't hide. I glanced to either side of me and knew why.

Lined up along the railway embankment were row upon row of German soldiers. A gauntlet of faceless figures that had watched me pick my way along the soot-greased sleepers of the marshalling yard to where Auban was waiting for me. They hadn't shifted a centimetre in all that time. The ones on the right partially obscured the low sun, their long shadows curling across the oil and grime of the railway yard, picking us out as we walked. To the left, hard young faces in bitter contrast stared impassively. I could make out an officer barely fifty metres away looking intently at me, his face expressionless. They were the first Germans I saw that day, some of the first to enter the city. They watched us now in silence, their machine guns pointing at the ground, the grey of their battle dress soaking the black clouds out of the sky.

'They been here all the time?' I asked Auban. He nodded.

We set off towards a group of half a dozen uniformed police waiting for us by some goods trucks. The normally bustling railway yard to the south of Gare d'Austerlitz was unnaturally quiet. No trains moved in or out. We picked our way through rubbish strewn along the tracks. In the streets nearby and all over the city, it had lain uncollected for weeks, left to rot while the Germans advanced on Paris and refuse was the least of anyone's worries.

Auban was right. It did stink. A smell of death and decay in the air. Whether it was the scene that I knew awaited me or the city itself, I couldn't decide. Under the scrutiny of the German soldiers, we walked past a dead dog lying on the jumble of tracks, its tongue swollen and lolling, its eyes wide open in panic. Flies rose and fell in a putrescent murmuration. I faltered for a moment. There was another smell, faint but acrid, lying underneath – like bitter pineapple doused in black pepper. Only it was different from how I'd remembered it. I shook my head to get rid of it.

I looked away from the dog to see a police sergeant hurrying towards us along the track. My breath caught in my throat and I almost stumbled. I glanced at Auban but he hadn't noticed. I looked back at the figure running at me and fought down my panic. His face was disfigured by a heavy gas mask and the smell that had been lurking outside my senses finally engulfed my memory.

His voice muffled, the sergeant held out a gas mask each for me and Auban. 'You need to put this on, Eddie.'

Fighting to stop my hand from shaking, I reached out for mine. It was standard army issue. Not much better than the ones we'd been made to wear the last time Germany went to war with us. Trying to keep control of my breathing, I struggled not to relive the same dark panic as when I'd last worn one a lifetime ago. I recalled another morning when I'd briefly felt the gas burn my nostrils and eyes before getting my mask on in time and peering through the yellow fog at the unlucky ones who'd left it too late slowly dying in the bottom of a trench.

'It's just a precaution,' I heard the sergeant say. 'The gas will have dissipated by now, but better safe than sorry.'

He led us towards half a dozen uniformed cops huddled in a tight circle, each one wearing a mask.

'Good morning, Eddie,' the only civilian there said to me. 'Not every day we have an audience.'

Bouchard, the forensic doctor, was only a couple of years older than me, but he always wore an old-fashioned cutaway suit and kept his salt-and-pepper hair combed back like a Belle Époque philosopher. Despite the mask obscuring his face, his presence calmed me.

'Tough crowd, I reckon. I'll let you take the hat round after.'

The sergeant signalled to us that we should follow him. Without a word, he led us to a row of three goods trucks parked in a siding, their sliding doors pulled shut. He pointed at the middle truck. The ventilation grille near the roof had been stuffed tightly with rags. A small gap showed, where some of the padding had come loose. I nodded to the sergeant to show him I understood the significance.

All three of us stepped forward to the truck. Auban hung back. The lock on the door had already been opened, a metal bar that had evidently been wedged to hold it in place lay on the ground. Cautiously, the sergeant slid the door back and leaned in, climbing on to the metal step and pulling himself up. He pointed at something by the far wall. A small mound of dark broken glass, a stain barely visible on the wooden floor around it. Yellowish dust motes, raised by the sergeant's movements, clung in the meagre light and slowly settled back to the rough planks.

'Chlorine,' he said, his voice distorted.

I climbed in, followed by Bouchard. I had to wait a moment for my eyes to get used to the gloom and to the unreal vision of the murky interior through the cheap glass of the mask. I wished they hadn't. I saw a man lying slumped on the opposite side, his hand still reaching up to the door. He'd died trying to prise the lock open. I looked at him and saw one more time the desperate, bulging eyes and swollen throat I'd hoped I'd never witness again. The same discoloured saliva dribbling down his chin onto his chest. My breath drew shallow in the tight mask.

The sergeant pointed to the left. Another scattering of broken glass lay on the floor. On the wall above it, a damp stain showed where the flask had shattered against the wood. A second man lay on the ground under the grille, some of the wadding in his hand, his face also red and swollen. The same look of torture and panic was etched on his features. Beyond him, two others lay. The planks at their feet scratched where they'd tried to get away from the gas, their heads huddled in final resignation against the far wall. I'd seen trenches filled with men like this, but few sights as despairing as the one in the grimy goods truck in a railway siding on the first real morning of my new war.

I felt a tightness grip my chest, not from the gas but from the feel of the mask clawing at my face. Unable to bear it a moment longer, I ripped it off and stood at the truck door, sucking in mouthfuls of air from outside. The sergeant lunged at me. Through his own mask, I could see his horror.

'Are you insane, Eddie?' I could just make out his words.

'The gas has gone. You said so yourself.' I spoke angrily to hide my fear. I turned to face inwards but stayed at the truck door. 'We can't work in here. Take the bodies outside and Doctor Bouchard can do his initial examination there.'

'This is not usual, Eddie,' Bouchard objected.

I looked at the scene around me, both inside and outside the truck. 'You're telling me. Get the bodies out.'

Reluctantly agreeing, the sergeant ordered some of his men to carry the four dead men out and away from the truck. 'One of you collect the pieces of glass from the gas canisters and put them in separate boxes,' he ordered. 'Wear gloves.'

'And keep your masks on,' I added. 'If this is chlorine gas, it's heavier than air. If there is any left, it'll be floating on the floor of the truck.' I needn't have spoken. I was the only one to have taken my mask off. 'And remove the packing from the windows and close the doors. We'll let the gas disperse completely and search the trucks properly later. It'll be too diluted with the outside air to do any more damage.'

Bouchard had stepped down from the truck and taken his mask off. He adjusted his semi-lunettes over his aquiline nose and looked up at me. I could see the concern on his face.

'I've seen all this before,' I reassured him. 'The gas has gone, I know. Will the forensic institute be able to get fingerprints from the rags?'

He looked doubtful. 'I don't know. Not that there's anyone left there to try. Not with this lot in town.' He gestured at the Germans and turned to follow the first of the bodies to a clear piece of ground some twenty metres from the wagon.

I jumped down from the truck and threw my mask to the ground. Walking away, I took in huge gulps of air, not worrying for once about the soot and corrosion that was suffocating the city. I looked up. Greasy clouds of black smoke clung to the dawn sky, throwing a shadow over Paris. They were from the fuel dumps outside the city. Burned, some were saying, by our own retreating French army. Others reckoned the American oil companies had set fire to their own depots. Either way, it had been to stop the Germans getting their hands on it. It didn't seem to be making any difference, not to the invaders. It was just us in the city who were suffering from the fingers of scum that clawed their way into your mouth and nose and on to your clothes. It had rained last night, the first we'd had in a month, and I had to walk gingerly between the tracks along the wooden railway sleepers, their usual coating of oil and soot thickened and made murderous by the coarse black dew that had fallen.

Looking around me, I saw Bouchard start a preliminary examination on the four bodies, laid out on tarpaulins on the ground. It was unusual, I knew, but the only option I saw possible. He'd carry out the proper post mortem at the forensic institute. Beyond the three trucks in a battery of sidings, the Germans continued to watch in silence. I'd almost forgotten them. Behind them lay a ragtag jumble of makeshift huts, thrown up over the years like a low-rise skyline, most of them illegally. Had the soldiers not been there, I'd have sent some of the uniformed cops in to take a look. North of the trucks lay the workshops and covered sidings, the passenger terminus past them again to the left. To the south, the tracks disappeared into the streets on their journey out of the city. I watched them narrow and fade, partly longing to follow them, partly not, I was surprised to realise. Behind me, I turned to see row upon row of tracks heading south to north. In the middle, stood a rickety tower reached by a narrow staircase that would have offered a view over the whole of the yard.

A uniformed cop came to fetch me, sent by the sergeant. He'd also removed his mask. Nervously, he hefted the rifle slung over his shoulder. Police in the city had been carrying rifles ever since the Germans had broken through the Ardennes, supposedly to defend on every street corner. Now it seemed like a worthless red rag waving provocation at the occupying troops. The policeman in front of me wore his rifle reluctantly.

'The workers who found the truck are over here, Eddie,' the sergeant explained when I rejoined him.

He led me to where a thickset man in his fifties wearing a leather jerkin over oil-stained blue overalls was standing. He looked like a pocket Mussolini, only with a full head of dark hair and without the pugnacious jaw.

'Le Bailly,' he introduced himself. 'I'm the union official for the Gare d'Austerlitz.'

'You should probably keep quiet about that right now.' I half-gestured to the Germans. 'Were they here when you found the truck?'

9

He nodded. The ground shook underfoot and Le Bailly and I looked at each other, both recognising the sensation. 'And now here's more of the bastards,' he added.

Underscoring the strange hush of the railway yard was the noise of lorries and tanks rumbling through the streets of our city, their tyres and tracks reverberating through the ground. In the midst of it, a telephone rang. I looked over to see the German officer talking calmly on a field telephone held for him by a soldier. He kept looking over at us and at the other police and nodding his head. I turned back to Le Bailly.

'See anyone else?'

'No one.' He gestured at two other workers standing a short distance away. 'We just noticed the smell and I told those two to get away from the trucks as quickly as possible. I was in the last war. It's not a smell you forget.'

I had to agree with him. I called Auban over and told him to go and talk to the two workers, a tall, lugubrious one with a moustache that had outgrown his face and a squat, bullet-headed heavy with an expression as hostile as Auban's grace.

I watched him go and looked at Le Bailly. 'Where had the trucks come from?'

'They were here overnight. They were going to be coupled to a train that was supposed to be leaving this morning, but nothing's running today.'

Before I could ask another question, I heard a sound. Le Bailly reacted at the same time as I did. Another memory of the last war. Rifles being cocked. I turned to see the German officer moving towards the group of cops nearest the trucks. His soldiers followed him, their weapons raised. I glanced the other way, the troops the other side were walking towards us. I felt my gun in my holster. The officer spoke to one of the uniforms, who pointed at me. He came towards me, flanked by four soldiers.

'You are the senior police officer here?' he asked me in passably good French. He'd unholstered his Luger and was idly pointing it in my direction. I'd seen so many of his type in the last war, on our side and theirs. They looked like they saw themselves permanently on a white horse, looking down at the rest of us festering in the mire. With his white blond hair and sculpted cheekbones, he seemed untouched by the soot and stench the rest of us faced.

'Yes. No need to ask if you are.'

'Why would that be?'

'You're not covered in shit like everyone else.'

He idly pointed his Luger more meaningfully. I could see him struggle between laughing uncertainly or shooting me. Composure and a faint smirk won. 'I am an officer in the Wehrmacht. You are mistaken if you think I will tolerate being spoken to like this.'

I pointed to the group of cops being shepherded by the German soldiers, their guns trained on the police. 'And I'm tired, angry and trying to do my job despite you and Adolf getting in my way. You're mistaken if you think I'll tolerate my officers being mistreated like this.'

The smirk went up a scintilla or two. 'I will remember that.' He turned and shouted a command at the soldiers. They backed off a little from the other cops and lowered their rifles. The officer turned back to me, his gun still raised, not enough to be directly threatening, but enough to say what he wanted to say. 'I am Hauptmann Karl Weber of the 87th Infantry Division of the Wehrmacht. I have to inform you that the German High Command has issued the order for all French citizens to be disarmed.'

'We are the police.'

'Including the police. I must ask you to surrender your weapons.'

I looked at the soldiers gazing at the cops like foxes in a hen house. I could see little choice. 'Do I have your word that the police won't be harmed?'

'You do.'

I signalled to the others to hand over their guns. The German soldiers quickly gathered the guns and rifles and carried them to a junior officer still standing on the perimeter. Hauptmann Weber kept his eyes on me the whole time, his expression an odd blend of aloof superiority and smiling insolence.

I surrendered my pistol to him.

'Thank you,' he said.

He shouted an order and the soldiers raised their weapons. I heard one cock his rifle and I looked at Weber. I could feel my anger rising, but with a faint smile on his face, he called a second order and his men fell away, drawing back to their original positions along the side of the railway tracks.

'I will leave you to get on with your investigation,' he told me, withdrawing to join his troops. 'I think we know where we stand now.'

'Why the fuck are they still there?' the sergeant hissed. 'We're unarmed.'

Bouchard and I couldn't help looking up. Silent as the heroic statues they seemed to love, the German soldiers were still lined up above us an hour later as we watched Bouchard checking the bodies of the four men. The only one speaking was the officer, a litany of asides lost to us in the ashen air that had the men either side of him sniggering.

'It's not because of us,' I told him. 'It's to secure the railway. Make sure our army can't use it to break in or out.'

'We have an army?' Bouchard commented.

A couple of young cops came over with a box each. 'The two gas bottles,' one of them explained. 'What there is of them.'

'Take them to the station,' I told them. 'Make sure Sergeant Mayer gets them.'

The relief palpable in the way they moved, they hurried to the police cars parked at the southern entrance to the yard and left the scene. Auban and eight other uniforms were standing nearby, waiting to take the bodies away when Bouchard gave the say-so. The three railway workers had been joined by half a dozen more and stood a small distance away, their curiosity overcoming their fear of the Germans.

The sergeant and I looked through the men's clothes. They were once good quality but now ragged. There was nothing in any of the pockets. No money and no papers to identify them.

'Robbed?' the sergeant asked. 'Or refugees?'

'Or both.' I found a tailor's label in one of the jackets and showed it to the sergeant. 'Probably foreign. This was made somewhere called Bydgoszcz.'

'Poland,' he replied. 'Seen it on the newsreels.'

Involuntarily, I looked at the four men and wondered what had happened to bring them here, to their death in a grimy railway truck on the edge of a strange city with no possessions and no identity.

'It'll be chlorine gas.' Bouchard cut across my thoughts. 'I'll know more when I cut them up, but we can take that as read.'

'Chlorine?' I wasn't certain. The smell wasn't exactly how I'd remembered it.

'How would they have died?' Auban asked the doctor. He was a few years too young to have served in the last war and had the morbid interest of those who wrongly felt they'd somehow missed out.

'Horribly, if you really want to know. The chlorine reacted

with the liquid in the lungs and turned it to hydrochloric acid. It simply ate away at them from the inside.'

'Christ,' the sergeant commented. 'It must be an agonising death.'

My voice almost broke at last. 'It is. I never thought I'd see it again. We can only hope this really is the last time.'

'Would you count on it, Eddie?' Bouchard asked, getting slowly to his feet.

2

I was alone in a river of tracks. The four bodies had been carried away to a waiting lorry by the last of the uniformed police. Auban had gone. Bouchard had snapped his bag shut and waited for me.

'Walk with you to the cars?' he'd asked me.

'I'll wait. When will you do the post mortems?'

'Tomorrow.'

'This afternoon.'

Bouchard had nodded and looked around us at the soldiers. They seemed to be growing restless. 'Don't stay too long, Eddie.'

I watched him go and shot a glance at the German officer. The sun was high now and a bead of sweat ran down my cheek. I rubbed it and saw a smudge of soot on my fingertip. Taking one last look at the truck seeping its wasted poison into the air, I scanned the yards before walking south towards the gate and my car, gunmetal eyes on me all the way. I heard a rifle bolt being pulled and I looked up to see a soldier standing next to Hauptmann Weber putting a bullet in the breech. Weber looked at me, the same aloof scorn on his face, and pointed his fingers at me like a gun.

I raised my hand in salute. 'Not if I get you first, you bastard,' I murmured with a smile.

Back in my car, my face crumpled and I held my head in my hands. The gas mask. I closed my eyes for a moment and immediately saw a cloud of smoke. A trench slowly emerged through the haze and the sound of shells and rifles quickly grew. I hurriedly opened my eyes again and the sights and sounds were gone in an instant. I could feel my whole body shaking. They were images I'd kept out of my head for over a decade. Ones I thought I'd seen the last of.

'If the bastards don't get me first.'

I looked around me. I was out of sight of the Germans. Reaching for the ledge I'd put in underneath the dashboard, I pulled out a Luger I kept in a clip and stared at it. It was one I'd liberated from a German officer in the trenches at Verdun. I used to keep it in my flat, part of a ritual I thought I'd got over. I knew I daren't close my eyes again. Shaking my head, I took out the little Manufrance pistol instead from another clip alongside the first. It always looked like a kid's toy but it could still do what it had to. I replaced the Luger behind the dashboard and shoved the Manufrance in my waistband inside my shirt.

'I'm a policeman and I carry a gun,' I said out loud, recalling the bright-eyed sneer of the German officer.

I drove off for the river and police headquarters. In the empty streets, one sense of unreality had given way to another. Our phony war had suddenly become a real one and each felt as illusory as the other. Paris had been a ghost town for the best part of a month and was now haunted by the crash of heavy tyres and boots on cobbles. I heard music, harsh and martial, echo through the halls of the city as I drove down lifeless alleys and along deserted boulevards, past empty apartment buildings and boarded-up shops like coins on a dead man's eyes. The richer the area, the emptier the streets. Millions had fled the city before the Germans came. Two-thirds of the population had gone. It was the old and the poor who hadn't been able to get away. And the cops. There was no life, no bustle. Paris was still there, but it was no longer Paris.

I turned onto a main road and came face to face with a German motorbike and sidecar flagging me down. I reached for the gun in my waistband, but the two soldiers simply turned away from me to watch a marching band dirge victoriously past a scattering of French civilians lining the pavement, a look of fearful defiance on their faces. A small boy leaned into his mother, not wanting to watch. An elderly couple cried silently. The band passed and the soldier in the sidecar signalled me to carry on my way. Our streets were now German, our role to move aside.

As the sound of the marching band died away, two German soldiers in a field-green truck following it pulled up in front of the local *mairie* and set up a loudspeaker. Curious, I got out to see what was happening. I stood next to an ancient guy in a grubby white shirt, its collar long gone.

The loudspeaker whistled into life and told us in accented French that German troops had occupied Paris.

'You don't fucking say,' the old guy next to me said. I decided I liked him.

The metal funnel then asked us to stay calm and told us that the request to stay calm must be obeyed.

'That should do the trick,' my commentator added.

We were also told that the German High Command would tolerate no act of hostility. Aggression or sabotage would be punished by death. Arms must be turned in and we were all to stay indoors for forty-eight hours.

'Just in case you find it hard to stay calm.' The old guy shook his head at me and slowly shuffled away. With a face like old army boots, he looked ancient enough to have been around the last time the Germans occupied us, back in 1870.

I watched the two Germans pack their truck away and head off, no doubt to the next district *mairie* on their list. The few people who heard the message melted away, heading for home to close the shutters and lock the doors if they had any sense.

I drove straight to the criminal investigation headquarters at thirty-six, Quai des Orfèvres, Thirty-Six as we all called it, where the first thing they told me was that I had to hand in my gun.

'Already done it,' I told the commissioner, explaining the incident with the German soldiers at the railway sidings. I didn't tell him about the Manufrance in my waistband.

The second thing they told me was that I had to put my watch forward an hour.

'We're on Berlin time now,' Commissioner Dax told me.

'I'm not.' I left my watch as it was. For some reason, the Germans telling us what the time was in Paris now they were here annoyed me more than anything else I'd seen that morning. 'They can wait for me.'

'The whole of the German army's going to wait for you?'

'They'll get used to it. It's either that or change it for me. Even then I'll only change it back.'

Dax just shrugged at that. A painfully thin man with a cassoulet and wine paunch and horn-rimmed glasses on a gaunt face, he was surprisingly expressive in his shrugs. It made up for the clipped paucity of his words. I told him about the four bodies found at the railway sidings.

'Do we know their identities?' he asked me.

'Not yet. They had no papers on them, but I think they're Polish. Refugees, possibly.'

'Or fighters. The gas was to attack the Germans and it broke by accident?'

'I don't see it. It takes more force to break the glass on a gas canister than just by accident. And they had no other weapons on them. I think they were simply trying to get out of the city and someone stopped them.'

'We also need to know where the gas came from, Eddie. Keep me informed. I don't want you doing anything without my knowing. Least of all now.'

'The Germans that were there. Can't we just charge them with it and have done?'

Dax rolled his eyes at me and went back to his office. I told you he was expressive.

I took a moment to stare out of the window in the main detectives' room. I should have seen barges on the river, cars weaving angrily along the road three floors below, men and women walking in a hurry to get somewhere, lovers kissing on the ancient stone bridge, police coming and going in and out of the building. Instead I saw nothing. No movement, no life. Grey streets under a cloud of black smoke from the burning oil to the north of the city. South across the river, the Fifth Arrondissement, my home, was a ragged film set waiting for the actors to return. But I could hear. A rumble of heavy vehicles still rolling through the city, more sporadic now, but enough to rattle the glass in the windows.

'Heading south,' Tavernier, an old cop told me, his voice numb. Until that day, he'd thought he'd been serving out his time until he retired. 'The Germans. A lot of them are stopping here, but most of them are crossing the city, heading south to catch up with the front.'

I just nodded. Barthe, a bluff Grenoblois with a drinker's bulbous nose, joined in. 'They say some of our boys got through down by the Porte d'Orléans, trying to make it south to join up with the army. The Boches missed them.'

The Boches. The word we'd used for the Germans in the last war had made a comeback since the start of the new one. Something else I'd hoped to see the last of.

'Good,' Tavernier replied, interrupting my thoughts. 'I saw a French unit retreating through my neighbourhood this morning. Running in panic. Mind you, I haven't heard anything bad so far about the Germans. Not like the stories you hear in Poland.'

'And the Netherlands. Let's hope it lasts. They bombed the shit out of Rotterdam.'

I didn't have the heart to join in so I went downstairs to see Mayer, the sergeant in charge of the evidence room.

'I've got something to show you,' he told me.

He made me wait a second while he went to soak a couple of rags in water from a glass flask. I was surprised he knew the old soldier's trick. He was too young to have fought in the last war. A slim, fine-featured man in his early thirties from the Alsace, he had the fingers of a concert pianist and the mind of a terrier denied a bone. Not for the first time, I wished he was a detective working with me and Auban was languishing down here in the basement. He handed me one of the pieces of cloth. I was reluctant to use it straight away.

'Any news from your family?' I asked him.

Like everyone else in Strasbourg, his parents had been evacuated last September between the Germans invading Poland and us declaring war on them. They'd come to live with Mayer in Paris, but had fled the city as the Germans got nearer. Since Adolf looked on Alsace as German, the ethnic French from the area were rightly fearful of what the invaders might have in store for them. Mayer had stayed, unwilling to believe the Germans would single him out in Paris.

'They're still in Bordeaux. I don't know where they're going to go from there.'

We covered our mouth and nose with the rags and he showed me to a walk-in cupboard where a metal box sat on a shelf. He took it down and opened it. Inside was the broken glass from the gas bottles that had been used to kill the four men.

He gestured to the rags covering our faces. 'It's most likely harmless now, but I'd sooner be certain.'

Me too, I said with my eyes. I could feel rivulets of sweat run down into them at the memory of ripping the mask off in the truck.

'What do you notice about it?' he asked me through the thin material.

'It's French,' I said in surprise. I could just make out parts of words embossed on the shards.

'Exactly. Phosgene gas. One of ours from the last war.'

I shook my head and led him back out into the main store room. I breathed in heavily after he shut the door and we put the rags down. Never had police sweat in a mouldy basement smelt so refined. 'I don't think it's phosgene. It smells of rancid pineapple, which makes it chlorine. Only it's different from how I remember it.'

'Phosgene or chlorine, it'll be over twenty years old, at least. Production of these ended after the war and the army no longer uses them. The smell must have changed as the gas deteriorated.'

'Does the army still keep a stock of them?'

'Not as far as I know, but it's impossible to say now.'

I let out a wry laugh. 'No stocks, no records, no army. So whoever used it had kept it as a souvenir from the last war.'

'Or they bought it from someone else who's got a cache of it somewhere. I'm surprised it didn't do more damage. It should have spread further.'

'That could be because of its age. It didn't work as well as it would have when new. That's also why I don't think it can be phosgene. That acts too slowly, it could take up to two days for any symptoms to show. If you were wanting to kill your victims quickly, you'd use chlorine. And there were yellow specks in the air in the truck. That's why the army stopped using chlorine, you could see the yellow cloud coming. Phosgene was colourless.'

Despite my argument, I still wasn't sure. The smell was wrong. I closed my eyes for the briefest of moments and saw again the cloud of yellow smoke drifting towards our trenches and the row upon row of men panicking for their lives.

'Why was it kept in glass bottles?' Mayer pulled me out in time.

'They were placed in the warhead of the shell. They burst when the shell landed and released the gas.'

'I thought firing gas in shells was supposed to be against the Hague Convention.'

'It was. But that didn't stop anyone.'

Mayer closed the box. 'And here we are again.'

'Not much.'

I'd left Mayer and gone back to the room I shared with three other officers, empty for the moment, and called Auban in to ask him what he'd learned from the two workers at the railway yard. That was his answer. Not much.

'Did you even get their names?'

He shrugged like it was the dumbest question he'd heard.

'Right, get back to the yard and question them both. I want their statements by this afternoon. And then check the buildings overlooking the sidings and make sure those trucks stay put until we say they can be moved.'

'Fuck's sake, Giral, they're probably just some refugees.'

'Then they're dead refugees. And it's our job to find out what happened and who did it. You're a detective, behave like one.'

He threw me a look that was supposed to intimidate me but thought better of saying anything more. I watched him peel himself slowly from the door frame and make to leave, but before he could, a flurry of hushed voices rolled through the main room behind him.

I stood up to see a figure in dress uniform at the other end of the long detectives' room. Following Auban into the outer office, I saw Roger Langeron, the Prefect of Police for Paris, standing at the far end. Tall and authoritative with a neat moustache and round glasses, he only had to wait a few moments for the room to hush and all eyes to fix on him. I came closer and saw that his face was grey, the harsh light above him reflecting off his bald head and casting gaunt shadows on his neck. Next to him, Dax looked even thinner and more elongated.

'I'm visiting all the police stations in the city to reassure our men,' Langeron told us, 'and to keep you informed of events. I have spoken to General von Studnitz at the Hotel Crillon and he has asked me if I can guarantee order.'

'Order,' a voice said.

'Indeed. Order. I told him that I could guarantee this if I was left to work in peace. He has reassured me that as long as order is kept, I can count on the security of his troops and that I would not be hearing from him.'

'So, as long as we play along, we'll be all right,' I commented. I couldn't help myself.

'Precisely, Inspector Giral. As long as we play along.' I could see the same sense of shame in his eyes that the rest of us felt at the fall of the city. 'I have also requested that they return your regulation firearms. I am still awaiting a reply. In the meantime, we have also asked the Germans to rescind the forty-eight-hour curfew that they have initially set. If they do, there will instead be a nightly curfew from nine o'clock.'

Everyone in the room took the news in, no one having anything to say.

'Is that nine o'clock our time or nine o'clock their time?' I asked.

No one laughed.

3

I stared at the scuffed wood of my office desk and was finally hit by the enormity of the new order of things.

Looking like he had the weight of Paris on his shoulders, Langeron had taken his leave, carrying on with his thankless chore of keeping the city's cops calm. With the weight of me on his back, Auban had left cursing for the railway yard shortly after.

And that left me in my office to ask myself where in the name of all that was holy was I supposed to begin an investigation with the city under occupation. Normally, I'd have tried to find out who the dead men were, but that suddenly seemed impossible. Especially in a city where thousands had fled in the exodus and thousands more had passed through as refugees, first in a trickle, then a flood as the Germans cut through Belgium and the Netherlands and crushed our own army on their way to Paris.

I thought of the people I would have spoken to in another age and looked helplessly at the telephone. I might have booked a call to the police in Poland to find out about any missing persons. I would have spoken to someone in our own army to track the stolen gas canisters. And I could have gone through the records of everyone at the railway company to look for anyone with a history that would point to their being involved.

As it was, they were all impossible. And there were no ministries I could talk to either. Not in Paris. They'd all cleared off before the Germans got here and had burned every last piece of paper before they left. I'd watched little spirals of smoke drifting up from the interior courtyards as officials carted wheelbarrow-loads of archives to the bonfires rather than let the approaching Germans get their hands on them. At least the police had had the sense not to put ours to the torch. We'd packed them all on a barge and sent them floating down the Seine. That way, we kept them out of the occupiers' reach. The problem was, it meant we also kept them out of mine.

With the realisation dawning on me that we might never know who the victims were, I decided my best next step would be to trace where the gas had come from. If someone was selling poisonous gas from the last war, someone else would know about it. But first, I figured I had one last go at trying to find out who the four men who'd died in a railway truck were.

Driving away from Thirty-Six, I saw there was nowhere open. All the shops were shuttered, the markets empty, the cafés and restaurants closed, their terrace tables and chairs stacked inside the gloomy interiors. At the Hotel de Ville, the Germans had already removed the tricolore from city hall and replaced it with a huge swastika, the blood-red banner rending a scar down the front of the building and seeping into the foundations. Anti-tank guns had been placed at each corner of the square and a gimlet-eyed feldwebel, a German staff sergeant, sweating in the summer heat signalled me to keep my distance. Mine was the only car moving. They could impose and rescind all the curfews they wanted, I thought; no one in their right mind would be out on the streets today of all days. Except me.

Sheltered on two sides by the railway lines and on the third by the Seine, the brick-built Institut Médico-Légal still looked like a nineteenth-century prison, from which there really was no escape. Less than a hundred years ago, when the mortuary was on the Île de la Cité, coming to look at the unidentified bodies laid out on black marble slabs behind a viewing window was seen as a fashionable day out. My first thought was we'd moved on since those days, but then I remembered the gas and the trenches and four men dying in excruciating pain because someone had smashed a glass bottle by them and I thought again.

Bouchard was on his own in the examination room. Two bodies lay under sheets on the pathology slabs and he was working on a third, rummaging around inside some guy's chest, looking for something, and staring intently in my direction as he did it.

'With you in a minute, Eddie.'

He popped something out and put it in a kidney-shaped tray, which seemed to please him. With the back of his right wrist, he pushed his semi-lunettes back up his nose and scratched an itch on the end of it before arching his back and stretching. I could see the tiredness in his eyes.

I gestured to the body in front of him and to the two under sheets. 'Where's the fourth?'

'These aren't yours, Eddie. This one's a floater, the two over there are suicides. Both brought in today.'

'Suicides?'

'Couldn't face defeat, I suppose. Or afraid of what the Germans might do. Who knows? We've all heard the stories from elsewhere.'

'So where are the men from the railway yard?'

Bouchard took a break from the dead man to wash his hands and gestured to the cold room. 'Through here.'

'And where is everyone? This place gives tombs a bad name.' There should have been two more pathologists on duty.

'Your guess is as good as mine. Lannes was here yesterday but no one's seen him today. Rougvie hasn't been here for the best part of a month, said he was going to get out of Paris before it was flattened. So it's just me here on my own cutting up poor souls who've slashed their wrists or injected themselves with poison rather than face whatever it is the Germans have got in store for us.'

He spared me the view of the rough stitching on the bodies and picked up his notes instead. 'As we thought, Eddie. The lungs were extensively damaged by acid, most probably caused by chlorine gas. And with the resources I've got right now, that's as much as I'm going to be able to tell you.'

I recalled the constraints I now had and knew I couldn't press him. 'Any other clues to their identity?'

'Only what you've already seen in their belongings.'

I looked again at the neat piles of clothing laid out on the table and found the label for Bydgoszcz again. I still doubted. 'You're sure it's chlorine?'

'With the amount of damage, it's impossible for me to tell if they drowned or suffocated in their own lungs. My guess is as good as any you're going to get. Chlorine.' He put the notes down. 'And there's no one here to test precisely what the exact substances were.'

We went back into the examination room to the sound of a door banging. Two bearers had come in with a stretcher, which they laid down on the slab nearest the door.

'Another suicide by the look of it, Doctor Bouchard,' one of the carriers said. 'Found dead in her home in the Tenth Arrondissement.'

Bouchard looked at me and raised his eyes. Equally frustrated, I left him looking around the cutting room in lonely dismay.

'You're going back out,' Dax told me when I got back to Thirty-Six.

'I am?'

'Report of a man's body found in the street on the Left Bank. Uniforms have been called, but I want a detective to see what it's about.'

'Why are you telling me? I've got the four bodies at the railway yard. And only Auban for help. Get someone else to do it.'

With a tired gesture, Dax pointed at the detectives' room behind me. Auban was back, and two or three others were there, but apart from that, the office was empty. Our numbers had been depleted slightly by some of the youngest cops being sent to the army as reservists, but there should still have been more of us in Thirty-Six. 'Take a look through there, Eddie. I'd like to think they're all out working, but would you put a bet on it? I want you to go. You're the only one who seems able to do the job today. Take Auban with you.'

'No, Commissioner, get someone else to do it.'

His voice hardened and he gave me a look I'd had to get used to over the years. 'I don't need to ask you again do I, Eddie?'

He turned away and that was that. I told Auban to get his hat, he was coming with me. He looked as pleased about it as I did.

'What did you learn from the two railway workers?' I asked him on the way.

'Nothing. Saw nothing, heard nothing, just four stiffs in a truck and a shitload of German soldiers. Waste of time.'

I was too tired to argue with him, so I drove. On the normally busy Rue des Écoles, we had to wait while an elderly woman shuffled ahead of us down the middle of the road, clicking her fingers at a tortoiseshell cat to entice it. She and the cat were the only living souls bar us on the street. At a quiet crossroads, we saw four old men sitting in silence on a bench outside a boarded-up café, stubbornly playing cards on an upturned box.

The only other creatures we saw, living and dead, were on Rue Mouffetard. Two uniformed cops stood tense guard over a figure lying near the gutter, no doubt eager to get off the streets to avoid any German troops. The figure was covered in a grey blanket blackened with wet blood. A heavy stream of red flooded the road and splashed the pavement, running in rivulets to a drain. All the shutters in the buildings overlooking the scene were bleak and drawn. A concierge was pacing up and down outside a front door, quietly moaning to herself. One of the uniforms told me that she was in charge of the building where the dead man had lived.

'She said he lived on the top floor,' the cop said, pointing up to a balcony. 'He jumped off that. That's as much sense as I've got out of her.'

'Go and talk to her,' I told Auban. 'Try and find out what she knows at least.'

I watched him saunter off towards her. The woman's left foot was encased in a heavy black boot with a built-up sole, her sparse white hair sprang shocked from a thin skull. It was a city of the elderly and the desperate. And under it all, you could still hear the Germans crashing along the streets around us like a distant gun breech endlessly loading.

Turning back to the body lying in the street, I took a deep breath and lifted the blanket. I saw the peaceful face of a man in his mid-thirties. Half a peaceful face. He was lying on his stomach, his head turned to one side. The profile I saw was intact, calm. Underneath, you could see where the impact with the ground had smashed his skull, ripping through flesh and compacting the far side of his features into the stones. Another suicide for the city to accept. I pulled the blanket back further. One leg was at an unnatural angle, both arms tucked under the body. Oddly, the thing that struck me most was that he was wearing a thick grey overcoat. A strange final ritual, I wondered. The day was far too hot and sapping for him to be wearing one normally. I tried to imagine why he would have put on an overcoat before taking his life. I asked the uniform if the Institut Médico-Légal had been informed.

'They said they were on their way, Inspector.'

Thanking him, I placed the coarse cloth back over the man. All around was dotted the jetsam of flight, things people fleeing the Germans had dropped or discarded in their rush to get away. It was the same all over the city. Lying on the pavement I saw a broken chamber pot, a tablecloth covered in the dust and grime of the street, and a child's teddy bear, one ear chewed, splashed with the dead man's blood. I had to tear my gaze away from it. Looking instead to where Auban was talking to the concierge, I saw him react suddenly in surprise. He called me over, more urgent than I'd ever seen him.

'Where's little Jan?' the concierge was wailing, over and over.

'Is his name Jan?' I asked, but Auban shook his head vigorously.

'She says he had a young son. That's Jan.'

I snapped my head to look up to the balcony and called the two uniforms over. 'Get upstairs to the man's flat. There's a small boy up there. Find him, make sure he's all right.'

The concierge started wailing more. 'He's not up there. I've been up to look. Little Jan isn't anywhere.'

I looked back at the figure lying under the blanket and closed my eyes for a moment. 'The coat.'

As I ran towards the body, Bouchard drove up and got out of his car. I ignored him and shouted to the two uniformed cops. 'Look along each side of the street.' Neither of them reacted, caught unawares, but I could see there was nothing to look for. I slowed as I approached the dead man. Bouchard reached him at the same time.

'What is it, Eddie?'

'We've got to look under the body.'

'I've got to check him first.'

'Believe me, we've got to look under the body.'

I pulled at the blanket, but Bouchard took over, lifting the material away and gently pushing the body on to its side.

'My God,' Bouchard exclaimed.

I closed my eyes for a second time and reopened them slowly.

Lying underneath the man, cradled inside the front of his heavy overcoat, was the body of his small son, crushed between his father's embrace and the rough cobbles of the empty street.

4

'I knew little about him,' Madame Benoit the concierge told me, clutching a frayed handkerchief. 'He was Polish, a refugee. Been here since November. Kept himself to himself, paid his rent, that's all. He seemed a good man, but always so sad.'

Another Polish refugee? 'Do you have a name?'

She and I were alone at a table inside her small apartment at the end of a gloomy corridor on the ground floor. I'd sent Auban and the two uniformed cops back to Thirty-Six, and Bouchard had left once the bodies had been taken away. Most of the elderly concierge's life was in this one room; table, cooker, faded sofa and forgotten mementoes. Two doors gave off, I supposed, to a bedroom and a bathroom.

'Fryderyk. I can't pronounce his surname. It's foreign. His son's Jan. I know his wife was killed in Poland and that he and Jan got away, but that's all. He doted on little Jan, but the boy wouldn't say a word. And he wouldn't leave his father's side even for a moment. They both used to be out at odd times most days. Fryderyk had a job and I think he didn't want to leave the boy here. I do know that he seemed terrified when we got news that the Germans were nearing the city.'

I imagined he was. And that was probably why he killed himself. Grief at the death of his wife, unable to face another

German invasion. I'd heard the same rumours as everyone else about what the Nazis had done in Poland, but like most I didn't know much and I didn't know how much to believe of the propaganda coming out on either side. He, though, probably had known. I tried to imagine how desperate he must have felt to step off a balcony holding on to his young son and I couldn't help letting out a long, sad breath. Just another suicide on a day filled with despair.

'I'll need to take a look in his flat,' I told Madame Benoit.

She climbed with me to the top floor but wouldn't cross the threshold. Inside, the apartment made my place look like the Hall of Mirrors in Versailles. Two mismatched wooden chairs at a kitchen table, a gas ring and a cupboard shared the same room as a pair of armchairs and a radio. It wasn't the life of ease enjoyed by the refugees flooding Paris that some on the right would have us believe. A glass door led out to a small balcony with an ornate iron railing. I stood on the narrow stone ledge and leaned over, trying to imagine Fryderyk's last thoughts before stepping out into space, his young son nestled against him in the warmth of his overcoat, not knowing what his father was about to do but trusting him to look after him. I had to shake off that train of thought and go back inside.

I searched the living room but found nothing. No personal belongings or final letter. Nothing in the kitchen area but two cups, two plates and two sets of cutlery, the third not necessary. In an awful moment of clarity, I could understand why he'd done what he'd done. A tiny bathroom held a shaving brush, a razor and a bar of soap. The brush and the razor had been good in their day, the soap was the cheap stuff you bought in the market. I wondered what the man's life before becoming a refugee had been like. Not as tough as it had become after, that was for sure.

Saddened by the deaths, I was nonetheless realising there was little we could do. In normal times, we always investigated suicides, but these were anything but normal, and I had a feeling Fryderyk and his son's deaths would go uncared for. I took a cursory look through the bedroom door and saw nothing more than a bed with a thin sheet draped across it, a small bedside table and an ancient wardrobe. Pushing the door open further, I felt it bang up against something on the other side.

It was a safe. An ancient and musty cast-iron safe on four small, solid wheels that squatted behind the door like a mud-encrusted toad. A pale handle drooped like a lazy tongue from the rusted dial on the flaked paint of the front. I could do nothing but stare at it for a moment and compare it with the Spartan sadness of the rest of the room. It was entirely out of place.

I called to Madame Benoit. 'Is this safe part of the furniture or did Fryderyk bring it with him?'

She crossed herself and the threshold. 'Neither. He bought it not long after he got here. My husband had to help him get it upstairs and he's not a young man.'

'I don't suppose you know the combination.'

I supposed right. I tried the handle, but it was locked. Even with the rust, it was sturdy enough to keep me out. Looking to see if I could find a piece of paper with the combination on it, I pulled the bedside drawer open. There was just one item in there. I took it out and sat down on the bed to look at it.

It was a Polish passport, with Fryderyk and Jan's photographs in.

'Gorecki,' I said out loud. Fryderyk's surname that Madame Benoit couldn't pronounce.

I looked from the document to the safe behind the door. Three things struck me.

The first was what would a refugee with little more than two coffee cups and a faded shaving brush to his name possibly be doing with a safe?

The second was the passport. For a refugee, it should have been as valuable as a gold bar. So what could be worth more to Fryderyk than his passport that he would go out and buy a safe to keep it in?

And finally, the words that were written in the passport. I understood little of what they said, but I did recognise one thing. Like at least one of the four men in the railway yard, Fryderyk was from a town in Poland called Bydgoszcz.

There was a present waiting for me when I got back to Thirty-Six. My gun. It was on Dax's desk.

'New order came through a short while ago,' he told me. 'Langeron's managed to get the Germans to agree to us being armed if they want us to keep order. And they brought the guns back themselves. All signed and accounted for.'

I wasn't sure I liked that last bit. He gestured for me to pick up my pistol, and I put it in my waistband without letting him see the Manufrance hiding there. I hoped my trousers would hold up.

'And the forty-eight-hour curfew has been lifted. But there's to be a nightly one at nine o'clock.'

'Eight o'clock.'

'Whatever you say, Eddie. Either way, it doesn't apply to the police so you don't need to worry.'

Leaving him, I put Fryderyk Gorecki's passport in my desk drawer and locked up for the day. There was little I could do in terms of any investigation, but I could at least look for any next of kin that I could tell.

I drove the short distance home across an empty bridge and

through deserted streets. It seemed like no one had told the rest of the city that the curfew had been lifted until tonight. I checked my watch. There were still one or two hours until it began, depending which time you chose. Outside my building, I put the Manufrance back in its hiding place. Staring at the dashboard and willing myself to get out of the car, I finally gave in. Reaching underneath again, I pulled the Luger out and put it in my pocket.

'Just hope you don't regret it this time,' I told myself.

Upstairs in my flat, I made a sandwich from yesterday's bread and last week's cheese and sat at my wooden kitchen table to eat it. For once, home seemed a palace after Fryderyk's tiny flat, and for a few rare moments it even felt like a safe haven.

I dumped the plate in the sink and went into the living room. Taking down an old tin box from my overloaded bookshelves either side of the hearth, I sat down with it on one of my two armchairs. I hadn't opened it for over a decade. Inside, I found what I was looking for: a bullet from a Luger, dulled by the years. Rolling it between my fingers, I found the slight indentation in it. I was unhappy to realise that the bullet still had the same power over me that it had always had. Carefully, I put it down on the low table between my armchair and the fireplace and placed the Luger next to it. Looking at them together, I remembered the ritual and I knew I had to get out of my apartment.

Outside, I roamed the streets at random. The Germans' curfew was approaching but I had my police ID in case I was stopped. I didn't much feel like paying any attention to their time anyway. The black smoke of the past few days still hung in the air, and in the warm evening I could smell the soot in the haze and feel the oil in my nostrils. A door in my memory that I had hoped was shut forever had opened a tiny crack, revealing a darker truth. It had begun with the gas mask that morning and the German uniforms lined up either side of me, the sight of the Luger in my car and the bullet in my fingers. And it continued now with thoughts of Jan, who had no doubt believed his father would always protect him and of Fryderyk who believed he couldn't and saw no alternative other than suicide.

Idly crossing a darkening Place Edmond Rostand that should have been teeming on a warm Friday evening, I thought of the shrouds on Bouchard's slabs and of the handful of Parisians today who'd also been unable to see an alternative. Fryderyk's was just one more suicide on a day that seemed to have spawned so many, his own in a foreign country soon to be forgotten. I wanted to question what had driven them all to their act. But I couldn't. I knew. I felt again the harsh metal of the Luger bullet and smelt its acrid tang. I closed my eyes as I walked, an aimless suicide attempt at any other time on the busy streets of the city, a futile and lonely gesture today. It wasn't my first.

A whine of brakes in front of me pulled me up short and I opened my eyes to see a German patrol. Four soldiers in a jeep eyeing me warily. They brought me back to a different reality.

'I'm so happy to see you,' I told an edgy gefreiter, a private, with an over-large forage cap resting on elephant ears. I even smiled. His three companions stayed in their jeep, the engine ticking over with a dull growl.

'Papers,' he said in accented French. 'It is after nine o'clock. You should not be out of your house.'

'I assure you I should.' I dug out my police ID and showed it to him. 'Police. No curfew.'

He examined it doubtfully and showed it to a bullish feldwebel, who was lounging over more than his fair share of the back seat, a rifle resting loosely in his lap. He simply nodded and handed it back to the gefreiter, who gave it back to me.

'That is all right, sir,' the young guy said, bowing slightly with an oddly polite formality. 'Please continue on your way.'

He smiled tentatively and returned to the jeep, which sped off the moment he got in.

'I plan to do just that,' I assured the vanishing exhaust fumes.

I watched the jeep disappear along the road towards the Odéon. Another four men in a vehicle uncertain of what was to happen to them. I'd been the same once, a young soldier gassing and shooting and bayoneting other young men across a field of mud and wire because I'd been told to. And then we'd all gone home and been given medals and told to get on with our lives. Not heroes, perhaps, but not villains either.

But put those other young men in a railway truck and throw the gas at the wall and it was murder. If this war was going to be anything like the last one, millions of people would die and millions of medals would be handed out to the people who killed them. But in Paris, my job was to seek justice for four men who died on a summer morning in a railway truck and excuse the unjudged murders of millions more. Outside, the purpose was to kill. Inside, the purpose was not to. And my purpose was to find a solution to the lesser evil of the two.

It was dark. I was walking further away from the river and home and deeper into Montparnasse. The blackout that the city had only half-heartedly observed for most of the phony war had suddenly descended. As the Germans had approached, we'd lived our evenings with a faint blue covering on the street lamps that had cast a ghostly pallor on frightened faces. Now the occupiers were among us, even that had descended into a greater blackness. Not even a candle was left shining in a window the way so many people had done in a strange and useless lip-service to not attracting the Luftwaffe while still lighting their own way home.

Always at the back of my mind as I thought of the four German soldiers and the four men in the railway truck was the gas. I wanted to know who had got hold of the gas. And to do that, I needed to know how. I looked at my surroundings. I was deep in the heart of Montparnasse. My random stroll through the deserted streets had been anything but random, my subconscious thoughts leading me to where I now stood.

I was at the entrance to a narrow street off Boulevard du Montparnasse and I knew where I was going. With more purpose, I burrowed into the backstreets. It was pitch black, but then the place I wanted was always pitch black, even in a Paris blackout. Finding the wood and glass front of a café, I peered more closely and saw that it was backed by a thick, black curtain. I could hear sounds from inside so I rapped on the door. A chink appeared in the heavy drape and a face I knew looked out at me. An ugly face with a bushy moustache and a nose broken in several places, once by me. He put the curtain back and opened the door.

'Eddie, we don't want any problems.'

'Open the door, Luigi, and you won't have any.'

He sighed and let me in. His name wasn't Luigi, but he was Italian and everyone called him that. He'd come to Paris twenty years ago, some said on the run from police and gangs in Naples, and his café was one of the best places for fencing stolen goods south of the Seine. And for information.

I followed him through the dense cheap cigarette fug, which had irrevocably stained the old wooden panels and glass panes separating the booths running along the wall opposite the bar, and saw that I wasn't alone for the first time all evening. Not everyone was pleased to see me. Some of the district's minor villains melted into the smoke as I walked by, others turned away from me. I was surprised to see some German soldiers at the bar and in a couple of the booths. Officers, not ranks. As usual, tolerating the misdemeanours of others as long as they got to do them too. Some of them looked at me incuriously and turned back to their conversations. It felt strangely comforting that the Nazis should naturally find themselves among the worst that Paris had to offer.

I found someone I wanted to speak to. He wasn't so keen, but he had no choice. I cornered him at the far end of the bar, where he'd tried to shrink away from me. The runt of a criminal litter, he wore a uniform of a cloth cap angled over one eye and an old-fashioned wing collar and thin black tie to match his thin white lips and dark-rimmed pale eyes. He was like a faded Pierrot from an unimaginative child's nightmare.

'How's it going, Pepe?' I asked him. Just like Luigi, Pepe also traded under a false name. He wasn't even Spanish. 'Gas. Who's selling it? Who's buying it?'

I saw no giveaway in his face. In happier times, he worked as a pickpocket and as a lookout for the find-the-lady sharks around the railway stations in the south of the city. 'Petty' was made to describe him, but he had his uses.

He didn't think so.

'Fuck off, Eddie. I've got nothing for you.'

That surprised me. It shouldn't have. 'Not nice, Pepe. After all I've done for you.'

He snorted and edged away, into earshot of a trio of blue-eyed Nazi wunderkinder using sign language to order a bottle of Luigi's least corrosive champagne.

'They're the future, Eddie, not you,' he told me in a loud voice.

'Give it up, Pepe. They don't understand.' I turned to them and raised his glass of indeterminate red at them. 'I hope it gives you the shits. It usually does.'

They raised their glasses back at me with the arrogant smiles of the youthful victor. They fed me their own insult in German, which was fair enough. I felt Pepe tugging at my sleeve and I gave him his wine back, wiping my hand on the counter.

'You're yesterday's man, Giral. No one cares about you anymore. Least of all now.' He smiled in his own turn at the young officers, who seemed amused. They turned to watch us.

'You think so?' I asked him.

Pepe became emboldened, his face close to mine. I got a front-row view I didn't want of teeth like a haunted graveyard. I fanned away breath that came straight from a mildewed tomb. 'Look around you. Germans. They'll put you in your place. No one worries about French cops anymore, not now we've got the Germans.'

'For as unenlightened a statement as you'll ever make, Pepe, that was incredibly astute. Well done.'

He looked pleased. He didn't know why. It was my turn to push my face in his, but Luigi came up to our end of the counter and repeated his earlier greeting. 'Please, Eddie, we don't want trouble.'

The three Germans began jovially repeating my name and clinking their glasses. They guffawed in that way that only the really entitled can. I glanced at them and then back at Pepe. I wasn't going to get anywhere with them there.

'Catch you later,' I told him and turned to leave. 'You'll tell me what I want to know.'

He waited until I was past the three officers at the bar before shouting, 'Yeah, well, fuck you, Eddie. You were an evil bastard once, but you've lost it. You don't scare anyone. Not before, not now.'

The Aryan super-trio turned to watch me go, sniggering schoolboy insults. I faltered for a moment but thought better of it and stepped through the black curtain into the fresh air of a soot-stained alley filled with refuse and shit. Everything's relative. Outside, I dragged in a deep breath and walked slowly back to the darkened Boulevard du Montparnasse. I could wait for Pepe to come out, I thought, but I didn't have the heart. Not today.

'Catch you later,' I muttered again and set off for home through an empty chasm of night.

Despite myself, I dwelled on Pepe's words as I walked. He wasn't scared of me, I realised, not like he used to be. There was a time that would have worried me, and another time it would have heartened me. With the Germans now in charge, I was no longer sure how it made me feel. Or what it might mean for me. I did what I'd done for too long now and pushed it from my thoughts.

At home, I walked through my apartment door and turned the light on in my living room. My breath caught in my throat. Standing on the low table, exactly where I'd left them, were the Luger and the bullet. I'd forgotten about them. I stood stock still for as long as I could, but I knew I wouldn't be able to stop myself. Approaching them warily, I sat down in my armchair and stared at the two icons of a lonely past. For the first time in many years, I picked the Luger up and pulled out the magazine. My fingers stiff, I removed the bullets and laid them out in a row on the table. My ritual.

After a few moments' hesitation, I picked up the lone bullet and examined it. It was worn smooth over the years. I smelt its coldness, the scent of the metal sour in my nose. I placed it in the magazine and clicked it into place in the pistol. Slowly, I raised it and looked down the barrel. A darkness I thought I'd forgotten lay there. Breathing heavily, I brought the gun closer to my eyes and held it over the bridge of my nose. The Luger was strangely warm against my forehead in the still night air.

I closed my eyes and squeezed the trigger.

Wednesday 20th May 1925

I squeezed harder. I don't know what I expected to happen but nothing did. No loud report, no lifting of a veil, no final sound. Curious, I squeezed a little further. It felt warm under my fingers but nothing more. No moment of thunder. No flashpoint that I'd expected.

I couldn't help feeling disappointed so I let go.

'You're fucking insane,' the man gasped at me. He clutched his throat now I'd relinquished it and tenderly rubbed it, gasping with pain as the air was forced back into his lungs.

'You're probably right,' I told him. 'Worrying, isn't it?'

'It's OK, Eddie,' Fabienne told me from behind. 'I can deal with it.'

'I'll have your fucking job,' the man promised me.

'That's going to be hard,' I told him. 'When you're flat on your arse on the pavement.'

I picked him up and carried him through the entrance to the street door. The pulsations of the drums and clarinets vanished in a heartbeat. He put up a struggle, but I cupped my hand and slapped him over the ear. The punters don't like that, they can't hear the music for the ringing in their head. And because it hurts like hell. Outside, I threw him to the ground.

'I'll have you,' he shouted at me.

'You do that.'

I nodded at Georges, the guy on the door, and went back inside.

'There was no need, Eddie, I'd have been all right,' Fabienne told me. She was putting her lipstick back on and drying her eyes, mopping up the make-up that had run. 'But thanks. He was a jerk.'

She leaned over and kissed me lightly on the cheek and I led her back into the heart of the club. A fraction of a moment after the heavy swing doors opened, a cannonade of music hit me like velvet bullets fired from a silver gun. Through a smoky gauze of swirling heads and illicit embraces, I saw the musicians on stage, playing a frenzied beat to a background syncopation of chattering glass and laughter. For a moment, I couldn't help smiling as I always did. I replaced it quickly with the passive look expected of me. That wasn't how the guard-dog was supposed to bare his teeth. Above the sweet smell of cigars, an aroma of perfume and the scent of champagne beckoned the hedonist. I took in a deep breath and watched Fabienne rejoin a group of young women and older men at a table. She kissed a man she didn't know on the lips and he called for a waiter. I looked around the tightly packed room. Dancers jostled noisily on the small floor in front of the stage, watched by the flirting heads at the crowded tables. Around three sides, a gilded balcony closed in on the downstairs revellers – the ones at the tables above more discreet but no less alive in their shadows. The glare cast on the musicians dissipated, away from the stage, through the filter of smoke and bodies. I'd started working on the door to make some extra money, but I'd grown to enjoy the contact with the musicians and the pleasure-seekers. It was happiness by proxy. I savoured the essence one more time and made my way through the tables.

'How's it going, Eddie?' one of the musicians greeted me when I got to the side of the stage.

His was the only voice you would have heard in this din. A gentle roar, it came from deep within his mountainous frame. He had a smile that would have melted the snow on the Pyrenees and an indomitable sense of joy that would have sent an avalanche thundering down. I grinned back, unsure he'd hear me. Like most of the musicians on stage, Joe was an American who'd served with the Harlem Hellfighters in the war. They'd been assigned to the French Army as many of the white American soldiers wouldn't fight alongside them. I asked him once why he hadn't gone home after the war ended.

'Home to what?' he'd replied.

Nodding now at the heaving crowd, he shouted, 'It's jumping tonight.'

I shook my head in that exaggerated way you do when you can't even hear your own voice. 'Bit quiet, I'd say.'

He laughed, a big-bellied sound that added an extra bass line to the music, and swatted me on the shoulder. I smiled back at him, but I meant it. I was hoping for another head to hit. I watched him turn back to follow the band leader and get ready for the next tune.

A few heads I'd have given a night's pay to batter were gathered in unholy array at a table near the stage. Each one sat atop a wiry body dressed like a drunkard had clothed them blindfolded. I looked at them all in turn even though theirs weren't faces their mothers would want to remember. They just stared back, expressionless. Cold, dangerous. A gang. Scrawny knife-wielders who scavenged and terrorised in their own little piece of heaven in Montmartre.

'What do you want?' one of them, an old guy with a neck like a dead turkey, finally asked me, his accent Corsican.

'Just letting you know I care.'

I smiled broadly, which unnerved him. Taking that as a result, I left them and carried on with my rounds.

A woman was standing at the bar, furthest from the sound of the band. A singer, she was new. I'd seen her a couple of times but never spoken to her.

'You're the one they call Eddie, aren't you?' she asked me.

I turned to her, surprised at her accent. 'You're not American?'

She smiled. A knowing smile that said she wouldn't brook any nonsense. 'I'm from Senegal. But they let me sing.'

'I've heard you. You sing beautifully.'

I cringed, but she had the grace not to make fun of me. Not with her words, anyway. Her look was enough.

'Got a light?'

She pulled a cigarette out of a small clutch bag in the same silver fabric as her dress and stared at me frankly. Holding the smoke in slender fingers to her lips, she waited expectantly, a slight smile at the corners of her mouth.

'I don't smoke.'

She reached behind her and lit up from a matchbook on the bar. 'Why's that?'

I shook my head and stared at the wisps that she blew out of her nose and mouth. I fought down my panic. 'I just don't.'

'I do it for my voice. It's what gives it the right tone when I sing.' She gave me one last knowing smile and moved away. 'Which I now know I do beautifully.'

I watched her slink through the smoke like a wraith vanishing out of reach and relived every word I'd spoken to her. A narrow sliver of guilt sliced through me.

'You're an idiot, Giral,' I concluded.

I hadn't even asked her name.

After the jazz club, the graveyard shift at the police station was dull, even with a few extra francs in my pocket, but at least it was quiet. My head was moving to the jazz but my body was on slow waltz time. I sat at a desk and moved two piles of paper around, stifling a yawn. I wondered if I could get through a whole night like that. Another cop sat at another desk doing the same thing. Where I moonlighted on the door in a jazz club, he did the same in a brothel. I got the applause, he got the clap.

Two cops came into the room and the other guy and I had to move things around less aimlessly. They didn't notice, but chattered instead about some drunk they'd just arrested and slapped about. Not every cop was as caring as I was. I stood their boasting for another minute and reached behind me to put the radio on. After it had warmed up, I fiddled the dial and found a station playing jazz. Inside, I started moving to the beat again.

'Jesus, Giral, turn off that Negro shit.'

I stared at the papers in front of me for a moment.

'Say that again.'

One of the newcomers came over to the radio and reached for the dial. 'You heard.'

'I certainly did.'

I got up and reached for the radio before he could get to it, but instead of grabbing the dial, I slapped him open-handed across the face. It was a trick I'd learned at the jazz club. An open slap works better than a fist, shocking troublemakers into stunned inaction but not seriously hurting them.

'Christ, Giral,' his friend said, 'what the hell is wrong with you?'

'More than you will ever know.'

I turned back to the first cop and watched his face redden. I felt the same remoteness that I'd felt in the club. He lashed out at me, but I dodged his fist and slapped him again, his humiliation complete.

'Leave it, Eddie,' the other moonlighter told me.

I only faintly saw him. Instead, I smiled at the cop in front of me and looked him in the eyes. He recoiled as I reached across his face, but I just turned the volume up on the wireless as loud as it would go and put my hand down.

'I just want to listen to the radio.'

Saturday 15th June 1940

5

I left the radio playing.

You had to hand it to the Germans. Their news was even less believable than ours had been. Right up until the day before yesterday, the newspapers had been telling us we'd turned the tide of the war and were pushing them back to Belgium. Then a German soldier rode into Montmartre on his motorbike and we realised we should have stopped reading the papers long ago. In the end, the best way to tell how far the Germans were advancing was by the licence plates of the cars streaming into Paris. The worse things got, the more you saw cars fleeing from areas nearer and nearer to the city. Until the vehicles coming into the city were German tanks and armoured carriers and motorbikes, by which stage even the government had got the message – except they hadn't hung around long enough to see for themselves.

I turned the dial across what channels there were. The few stations not playing military music or German propaganda just carried on fobbing us off with more empty hope about our troops rallying south of the capital. But even the sound of stupidity is preferable to a hopeless silence, so I left the noise playing while I worked out how to make breakfast with no eggs, no bread and no milk. I called it coffee. I turned the wireless off and took the cup into the living room.

The gun was on the table where I'd replaced it after the cold metal click of the night before. The bullet was standing on its end next to it. The bullet that had saved my life one winter's morning in a long-ago trench. A German officer had held the Luger centimetres from my head as I'd fumbled for my rifle. With no expression on his face, he'd pulled the trigger, only to hear the click of the firing pin jamming. The same click I'd heard last night. The sound that had blemished five years of my life in this same armchair, a succession of bleak nights in which I'd pretended I'd wanted release but had been too afraid. It was a sound I thought I'd cured myself of hearing some ten years ago. I saw again the look of surprise on the officer's face as I turned my rifle to him and fired it up into his chest. His odd look of disappointment as his legs gave way and he fell into the mud of the trench. Another pointless death.

It had been my ritual. My escape from far more painful memories and the guilt of surviving a war and other moments of horror and despair. Once again, I had some understanding of why Fryderyk Gorecki had done what he'd done to himself and to his son.

I picked up the Luger that I had taken out of the dead German's hand that day. I'd kept it oiled and serviced ever since and I knew it worked with other bullets. With that thought, I scooped up the other rounds and replaced them in the magazine. It was now a working weapon again. Taking it into the bathroom, I reached for the loose tile above the washstand and pulled it away to reveal a gap. Inside, there were already two ammunition boxes, one for the Luger, the other for the Manufrance. I shifted them along and hid the Luger in the space remaining. With the Germans in town, who knew when you might need a back-up plan.

Returning to the living room, I thought of putting the bullet back in its tin. It should have been a lucky bullet, the one that had saved my life that day, but I could never think of it as that. There'd been so many times that I'd wished it had done its job. Both on that day and on other desperate nights since. Not last night, though, I realised. Instead, I picked it up, feeling the slight indentation that was either the cause or effect of the day the Luger jammed and I put it in my jacket pocket. On the radio, the announcer was telling me of a brand-new dawn, so I turned the set off and went out.

One floor below, Monsieur Henri, my downstairs neighbour was on the landing. He was just coming in.

'Been out looking for bread,' he told me. 'Nothing. Have you heard the radio? The government's just left Tours for Bordeaux.'

'You believe it?'

'I believe that. The sons of bitches have abandoned us like they always do. The whole lot of them: the government, the army, the British, Roosevelt. They've all left us to our fate.' He tutted vigorously. I was hoping to be spared one of his rants. He had more gossip than Gertrude Stein. He unlocked his door. 'They say the Germans are cutting the hands off young boys so they can't grow up to hold weapons against them.'

'Is that right?' The Nazis could have saved themselves a fortune on Goebbels' salary.

I walked the five minutes to Thirty-Six. I sometimes thought I should move further away, but I'd got used to my apartment. I'd moved there in 1925 when I couldn't afford much, and I'd never got around to moving on. And I liked the name of my street: Rue de la Harpe. I'd needed music in my life at that time. It suited me for all sorts of reasons. And I also learned that the street had once been where refuse ended up, which also suited me at the time. Then I learned that that didn't include the part of the street where I lived, which suited me by the time I discovered it.

It was Saturday morning and the city was as sad as a forgotten friend. A pale sun rose, struggling through the rolling clouds of burning oil, the summer warmth made oppressive by the blackened mantle suffocating the city. The air was heavy in the back of my throat. Crossing the lonely bridge to a spectral Île de la Cité floating on the dark-reflected Seine, I had an odd and illogical feeling I was heading for safety. In my mind, the police station being on an island in the river gave us some protection.

'Won't last,' I told myself.

I was right. I went into my office to find a German at my desk. Sitting on my chair. Looking out of my window. He stood up and saluted me. Lazily, but it was a salute. I scanned my papers to see if anything looked out of place.

'This is Major Hochstetter,' a voice behind me said. It was Dax, standing in the doorway. He looked older and even more gaunt than the previous day.

'And you are Inspector Giral,' the German said to me. 'Or may I call you Édouard?' He spoke perfect French, which annoyed me.

'I'd sooner you called me from Berlin.'

Hochstetter examined me closely before giving a small laugh. He moved out from behind my desk, each step measured, the natural soldier. Too young for the old war, too eager for the new one. Curious how senior German officers always reminded me of the senior French officers I'd served under in the last war. He was tall and patrician, with regulation brown hair, regulation firm jaw and regulation dark, probing eyes. I caught him examining me, specifically my top lip. I had a scar there, from when I was young and played rugby in my home town, but it made me look like a boxer, someone most people wouldn't consider bothering. I sometimes forgot how much a small line of puckered white skin could determine people's reactions to me. It was a good job he couldn't see the other scar under my ear. He looked back up at my eyes.

'You speak good French,' I told him. Building bridges.

'I studied at the Sorbonne in 1934 and 1935.'

'So you've been planning this for some time.' Burning bridges.

'I think we shall get on just perfectly, Édouard,' he decided, his lips lining out in a dry smile. He came and stood on the blunt side of my desk, allowing me to go round to the business end. I straightened my chair, quickly looking to see if any drawers were left open or any papers touched. Everything looked all right, which probably just meant he was good at what he did.

'Major Hochstetter has been appointed to liaise with the criminal investigation department,' Dax explained. He and Hochstetter remained standing, so I sat down. Hochstetter followed suit, that half-smile still on his face, as did Dax a moment after him.

'I should introduce myself properly,' Hochstetter said. 'I am a major in the Abwehr, which I am sure you are aware is German military intelligence.'

'Were you a cop before the war?'

'A soldier. I have worked for most of my career in intelligence. I am aware a Paris police detective might not regard that as proper policing, but we share many of the same skills. I am sure I can be of assistance to you in your work. Please see me as a conduit for smoothing the path between your investigations and our administrative procedures.'

'I haven't had a conduit before.'

Dax shot me a look.

'I should also apologise for being in your office. In my new role, I am presently touring the whole of the criminal investigation headquarters, acquainting myself with how the French police work. You will have to excuse me if I ask questions. Might I ask if you have any investigations at the moment where I could be of service?'

I looked out of the window and considered how much I should trust my new-found conduit. I explained very quickly about the four men found gassed in the railway truck the previous morning. 'We're still trying to ascertain their identities and find out what people in the yard saw.'

'They were gassed, you say?' Hochstetter asked.

'Like in the last war. I was in the trenches when your army used gas on us.'

'Those were other times, Édouard.'

'There were German soldiers in the vicinity of the murders. At any other time, I would be wanting to question them to ask what they might have seen.'

'As an investigator, I understand your concerns.' Hochstetter folded his legs in an economical, graceful movement. 'And normally I would be happy to accede to your wishes in the interests of mutual cooperation, but you must understand that there is a great deal of confusion at present. Many of our forces are simply passing through the city on the way to the front. I would be unlikely to be able to verify exactly which troops were at the yard and at what time, and it is not at all impossible that they are no longer in Paris. As I say, it is not that I would not wish to accede to your wishes, but that I don't see that it is feasible for me to be able to do so.'

His French might even be better than mine.

'A Hauptmann Karl Weber,' I told him, 'of the 87th Infantry Division of the Wehrmacht. He was the officer in charge.'

'Weber.' Hochstetter studied me before continuing. 'Very well, I will see what I can do.'

'Finished, Eddie?' Dax finally asked. He turned to the German and stood up. 'Thank you, Major Hochstetter, I'm sure we both appreciate your cooperation.'

Hochstetter looked at me thoughtfully and rose to follow Dax out of the room. I turned back to thoughts of my investigation, but was interrupted by Dax making an announcement in the main room. Getting up to look, I saw him calling for silence so that he could present Hochstetter to the other detectives and so that Hochstetter could make a nice speech.

'I do not see,' Hochstetter told us after he'd introduced himself, 'that there should be any need for any change to your daily work. I am simply here as an advisor. You will carry on as you have been until now and I shall be overseeing the affairs of the criminal investigation department to make sure it falls in line with the overall policy of the German High Command in Paris.'

As he spoke, he looked at everyone in the room, no doubt observing and evaluating the reactions he saw. I did likewise. With their right-wing sympathies, Auban and one or two others looked doe-eyed, their adoration of Adolf outdoing their rampant patriotism. A small handful uneasily hid their defiance, while most simply looked numb. Hochstetter now knew where he stood. So did I.

When he finished, I went back into my room and took Fryderyk Gorecki's passport out of my drawer. Something nagged. I studied the pictures in the document and wondered again what could be more important to a refugee than the passport that he should keep it in a safe.

I rang Bouchard at the forensic institute.

'The Polish guy who committed suicide,' I asked him. 'Have you found any papers on him? Anything with a series of numbers?'

Bouchard told me he'd found nothing.

I heard a noise and looked up to see Hochstetter come in. Before I could stop him, he'd picked up the passport.

'I'll ring you later,' I told Bouchard and hung up.

'I came in to say how much I am looking forward to working with you,' Hochstetter told me. He gestured with the passport. 'Is this to do with your investigation into the deaths at the railway yard?'

'No, this is unrelated.' I reached across my desk but he held on to it.

'Bydgoszcz,' he recited, looking thoughtfully at the address. 'Poland. In the Reichsgau Danzig-Westpreussen as it is now. Unrelated, you say.'

I decided it didn't really matter if he knew. 'A suicide. Yesterday evening. A man and his young son. I was hoping to be able to find the man's next of kin to inform them of their deaths.'

He put it down and turned to leave. 'You're a good man, Édouard. I hope that doesn't prove to be your undoing in these difficult times.'

6

I picked up my Citroën from outside my apartment building. I wanted to take another look at the scene of the killings at the Gare d'Austerlitz. The gas should have dissipated completely by now, so it would be safe to search inside the goods trucks properly. We'd left all three of them sealed and I was hoping there'd be no Germans around today so I could take a look in peace.

As it was, there were no Germans and no goods trucks.

'Where the hell are they?' I asked Le Bailly, the union official I'd spoken to yesterday. The same two workers from before were with him. 'There were orders to leave the three trucks until we'd been back.'

'We didn't get any orders. The only one we had was this morning telling us to put them back into service. They were needed for a train heading for the front line. The German front line, not ours.'

'So where are they now?'

'On their way to Bordeaux as far as I know.'

I shook my head in frustration. 'Did you see Detective Auban here yesterday afternoon? The detective who was with me.'

'I haven't seen him since.'

I mentally cursed Auban and asked them the questions he

was supposed to. 'Do you recall anything else that you saw yesterday morning?'

'The Germans were looking through the sheds and the trucks when we got here,' the taller of the two workers said. As he spoke, his moustache dipped up and down over thin lips. It made him sound like he was speaking through a private fog.

'Your name is?'

'Marcel Font.'

The other looked more reticent to speak, to me or to Le Bailly. Shorter, he was much stockier with a boxer's eyes and a sullen expression that reminded me of the old photos of the turn-of-the-century Apache gangs.

'And you?'

'Thierry Papin,' he finally told me.

'Did you see anything?'

'I don't know anything.'

'You don't say.'

He clenched his fists and glowered at me, but Font laid a hand on his arm.

'Back to work, the pair of you,' Le Bailly told the two men, which seemed to displease them more than I did.

'We helping the Boches now?' Font asked.

'No,' Le Bailly replied. 'I'm trying to help you. If you don't do your job, they'll have you up against a wall with a rifle in your belly. You want that?'

The two men sloped off, cursing. Le Bailly watched them go, shaking his head. 'And they'll line me up against a wall before they do you,' he grumbled after them.

'Why so?'

He looked warily at me and beckoned me to follow him. He led me across the tracks to the tower in the middle of the yard, little more than a hut raised on stilts. Together, we climbed a flight of rickety steps to the small wooden cabin and he let us in. It was stifling and smelt of coal and sweat.

'Because I'm a trade unionist. That's why I've got to keep my nose clean and why I've got to make sure they toe the line. Coffee?'

A blackened pot simmered on an old stove in the middle of the hut. It was no wonder the air was sweltering inside. Outside, the burnt-oil sky acted like cloud cover, oppressing us under the heat of an already warm summer's day. He poured us both a small shot into two grimy enamel cups. It looked like treacle and tasted like tar. I pretended to drink it while looking through the windows that covered all four sides of the hut. Up here, you got a view that was impossible to get at ground level. Below us, the lines came in from the south, leading into the marshalling yard all around our feet. In front of us, to the east, were streams of sidings filled with goods trains and where the trucks with the dead men had been found. Beyond these was a sprawl of makeshift huts that stretched away from the tracks as far as the perimeter. They looked like they'd fall down the next time a train passed. You could say the same for the bird's nest we were in. It swayed in what little wind there was. Behind me, to the west and beyond the railway yard, was the ancient sprawl of the Salpêtrière Hospital. And to the north was the terminus, with the warehouses and workshops to the east of them. I could see Font and Papin slowly making their way to a group of other workers. None of them were in danger of breaking into a sweat.

Le Bailly gestured at them with his beaker. 'Normally I'm stuck in the middle between this lot and the management. Now I've got the Nazis to contend with too. I know the workers don't want to help the Germans. *I* don't. But it's my job to protect them, and if that means going along with the Boches for the time being, then so be it.'

I waited but he'd said all he was going to. I had a feeling there was something else he wasn't telling me.

'Who gave the order to move the trucks?' I asked him.

He turned and picked up a notebook covered in notes scrawled in stubby pencil. 'Management. Here's the log.'

He showed me the current page. A handwritten note showed a call had come in just after six that morning to let the Germans commandeer the trucks.

'Did you take the call?'

'Yes, but don't ask me who it was. It wasn't a voice I recognised, but that's not surprising these days. Couldn't even tell you if they were French or German.'

I looked briefly at the note and put my coffee down. 'Not exactly evidence, is it?'

'It's as much evidence as you're likely to get.'

'Who was it who found the bodies in the truck?'

'That was Font and Papin. They were supposed to be doing maintenance work but were skiving off when they found them. They fetched me and I called the police.'

'What about the Germans? When did they turn up?'

'They were already here by the time I got to work.'

'Who would know that the train wasn't going to be leaving the yard yesterday morning?'

'No one. No one would know if it was going to be leaving, or when.'

'But it would eventually run? And anyone hidden well enough on the train would get out?'

'I suppose so, but it's not reliable. Or safe. If I were trying to get someone out of Paris, it's not the way I'd choose. I work here, I'd know.'

'Have you heard any of the workers talk about helping people leave the city?'

'Nothing. They wouldn't tell me. Some of them might, although the likes of Papin and Font would only do it for what they could get out of it.'

The rarity of a train came slowly into view, black smoke gouging through the remnants of the soot floating in the sky. Le Bailly sighed and got up.

'Work to do,' he said, taking my undrunk coffee from me.

We climbed down the rickety stairs from his hut and I watched him head for a group of workers standing idle. I didn't envy him his job.

Crossing the yard, I went to stand in front of the huts. We couldn't get to them yesterday because of the Germans, and having just seen the extent of them, I knew searching them would be a huge task. Even so, I wondered what secrets they held. And if those secrets included a spot of poisonous gas left over from the last spat with the neighbours.

I left the yard to drive across the river to the SNCF railway company offices. I wanted to know where the order to release the trucks had come from. Driving past the Opéra, I slowed down to stare at an untimely Christmas tree of German road signs that had sprouted overnight outside the ornate beauty of the theatre. You had to admire their efficiency. They knew where they were going. Unfortunately, a feldwebel with a thick neck and massive hands wanted to know where I was going and pulled me over.

'Papers,' he demanded, his voice as deep as the shine on his boots, his French as new and uncomfortable. 'Why are you stopping?'

'I'm a cop. I wanted to know what the signs said.'

He glanced over his shoulder at the cacophony of words. 'They are for Germans, not French.' He handed my papers back to me and signalled me to move on.

'At least I know where to find the Zentral Ersatzteillager now,' I told him.

I carried on to where the SNCF offices hid behind its ornate clock gateway in the Ninth, the deeply shaded road darkened even further by the cloud of ash overhead, the pavement sprinkled with a fine dusting of soot. The burning fuel dump outside the city showed no sign of abating.

At the railway company, I found someone behind the second door I tried. He was staring at a sheet of paper on his desk, his hair ruffled where he'd run his hands through it. He did consternation well. He should, he had two German officers in the room with him who didn't have an expression between them. I swear the one on the left had died and not told anyone.

'The three goods trucks that were the scene of the killings yesterday morning,' I asked him. 'Was it you that rang Le Bailly at Gare d'Austerlitz to tell him the trucks could be put back into service?'

He shook his head. 'Besides, at the moment, it's the Germans who would decide whether they were to be used or not. Nothing is running without their say-so.'

I looked at the Germans. 'Can I ask these two?'

'You can try.'

I'd already decided to ask the one who was still alive, when Lazarus piped up before I could get the words out. He spoke with a clipped politeness that was at odds with his harsh appearance.

'As far as we know, the German High Command did not issue any order to that effect.' His French was good. If we ever decide to start invading places again, we'd better start learning some languages.

'Could an order possibly have been given without you knowing?'

'It might be possible,' he said grudgingly.

'So, it is possible that trucks would be requisitioned to take troops and supplies southwards to the front, but you have no idea if that's the case here?'

'They have none whatsoever,' the railway official replied for him, his voice a monotone.

I left the three of them in their stalemate. I had no idea whether an order had been given to move the trucks, or who'd given it. I got the feeling this was what much of my job was going to be like from now on. I needed a coffee but there was no café open outside, so I headed back to Thirty-Six. I passed the feldwebel and the road signs outside the Opéra and revised my opinion of German efficiency. They knew where they were going, they just didn't know what to do once they got there.

Back at the Quai des Orfèvres, I looked for Auban. I caught him on the stairs between the second and the third floors.

'I told you to question the workers at the railway yard.' My face was centimetres from his. I could feel the hate he gave off. 'I told you to make sure the order not to move the trucks was given.'

'Jesus Christ, Giral. No one cares.'

'I care, Auban. Four Polish refugees were killed in a railway yard and I care.'

He smirked at me. 'Polish? I care even less now, and so should you. There are more than enough French suffering without us worrying about immigrants and refugees. I'm not wasting my time on four Poles. If they don't like the Germans so much, why don't they stay there and fight like men instead of running to France and bleating about how bad the Nazis are?'

I clenched my fists but held them firmly at my sides. 'Like you're doing, you mean? I don't see you in uniform, Auban. The only effort you're putting in is skulking hundreds of kilometres from the front telling others how they should be fighting for you.'

'Fuck you, Giral.'

I brought both fists up to his throat. My hands shook as I tried to control them. Cursing, I turned and walked away, back up the half-flight of stairs to the third floor. Behind me, Auban called out.

'That's it, Giral. Walk away like you always do. You're as cowardly as these fucking Poles you love.'

His voice was blotted out as I went through the doors. Stopping to let my breath out, I lifted my right hand to look at it. I'd drawn blood in the palm where my nails had dug in. Making sure no one was around to see, I wiped it on my handkerchief and went back to my office.

Dax was waiting for me.

'What's happening, Eddie?'

I thought he meant with Auban, but he was asking about the investigation.

'I want to know where the gas came from,' I told him. 'I've looked at the huts in the railway yard, and we need to mount a proper search.'

'Be serious, Eddie. Who with? We don't have the manpower.'

'Anything could be hidden in them. We need to find out if that's where the gas is being kept.'

'Not going to happen, Eddie.'

I left it. Dax's first answer was always a no, but if I pestered him again, he'd probably fold. I tried something else. 'The suicide from last night. He was from Bydgoszcz, the same town as at least one of the men in the railway truck.'

'That doesn't have to mean anything. There'll be thousands of people from every village fleeing the Germans and the Soviets.'

'I know. It's just odd they're from the same place, that's all.'

68

'Do what you have to, Eddie, but don't get obsessed. And don't see connections where there aren't any.'

I nodded. We both knew I'd ignore every word he'd just said. We had a visitor.

'Oh good, it's Major Hochstetter,' I said. 'You might actually be able to do some conduiting here.'

Dax gave me a warning look.

'How so, Édouard?'

'The order was given for the trucks at the railway yard to be sent to the front. Le Bailly, the supervisor, claims the management told him to move them. Management say they have no knowledge of it and the two German officers at the SNCF offices didn't know if an order had been given by them or not.'

'That is quite probable. The transition to the new order of things is perhaps not going quite as smoothly as we had envisaged. There are occasionally gaps in the information that we provide to the French authorities. And among ourselves. I'm afraid there is a lamentable scope for misunderstandings.'

'Would you be able to find out? To rule out any question of Le Bailly deliberately misleading us for any reason.'

Hochstetter looked directly at me. The light from the window behind his tall form cast shadows on dark eyes and high cheeks, his expression as cold as a skull.

'I can normally get most of the information I want, Édouard. The question is whether you would really want me to.'

7

'Why do you need to speak to this German officer?' Dax had waited until Hochstetter had gone before asking.

'Because this is a murder investigation. I need to know what Weber saw to have a better idea of what time the events happened and to verify the workers' stories. I also still need to know who gave the order to have the trucks moved. Without that, I can question the workers as much as I like, but I can't fully rely on their versions of what happened.'

'What do you think happened?'

I looked out of my office window. Traces of the black smoke from the burning oil depot still hung in the sky. 'I think someone took the Poles' money and promised to get them out of the city. And then it was either that person that killed them, or someone else found the Poles waiting and killed them before the first person had the chance to help them.'

'Why, if it's the second one?'

'I don't know. To rob them perhaps. Either way, if that's the case, I don't just have to find the killers, I also have to find whoever might be trying to get refugees and deserters out of the city.'

Not to stop them, I didn't add, but to warn them to find a safer way.

*

I left Thirty-Six, tired at the end of the afternoon, and walked out into the filtered sunlight. I'd always loved this time of day, the streets filled with noise and light and bustle, walking anonymously through the crowds, all the misery and fear I'd seen in my working day sloughed off by the passing of strangers. But the city had changed. There were more people out on the streets than the previous evening, but there wasn't the hubbub. The movement and chatter had been drained out of them. Everyone walked in grey, hunched and subdued under the weight of the sky. And it was too early, too light for Paris on Berlin time.

Instead of home, I crossed the river to the Right Bank. Dax had told me not to see any connections that weren't there, so I ignored him and made for the Marais. My mind had kept returning to Bydgoszcz, a town I'd never heard of until less than twenty-four hours ago. And now in under a day I'd come across it twice, both times to do with the violent deaths of people who'd escaped from the Nazis, only to die on the day the Nazis caught up with them.

Isaac l'Aveugle, Isaac the Blind, lived in a scruffy apartment at the end of a dingy passage with his middle-aged daughter. She was his eyes. She was often also his mouth.

'He's not coming with you,' she told me at the door, refusing to let me in.

I could see Isaac in the hallway behind her. The front of his cleanly starched shirt was obscured by the luxuriant grey beard that hung down over much of it. The beard made up for the lack of anything but an ancient Homburg hat on his head. He was putting on his smart suit jacket.

'Look at him, he's bored. Trust me, he can't be arrested if he's with me.'

Isaac squeezed past his daughter with a brief and sheepish smile in her direction.

'I want him back in one piece,' she yelled, slamming the door behind her father.

I led Isaac by the arm across the river. 'She means well,' he told me, 'but I do like a bit of excitement at times. I miss the old days.'

We passed a German patrol. 'You and me both, Isaac. Which is why I've got a little job for you.'

He smiled, the most innocent and beguiling smile I knew, which was odd, as in his time he'd been one of the most notorious safe-crackers in Paris. Providing you gave him a helping shove, given his blindness after a shell went off near him at the Battle of Tientsin in China during the Boxer Rebellion. The things we do for war.

At Fryderyk's building, Madame Benoit wiped her hands on a faded apron tied around her waist and gave me the key. Behind her, seated at the kitchen table, I could see a man's back; I presumed he was her husband.

'Is someone meeting us in there?' Isaac asked at the top of the stairs.

I looked at him in puzzlement and then heard the hushed and hurried sounds coming from Fryderyk's flat that I'd missed. The door was ajar. Leaving Isaac safely in the corner of the landing, I pushed the door open and walked slowly in. I could see that the door to the balcony was open, as was the one leading into the bedroom. The noise had stopped. Pulling my service pistol out, I went over to the bedroom and gently eased the door open a bit more, looking through the crack between the door and the frame.

I could see nothing.

I pushed the cheap wooden door open further, when I heard

a sound from behind me and felt a punch to the small of my
back, which sent pulses of fluorescent pain through me. I fell to
my knees as a foot reached from behind me and kicked the gun
out of my hand. I twisted as I fell, just in time to see a man run
out of the front door. I caught a glimpse of his face. He must
have been waiting on the balcony, tucked out of sight against
the wall. Wasting seconds, I retrieved my gun from underneath
the bed and chased after him as well as I could with the bitter
ache spreading through my muscles and bones. I knew from
past joys I'd be pissing blood for days.

He was already down at the bottom of the stairs by the time
I got to the landing. He tripped and fell as he took the steps a
flight at a time and I heard him yell something in anger before
he got up again and crashed out of the heavy downstairs door.
I knew he'd be long gone by the time I got back into the flat to
look over the balcony, but I did anyway. The street was empty.

I went back to help Isaac in. 'I don't suppose you got a description?'

'He smelt nice.'

I sat in one of the armchairs and waited for the worst of the
pain to pass. It subsided to a numb misery and I started to feel
how uncomfortable the chair was, so I realised it was time to
get up. My mind started to work again. He had yelled in anger,
but it hadn't been in French. I don't think I'd ever heard Polish
being spoken, but I was happy to bet that that was the language
he'd used. I hobbled over to the sink and ran myself a cup of
water. It hurt on the way down. Not as much as it would on
the way out.

'Seems like someone else was after the same thing you are,'
Isaac said.

'Whatever it is.'

Even more curious now, I showed him into the bedroom and

73

guided him to the ancient safe. His fingers slid over the surface before he moved to the combination dial. He turned it one way, then the other.

'Nice. Give me ten minutes, Eddie. Soon be done.'

I stood on the balcony while Isaac worked. I'd left the door open so I had a clear view of him. He might look sweet, but he'd pinch anything of value if he thought he could get away with it.

Glancing down at the street below, I recalled the sight of Jan tucked inside his father's heavy coat. I imagined Fryderyk saying quiet words of comfort to his son as he walked them off the balcony, cradling the boy in his overcoat and holding his head to his chest to shield him from the terror of what he was about to do. Some of the jetsam from the previous evening was still in the gutter, other pieces had already been scavenged or retrieved. I remembered the teddy bear, covered in blood, and wondered if it was Jan's. It was gone now. I pictured Fryderyk giving it to him for something to cling to in the last moments, perhaps the one toy he was able to save as they fled home, and I wondered again what would possibly drive a father to do that to himself and to his own child. What level of desperation. What he must have witnessed in Poland.

I could hear from inside the bedroom that Isaac had finished. I hurried in just as he was pulling the heavy door open.

'Don't you trust me, Eddie?'

'Would you?'

I reached past him to look inside. There was nothing but a small pile in the centre of the safe. A piece of thin card folded in half on top of what looked like three books. Surprised, I reached in and pulled the card out to find that it held a tight stack of old envelopes. Oddly, the bottom edge of each one was sewn to the fold in the card, so they concertinaed out when I opened the folder, the open side facing up at me. The envelopes were all in the same hand, all yellowing with age, all posted to Fryderyk at an address in Bydgoszcz.

'Any money?' Isaac asked.

'Not a bean.'

I took the first letter out of its envelope and scanned it. I couldn't understand the Polish, but it had the look of a love letter. It was signed 'Ewa'. I presumed that was Fryderyk's wife.

Taking the three books from the safe, I saw that the top two were in Polish. I didn't understand either title. What took me aback was the bottom book in the pile. And not just because it was in French. I stared at it for a moment. *Journey to the End of the Night* by Louis-Ferdinand Céline. It was a book that many French readers found tough going, so I wondered why a foreigner would buy it. Stranger than that, though, was that Céline was an admirer of Hitler.

'What's in there, Eddie?'

'Books. Three of them.'

There was another piece of folded card that had been at the bottom of the pile. Similar to the folder containing Ewa's letters to Fryderyk, this one just had two photographs inside, sewn and glued to the fold in the middle. The first was of a man and woman holding a small boy between them. It looked like summer, and they were smiling in happier times. I recognised the man in the photograph as Fryderyk. The boy was Jan, the woman Ewa, I presumed. The second photo was similar to the first and looked like it had been taken on the same day.

Isaac shoved his hand inside the safe and rummaged around. 'Nothing,' he said in disgust.

Three books, two photos and some letters, I thought. And they were more important to Fryderyk than his passport. I quickly flicked through the three books but found nothing in the first two. The third one, the Céline book, contained an even odder find. A pamphlet, also written by Céline, *The School of Corpses*, published a couple of years ago and which had kicked off a lot of controversy because of its raging anti-Semitism. It seemed a strange book for a foreigner to use to brush up on their French, and even stranger for a victim of the Nazis to possess. Maybe Fryderyk had been trying to understand why his life had been torn apart.

'That's your lot, Isaac.'

'You said I'd get paid.'

'You'll get your money.' We'd agreed a fee on the way there.

'What was the noise?' Madame Benoit asked me when I returned the key.

'There was someone in Fryderyk's flat, but he got away. You didn't see anyone going upstairs?'

She crossed herself a few times before answering. 'No. I would've told you.'

'OK, but best to keep an eye open. Can you box up Fryderyk's belongings and keep them down here for the time being? Someone from the police will let you know what to do with them. Don't worry about the safe.'

I dropped Isaac off with his angry daughter and went back to Thirty-Six. The third floor was empty, any officers on duty congregating downstairs. I locked the books and other things in my drawer with Fryderyk's passport and left for home. I probably wouldn't be able to track down any next of kin, but at least I had what Fryderyk had felt to be of value, even if it was only sentimental. Although I couldn't see how the Céline book could have any emotional value to him, and the effort in buying a safe to store such an odd array of items also tunnelled its way into my mind.

With the memory of the sad little apartment, I couldn't face home, so I carried on towards the Jardin du Luxembourg. There were no bands playing in the bandstand, no children running excitedly around groups of adults talking. Just dust blowing on the parched ground and branches aching in the low breeze. No one was promenading. The few people still out were hurrying home, looking at watches, making sure they beat the curfew.

'Good evening,' I said in reflex to a couple going the other way, but they didn't look up or reply.

I left the park and walked through silenced streets. I was alone as night finally began to fall and I wondered with a growing anger if I'd ever stroll among crowds of idle walkers through our streets again.

A car pulled up behind me, the heavy throb of a diesel engine pounding in my head. Another German patrol demanding my papers, I thought, my annoyance rising. I turned to look.

8

'My favourite Abwehr major,' I said, anger giving way to irritation.

'Édouard,' Hochstetter called to me from the back of his open-topped staff car. 'Such a splendid evening for a spin in this romantic city. Do get in.'

'I'm fine walking, thanks, Major.'

'No, Édouard, really. Do get in.'

A gefreiter in the passenger seat jumped out and opened the back door for me. Hochstetter looked at me expectantly, the half-smile there as always. I sighed and stepped towards the car.

'It will make the war worthwhile.'

I sat down gingerly on the wide leather seat and the driver smoothly accelerated away. Even with the best suspension and softest upholstery Nazi technology had to offer, I had to avoid wincing from the pain in my back every time we went over a bump in the road.

'Although I'm afraid we've missed the best of the daylight,' Hochstetter added.

Well, this was nice. The invaders' guide to Paris. 'Just passing, were you, Major?'

He laughed. 'Of course not, Édouard. I leave nothing to chance. Apparently, there's somewhere delightfully revolting that all our officers are talking about and I thought you might like to accompany me there. You might even meet someone of interest to you.'

I would never have admitted it, but I was intrigued. Especially as it became apparent that out of all the places they could choose from in Paris, the Germans' new favourite night spot was Luigi's bar. The driver pulled up at the end of the narrow street and Hochstetter invited me to follow him.

Louder, bolder music than the previous night spilled out into the dusk as Luigi pulled the drape aside to let us in. His initial surly grunt on seeing me was transformed suddenly into an unctuous bowing and scraping at Hochstetter.

'Let me show you to your table,' the Italian said.

'You have tables now?' I asked him.

He laughed and clapped me on the back. When you're sucking up to the organ grinder, you can always throw a nut or two to the monkey.

'I see my table, thank you,' Hochstetter told him.

We walked through the murk. No matter how low you put the lighting, you could never hide the squalor of the café and its patrons. The place was heaving, far busier than the previous night. Behind us, the door opened again and dribbles of night-life continued to pass through the curtain even though it was gone nine o'clock. The German officers, more numerous still than the night before, seated at tables and standing in raucous groups appeared not to be too concerned with upholding their own rule. I recognised more faces from the city's underworld, minor figures cosying up to the occupiers and carmine-lipped prostitutes cooing at the Germans' every word. Most of them turned away from me as we passed by.

'You're not popular here, I see,' Hochstetter told me.

'We all find our level.'

He laughed. 'I do admire your style, Édouard.'

The same three blindingly blond officers from the previous night were standing at the same spot at the bar as before. I wondered if they'd been home yet. They failed to notice me as Hochstetter and I went past as they were too busy miming a bottle of champagne to Luigi. They'd obviously been sitting at the back during the Thousand-Year-Reich language lessons.

One German who did notice me was a disturbing vision. He had one of those faces that either looked like an old man with an unnaturally young face or a young man who'd aged prematurely. It gave him the appearance of having a round and quizzical baby's head on an adult's body. Even his hair was fine and wispy like a newborn's. The whole picture was strangely unsettling, like the cruelty of children imagined by a Surrealist artist.

'Odd how so many Nazis don't look as Aryan as they want everyone else to,' I told Hochstetter.

'I beg your pardon?'

He looked annoyed, but then you can't please everyone.

We reached our table and I found who Hochstetter thought I might be interested in meeting. Hauptmann Weber, the officer who had taken our guns at the railway yard yesterday morning, was seated at the opposite end. He hadn't seen me. He was far too drunk on Luigi's version of champagne.

'You wanted to question him,' Hochstetter explained.

'When he's like that?'

'I may not be able to give you another chance.'

Before I could answer, a tinny piano began to strike up a tune. In the corner of the room, Luigi had put up a makeshift stage, the piano occupying one side of it. A young woman was standing in the centre, and she began to sing 'J'ai Deux Amours'. Softly at first, but rising. I'd heard Josephine Baker sing it when

I worked on the doors in the jazz clubs and it always took my breath away. This kid was good, singing beautifully, but in her own way. It was wasted on this audience. The German officers carried on talking in loud voices, swapping stories of war and striking up deals with pimps and prostitutes. I watched the woman singing and felt sorry for her. I waited to see how the audience would react to the line at the end of the first verse where she sings of having two loves: her country and Paris, except it didn't go how I expected. As she sang the line, she rolled down the long glove on her left arm and threw it into the audience. I sighed. I might have known Luigi hadn't suddenly found the arts. It was only after the second glove had come off and she started unzipping her tight dress that the room took notice. The murmur of voices gave way to catcalls and coarse encouragement.

I looked around. At the other end of the table, Weber hadn't yet noticed the singer and was deep in drunken conversation with a thickset man in civilian clothing sitting next to him. Equally drunk by the look of him, his companion had noticed the show on stage and was staring eagerly at her, ignorant of much of what his companion was saying. On Weber's other side was a woman. I thought at first she was another of the prostitutes who'd come to sit at the table with the German officers, but her bearing made me stop and look closer. She was doing the same as I was: looking around at the other people in the room rather than joining in any conversation or watching the steadily more naked singer on stage. She caught my eye and raised her glass at me with a drunken smile. I raised mine back.

'Except you're not as drunk as you want everyone to think you are,' I said to myself.

I continued to watch her without her noticing. With medium-length blonde hair swept back the way Marlene Dietrich wore hers and wearing a tight sleeveless sweater that rose to her neck, she looked as out of place as I hoped I did. Her gaze carried on surreptitiously sweeping the room, and I looked away every time it was about to embrace me.

On stage, the singer hit the final note in her song and stood tall, her arms raised wide, not a scrap of clothing left on her body. The audience clapped loudly, but not, I suspected, at her singing. She bowed low and turned to hurry off the rickety stage.

When the singer had gone and the pianist had packed up for the time being, the room settled once more into the general hubbub. The woman opposite looked at me more frankly and I held her gaze.

Next to me, another German officer, more sober than Weber, spoke to me in good French. He had the studious look of a junior doctor.

'I have always wanted to visit Paris,' he told me. 'I love French culture. I hope our two great nations can find a way to coexist.'

'We already had.'

Opposite, Weber was becoming more animated in his conversation with the male civilian. I could hear them for the first time, now the music had abated. The two men were talking in German, but I couldn't place the other man's accent. He appeared to be in a contest with Weber as to who could be more obnoxious. Le Dingue – a small-time crook who was infamous for still carrying the old Apache gang weapon of combined knife, knuckleduster and revolver – was walking past them as the civilian made an expansive hand gesture and spilled his wine over his shirt. Le Dingue looked like he was going to make something of it, but quickly backed off when he saw the other people at the table.

'Please accept my most humble apologies,' Weber's friend

said in profuse drunkenness, bursting into cackles of laughter. He said it in French and I was finally able to place his accent. I wondered what an American civilian was doing mixing with German officers. As I was looking at the American, Weber finally saw me and called across the table at me.

'The policeman. Of what use are you now, policeman? Now that the Wehrmacht is here to do your job for you.' He stood up and walked unsteadily over to me, his eyes bright with alcohol. 'You are redundant. The Wehrmacht will be in charge of law and order from now on.'

'That's wonderful, Hauptmann. But who'll be in charge of justice?'

Glancing over, I could see the woman staring intently at us.

'Hauptmann Weber,' Hochstetter admonished him. 'Perhaps you should temper your attitude. Your behaviour is unbecoming of a Wehrmacht officer. We need the French police for their expertise and knowledge.'

Weber sat down heavily next to me and smirked. 'Expertise?'

'Expertise, Hauptmann Weber. I have great regard for Inspector Giral's excellence as a detective. And his tenacity. He is determined to bring the killers of these four Polish men to justice. You as an officer in the Wehrmacht should congratulate that.'

Weber wasn't to be cajoled so easily. 'Polish scum,' he muttered and belched.

'And I believe that Inspector Giral is an honourable man. The Reich has need for men like him. He is also pursuing the suicide of another man. Another Pole. A man he doesn't know from a town he's never heard of. Bydgoszcz.'

Weber's head snapped up at Hochstetter's last comment and he glared at me. 'Polish scum.'

'Maybe now is not the time,' Hochstetter said, looking

intently at Weber, 'but I will be requesting your commanding officer to allow you to assist the French police with their investigation into these deaths.'

Through his stupor, Weber evidently caught something in Hochstetter's tone. Meekly, he nodded and got up to return to his companions.

'I will do what I can, Édouard,' Hochstetter told me. 'I think it is important for all concerned that we should be seen to be assisting the French authorities.'

I needed some fresh air so when Hochstetter started talking to the Francophile officer, I got up and went to talk to Pepe in his mouldy corner of the room.

'Miss me, Pepe?' I asked him. He hadn't. 'Sadly, we were interrupted yesterday when you were about to tell me all about gas and what happened at the Gare d'Austerlitz.'

'The Poles, you mean?'

'You know they're Polish?'

'Everyone does. But that's all I know.' A group of German officers, new to the party, walked past us to join some compatriots at a table. Pepe raised his voice as he carried on talking and glanced sideways at the soldiers. 'Anyway, who wants Poles in the city? Refugee scum, they got what they deserved.'

'You might have found a few thousand kindred spirits have hit town, Pepe, but don't push it with me. What do you know?'

He snorted at me. 'What do I know, Eddie? I know you're washed up. In the past, you'd have had me by the throat for saying that.'

I smiled at him. 'You're probably right, Pepe. But I'm older now, and wiser. I've set my sights much lower.'

Hidden by the crowd of people and the zinc-topped ornate wood counter, I caught hold of his balls and pulled him towards me. His breath caught in pain, the sneer frozen on his mouth.

'You may impress the Germans,' I whispered to him, 'but don't let me hear you talking like that again. There are plenty of people in this city we don't want, and the list doesn't start with refugees.' I gave an extra squeeze. He tried not to let the others in the bar see the tears that had come to his eyes. 'Now, gas. You must know who'd be selling something like that.'

'I don't know, Eddie, honest.'

'Come on, Pepe. It's pretty niche. There can't be that many people selling military gas. Give me a name. And who's in the market to buy it?'

I could see him frantically casting through his mind for something to give me to stop the pain. 'I don't know about any gas,' he gasped. 'Honest. But the Gare d'Austerlitz. There are all sorts of sheds that the railways aren't using where stuff is being stored.'

'Tell me something I don't know, Pepe. At least if you're planning on having any little Pepes to keep the courts in business.' I squeezed tighter.

'There's more going on there now. Since everyone left Paris. More stuff's being kept there.'

'Stolen?' He nodded. 'And people?'

'I don't know.'

'And what about the gas? I think you know something.'

'I don't. I really don't.'

'Give me names?'

'I can't. It's all changing since the Germans. I don't know who it is.'

I studied his eyes. Through his tears, I sensed he wasn't keeping anything from me. I let him go and he staggered back slightly before catching himself. He looked around quickly, making sure no one saw him lose face.

I finished my drink and told Luigi that Hochstetter was paying.

'See,' I told Pepe. 'Helping the police needn't be painful.'

I left him and went outside, Luigi carefully closing the door behind me. I gulped in the untainted air of the street, glad to be away from the smoke and the noise and the smell of the bodies in the café. I stretched, my back aching more acutely after so long on one of Luigi's chairs.

Walking back to my apartment through the intense dark of the blackout, I considered what I knew. The first thing was that we needed to search the huts in the railway yard, despite Dax's refusal. Pepe had no idea who was selling the gas, so the next best bet would be to look for where it was being stored.

I also recalled Hauptmann Weber's face when Hochstetter had mentioned Bydgoszcz. 'You know the name.' My voice was loud in the gathering shadows.

The final thing I knew was that I was being followed. I'd been a cop in Paris too long not to pick up on that. I walked out into the centre of Boulevard du Montparnasse and stood there, waiting for someone to show themselves to me. I gazed calmly into the darkness. I couldn't see anything, but whoever was tracking me would know I knew they were there.

'Goodnight,' I called to them. 'I'm off home now.'

It was only once I'd closed the street door to my apartment block behind me that I let out a breath of relief. The sweat coursed down my back as I climbed up the four flights to my door in semi-darkness.

As I put the key in the lock, I felt a change in the flow of air from the stairwell behind me and I heard a low rustle. Turning, I saw a young man's face emerge from the shadows of the stairs leading to the roof.

Each step he took revealed another feature. One by one as he came near.

I felt a chill run through me.

9

My hand shook and I laid it flat on the kitchen table before carrying on. I could hear him moving about in my living room. I wondered what it looked like through his eyes. When I'd calmed down again, I picked up the bottle and hefted it, judging the weight. A simple task, but I couldn't get the balance right. I wasn't sure I could do this. Taking a deep breath, I walked from the kitchen into my living room.

I'd been saving the whisky for a special occasion. I had no idea what that was ever going to be. This was it. The young man was looking at the books on my shelf. He turned when I came in.

'Mum always said you had better taste than you should,' he told me. 'I never knew what she meant by it.'

I nodded silently. Neither did I.

He moved about restlessly. I'd only fetched the whisky and my two cleanest dirty glasses for something to do, but now we were in the room together, there was nothing left to do but talk. The first time that had happened in fifteen years. I'd often wondered lately if I'd recognise my own son if I were to pass him in the street. He was five the last time I saw him. Now he was twenty and wearing a grey serge jacket that was too big for him over khaki green army trousers. It turns out I would have recognised him in an instant, as I had done on the stairs.

'You're in the army?' I asked.

'A *poilu*. A private. Cannon-fodder if we knew where the cannons were.'

He told me he'd been serving in the Meuse area. Not one of the elite troops stationed on the Maginot Line, because the French military command had supposed that they wouldn't be needed on the Meuse. They were wrong. The Germans didn't play by the same rules and went round our defences and our best soldiers and trampled through the Ardennes to the Meuse, where we kept our most inexperienced and unprepared soldiers. And they crushed them and killed them in their thousands and scattered them to their fate. Just like Jean-Luc – my son, who I had left to his and his mother's fate when he was five years old.

I gave him a glass of whisky and we paused a moment before drinking, both unsure whether to propose a toast. We didn't. We just drank awkwardly. We hadn't embraced. I watched him. He had my height but his mother's finer features and wide mouth. His mother's colouring, thick hair the shade of sand that had reminded me of my home when I'd needed it. But he had my eyes, the soft gaze that could turn into a killer's if uncontrolled. The one thing I wish I hadn't given him. I caught him staring back at me and we both looked away. I tried to imagine what he saw.

'I can't find Mum,' he explained. 'Otherwise I wouldn't have come. I can't get into our flat because I lost my key. I have nowhere else to go.'

'You can stay here.'

He nodded and held his glass out for more whisky. I poured some for him and for myself.

'She's not at home. One of the neighbours two floors up says that she left with everyone else before the Germans got to Paris. They wouldn't let me in because I was a *poilu*. On the run.'

He sat down on my favourite armchair, so I took the other one. It wasn't as comfortable. It hadn't moulded to me over thousands of empty evenings and almost as many nights when I hadn't made it to the bedroom. Or hadn't wanted to.

'I'll make up the bed in the other room.'

'Leave it for now. I'll help you do it.'

He went silent. He was still a kid. Just like I'd been when I went to war. Younger even than he was now.

'Mum never talks about you now.' I didn't know what to say. 'She did when you first left, and for years after. She hates you, you know.'

'Do you?'

'I don't know.' He pointed at his army trousers. 'But now at least I can understand you.'

For the first time, I saw the dark stain of blood on what remained of his uniform. Someone else's blood, he told me, a friend's.

'I know what that means,' I said, blotting out memories of my war. The memories that had brought me to Paris to be cured of my shell shock and sent me back to the front when the doctors and officers decided one morning that I was no longer suffering. I kept my eyes open, waiting for the images to pass. The one person who saw that I wasn't ready was Sylvie, Jean-Luc's mother, the nurse who was too young to be expected to look after damaged men who were too young in turn for what was being asked of us. And now it was happening to my son.

'Mum always said you were a dreamer. That's why you ended up living here, on the Left Bank. She always said it was no fit place for a policeman to live.'

'She's probably right.' But it suited the romantic notion

of what my life should have been before the war changed everything. I stared over my glass at my son. I knew I had to say something but I wasn't sure what.

I'd imagined this meeting so many times, but it was never under these circumstances. I'd expected anger. Or recrimination. Or even coldness. Instead, he regarded me like I was an old family acquaintance. A distant relative who'd lost touch. The realisation that that's what I'd become pierced me.

'I couldn't stay with your mother,' I finally explained. 'I fell in love with her when she nursed me in Paris, but it wasn't the real me that fell in love with her. I couldn't live with that after the war.'

'Or me?'

I had to pause for breath. This new war was opening up too many old wounds.

'Anyone. Most of all myself.'

He looked around my room, empty but for books and faded furniture, and nodded. He didn't know, but he was the first person other than me to sit in one of my armchairs in over ten years.

'Don't let this war do the same to you,' I told him.

'I won't. I've lived with things you haven't. And now, my generation has to live with defeat. Yours lived with victory. You killed in the last war. You knew honour. I lost without firing a single shot. I didn't see a German until I was running to Paris, hiding from them by the side of a road. You have your own shame, I have mine.'

'You don't have the shame of killing, Jean-Luc. There is no greater shame than that.'

He stared back at me. I could see he didn't believe me.

I tried to explain. 'War creates strangers of ourselves, Jean-Luc. We never come back from that.'

Sunday 24th May 1925

I watched my son sleeping.

His head was bent back so far, his neck was a taut, straight line from chin to chest. His mouth was open, his pale lips quivering very slightly. I wondered what his dreams were. I hoped they were different from mine. I had to fight the urge to push his head forward so he'd be more comfortable. He was tall for his age, just five years old, but he always looked small and helpless in bed. The boyish bravado gone for the night, the vulnerable child in his place. He was too much like me.

I backed out of his room, not wanting to wake him, and went to the bedroom I shared with Sylvie. She was asleep. Or pretending to be. I never knew anymore. I turned away and tried to recognise what I felt. Sadly, I wasn't even certain I cared.

It had been a bad shift. The buzz of the jazz club had been replaced by the bleak ache of a night spent hustling the prostitutes and their pimps around Pigalle. Hopeless alleys where drunks were rolled for five sous and streetwalkers were beaten for fun. Tonight was one of those nights when Paris was a city of dark. A pimp had cut the face of one of the women he controlled because she hadn't earned enough money. I'd been the one to take her to the hospital. Mercifully, she was too high on whatever drug her pimp had forced down her throat to feel much pain. I'd watched as a tired doctor had sewn up her face, his delicate fingers taking care over each stitch.

'You're going to have to find other work,' he told her matter-of-factly when he'd done.

She looked horrified, the drug wearing off. 'He'll kill me.'

I'd taken her from the hospital to a poky room in Montmartre she shared with two other girls and stared out of the window while she got a bag together.

'I'm taking you to the station, Marianne,' I told her. She'd told me once it wasn't her real name, but that it appealed to the patriotism of her lonely punters.

'It's no use. He'll find me.'

I lost her at the Gare d'Austerlitz. She said she needed a pee and disappeared into the toilets. After ten minutes, I went in to find the window open and Marianne gone.

I thought of her again at home as I pulled a blanket out of a cupboard and settled down for another uncomfortable night on the small living-room sofa.

'Some people can't be helped.' I punched the cushions into shape and looked around the gloomy living room filled with ornaments I didn't remember and wondered if it was her or me I was talking about.

I woke up to find Jean-Luc staring at me. He was holding the tin soldier his maternal grandfather had given him and that I hated. He looked at me like he didn't know what sort of creature I was.

'Papa's awake,' he called, running off to the kitchen.

I got up, my back stiff, and stuffed the blanket back in its cupboard.

'Why didn't you come to bed?' Sylvie asked me when we sat down to breakfast.

'You were asleep.'

She sniffed at that and buttered a chunk of bread for Jean-Luc, her movements brusque, leaving thick waves of fat on the coarsely ripped piece of baguette.

'What did you do in the war, Papa?' he asked me as he waited.

'Don't ask your father that question, Jean-Luc,' Sylvie told him.

I tried to thank her with my eyes, but she'd already turned her angry attention to the coffee pot. I smiled at Jean-Luc, but he was caught up in his food, his question of a few moments ago mercifully forgotten. Instead, I stared out of the window at the grey building opposite and tried to want what I had.

Sylvie only thawed when she saw the main promenade of the World Fair. She hadn't wanted to go. I'd had to chivvy her to leave the flat more than I had Jean-Luc.

'What's there for Jean-Luc?' she'd demanded a dozen times on the Metro.

'He'll love it,' I'd told her, unsure he would.

But there were merry-go-rounds and rides and a miniature village, and sweets and chocolates and other children running around. And there were pavilions of all the major stores on the Esplanade des Invalides: Galeries Lafayette, Bon Marché, and Printemps.

'I love the roof,' Sylvie gasped when she saw the Printemps pavilion.

'Lalique made the glass pebbles.'

We both stared in awe at the building, the roof a simple glass and concrete reworking of Lalique's own elaborate stained-glass cupola on the store on Boulevard Haussmann. It looked savage and rough, a bare shell, and it was beautiful. A lot of people hated it. I glanced quickly at Sylvie and remembered falling in love with her so long ago, when she looked the same way I did upon a world gone mad. I reached for her hand, but she'd already moved away to take Jean-Luc's.

'You go and look at whatever it is you wanted to,' she told me. 'I'll take Jean-Luc to the rides.'

I watched them go, an easy swing to the way they held hands, and I carried on looking after them long after they'd been lost to me, swallowed up by the crowd.

Much as the Printemps pavilion had spoken to me, I crossed the river and made my way to the edge of the exposition site. Rising through the trees was the sight I'd come to see: the Esprit Nouveau. The organisers had been horrified by its starkness and had given it the worst spot possible. It was near the Grand Palais and they hadn't allowed any trees to be cut down, so Le Corbusier had simply built among them. In one case, he'd even built around a tree. I stood outside and stared in wonder at the trunk and leaves rising through a hole in the floor and ceiling. He'd broken the rules that others had put in his way. He'd even made it out of wood, and then covered it in white stucco. A thin veneer over a fragile structure and it still had the strength to withstand. I turned to go. I didn't need to see inside.

We had lunch at one of the temporary restaurants set up on the banks of the Seine. Jean-Luc and Sylvie had little appetite after an ice cream, and I wasn't hungry either, but we all three fought our way through our food. My wife and son were laughing at some funfair memory.

'What did you do in the war, Papa?' Jean-Luc suddenly asked again.

I folded my serviette slowly and put it down.

'I killed people,' I told him. 'I stood in mud and blood and shit and I killed people so they wouldn't kill me. And I killed people because I was told to kill people and I didn't know enough to know that I didn't have to obey their rules. But I did, and I killed people again and again.'

'For Christ's sake, Édouard,' Sylvie interrupted, but I wasn't to be stopped.

'And I saw bodies of men being eaten by rats and I felt my friends' blood on my face when their heads were blown off. I heard young men at night, lying in no-man's-land, crying out for their mothers. Every night, I'd hear them. Calling for their mothers because they were dying and afraid. And I'd eat my breakfast with the smell of burnt flesh in my nose and I'd panic every time I saw smoke because I didn't know if it was poisonous gas or not.'

'Stop it, Édouard.' Sylvie banged her knife onto her plate, the sound harsh in my head, but I couldn't.

'And still I killed people. With bullets through their heads and bodies and bayonets in their stomachs. I felt their blood run down my hands and I saw their eyes stare back at me for that one moment. And then I was taken prisoner and it was a relief. I thought for a moment that at least now I wouldn't have to kill anyone again and no one would kill me. But they put me on a train with other soldiers and drove us kilometres through the country. And we were still standing in mud and blood and shit, and all the time, I realised they might kill me any time they wanted to. And when they put me in prison, every day I got up and I thought, this is the day. This is the day they'll kill me. And I was afraid. Every day, I was afraid. Because I deserved it. I knew I deserved it.'

I thought I heard myself crying. Only it wasn't me. It was my son. He looked at me in fear, his face seared with terror at what I was saying and he cried until his cheeks turned red and his eyes disappeared tight shut.

'Shut up, Édouard,' Sylvie was hissing at me. 'Shut up. He's only a child.'

She picked Jean-Luc up and left me alone in the restaurant. The people at the tables around me were silent. Another child nearby was also crying. I neatly folded my serviette before getting up to leave.

I didn't go home until it was dark and I'd finally grown too cold sitting outside in the Jardin du Luxembourg.

'Where have you been?' Sylvie asked me.

'I found a book on a chair in the gardens and I stayed to read it.'

She looked exasperated in that way I think I once loved. She pushed back the strand of hair that always fell over her face when she was worried or angry. 'A book? I could understand it if you drank, Édouard. But a book? I don't know what's normal with you.'

'Normal?' Nothing of what I feel or do is normal, I wanted to tell her, but couldn't. 'Shall I sleep in the living room?'

'Come to bed, Édouard.'

I lay awake until I heard her breath come in slow whispers before getting up and going into Jean-Luc's bedroom. He lay asleep. He'd thrown the cover off, his arms and legs splayed in innocence. I watched him for as long as I could bear before bending down to kiss him lightly on the head. He smelt safe.

'Why can you never do that when he's awake?'

Sylvie's voice behind me startled me. I hadn't heard her follow me into our son's room. I looked at her and then back at Jean-Luc but said nothing. I heard her turn to leave.

'Or when I'm awake?'

'I don't know,' I said, low enough so she wouldn't hear me.

Sunday 16th June 1940

IO

Jean-Luc was gone from his bed by morning.

It was the first Sunday under German rule and the sky was unnecessarily blue and hopeful. Even the clouds of soot had dissipated a little overnight and were conspiring to imbue us all with a false cheerfulness. I walked away from my building, lost in my own fears. A sprinkling of smartly dressed believers were walking in all directions to their various churches for Mass, their faces fixed in steadfast faith. It made me want to give up before the day was born. I looked for Jean-Luc, but knew I wouldn't see him. An elderly couple walked past me, their hands held tightly. They avoided making eye contact with me or anyone else, but I could see the look of underlying fear on their faces. It made me look more closely at the churchgoers and the bread-buyers and the stilted Sunday strollers trying to do one thing normal and I saw at last the constant murmur of anxiety below the surface.

I was surprised to find a café open by the Jardin du Luxembourg, the terrace tables and chairs set out as though we'd suddenly gone back to normal. I sat at a table and closed my eyes and for a moment we had. I was no different from anyone else out on that Sunday morning. The unusually muted sounds of Paris drifted away from me. Jean-Luc's bed had been empty when I'd gone through to see him and I'd cursed myself for the rarity of sleeping well. Waiting for him to return, I'd listened to the radio. They'd given up lying to us and just played dance music so I'd turned it off. After a time, I'd realised my son wasn't coming back and I had to get out.

The waiter brought me my coffee and I opened my eyes with a start to see two tall, blond German soldiers at a nearby table. They were flirting with two young Frenchwomen, who giggled in time as they spoke. There were no Frenchmen their age in the city, all of them gone to war and loss, or running bewildered like my son. The soldiers joined the two women and I stirred the froth into my coffee. At another table, a smartly dressed couple, flanked by two tables of German officers and obstinately keeping up appearances, complained to the waiter about the quality of the croissants.

'This isn't real butter,' the man said.

'There is no real butter,' the waiter replied, a southerner like me. He stopped by my table on the way back inside and muttered, 'Only a Parisian would complain about butter when we're surrounded by Boches.'

An enterprising ice-cream vendor ready to try his luck had stopped his cart by the park gates and a group of four soldiers stopped to buy ice creams.

'Take the uniforms off them and they'd be kids,' an accented voice said next to me.

I turned to see a grizzled German NCO sitting on his own watching the scene. He was picking up his change and getting ready to leave.

'They don't know what war is,' he went on, facing me. 'Not like we do. We saw things they'll never see.'

'They chose to. We didn't.'

He paused to look at me before answering. 'We don't all

want to be here.' I watched him slowly walk away and suddenly felt sorry for him. He looked a lonely man somewhere no one wanted him.

The four young soldiers with their ice creams stopped at the park entrance and fussed over a French baby in its pram before moving on slowly into the gardens. Another waiter brought me my change and said something about the atrocities we'd all been hearing of since war had been declared.

'They seem civilised enough to me,' he murmured. 'No worse than the clowns running the country till now.'

'We'll see.'

Over the road, the newspaper kiosk was closed. They had nothing to sell, there were still no papers being printed. For all the good they'd done us. The prevarications of our politicians and the easy lies of the press of the twenties and thirties were universal laws of physics compared with the fake optimism and blatant untruths of the last six weeks.

I picked up my change and walked back home to see if Jean-Luc had returned. He hadn't, so I left a note for him in the living room and went back out. Downstairs, Monsieur Henri was just coming in. He brandished two baguettes at me, his neat moustache bristling with excitement. 'Baker's open on Boulevard Saint-Michel. Queued twenty minutes for these.'

I watched him close his door with a triumphant flourish. I tried sneaking past but he opened it again almost immediately.

'The British have parachuted in on bicycles and they're cycling up the Champs-Élysées. I'm staying in.' He nodded at me and slammed his door shut a second time.

'Thanks for that.'

In the narrow streets on my way to the river and Thirty-Six, I heard a stone scrape on the pavement behind me, like when it catches under a shoe. I turned round, but there was no one there.

No one was moving on the street, the Sunday faithful already safely back indoors. I walked on. I heard no more sounds. Our police station on an island in the Seine seemed a safe haven.

Except Hochstetter was in Dax's office when I got there. 'Good morning, Édouard,' he greeted me, far too warmly.

'Why are you here? Surely whatever plum hotel the Abwehr has requisitioned has to be better than Thirty-Six on a Sunday morning.'

My petulance was lost on him. 'Thank you, we are in the Lutétia. It is most splendid. I really must invite you for coffee one day.' He turned to Dax. 'Édouard and I enjoyed a most convivial evening in one of your city's low spots last night. It's very important that we all work together, don't you think? I feel Édouard and I are really beginning to get to know each other.'

Dax looked at me in surprise.

'I don't think I had much choice.'

'You always have a choice.' He stared frankly at me. 'Ah, Detective Auban, you're here.'

I turned around to see Auban in the doorway. Hochstetter took his leave and vanished into the depths of the detectives' room with him.

'That's a marriage that should worry us all,' I told Dax.

'There's something else you're not going to like. Don't bring your car to work tomorrow. The Germans have ordered that all private cars are to stay off the roads until they're issued with a German licence.'

'You are joking.'

'I wish I were. Just pray they don't requisition it. That's what's going to happen to most people, I've heard.'

My head dropped. I noticed a bumble-bee crawling in tight circles on the floor, trapped and sleepy in the dark of Dax's office. 'I want to search the railway yard.'

'We've been through this, Eddie.'

I told him about what I'd learned from Pepe about the huts being used to store stolen goods. 'I want them searched to see if it's where the gas canister came from. And to see if there are any more refugees hiding out in them.'

'Do you realise how many men it will take to search that area? With everything else that's going on?'

'We can't do much about all the other stuff going on, Commissioner, but we can do something about this.'

He let out a deep sigh, the skin on his cheeks stretched tight. 'All right, Eddie, get a team together. You've got until the end of today, that's all. Is there anyone worth bringing in for questioning yet?'

I shook my head. 'There are a few I want to check up on. Le Bailly, the union official. The two workers, Papin and Font. But it's too early to say any of them is the main suspect. And I want to speak to the German officer, Weber. He could have seen something and he might know if it was the German military who ordered the trucks to be moved.'

'So you do see a possibility of a German hand in the murders, Édouard.' Hochstetter's voice in the doorway startled us both. Auban wasn't with him.

'Now wouldn't that be nice?'

'Including Hauptmann Weber.'

'No, I don't. Should I?'

Before Hochstetter could answer, Barthe, his nose red after his breakfast brandy, came into the room with some news. 'Reynaud's resigned as Prime Minister. We don't even have the remnants of a government now. And the Germans have reached the Swiss border.'

In the silence, Hochstetter saw the bee and casually stamped on it. I heard its body burst. He wiped his boot on the floor next to the insect, leaving a yellow stain. My eye caught him looking at me. We stared at each other in silence, both knowing that the roles of the occupier and the occupied were becoming progressively more cemented.

II

'Goddamn Sunday rooting through this shit,' a uniformed cop grumbled as I walked past.

'Four men died ten metres from where you're standing,' I told him. 'Tell me you don't want to find who did it.'

Without a word, he and his partner went back to searching through a rickety shed. I looked across the yard. Two dozen uniforms and detectives were slowly working their way through the muddle of huts made of brick and wood and old rubbish that had grown up around the marshalling yard and along the tracks. The buildings were six or seven deep in places, each obscured by another, and the cops had to negotiate their way through a tangle of brambles and junk and rusted metal.

And just like Friday, we had an audience of German troops. They'd turned up in a freshly laundered lorry a short while after I'd organised the cops into search teams and were lined up along the tracks. I saw Hochstetter's hand in it.

We'd found nothing we'd wanted yet, but steadily rising at the edge of the yard was a pile of items taken from some of the huts that had to have been stolen and stored there. Mayer, the evidence sergeant, held up a fedora hat to show me.

'Boxes full of them, all about fifteen years old. Shed over there with crates of brand-new men's clothes, all good makes.

And these.' He put the hat down and took a church candle the size of a horse's leg out of a wooden box.

I looked at it. 'Probably why we're losing the war. All those unlit prayers.'

He grinned and led me towards the huts. 'Something else you should see. You might want to cover your nose.'

For a moment, I panicked at the thought of more gas, but he took me into the maze of shacks, to where two uniformed cops were standing by a more substantial hut than the others. They were pinching their noses. Mayer gestured me forwards. Cautiously, I peered in, the stench from inside making me retch. Through the gloom, I could see row upon row of vegetables stacked in market boxes the height and length of the shed. All of them had gone to waste, rotted in their cheap wooden crates.

'And we've been going without food for months.' Mayer shook his head in despair.

I had to agree with him. We'd put up with food shortages all year. And I didn't see that situation improving any now that the Germans were in charge of everything that would be coming in and out of Paris. I went back out and took in a deep breath. Paris was becoming a city of dead aromas. Papin and Font were there, so I called them over and asked them what they knew of the huts.

'Nothing,' Font said, his moustache roaming his face as he spoke. Papin stared in surly boredom at a point over my shoulder.

'Who uses them?'

Font shrugged. 'Anyone who wants to. They're nothing to do with us.'

'You must see people going in and out of them.'

Papin spoke. 'Too busy doing our job to be standing staring.'

'Now I know you're lying. Who was it who told you to move the trucks?'

The two men looked at each other and shrugged.

'Management,' Font said. 'I don't know. We just knew we had to couple them to a convoy for the Germans.'

'It was Le Bailly,' Papin added. 'He told us.'

'Suddenly you want to be helpful,' I commented.

'You asked. I answered. All I know is, Le Bailly told us to hook up the trucks. Doing the Boches' work for them.' Font and Papin shared a satisfied look with each other. 'Anything else?'

'Where is he now?' Again, the shrugs. 'Stay where I can see you.'

I watched them slouch off. Mayer signalled me over, trying not to let the Germans see what he was doing. I walked over to him slowly and followed him into a second row of makeshift buildings. Two uniformed cops were standing in the doorway of a newer-looking hut. They stood by to let me in.

Looking terrified in the corner were three young men. As my eyes got used to the dark, I saw they were wearing French army uniforms. Muddied and torn, but uniforms all the same. I told the two cops at the door to make sure no one came in.

'We got separated from our unit,' one of the *poilus* told me. 'We were stationed at the Meuse, but when the Germans over-ran us, we got lost. So we made our way back to Paris to try and find someone to tell us what to do.'

'And then the Germans reached Paris,' the second one said, 'and we were trapped here. We couldn't get out and we couldn't find any officers to report to.'

Even in the darkness, I could see that they were kids, not yet twenty by the look of them. I knew what going to war at that age felt like. And now I knew how it felt to have a son in the same boat.

'Does no one know you're here?'

'We're not from Paris,' the third one finally spoke. He seemed close to tears. 'We don't know anyone here.'

I asked them if they'd seen or heard any activity on the Friday morning, but they said they hadn't. 'Have you tried to get on a train since you've been here? Or spoken to anyone about it?'

'There've been no trains running. We haven't spoken to anyone since last week.'

I told Mayer to go to the hut with the clothes and bring enough for the three *poilus*. 'Don't tell anyone what you're doing.'

He came back with a box of trousers and shirts and I told the three young soldiers to find clothes that fit them. In the end, they looked decent, if unfashionable. They stashed their uniforms in their packs with what was left of their army rations.

'There are German soldiers along the railway track,' I told them. 'They will go after we do. As soon as you hear us leave, wait an hour and then head west or south-west out of the city. The Germans have got as far as the Swiss border, so if you're going to meet up with the army again, it's most likely to be in the south. There is a nine o'clock curfew in the city. You need to be out of here by that time.' I also told them we were now on Berlin time, but they refused to change their watches.

'We'll remember,' the first one told me.

I wished them luck before leaving. Outside I rejoined Mayer and the other two cops. Auban went past and I waited till he'd gone before saying anything to them. 'No one speaks of this. Keep an eye on the hut. Make sure no one goes in there.'

I heard my name being called from somewhere further inside the more densely packed shanty. A uniform ran over to me and told me they'd found something. I followed him into the maze to where half a dozen cops were looking excited.

'In there, Inspector.'

I went inside a hut that looked like it dated from before the last war. Mayer followed me and we approached a pile of wooden crates stacked in a corner. The sergeant who'd accompanied me into the truck on Friday morning was holding back a tarpaulin that had been covering the boxes.

'There's one missing,' he told me.

I counted the crates. There were eleven, stacked on the floor in three columns, the top left one absent where it looked like a twelfth should have been. The sergeant shone a torch on the pile. The remaining two boxes on the top tier were thickly coated in dust. They'd lain untouched for years. The lid on top of the short stack lay at an angle and was clean of grime.

'I took the lid off this one to check,' the sergeant explained, 'which is when we found this.' He removed it for me to see and shone the torch inside. 'Chlorine gas. Twenty-four canisters to a crate.'

I saw for the first time the army stencil, faded on the sides of the crates. 'Which means the killer's got twenty-two left in the box that's missing.'

The sergeant replaced the lid. 'There's more.' He showed me another smaller pile of boxes coated in dust against the far wall. Inside were flares and fireworks. 'Also old military. None missing, though.'

'Clear the shed,' I told him. 'I want everything at Thirty-Six. All accounted for.'

I went to see Le Bailly in his raised hut.

'There's nothing to tell you,' he said. 'Anyone could have stored the gas canisters there. You've seen what it's like. There are a lot of abandoned sheds. They could have moved them about and I'd never have known.'

'Turning a blind eye?'

'I swear to you, Inspector Giral, I knew nothing about any

thefts or stolen goods. Sure, I've come across boxes and items in some of the huts that I thought were a bit suspicious, but it was nothing to do with me.'

'You didn't think to report it to the police?'

'I'm a trades unionist. I tend to get short shrift when I try dealing with the police, so I've learned to keep myself to myself.'

'There's a possibility that some of the people involved in stealing these goods were also behind the scheme of getting refugees and deserters out of the city by rail. Possibly even of killing them. If that's the case, it would point to an organised gang with people on the inside. People with expertise.'

'Railway workers? Impossible. I mean, Font's a dark horse and Papin's a bit of a troublemaker, but it's a big leap from that to murder.'

'And you?'

'You can't think I was involved with a gang. The only trouble I've ever had with the police is because of my politics.'

I got back to Thirty-Six in time to watch Mayer oversee the crates being stored in a separate room. I watched him and the sergeant and two uniforms carefully stack the flares and fire-works away from the eleven boxes of gas canisters. When they'd finished, the other three left, leaving me and Mayer alone with the ancient ordnance. Mayer carefully removed the lid from the box we'd already opened.

'Much as there are times I'd like to see this place go up in a ball of poisonous flames,' I told him, 'best not to let it happen on our watch.'

'I'm touched by your concern, Eddie.'

'At least not while I'm here.'

He narrowed his eyes at me and looked inside the crate. 'So, it was chlorine.'

Something still didn't feel right though, I thought. The smell had been wrong. Gingerly, Mayer took out one of the bottles and held it up in the weak light in the room to look at the markings.

'Chlorine and phosgene mixed.' I sighed. *'That's why I didn't* recognise it.'

'Why mixed?'

'Phosgene was deadlier, but too slow-acting to be of any use in battle. And you could see chlorine coming because of the yellow smoke. So they mixed the two, to make it colourless. The chlorine incapacitates you straightaway and the phosgene finishes you off. Quicker than phosgene and more agonising than chlorine. They always did have our best interests at heart.'

'Did you experience it?'

'Not this stuff. I only saw chlorine attacks. I'd been taken prisoner by the time this was widely used. They called it white star, because they used to paint a white star on the shells that contained these little beauties. It was a green cross for chlorine or phosgene, a yellow cross for mustard and white star for this. The army always wanted to brighten up our day. Still, I'm sure you'll be all right down here with it.'

I left him glancing nervously at the door to the room where he'd stored the boxes and went up to the third floor to tell Dax about the gas.

'At least we've cut off his supply,' Dax decided. 'Whoever it is who's selling it.'

'He's still got another twenty-two bottles to play around with. And I'm not so sure it is someone dealing in it. The way just the one box was taken and the amount of dust on the other boxes makes me think it was opportunistic. Someone found a forgotten stash and took what they needed.'

'Why now?'

'Part of a con to rob and kill people escaping the Germans? Someone who doesn't like refugees?'

'It's got to be someone who knows the railway yard and the huts. One of the workers?'

'I spoke to Le Bailly. Anyone could have had access to them, including the gangs my informant told me about. They're having a field day with all the empty flats in the city. We've seen that in the amount of stolen goods we found.'

I went back to my office and stared at the wall. It was an investigation that would have been challenging even without half the German army tramping through the city, all our files floating off downriver and a ragtag, drifting population. And all the time, a name kept nagging at the back of my mind. Bydgoszcz. Four murders and one suicide, all linked by the one town.

And why a refugee would keep books and letters in a safe, but not his passport. On instinct, I opened my desk drawer to look at the letters Fryderyk had left. On their own, I wouldn't have spared them a second thought, besides looking for someone in Bydgoszcz to inform of Fryderyk and Jan's deaths, but the discovery of the safe and the intruder searching through the apartment cast a new light on them. Before the Germans had come, I might have found someone to translate them in case there was something more to them, but that was now almost impossible. Of course, had the Germans not come, there'd have been no need.

I became aware of a figure standing in the doorway. It was Hochstetter. I had no idea how long he'd been there. He felt like a dose of the clap that just wouldn't go away. I didn't tell him that.

'I have good news for you,' he told me. 'You are to be issued with a licence for your private vehicle. You will have to have an SP plate put on your car by a Wehrmacht mechanic to authorise your car to be on the road.'

I closed the drawer, leaving the letters where they were. The first thing I thought of was the gun hidden behind the dash-board of my Citroën. 'Thank you, Major Hochstetter, if you'll tell me where to take it, I'll do just that.'

'Why wait, Édouard. I will accompany you.'

'There's no need.'

'I insist.' He didn't move a centimetre from where he was standing.

'Is that a polite and friendly "I insist"? Or a come with me, I'm German "I insist"?'

He stood and smiled in that remote way a cat teases a mouse. 'Guess.'

I sighed and followed him downstairs to my car. I could feel the Manufrance burning a hole in the dashboard, eager to hand itself in to Hochstetter. We set off and I glanced in the mirror.

'I take it that's your staff car following us.'

'We will need a way to get back to your police headquarters after you leave your car with the Wehrmacht.'

'You think of everything.'

I glanced sideways to see him looking at me in wry amuse-ment. It was more unnerving than any single word he could have said in reply. I wished I was in the basement with Mayer and several kilos of gas and gunpowder.

Outside the Opéra, the same feldwebel who'd pulled me over the previous day made to stop me again but thought better of it when he spotted Hochstetter. As we went past, he raised his thick arm in that cheery wave that Adolf taught them all. Hochstetter's own salute was lukewarm in reply.

'You've all got your own jobs you stick to, haven't you?' I commented. 'He was doing the same thing yesterday.'

'That's why it works, Édouard. Why Germany works. Every-one knows what is expected of them. Where they stand. Which is interesting, don't you think?'

'Somehow I don't think so.'

'Take our relationship, for example.'

'If you insist.'

'I always insist. Although I should hope I won't have to. As you are aware, I'm here to help you in any way I can. A link between the German High Command and the French police. My job is to smooth your path. Your watch, for example.'

'My watch?' Instinctively, I glanced at my hand on the wheel and shrugged my wrist up into my sleeve.

'It is set to the wrong time. You might think I don't notice these things, Édouard, but I can assure you I do.'

'Old watch, Major. You can't teach it new tricks.'

'Everyone and everything can be made to learn new tricks. It is really not that difficult. You have been ordered to set your watch to Berlin time, yet you evidently refuse to. Now, some might say that that is an act of defiance. Even rebellion.'

I turned a corner, letting my sleeve ride up my wrist again. 'We're in Paris. This is Paris time.'

'Maybe so, but I have no doubt that many of my fellow officers would not see it that way. For my part, though, I understand that if I let the relatively trivial matter of your watch go, you might be more amenable to other demands I might care to make of you.'

'Why am I starting to feel like a streetwalker on Pigalle wheeling out the lubricant?'

'That's really quite apt. Because I can smooth your path, Édouard. Or I can fuck you.'

I almost swerved into the path of a German lorry. Both the word and the sentiment were all the more shocking for coming from Hochstetter. I'd got used to his threats being much more polite.

'And I will fuck you, if I have to,' he carried on. I struggled to stick to my side of the road. 'You should be aware that people who become of no use to me, become of no use to me. If you catch my drift.'

'I think I liked you more when you were just menacing, Major Hochstetter.'

'I am just menacing. Your job is to make me stay that way. Your job, in exchange for my forbearance with your little investigations, is to provide me with the loyalty I shall be affording you. For as long as you earn it.'

We drove through colonnaded streets. Somehow, the city didn't look quite so beautiful now the Germans were here. I turned to face him. 'You want a deal?'

'A quid pro quo, Édouard. Deal sounds so vulgar.'

I remembered the promise to fuck me and let that one slide.

'And all I have to do is show you the same loyalty you show me?' Out of the corner of my eye, I could see him nodding. 'I think I can manage that.'

I'd gone a full block in triumphant silence before he replied, 'Don't make the mistake of thinking Germans don't understand sarcasm.'

At the Wehrmacht garage, Hochstetter wouldn't get out of the car until I did, so I didn't have a chance to retrieve the Manufrance. I took one last surreptitious look at the dashboard and hoped it wouldn't give up its secret. We drove back to Thirty-Six in silence, the driver fortunately hampering any further discussion. Hochstetter made him drive up to the main door, the diesel engine ticking loudly. I got out and looked up to see Auban staring out of the window at me.

'We will speak again, Édouard,' Hochstetter told me as his driver roared off along the riverbank.

'I'm sure we will,' I mouthed after him.

I watched the car disappear across the bridge. There was no

other vehicle in sight, but there was a sound, one I couldn't place. Looking around me, it was a few moments before it dawned on me it was the river. In the absence of the life we knew of the city, the Seine murmured in soft comfort through the midst of us. I crossed the road to look and listen. I'd never heard it before. Paris was normally too noisy. I stood and watched as long as I could bear it. The river was telling us it was still there and so were we.

So was Auban. 'Cosying up to Hochstetter, Giral,' he commented after I'd climbed to the third floor.

'I'm sure he'll fuck you too if you ask nicely.'

I closed my office door on him and sat down. I was sorely tempted to go back out and ask Barthe if I could have a nip of the brandy we all knew he kept hidden in his drawer. There was a scrawled note on my desk. Madame Benoit had come to the station, it said, and asked for me. I'd decided Fryderyk's death might bear a relation to the investigation of the four murders, although probably not enough to satisfy Dax, so I spared him any knowledge of it and left Thirty-Six for the day, crossing the river for Rue Mouffetard.

'A foreign woman wanted me to let her into Fryderyk's flat,' the concierge told me when I got there. She was wringing an ancient handkerchief in her hands. 'I wouldn't let her, though, not even when she offered me money.'

'Where was she from, do you know?'

'Foreign. I wouldn't let her in. Not after last time.'

'You did just right. Can you describe her?'

'Tall, blonde. Bit brassy for my liking. Pushy.'

'Did she have an accent?'

'Yes, foreign, but I can't tell what. They all sound alike to me. I told her she had to talk to you at the police station if she wanted to see Fryderyk's flat. I didn't tell her about all of

Fryderyk's stuff in my rooms either. Did I do the right thing, Inspector Giral?'

'Just perfect, thank you. Where are Fryderyk's belongings?'

She gestured to a cupboard in her kitchen. 'I stored them, like you asked.'

I took a quick look at the scant clothes and possessions in the box. 'Was there anything else of Fryderyk's?'

'I don't know what you mean. I just put everything in a box like you asked.' She wrung her handkerchief more vigorously.

I quickly checked Fryderyk's flat again, searching through the safe with my fingertips, glad I'd told Isaac to leave it open. As I thought, I'd missed nothing the first time, its only contents now resting in my drawer at Thirty-Six.

Leaving Madame Benoit to her wrung-out handkerchief, I walked towards home, annoyed I didn't have my car and worried about the Manufrance hidden in it. Distracted, I thought of Fryderyk and of two people in two days looking for something. There did seem to be an awful lot of interest in his flat.

Behind me, a car engine slowly growled. With so little traffic, it should have sailed past. The moment I turned, I heard the sound of it braking and a door opening. A hand clamped on my right arm and a man in a grey uniform wheeled in front of me, his face close to mine. I felt something dig into my ribs and looked down to see he was holding a pistol. He released my arm and quickly searched for my own gun, removing it from its holster. The car slowly drew up alongside, the passenger door wide open. The man with the gun signalled to me to get in. He had no expression on his face, like a dead fish baring rows of sharp teeth on a slab in Les Halles.

I wouldn't move, so he spun me round by my shoulder and pushed me into the back seat.

12

The driver gunned the engine and raced off, scattering a trio of cyclists that had gone past, their heads down, as I'd been bundled into the car.

I wasn't alone in the back seat. Next to me was another man in a similar grey uniform. They weren't like the ones Hochstetter or Weber wore. These had sky-blue piping on the epaulettes with the initials GFP. The guy by my side was wearing a cap with the Nazi eagle and the same sky-blue piping. He also had a gun of his own, digging into my side.

'Not sure the blue works,' I told him. I don't think he understood.

I recognised him. I had to dredge up where I'd seen him, but then I remembered him from Luigi's. He was the one I'd seen last night, with the baby's head on the man's body. Up close, he was even less appetising. I didn't tell him. He obviously didn't go for style tips.

'If you'd just drop me off at the next stop,' I tried instead.

The one in the front passenger seat who'd manhandled me into the car holstered his gun and turned to me. He had a face cratered with old acne scars that looked like it had been badly hewn out of low-grade granite. A cold man of the Inquisition, his expression was a torturer's mask. I couldn't help thinking of him as Gargantua to my back-seat companion's Pantagruel. I couldn't see the driver. He was too busy ignoring the Germans' own speed limit through the empty streets of the city. Neither did I see Gargantua reach across and hit me in the face. Not too hard, but sharp enough to make me wince. I clenched my fist, but Pantagruel put his free hand on my arm.

'You had probably better not,' he told me in good French. I looked into Gargantua's eyes and saw nothing. Not even enjoyment. 'He will kill you with the same efficiency. Please listen to what I have to say. My name is Kommissar Müller. My colleague is Inspektor Schmidt. You are a police detective in Paris. Paris now belongs to the Third Reich. That means you do too. We will expect to receive a commensurate level of obedience from you in your dealings with us. Is that clear?'

'I am a police detective in Paris. That is perfectly clear to me.'

'And your obedience?'

'To the people of Paris and to my superiors.'

'We are your superiors now.'

I looked from baby man to the pockmarked kid. 'You really think so?'

From the front seat, Schmidt, or Gargantua as was, gave me another slap. Next to me, I heard Müller cock his pistol. I looked straight at him. 'If you kill me with or without efficiency, I'll be showing no obedience to anyone.'

'You have spirit and courage,' Müller told me. 'I like that. We can break them both.'

'What do you want?'

'You know an American journalist called Groves.'

'No, I don't.'

That earned me another slap. Same face, different spot. Schmidt evidently knew his way around battering suspects. I could feel blood begin to flow from a cut above my left eye. My nose was already bleeding into my mouth.

'What is your relationship with Groves?' Müller insisted.

'I don't have a relationship with him because I don't know who he is.'

Schmidt punched me, in the ribs this time. I was grateful we were in a confined space as he couldn't get a good run-up to it, but I still felt it through to my backbone. At least it was taking my mind off the ache in my kidneys.

'We know you met him at a bar in Montparnasse. Please don't be stupid.'

It clicked who they meant. 'The American? He's a journalist? I don't know him. He was on the same table, but we didn't speak. He was drunk, he wouldn't have made much sense anyway.'

The car went over a pothole and we were all jolted in our seats. It felt like someone had skewered my kidneys with an Inquisitor's poker. Müller was pushed away from me to the corner of the back seat and I instinctively looked at his hand on the gun. His finger was resting lightly on the trigger. The gun was still pointed at me.

'We'd get along a lot better if you put the gun down. I'd hate it to go off by accident before I could show how obedient I can be.'

'Then the sooner you satisfy our curiosity, the sooner you can leave the car and not be exposed to the perils of your barbaric roads. What about Hauptmann Weber? What is your connection with him?'

'Weber? I don't know him.' I saw another punch coming my way so I held my hand up. 'I mean, I know who he is, but I don't have any connection with him.'

'What is the connection between Weber and Groves?'

'I wouldn't know. I just saw them in the café in Montparnasse. They looked like drinking partners.'

Schmidt hit me again and Müller asked me if I was sure.

I held my arms tightly against my chest to numb the pain. 'I couldn't be any more sure.'

Schmidt readied himself for another punch, but Müller motioned him not to. Instead, Schmidt asked me a question. 'Why is Bydgoszcz important?'

'Are you sure you can ask questions and hit me at the same time?'

I only asked it to hide my surprise at the question. I probably shouldn't have. It got me another punch to the ribs. In exactly the same place as last time. He certainly knew his stuff. In friendlier times, he could have got a job with us.

'Why is Bydgoszcz important?'

I thought I'd better give them something, so I told them about the four men in the railway yard being from Bydgoszcz. Müller's next question told me I'd made a mistake.

'So who is the man who committed suicide? He was from Bydgoszcz too.'

'Just a suicide. How do you know about him?'

'I heard Major Hochstetter mention the name in your seedy Parisian brothel last night. Unlike you French, I'm interested in information, not some whore disrobing.' He saw me clench my fist and nodded to Schmidt, who gave me another slap across the ear. I'd forgotten how much that hurt. 'Do you know of any link between Weber and Groves and the man from Bydgoszcz?'

I was having to speak between gasping for breath. I could hear my chest rasping and hoped they hadn't done too much damage. Each intake of air I needed to speak was painful.

'No, none.' Not yet anyway. That at least was true. 'And I

hope you haven't got any more questions, because I can't hear a fucking thing now.'

They both fell silent for a moment and then spoke to each other in German. I hung my head, pretending I didn't understand. I did. I'd spent part of the last war in a German PoW camp. I knew enough to follow a conversation. They disagreed on what I knew. Müller seemed happy with what I'd said. Schmidt wanted to push me a bit more. I almost forgot myself and told him to pay attention to what Müller was saying. He argued that there had to be some connection between Bydgoszcz and Weber and Groves, but that I knew less about it than they did. He finally convinced his partner and told the driver to head back towards the Left Bank. I closed my eyes to hide my relief. They drove into my street and pulled up right outside my front door.

'I don't suppose you could drop me off at the shops,' I asked them. 'I haven't got a thing in.'

Schmidt gave me a farewell slap and pointed up at my apartment to tell me they knew where I lived before hauling me out of the car. I managed to stay on my feet as he got back in. He tossed my gun and the magazine out of the window and the driver sped off. I watched them go, wiping the blood out of my eyes, and picked up my gun, checking the magazine and sliding it back in place.

'I'll take that as a no, then.'

13

I ached all the way up the stairs and had to stop halfway to ease some air into my lungs without feeling my chest was going to melt with the pain. I gave thanks that Monsieur Henri wasn't loitering outside his front door. I'd had enough for one day and I wanted to see if Jean-Luc was waiting for me. I also had some whisky left with my name on it.

Inside, I locked the door behind me and kept my gun in my waistband when I took my shirt off. A bruise was already coming out on my stomach and chest. I went into the bathroom and cleaned up the blood from my face. Nothing broken, and the cut above my eye looked worse than it was. I'd probably have another small scar to call my own, though, so I went to pour myself a glass of whisky to mark the occasion. I looked at the amount left in the bottle and wondered whether I'd be able to afford another scar.

Jean-Luc wasn't there.

I'd felt the bullet in my pocket when I'd taken my jacket off, and I'd glanced just once at the Luger's hiding place when I was cleaning myself up. Luckily my need for whisky had been greater. I didn't want to weaken now while I was waiting for my son to come.

Only he didn't come, and two hours later, the glass of whisky was gone and the Luger wasn't. In my fear of being alone with the damaged bullet, I took myself off to walk through black and deserted streets to Luigi's bar. I figured if I couldn't stay in my own flat, I'd dig around in Nazi Germany's home from home to find out something more about what was going on at the railway yard. There were no German patrols to stop me. But that still didn't mean I was in any better a mood when I got there.

'I don't want any trouble, Eddie,' Luigi begged me.

I forced my way past him and took in the fauna in his bar. 'And I want a Paris free of arseholes, Luigi, but that's not going to happen either.'

Next to me at the bar, two prostitutes were eyeing a table full of youthful officers looking like acne in a uniform.

'Duty calls,' one of them commented, moving in on the kindergarten Nazis.

I watched them enter the shadows and fought down the pain in my ribs and back. The walk had introduced them to each other and now they were ganging up on me. Taking in shallow breaths, I let the ache subside and drank a shot of the cheap whisky that Luigi had put on the counter in front of me. I turned to face the room. Weber and the woman who'd feigned drunkenness the previous night were at the same table, their heads together in whispered conflab. They hadn't seen me, so I was able to watch them as I took a slower draught of my drink. They were very close to each other, their legs touching but their hands apart. Both of them kept their faces lowered, turned to speak into the other's ear in a strange dance of heads. They were lost in each other, but they weren't lovers. My memory was still good enough to know what that looked like.

'So what are you cooking?' I asked. I decided to go over and find out.

The woman spotted me first. Her face registered brief irritation, along with something more. Frustration? Weber did as Weber does and sneered at me.

'What do you want?' he demanded.

I sat down opposite them with my whisky. 'So what is it about Bydgoszcz that worries you?'

His eyes flared in anger. 'Leave now, policeman.'

'Because there's clearly something about it that worries you. Or annoys you. I just haven't worked out what yet.'

'I will not warn you again. You carry no jurisdiction with German officers.'

'Or is it alarm? I don't think it's fear. Anger, maybe? But there's definitely something about the mention of Bydgoszcz that affects you.'

As I spoke, my eyes flickered towards the woman. Instead of watching me, as I'd expected, she was staring intently at Weber. I still couldn't work out their relationship.

He stood up. 'Major Hochstetter isn't here now. You can't rely on him for protection.'

I finished my whisky and looked up at him. 'And there's something *you* can't rely on, Hauptmann Weber. I'm probably not something you've encountered before. I'm not afraid of your uniform.'

His anger looked to be at the point of boiling over, but the woman touched his sleeve lightly. It seemed to calm him, despite his obvious natural inclination otherwise. He sat down again and spoke, the usual smirk back on his face. 'You really should be.'

Any reply I might have felt like making was instantly blotted out by the sound of Luigi's off-key piano loudly clattering. I turned to see the singer from the previous night. The same dress, the same gloves, the same song. It was either a beautiful song cheapened by the falsely erotic, or a low striptease emboldened by a harmonious act of defiance. Opposite me, the woman indicated to Weber that they should leave. I watched them go. Weber couldn't help scowling at me from behind her back. I simply watched them. Theirs was a relationship I was probably going to have to get to the bottom of if I was to find out what Bydgoszcz meant to him.

The singer finished her song, as naked as the night before, and tried to flee the audience as quickly as she could, but an officer who'd availed himself too freely of Luigi's toxic champagne stood in her way. His right hand lunged for her breasts. I was standing in front of him by the time his left hand had finished the same journey. In a long-forgotten instinct, my own hand reached for his throat, but something made me falter at the last moment. Instead, I grabbed his right arm firmly and pulled it down. Through his haze, he looked shocked.

'Eddie, please,' I heard Luigi plead.

'I am an officer in the Wehrmacht,' the German said with as much dignity as his drunkenness would allow.

'Good for you. I'm a French cop and you're assaulting this lady.'

'Lady?' He sniggered.

I gripped his arm more tightly and he winced in pain. Two other officers stood up and came over. One of them began to undo the holster on his belt.

'It's OK,' the singer said. She was forcing back tears and desperately trying to cover herself with her dress.

'No, it's not.'

The German had pulled his Luger and was pointing it at me. I looked at the familiar shape of the pistol and felt a sudden calmness.

'That's really not going to work,' I told him.

He looked nonplussed. Another figure approached in my peripheral vision.

'That'll do,' a voice said in German. I turned to see the officer from the previous night who'd told me how much he'd wanted to visit France. 'Put your gun away, Hauptmann, and sit down.'

From all the bright bits on their respective collars, I could see that my new friend was higher up the pecking order than the three officers facing me. He told them again to sit down and turned to speak to me in his fluent French.

'I apologise, Inspector Giral. Their behaviour is not becoming of a German officer.'

I had my own heights to descend before I could reply. The singer hurried away, helped into a back room by the prostitute who'd spoken earlier.

'Thank you.'

He bowed. I didn't think they really did that. 'May I suggest you leave now while matters are calm? I think it would be in your best interests.'

I could see the three Germans licking their wounds at their table, numbing the attack on their pride with more champagne.

'You're probably right.' I surprised myself at how calmly I accepted his intervention. I looked around me to make sure the singer was safely out of the way. The friendly officer accompanied me to the door, past Luigi who was wringing his hands in indecision.

'I do hope we can work together,' the officer said. I couldn't find an answer to that. Instead, I pulled the curtain aside and wished him goodnight.

I walked home through the darkness, all the time checking there were no drunken officers following me. Near the end of Boulevard du Montparnasse, I stopped in a doorway and leaned heavily against the metal frame. I was shaking, my breath shallow, my ribs hurting again. The officer's Luger appeared in my memory, and I retched at the thought of my calmness on seeing it. In the silent dark of the street, I felt a lid shift. A lid that I'd pulled over me after the effects of one war, only to find that another war was trying to prise it off again. I knew I had to hold onto it for as long as I could.

I carried on walking home. All I could see was the Luger in Luigi's and the Luger behind the tile in my bathroom. For so many lonely moments, I'd longed to die – wishing I'd died in the last war – and I'd exposed myself to the possibility of it so many times. For so long, I'd had nothing to live for. Until I realised I had nothing to die for, either. I didn't want that to change.

Jean-Luc was asleep in my spare bed.

In silence, I stood and watched him. I recalled the times when he was a child that I'd stand by his bed and look on him in an act of love I felt unable to show him. I used to kiss him while he slept. I moved forward to kiss him now but stopped myself. I'd lost the right to do that the day I walked out on him.

With a shock, I saw the seed of change. Whether it was welcome or not, I don't know, but I felt an incipient fear and concern that I'd lived without for years. A vulnerability restored. I backed soundlessly out of my son's room and closed the door.

Thursday 28th May 1925

I felt no fear or concern.

I felt only the flesh cede to the tip of the blade that pierced it. The brief moment of resistance to the metal and the short journey of the knife through the skin.

If I felt any emotion, I felt elation.

Marianne's pimp had beaten another of his women, more savagely this time, and we were searching for him in the streets and dives of Pigalle. We didn't know yet that Marianne was gone too.

'I haven't seen her since Choucas beat Sophie,' a prostitute told me. Too afraid to be seen talking to a cop, she'd led me to a darkened doorway away from prying eyes. 'Marianne tried to help her when he was attacking her.'

'Did you see what happened after? Did Marianne go with Choucas?'

'I don't know,' she said in tearful gulps of air. 'I got away. I didn't see what happened, but when I went back to help Sophie, both Marianne and Choucas were gone.'

I left her and grabbed two other cops, taking them with me to Marianne's apartment.

'If she hasn't been able to get away from Choucas, he might be holed up there with her,' I explained.

He was. The door to her flat was barricaded but we beat it down and got in. Choucas was in the corner of the dingy room with a knife to Marianne's throat.

'I'll kill her if you come any nearer,' he told us. He had a rasping voice that the local criminals said came from when he was cut in a knife fight in *le bagne*, the penal colonies in French Guiana. One of the few to return to France, which instantly made him an object to be feared, he was called Choucas because of a tattoo of a jackdaw on his chest. Around his neck, he bore another penal colony tattoo, a dotted line and a motto saying, 'Cut here and be damned.'

In the stand-off, I found a voice that surprised me. 'Let her go. Take me.'

Choucas' leather-tanned face split in a skeletal grin. 'Hold a knife to a cop's throat? Deal. It's been a long time since I sliced a *poulet*.'

The other cops tried to stop me, but I approached Choucas. Her face still bandaged from when he'd cut her, Marianne was frozen with fear. I told her to stay calm and we crossed over to each other's side in a slow-motion danse macabre until she was free and I was held in Choucas' grip, his knife pressing into my throat near my left ear. In front of me, Marianne fled the room while the other two cops stood motionless. I could see they had no idea which way this would go. Choucas made that clear. I could smell cheap red wine on his breath as he spoke.

'I've been to hell once, and I'm not afraid of going back.'

He slowly sliced into my throat, my flesh ceding to the tip of his blade. I felt the icy pain as my skin parted. I felt no fear, no concern, just an elation, a sense of ease.

I spoke to him in a whisper. 'I've been to hell, too. I don't care whether I live or die.'

His hand faltered and I was able to turn to him. I saw a

momentary fear on his face, the fear of someone when they see you care nothing for your own life, the fear when they know they have no hold over you. It gave me the split second I needed to twist out of his grasp and stamp on his shin. I heard the bone shatter as I felt his leg give way unnaturally beneath him. He screamed, the sound blocking out the thud of the knife falling to the floor and embedding itself in the wood. The two cops were on him before he fell completely and beat him in a way he could only dream of beating the women he victimised.

Afterwards, one of them went with me to the hospital, where a doctor stitched my neck up. 'You're a very good cop, Giral,' he told me when the medic had done, 'so why are you such a waste of fucking breath in every other way?'

I wore a roll-neck sweater to the jazz club the next night. It was too hot and it itched like hell, but it covered up the bandaging over the scar. To relieve the pain, I took some powders and a whisky and scowled at anyone who annoyed me. The cop's words still rankled.

'So why do they call you Eddie?' the Senegalese singer asked me, shaking me from my world. Her face was so close to me, I could smell her lipstick. For a brief moment, I imagined the feel of her mouth on mine.

'The American musicians. They reckon Édouard's too much of a mouthful, so they call me Eddie. Now most people do. Except my wife.' I regretted my last utterance the moment I said it. And I felt immediately ashamed at my regret.

'You have a wife.' She shrugged. 'But then I have a husband. And a kid.' She smiled at me and walked off, turning to face me as she left. 'But don't worry, I'm not the jealous type. My name's Dominique, by the way, since you won't ask.'

I watched her leave to get ready to sing. Her words rattled

around my head, making whatever sense I wanted them to make. On stage, she picked up the mic, but the noise in the room didn't abate. Tonight's was an uneasy crowd, raucous as Dominique tried to make her song heard over the din. The wound in my neck ached in time with my anger. Two men at a table began to argue, one of them rising to his feet. I went over and grasped them both by the back of the neck, forcing the first one down and holding the second one firmly in his seat. I leaned down and whispered in their ears.

'I'm tired and in pain. If you don't shut up and listen to Dominique singing, I will make sure you are in much more pain than I am. Do you understand?'

I twisted their necks so they both faced me and waited for them to nod before releasing them. The smell of industrial drink on their breath almost made me reel. I glared at their companions, each one equally drunk, equally argumentative. Dominique finished her song and the lights flickered out before coming on fully. Some of the audience cheered the brief black-out, their voices harsh under the renewed glare. I saw Fabienne at another table, putting up with her male companion squeezing her leg too tightly under her dress. She shook her head at me when I went to help and smiled in false complicity at the man.

I had to leave the main room to go backstage. The ache from the cut and the painkillers and whisky were casting an ugly glow on the room, the music no balm against the misery of the night. I passed the Corsicans at their table. They stared coldly at me as I went by.

Dominique was disappearing through the door to the side of the stage. Ahead of me, one of the Corsican gang followed her. I went after them to see the man tap Dominique on the shoulder and say something to her. She shrugged his hand away and went into the dressing room. I caught up with the man.

'What did you say to her?' I demanded.

'Fuck you.'

He tried to get past me to go back to his friends, but I caught hold of him around the throat and dragged him outside, into the alley behind the club.

'Whatever you said, you won't be saying it again,' I told him.

I was breathing hard when I heard the door open. I looked up to see Dominique coming out and had a realisation of my own, more frightening than any that the man now lying bloodied and unconscious at my feet had had. I looked down at him, my left hand still clasping his shirt front, and felt a deep shock. I saw my hands covered in his blood and looked back up at Dominique. I saw fear in her face. Fear of me. And horror.

'Is this what you think I want?' She shook her head in disgust and went back inside.

I looked down at the man one last time and closed my eyes. He stirred and groaned. I went to get some water from a rain butt by the door and cleansed his face with it, washing the blood from the cuts. I used my handkerchief to clean the wounds and stem the flow.

I closed my eyes again and saw the slow death of the little that was good in me.

Monday 17th June 1940

14

There was no priest, no eulogies and no wreaths. Just a perfunctory burial of two flimsy coffins in an unmarked trench in a municipal cemetery and a functionary who turned away when it was all over. That just left me and two others, a man and a woman, standing silently at the funeral of Fryderyk Gorecki and his three-year-old son Jan. A hasty interment in the summer heat for two forgotten victims at a time when there was no one left to care.

I could feel my hands shaking as, inevitably, I thought of my own son. After so long denying any part for him in my life, I was shocked at how much I needed to make sure he was safe. When I'd woken this morning, I'd found the Luger on the low table in front of my armchair, the bullets lined up in a row, the dud inside the gun. I had no recollection of the ritual that had also suddenly returned to my life. I'd only just tidied everything away when Jean-Luc had come out of his room, clothed and ready to leave. He refused to tell me where he was going, and I had no right to know.

I re-emerged from my thoughts to see the man and woman on the opposite side of the grave turn and walk away. Hurrying after them, I caught up on the main path leading to the gates. The man said something to the woman. In reply, she shook her head almost imperceptibly.

'Did you know Fryderyk Gorecki?' I asked them.

The woman gave an apologetic smile. 'No French.'

She was tall, with blonde hair and eyes that were constantly searching my face. The man was equally tall, with an old-fashioned cavalryman's moustache that hid his top lip, and eyes that hid even more.

'You're Polish?' I knew before speaking to them that they had to be. 'Fryderyk Gorecki. You knew him? Bydgoszcz.'

The woman smiled and nodded her head. 'Bydgoszcz. Fryderyk.' She went into some lengthy explanation about something in Polish. 'No French, no French.'

It was pointless, so I let them go. As far as the gate. Then I followed them. They led me through a labyrinth of narrow streets south of the cemetery to a small, cobbled lane, where they vanished into a dark passageway between the buildings. Cautiously, I tracked them inside, my eyes growing accustomed to the gloom, before the alleyway opened out into a damp courtyard littered with junk. Looking up, I scanned the balconies to search for them. Maybe I should have looked behind me. Because that's where whoever hit me and thrust a rough canvas sack over my head was waiting.

My head was wet when I came to. I tried to put my hand to my face to see if I could feel blood, but they were tied firmly behind my back. The movement sent a stab of pain through both elbows and I let out a yelp. The small of my back where I'd been punched the other night and the bruises on my chest where the Germans had hit me were also complaining. I now had an ache behind my right ear to keep them company. The old scar under my left ear came out in sympathy and began itching. Some of the liquid from my face dribbled down onto my lips. I tasted it. Water, not blood. That was a relief. So much so, I thought I might try opening my eyes. I waited, not sure I'd want to see whatever it was I might find. That was a mistake. Someone threw a second bucket of water into my face.

I spluttered into full wakefulness and tried to blow the icy water back down my nose so I could breathe. A hand pulled my head up and a face appeared in mine. It was a face I had a score to settle with. Two, now. It was the face of the man I'd stumbled upon in Fryderyk's flat, who'd hit me in the small of my back. My kidney went into spasm at the memory.

Another face appeared in its place and I tried to sit up. I realised I was tied to a chair. This face was much more welcome. The woman from the funeral. Attractive, firm jaw and high cheekbones. Deep, dark eyes. There were places in Pigalle where some men would pay for this.

'Who are you?' she asked me in French. She had a foreign accent but spoke fluently.

I tried to answer but I started coughing, so she called out something and a hand appeared with a glass of water, which she held to my lips. Most of it spilled down my chin but I got some in.

'Who are you?' she repeated.

Over her shoulder, I could see more of the room I was in. Barer than mine, with a plain wooden table and three chairs. I was on the fourth. The window was shuttered, the light shining through the slats casting thin strips high up the opposite wall. Still morning, I reckoned. I'd probably only been out long enough for them to bring me here. Wherever *here* was. I had no doubt it wasn't the building I'd followed them into.

I could see four other people in the room. All men. The man who'd hit me was standing behind her, next to the one who'd been with her at the funeral. Two other men were sitting at the table, looking over, but I couldn't make out their faces clearly.

I'd seen my ID and gun on the table.

'I'm a cop, but you know that.'

'Working with the Germans.'

'Working in spite of the Germans.'

'Why were you in Fryderyk Gorecki's flat?'

I looked at the man who'd punched me. 'I could ask you the same question.'

'What were you looking for in Fryderyk Gorecki's flat?' she asked again. 'Why were you at his funeral?'

I looked straight back at her and decided to go for the truth. 'I wanted to find something that would explain why he did what he did. He killed his son. I wanted to know why.'

'With the Germans occupying Paris, you want to know why a Pole would kill himself?'

'I wanted to know why he didn't try to get away.'

'You know about his wife?'

'I know she was killed in Poland, that's all. I understand why he would kill himself. I can't understand why, if he had a son, he wouldn't have tried to find another way out.'

She looked at me uncertainly. 'I don't know the answer to that, either. What did you find in his flat?'

I decided I'd told them enough. 'Nothing. He had nothing.'

'What was in the safe?'

'His passport.' I had to hope they hadn't had time to search the bedside table.

She studied me closely and said something to one of the men at the table, who pulled a knife out and handed it to her. I flinched as she drew it near to me, but she simply cut through the rope tying my legs to the chair and through the bonds behind my back. The blood flooding back into my hands stung like ants and I shook them to hurry the circulation along. The man at the table poured a clear liquid from a bottle into a glass and brought it over to me, motioning me to drink. I thought it was water and took a deep gulp to find it was vodka. I coughed and spluttered and the man laughed and said something that made the others laugh.

'He says you're soft through too much fine wine,' the woman explained.

'You know me so well.'

They let me get up and walk about to restore movement to my legs. My head was still aching from where they'd hit me and layers of pain from the various beatings I'd had were queuing up to have another go.

I looked at the man from Fryderyk's apartment. He was sleek like a roadster, his face a gauze of tight skin drawn over narrow bones. 'I have a score to settle with you.'

He held out his hand. 'I am sorry. My name is Janek. I thought you were Gestapo.' Isaac was right. There was a faint air of eau-de-cologne about him.

'That hurts even more.' I shook his hand.

It was my turn to ask some questions. I sat down at the table and poured myself some more of their vodka, which I sipped slowly this time.

'Why would you think I was the Gestapo? Who was Fryderyk Gorecki?'

The woman brought the chair to which I'd been tied to the table and sat on it. 'How much can we trust you?'

'As much as I can trust you.'

She seemed happy with that. 'It's not who he was, but what he knew. Or more precisely, what evidence he had of what he knew.'

'So who are you?'

'My name is Lucja. I was a lecturer at Warsaw University. My companions here were in the Polish Army. We fled Poland after our country fell to the Nazis and we followed our government to Paris. When the Nazis broke through the Netherlands and Belgium, we stayed behind in Paris after our government left for Angers. The government has since left Angers and we believe that it will now seek an agreement from London to set up there. Our role here is to assist any Polish servicemen left in Paris who are trying to get away to rejoin the fight against the Nazis and any civilians who want to escape the Germans.'

'What was it that Fryderyk knew? Was he with you?'

She shook her head. 'He was a printer and bookbinder. He ran his own small company in the town of Bydgoszcz. What do you know of the Nazis' invasion of our country?'

'I know about Warsaw being bombed, that's about all. What's special about Bydgoszcz?'

'Sadly, nothing is special about Bydgoszcz.' She poured herself a glass of vodka before carrying on. 'You will have heard the rumours coming out of Poland. Of atrocities that have been carried out on certain groups. Fryderyk was married to a schoolteacher. When the Nazis invaded in September, she and a large number of other teachers from the town were taken into a field and shot. Simply because they were teachers. Other groups are suffering the same fate. Intellectuals, artists, writers, Jews. And the world doesn't know about it. And it is happening in towns and villages and cities all over Poland. So no, there is nothing special about Bydgoszcz.'

'The world doesn't care,' the man from the funeral added, 'and does nothing about it.'

'The world wants proof,' Lucja continued. 'And Fryderyk claimed that he had it. Documents and pictures that show the extent of the massacre in Bydgoszcz and worse. He was also supposed to have been killed, he claimed, but he was at the doctor's with his son when the SS came to find him. He spoke to a man who witnessed the killings, and who had photographs of them, and he escaped to Paris with them.'

'Why haven't we seen them?'

'The French authorities wouldn't listen to him. He showed them some of the evidence he had, but they kept it and did nothing about it. When he asked for them to be returned, they refused.'

'Any evidence the French ministry had will have been burnt by now. Why didn't he take it to your government in exile?'

'He didn't think it would serve any purpose. He wanted the evidence to go to a foreign government or journalist as a neutral would be more likely to be believed than the Polish government in exile. He thought it would be dismissed as propaganda if we were to publish it. That's why he wouldn't show any of it to us.'

'You haven't seen it?'

'We have no idea how authentic or extensive it is. We assume it's photographs or even film, but we don't know for sure. He said he kept most of the evidence back from the French authorities, but we have no idea what he did with it. If it exists, we need to find it. The world doesn't know about the atrocities that the Nazis have committed in Poland. There are many stories coming out, but no hard evidence that will force other countries to act. That will force America to come to our defence and the Soviet Union to break its pact with the Nazis. That will force countries that are sitting on the fence to join in the fight against Hitler. We hope that this is it.'

'Why didn't he do something with it when the Germans occupied Paris instead of killing himself? Surely then his wife's death would have been avenged in some way.'

'We think so too. He was extremely depressed about his wife's death and his life here. And at not being taken seriously by your government. He came to see me on Friday. I thought it was to offer me the evidence at last, but he was very agitated.

He was afraid and kept pacing up and down, clutching his son. He wouldn't let him go for a moment. I asked him to give me his evidence but he wouldn't. He was desperate but confused and refused to stay with me and try to calm down. The next we heard, he had killed himself and Jan.'

'Which is why you were searching the flat.' I turned to Janek. 'Did you find anything?'

'Nothing. I'm not convinced there is anything worth finding.'

'Janek doesn't believe Fryderyk really had any evidence.'

I recalled Madame Benoit's description of the foreign woman. 'Why did you go back to his flat?' I asked Lucja.

She looked surprised. 'I've never been there. Janek's the only one.'

'If he'd had anything of value,' Janek argued, 'the French authorities would have taken it seriously. And why didn't he let us see it if it was worth something?'

The man who had been at the funeral with Lucja spoke. 'In my village, the Nazis did the same thing. They took the teachers, the mayor, the doctor and the solicitor and shot them. I didn't witness it but I saw the bodies lying in the village square afterwards. I saw what the Nazis did. We need to find Fryderyk's evidence before they can suppress it.'

'And you're certain Fryderyk didn't destroy his proof of the massacre?'

'No, we can't be certain,' Lucja said. 'But what we can be certain of is that if it does still exist, we have to find it before the Nazis do. If we don't, no one will believe what is happening before it becomes too late for us and for the rest of the world.'

They let me go. Janek wanted to blindfold me so I couldn't find my way back to their apartment, but Lucja argued that I was to be trusted.

'We have to trust you,' she told me.

She walked with me through the tunnels of crooked buildings and narrow cobbled lanes of the Pletzel, the poor quarter where many of the city's Jewish population lived.

'This should be teeming with people,' I told her.

'There are still more people here than there should be. If the Jews of Paris had any real idea of what was happening to the Jews in Poland, they would all have fled long before the Germans got here.'

We stood aside on the narrow pavement to let an elderly man wearing a yarmulke pass and I felt unutterably saddened at the thought of the Paris melting pot to which I'd come to lose myself so many years ago being irrevocably lost because of the Nazis.

'Are the rumours really true?'

'True and more. But to the outside world, they are still only rumours and hearsay. We have no evidence. But many of us have seen what they're capable of, and we all know people who are missing and we've all seen the soldiers in my country and know the stories of people like Fryderyk and of so many others. Believe me, they are true.'

'You say they killed teachers.'

'Teachers, doctors, writers, artists, Jews simply for being Jews. The Nazis are afraid of elites and intellectuals so they take them away or they kill them. There are so many people missing.'

'Elites?'

'Elites can be anyone they want them to be. Nearly every lecturer in my faculty at the university was shot or imprisoned. The Germans came one day in half a dozen trucks and arrested them all. A Jewish professor, a gentle man in his seventies who had taught philosophy and peace all his life, was kicked to the pavement outside and beaten to death with clubs. They were organised, disciplined in who they took, cold as machines, only to become savages in their anger when a quiet old man stood up to them.'

'Why didn't they take you?'

'There was a mop and bucket in the corridor when the Germans came so I picked them up. I'm a woman. The Nazis didn't think I could be a lecturer. They didn't even see me.'

We walked in silence. Some businesses were boarded up, but others had reopened like any other Monday. Kosher butchers and Parisian bakers alike.

'There's a pharmacy here,' she suddenly said. 'You look dreadful. I am sorry. Janek can be quite enthusiastic when he thinks he's dealing with the Gestapo.'

She was right. I had a headache that was blasting its way through my skull, so we bought some powders for the pain. Outside, I dissolved them as well as I could in my cupped hands under a drinking fountain and swallowed them, licking the last bits of residue off my palms. I closed my eyes and leaned against a building. The pain of the blows to my head and the shock of being grabbed and trussed were just hitting me.

'We'll go and sit somewhere while it passes,' Lucja said.

I took her to the Place des Vosges, to a bench under the trees dense in leaf. The city and all that was happening in it seemed for once to be shut out by the ancient glory of the faded buildings protecting the square and the once-ornate gardens in the centre. A small circle of sunlight shone through the trees and Lucja closed her eyes and held her face up to catch the warmth. I studied her for a moment. Now that the anger and fear that I'd seen in the depths of her dark eyes were hidden for a brief moment, I saw the tiredness in her face. The powerful cheekbones and strong jaw simply looked stretched and gaunt, her neck taut with tension, her face sallow and tired. Thick, blonde hair that I imagined usually tumbled richly around her face looked drained of life. I closed my eyes too.

'I used to come to this bench and read,' I told her after a while. 'A lifetime ago. When I first moved to the city after the war. It was my escape.' She didn't reply and I kept my eyes shut, or my chance to speak would be gone. 'It's rundown and unloved and it suited me because of that. I haven't sat here for a long time.'

I opened my eyes and I missed that time with an ache stronger than the physical one in my head and chest and back.

There were German soldiers in the square. I sat up, alert. Lucja was already watching them through eyes devoid of expression. But the soldiers weren't parading or standing guard or issuing orders. They were sightseeing. One of them set up a camera on a bench for a timed exposure and ran to stand next to five smiling companions. They were kids let loose on a foreign city as junior conquerors. I imagined six copies of the photo being sent home in six letters to proud parents and girlfriends. Near to them, two time-serving feldwebels strutted past a French policeman in uniform before stopping to go back to him. One of them prodded the cop on the shoulder and spoke loudly into his face until he saluted them. I tensed, but Lucja put her hand on mine. Satisfied, the two feldwebels walked away. The six German soldiers warily eyed them, making sure they did nothing to earn a reprimand. The cop turned away, rubbing his saluting hand as though to clean it.

'It's called the *grusspflicht*,' I explained to Lucja. 'The Germans have ordered that French police have to salute German soldiers.'

'One day that will be the least of your worries.'

I watched the young soldiers move on across the square.

I decided I had to trust her. 'I found some letters from Ewa to Fryderyk in the safe, but I can't understand them.'

She studied my face for a moment. 'Meet me on this bench at seven this evening. Bring the letters with you.'

'Is that seven our time?'

She looked puzzled. 'German time. As I said, Eddie, one day all that's going to be the least of your worries.'

She left the square first and I watched her go. I saw no one follow her.

It was me that was being followed.

15

Keeping my head down as I passed the two German feldwebels in the sunshine, I crossed the square and stood under one of the narrow arches where Rue de Béarn emptied out into shaded streets. I let my eyes get used to the sudden gloom and waited. The sound of footsteps came near and a figure emerged from behind the weathered stones. I waited until I knew they'd be unsighted by the change in light and barged them heavily into the wall. Hidden from view from the square, I turned them so they faced the wall and held their head firmly, twisting their face around so I could see who it was.

'Jesus, you don't mess around.' It was a woman's voice.

Still holding her firmly against the wall, I took a step back to take a look at her. It was the woman I'd seen with Weber at Luigi's bar.

'Why are you following me?'

'I'm not. You just happen to be going the same way I am.'

'Wrong answer.' I didn't loosen my grip on her and left a silence, waiting for her to speak next.

'OK, OK. Let go. I'll talk to you.'

Out of instinct, I checked she wasn't carrying any weapons and let her free. She patted herself down, all the time staring at me. She was wearing a light summer jacket, which had ridden up over a man's check shirt, and she was slowly putting it back in place. It looked more like it was to steady herself, to think of what she wanted to say. Underneath, she wore wide-bottomed trousers. Even I knew they were the latest fashion. I waited until she spoke.

'Good technique,' she finally said. 'Shut up and let me incriminate myself.'

'Who are you? Why are you following me?'

She carried on sizing me up. 'Yep, I reckon you're a good cop. Whatever that means. My name's Ronson. I'm American. A journalist.'

Her French was good. It was only now that I noticed a trace of an accent.

'Just Ronson?'

The look I'd noticed the first time I saw her, when she was surveying her surroundings in Luigi's, was back. Cool, deliberating, amused. She gave a slight mock-bow. 'Kitty Ronson to my mother, Katherine Ronson to my father, Kate to my lovers, Ronson to the rest of the world. And you're Eddie Giral, Paris cop. Except to Major Hochstetter. He likes formality.'

'Sweet. Why are you following me?'

'I told you, I'm a journalist. I'm just sniffing out a story.'

'What story? What did you expect to find?'

'You tell me, Eddie Giral. Because there's sure as hell a story here someplace.'

'Who do you work for?'

'Anyone who pays. I'm freelance. I'm just after a story to pay my rent, that's all. Any story. You've got the Nazis spooked, so I thought I'd take a look for myself. See where you took me.'

'Did Weber get you to follow me?'

I've had pitying looks thrown my way in the past, but none like the journalist gave me now. 'Oh, Eddie, Eddie, that is never going to happen. No one ever gets me to do anything I hadn't planned on doing in the first place.'

'That's the first thing you've said I believe. So what *is* your connection with Weber?'

She shook her long blonde hair out and shrugged her shoulders. 'I'm a journalist, he's a German officer, I ask him questions, he answers some things, lies about others, I wire stories back home about what the Nazis are doing, magazines back home wire me money.'

I remembered the concierge's description of the foreign woman who'd tried to get into Fryderyk's flat. 'Was it Weber who wanted you to take a look at Fryderyk Gorecki's flat?'

She broke into a grin. 'I thought for a moment you weren't being such a good cop, but you are, aren't you, Eddie? No, Weber didn't ask me to go there. And yes, it was me who tried. And before you ask, I was after a story, the same one I must be after by following you.'

'You haven't told me what the story is yet.'

'That's because I don't know what it is yet. But when I do, I'll be sure to let you know. Do you want to follow me now?'

'Why? Where are you going?'

'Back to my hotel. Not so hot on room service these days but they still do a good Manhattan.'

'I'm sure that'll be a relief to us all. Which hotel?'

'You're the cop, Eddie Giral, find out.'

She grinned at me one last time and headed off away from the square. I watched her go. I didn't follow her.

At Thirty-Six, I found everyone in the detectives' room huddled around a radio. They were listening to Marshal Pétain, who'd taken over the government when Reynaud resigned. His old and tired voice was telling us all that he was going to ask the

Germans for an armistice. He urged everyone in France to cease fighting.

'Finally, a hero and a patriot running the country,' one cop commented. 'It takes a soldier to do what the politicians are too scared to do.'

'What? Surrender?' Barthe asked.

'Throw our lot in with the Germans. Make France great again. I don't agree with putting Weygand in charge of national defence, mind. He was the one who declared Paris an open city. Told the Germans to just march on in.'

'And saved tens of thousands of lives in the process,' Barthe replied. 'It was the only solution he could have taken at the time.'

'Like Pétain now.'

'The Nazis have got the right idea,' Auban said. 'They're a bloody sight better than any of the corrupt, useless bastards we've got. And the Yanks and the Tommies did nothing for us. Now we can round them up and send them home. Then the Jews.'

He looked sideways at me, but I wasn't going to stoke Auban's fire right now. He could wait. I turned the radio off and told them to get back to work. They walked away, grumbling, reluctant to get on with anything. As they dispersed, I saw Hochstetter emerging from my office. Try as you might, you couldn't flush him away.

'You look like you've been in the wars, Édouard.'

'A German with a sense of humour. Just what I need right now.'

He gestured to the cuts on my face and asked what had happened.

'Your lot happened.' I told him about the two Germans who'd shoved me into the back of their car. 'I hope it wasn't your doing.'

'Hardly.' Despite his cool response, he looked mystified. 'You say they had GFP on their epaulettes? The Geheime Feldpolizei. They're the Wehrmacht military police, but I have no idea why they should want to question you. What did they want to know?'

'They were asking about Hauptmann Weber.'

'I see. What were their names?'

'Kommissar Müller and Inspektor Schmidt.'

He let out a laugh, like a seal in the zoo barking. 'Müller and Schmidt? Two of the most common surnames in Germany? I will look into this for you, Édouard. I think they're billeted in the Hotel Bradford. We might even get an apology out of them.'

'I'll be sure to hold my breath. Why are you here?'

'Direct as always, I see. Maybe we should use your office.' He led me to my own room before continuing. 'Unfortunately, all my efforts to bring about your wish to question Hauptmann Weber have been unsuccessful.'

'I simply want to ask him what he saw at the railway yard. This is a murder case.'

'I should perhaps tell you a little more about Hauptmann Weber. One thing that you do need to know is that he was formerly a member of the Nazi Party. He was so since 1933.'

'But he isn't anymore?'

Hochstetter gave one of his half-smiles. The one that let you know you weren't in on the joke. 'It's perhaps a vague concept, Édouard. When Weber joined the Wehrmacht, he would have been prohibited by law from having any political allegiance, even to the Nazi Party. Although those rules have since been relaxed, there are still some of us who believe that the army has to be separate from government and from political sympathies. We are not all Nazis. We simply serve Germany.'

'And whichever lunatic is in charge.'

'You really must be more careful. One day you will make such a comment to the wrong German. Either way, to return to Weber, what is essential for you to remember is that although he is no longer an active member of the Nazi Party, he still has friends among the Nazis who will stand by him. That makes him quite untouchable. Even by me.'

'So I can't even question him about what he saw?'

'Not for the time being. And I know your tenacity will lead you to question him unofficially, so I'd ask you to wait while I persevere. I'm afraid you're just going to have to trust me on this one, Édouard.'

It was my turn for the seal impression.

'I have some other information for you about Hauptmann Weber if you are interested,' he continued. His assured smile told me he knew I would be. 'You should perhaps know that before coming to Paris, he had been on leave in Berlin for some months. To put it delicately, he was kept there while the Wehrmacht made up its mind as to what exactly was to be done with him. Prior to that time, he had served in Poland. There were some concerns voiced by his senior officers regarding his behaviour during his time there. There were rumours.'

'He wouldn't be the only German soldier there were rumours about.'

'That is true. I should perhaps explain the way some of us in the Abwehr and the Wehrmacht feel. We regard ourselves as the army of Germany. The SS is the army of the Nazi Party. The rules by which the SS chooses to live are not necessarily the same that the Wehrmacht seeks to observe.'

'And Hauptmann Weber chose to live by SS rules.'

He nodded once. 'It is also true that the SS somewhat took the lead in certain lamentable events in Poland that the

Wehrmacht would not normally countenance. Members of the SS were ordered to do what they had to do and they did it. It is not my place to judge that. Regrettably, some members of the Wehrmacht abetted them in this, and I feel as a soldier that I must judge that. While we are on this subject, I should assure you, Édouard, that those same orders have not been given for France. You should perhaps be grateful that German command here is military rather than civilian. Wehrmacht rather than SS. Indeed, German rather than Nazi, I will make that distinction. You will have to hope that that situation lasts.'

'Why are you telling me this?'

'Hauptmann Weber is not one of my officers, but he is a Wehrmacht officer. And while he still has friends in the party, our policy towards France might mean that I would be able to pull a few strings and allow you to question him more formally. But for that, I might also need your support in other ways.'

Before Hochstetter could tell me how much of my soul I'd be selling, we were interrupted by Auban appearing in the doorway.

'The suspects are here,' he said. The only thing being was that he was talking to Hochstetter, not me.

'Suspects?' I asked.

Hochstetter turned to go. 'Yes, the other reason I am here. Detective Auban has kindly brought in the railway workers at my request. I wish to question them at Abwehr headquarters. If we are unable to speak to Hauptmann Weber, I at least can find out what your suspects know.'

Dumb with anger, I followed them downstairs to find Le Bailly, Papin and Font being handed over by half a dozen uniformed cops to four German soldiers. Fear curled off them like smoke.

'These are not formal suspects,' I told Hochstetter. Dax

appeared in the hallway, catching his breath after running down from the third floor.

'Then I shall question them informally,' the German replied. 'And perhaps afterwards I can arrange for you to question Hauptmann Weber. Quid pro quo.' He looked at me, challenging me to react.

'They are not your suspects. You have no jurisdiction over them.'

A vulpine smile on his face, he held one finger up in the stalemate. 'You hear that, Édouard? That's the sound of occupation. Of my having jurisdiction over whatever I want, whoever I want, whenever I want.'

'I have to make a formal complaint, Major Hochstetter,' Dax butted in. 'You have no right to question these men.'

Hochstetter looked as surprised as I felt. 'Then go ahead, Commissioner Dax, and make your formal complaint. And the Abwehr will issue a formal rebuttal.'

I saw Dax glance at the three workers. Le Bailly's head was lowered, but Papin and Font looked helplessly back at him. 'Then I will take it higher.'

Hochstetter stood in front of him. 'Do you really think the German High Command will look kindly on an act of rebellion by the French police so soon in our amicable relationship?' Dax struggled to hide his nervousness. 'I thought not.' Hochstetter signalled to the soldiers to lead the three men out of the building before turning to me. 'Oh, and by the way, Édouard, your car is waiting for you outside with your SP plate.'

16

'You're still a French cop,' I told Auban. 'You don't hand Frenchmen over to the Germans.'

The sneer was back, which was impressive, considering his head was pushed back as far as I could get it to go against the cigarette-stained wall and my own snarl was centimetres from his.

'What's the matter, "Édouard"? Don't want anyone else sucking up to Hochstetter?'

'Don't push me, Auban, because so help me ...'

He laughed. Small flecks of his spittle spattered my face. 'So help you what, Giral? You might have been something once, but that was back in the day. You're a spent force. Everyone knows it. You lost your teeth years ago.'

'Funny you should say that.'

I leaned back to launch a punch at him, but I felt a hand grab at my arm from behind. I turned to see Dax looking at me, his face red with anger.

'Detective Auban,' he said, his voice barely under control. 'Go to my office, I will deal with you there. Giral, come with me.'

We watched Auban slink off up the stairs and then Dax walked with me to my room. Through the window, I saw traces of the black smoke from the burning oil depot hanging in the sky. Dax turned towards me. His face was darker. I waited until it had calmed to an off-white rage before I spoke.

'I admire the way you stood up to Hochstetter, Commissioner.' It didn't work.

'Cut the crap, Eddie, I know you.' He strode up and down my room to let off steam. 'Look, I know you're as angry about this as I am, but keep your antagonism with Auban to yourself. These times are difficult enough without you brawling with your subordinates. You're one of the few detectives I can rely on, don't betray that. I need you to get on with your job.'

'I'm trying to, but you can see that Auban is hindering it every step of the way.'

'Deal with it, Eddie. And not like this. We both know what you're capable of.' The look as he said it was full of meaning. I could only pull the mask over my face and back down. We stared at each other for a few seconds until his own expression finally calmed.

I was the one to break the silence. 'Although it would have been nice if you'd waited a moment longer so I could have thumped the little bastard.'

He was about to say something, but I held my hands up in fake apology, which seemed to do the trick.

'Thanks for trying to stop Hochstetter,' I repeated. I almost meant it this time.

He stopped his pacing. 'Yes, well, it's the thin end of the wedge. We can't have them overruling us. I'll do everything I can to get the three workers released.' He turned to leave but stopped. 'This Weber. Is it really necessary for you to question him?'

'Probably not. But it's worth it to keep Hochstetter rattled.'

My car was waiting for me outside as Hochstetter had

promised, shiny new SP plates fastened front and back, allowing me to drive in my own city. As impatient as I was to check behind the dashboard, I didn't dare go searching for the Manufrance in front of Thirty-Six. Instead, I recalled Hochstetter's mention of where the GFP were billeted and drove off towards the Eighth Arrondissement. I got as far as a quiet backstreet on the Right Bank before I couldn't stand it anymore and stopped. Checking no one was around, I leaned down to reach underneath for the clips.

Nothing.

Just an empty space where the small pistol should have been.

I searched under the seat and in the wells, but I knew I wasn't going to find it. Instead, I saw again Hochstetter's challenging look as he told me my car was ready and I swore. Locking the stable door, I carried on as far as the Eighth. So did the swearing.

I checked out the hotel Hochstetter thought my German assailants might have been staying in. It was on a quiet street in a fancy part of the city. The Germans knew how to look after themselves. I walked into the lobby, where a handful of officers sat in armchairs chatting while other ranks scurried around them. It was all very amenable as invasions go. There was no receptionist, just some hook-nosed guy in uniform. I recognised the blue piping but not the wearer. I still didn't like it.

'I'm here to see Kommissar Müller,' I told him.

The German looked me up and down like I was going to steal all Adolf's secrets. 'And you are?'

'Here to see Kommissar Müller. I just said.'

He snapped his fingers at a couple of NCOs lurking, who grabbed me from behind and frisked me. They found my service pistol and took it. The officer came out from behind the desk and drew his Luger from its holster.

'You know it is against the orders of the German High Command for French people to carry weapons?'

'Tell these two to search a little better and they'll find my ID. I'm a police officer.'

I showed him my warrant, which he held onto, along with my gun, and they took me along a corridor to an office. Behind a desk was a man about my age with a thin face raw from shaving and eyes as cold as a Berlin winter. He was dressed not in uniform, but in a dark suit with a swastika lapel badge. I hate to admit it, but the sight of civilian dress amid so many soldiers was surprisingly unsettling. A plain-clothes zealot. The first officer explained to him in German why I was there while mufti man slowly drummed fingers as fine as a surgeon's on the leather desk insert. He stopped drumming and spoke to me in French.

'Why do you want to see this Kommissar Müller?'

I pointed at the cut over my eye and the bruises on my face. 'Because he did this. And I'd like to know why.'

He looked at my ID. 'I'm afraid you are mistaken, Inspector Giral. We have no Kommissar Müller here with us.'

'He was with an Inspektor Schmidt. They were wearing the same uniform these men are.'

I thought it best to keep my fashion sense to myself for now, but he just shook his head and handed me my ID with a sharp finality. 'We have no one of those names and ranks in the Geheime Feldpolizei. I'm afraid I cannot help you.'

'They wore GFP insignia and gave their names. They are your officers. I am a French police officer. I want to speak to them.'

'Fortunately for you, I am finding this mildly intriguing. Otherwise, I really wouldn't be too optimistic about how this whole affair will go for you.'

'Beaten up in the back of a car is not what I'd call intriguing.

If you won't let me see them, I'll have to ask you. Why did you have your officers attack me?'

'Inspector Giral, I can assure you, I did not have any of my men attack you. However, I can also assure you that I would order your detainment and beating without any compunction. I do not care for one moment that you are a French policeman. You are also a subjugated individual of the German Reich, and as such, you have whatever rights and whatever punishments I see fit to give you. Now, I suggest you leave.'

He made some hand signal and the two NCOs marched over and gave me a hefty punch to the stomach each. I doubled over and had to fight down a need to be sick. Between them, they frogmarched me to the front door, where they handed me my unloaded gun and ID before shoving me out into the street.

'That's one more freedom gone,' I murmured on my gut-aching way back to the car. In more peaceful times, I'd have been back to batter the shit out of them. In more peaceful times, I wouldn't have had to.

Gingerly getting into the driver's seat, I pondered on the man behind the desk denying any knowledge of Müller and Schmidt. Something about his glacial lack of care led me to believe him.

By now, I'd got a taste for Nazi officialdom, so I tried the Lutétia next as that's where Hochstetter was hanging his 'God's-on-our-side' belt buckle. The hotel that German military intelligence had bagged as its home from home in Paris, it stood on what was normally the busy junction of Rue de Sèvres with Boulevard Raspail. Years ago, Raspail had been known as Boulevard d'Enfer, Hell Boulevard. I might tell Hochstetter that one day. I parked the car wherever I wanted, which almost made being occupied worthwhile, and looked up at the un-nervingly undulating balconies and arched roofs like quizzical eyebrows. The building looked as baffled as we were at what was happening to our city. I got the same questioning look from the two German soldiers on the door, only less giving.

'I'm here to see about three French workers that Major Hochstetter has taken in for questioning,' I told them. Neither soldier looked like they understood and I almost forgot myself and spoke in German. Instead, I tried sign language. Actually, I tried barging past them, but the two soldiers pointed their rifles at me and ordered me to leave. 'Go and tell him it's Inspector Giral. He'll see me.'

'He is unavailable.'

They tried some sign language of their own and cocked their rifles at me. It seemed to work. The one who hadn't spoken pushed the stock of his against me, forcing me back down the steps until I was on the pavement. It felt more coldly degrading than being punched by the two NCOs. Looking from one to the other, I had to push down a sudden rise in an anger I hadn't experienced in years. Returning to my car, I felt myself begin to shake at the memory of rage. I drove away before it took me over.

I collected Ewa's letters from my desk drawer at Thirty-Six. Closing it, I sensed that something wasn't right, so I opened it again and saw what it was immediately. Fryderyk's passport wasn't lying on top of the books where I'd left it. I rummaged through and found it had gone. I recalled seeing Hochstetter emerge from my office earlier and cursed him more imaginatively than usual. I also remembered Lucja telling me about the evidence Fryderyk claimed to have, so I gathered up everything of his that was in there and took it with me. I had no idea if any of it had any significance, but there was too much interest in Fryderyk's belongings to leave them unprotected. And there was the small matter of the contents of the safe. I was glad Hochstetter had only had eyes for the passport.

Before leaving, I reloaded my pistol after the Germans had taken the last bullets. I also pinched a box of ammunition and put it on the ledge behind the dashboard in my car. I just had to hope Hochstetter wouldn't find an excuse or an opportunity to go looking there again.

Dropping everything but the folder of letters at home, I could see that it was getting near seven o'clock, so I hurried to Place des Vosges. In the evening sunlight, it would have been glorious but for the thin swastikas hanging from balconies like bodies strung from the highest windows. As I got nearer the square, my mood darkened further with my surroundings. One of the things that had surprised me when I first came from the front line to the hospital in Paris in 1916 was the grime. I'd been told of a city of light, but I'd rolled in my own darkness in a train through buildings blackened by years of smoke and industry. The buildings by the square were among the dirtiest, the ash and soot of years congregated in their cracks and seams, the grit augmented by the pall hanging over Paris.

Slowing my pace as I emerged from under the arches onto the square, I saw Lucja on the same bench we'd sat on that morning. Surprisingly, she got up when she saw me and walked towards me, giving me a kiss on both cheeks when we met.

'One of the first things I learned,' she told me. 'Nothing looks more suspicious than two people pretending not to be meeting each other.'

She led me back to the bench and we sat down. Janek was waiting there for us. I handed him the folder while Lucja and I spoke. He began to look through the concertina of letters but soon closed it.

'This looks too strange,' he said. 'Me taking each letter out of

163

the envelopes and you two talking. I need to take them with me to look at them properly without anyone seeing.'

I was doubtful, but Lucja mentioned that Janek had worked with Polish Intelligence. 'He wasn't a code-breaker, but he knows enough to know if there's anything that would be interesting.'

'So far,' Janek added, 'they just look like innocent letters, but I need to look at them with time and compare them.'

I wrestled in my mind. I had no other way of finding out what the letters said, so I knew I had to take a chance. 'Take them, but meet me here tomorrow at noon.'

We left the bench like friends taking their leave and went our separate ways. At the edge of the square, I couldn't help looking back, wondering if I'd done the right thing. The two figures had already gone.

I went home to find no sign of Jean-Luc. Checking his room, I was surprised to see his key on the bedside table. I simply stared at it. It either meant he'd got into his mother's flat or he'd found refuge with friends. Either way, he wasn't coming back. I knew I had no right to be saddened, but I wasn't ready for him to go. Not yet.

I left his room and closed the door behind me. It was back to being my ever-empty spare room and I didn't want to be reminded of that. I sat down and felt the mask I'd created for myself settling back into place. Over twenty years ago, and also less than five days ago, I'd swapped a gas mask for one that only I saw – one I wore all the time. Ever since the last war. I wore it at work and I'd worn it in my short marriage to Jean-Luc's mother and I wore it in the grocer's and in cafés and on the street. I only took it off in the dark and chattering corners of my bedroom, flooded with the ghosts of the trenches. It was the only place that truly frightened me. I wondered what ghosts had hidden in the corners of Fryderyk's room to drive him off the edge of his balcony with his son. I'd walked out on my son to spare him that. And myself.

And now he'd gone. It was his turn. And I deserved it.

I got up. I knew that if I didn't do something, I'd awake in the morning to find I'd prised the bathroom tile off and placed the Luger to my forehead. I picked up the books I'd brought home, but put them down almost immediately. I knew I wouldn't settle.

Instead, I drove to a seven-storey grey apartment block in Ménilmontant. Sheer like a mountain, with no balconies to break the façade, it looked an even poorer relative to the faded wrought-iron of the neighbouring buildings. Inside, I climbed to the third floor and picked the lock to get in.

I noticed the familiar dampness of the walls despite the summer warmth, the faded scent of old furniture, the sad smell of clean sterility. I knew immediately Jean-Luc wasn't there. No one was. Just acrid memories of my old life.

There were photos of Jean-Luc in the living room, on all the walls and on every piece of furniture. Pictures of him at school, playing rugby, standing on a beach somewhere. I had to look away from them, the guilt and the sorrow punching their way to the surface. My ex-wife had changed everything from the way it was the day I walked out of her life, but for the briefest of moments, I had the sensation I'd never left. For fifteen years, we'd lived just a few short kilometres from each other, but our paths had never once crossed. That was one of the reasons I'd come to Paris in the first place; to lose myself in an anonymity of my choosing. The problem was I wasn't the only person I'd lost.

Checking the kitchen, I found a note from Sylvie addressed to Jean-Luc, dated just ten days ago. She'd obviously waited as long as she'd dared before fleeing the city. I instantly felt another jolt of guilt. The note said she was going to try and make it to Perpignan, which shocked me. It said he was to meet her there.

'Perpignan?' I whispered in the silent flat. My home. She'd hated it, itching to get back to Paris the one time I'd dared take her there to visit my family.

I pocketed the note and went into the living room, where I peered out of the window to the street below. Rue des Pyrénées. Perfect, Sylvie had said the day we'd found it. I'd thought so too at the time. A Catalan living in Paris, I should live on a street named after the Pyrenees. It wasn't choice, it had just happened that way. But then I got to the point where even the name of my street was too sorry a reminder of all that was wrong with me. So I moved on my own to the Left Bank and my wife never forgave me. She told everyone I thought I was too good for the humble roads of Ménilmontant. Only I knew the exact opposite to be true.

Closing my old front door, I hurried downstairs and out of the building, the darkness of the stairs whispering too many memories at me of the shared unhappiness I'd created.

On the way home, I stopped myself from dwelling on Jean-Luc and the past by recalling what Hochstetter had told me about Weber in Poland. I'd witnessed dreadful cruelty in the last war, but Hochstetter and Lucja seemed to be talking of actions much colder and more calculating than anything I'd ever seen. Lucja spoke of people simply taken from their homes or their work and shot in a way that I found hard to imagine. And Hochstetter's story of the SS in Poland implied that it went beyond the heat of battle that I had experienced to a deliberate plan to exterminate. I had no idea if he was speaking of soldiers being killed or civilians. I closed my eyes, unable to keep them open, the thoughts too much to take in, an enveloping tiredness hitting me.

I heard tapping. I opened my eyes. I was back in my flat, on my faded armchair, my knees curled tightly under my arms, my head in my hands, and I was moaning, an animal sound from inside my chest that ached again and again. Tapping. The sound I was most afraid of. It was late. I'd fallen asleep and a dream I hadn't allowed into my head in over ten years had come calling. And still I heard the tapping.

It was coming from the door. Someone was knocking, gently, not to make too much noise but to call me. I jumped up. As I began to pull open the door, I hesitated but then pulled it open wider. Jean-Luc was standing on the landing in the shadows. He looked scared when he saw me.

'What is it?' he asked me.

'You're back.'

17

'I forgot my key when I left this morning.'

We sat down in our armchairs, both with a glass of whisky, both silent for a moment, gathering our thoughts. I watched him. I'd been a cop for too long.

'That's not true, Jean-Luc. What happened?'

He shifted uncomfortably. 'There were Germans in the street this morning. In a lorry. I saw them from the balcony.'

'Where were they going?'

'I didn't stay to find out. I got out over the roof in case they were coming for me.'

'What is it you're not telling me?'

'Everything. You can't know what I'm doing. What was happening to you?' He looked at my face. 'What's happened to you?'

I couldn't tell him. Probably just as he couldn't tell me where he went. 'Just an argument. I fell asleep, woke up feeling sore, that's all.'

I drank from my glass and pushed the memory of the incipient nightmare to the back of my mind. I thought of the doctors in 1916 telling me I was ready to go back to war and I almost laughed. I shifted my shoulders to get comfortable in the spare armchair. Jean-Luc was in mine.

'I have to do something,' he suddenly told me. 'I can't just stay here. I'm a soldier. I'm supposed to be fighting the Germans. Instead, I'm hiding from them in my own city while they do what they want with us. And no one stops them.'

'What are you going to do?'

'I can't say. You can't know.' He saw my look of surprise. 'You're a cop. You're working with the Germans. I don't know how much I can tell you.'

My ribs and stomach ached and I reflected on my working relationship with the Germans. 'I'm not working with them. Or for them. I'm a cop, I'm doing my job.'

'For the Germans.' I heard the scorn in his voice.

'Doing the same job I was doing before they came. I haven't changed anything. How can that be working for the Germans?' He didn't reply, so I tried another question. 'Where are you going to go?'

'I have to try and get out of Paris. Don't ask me how.'

'Just promise me you'll be careful. Don't trust anyone. Stay away from the railways.' I told him about the four Polish refugees found dead in the sidings. 'I think they paid someone to get them out and they got murdered instead. Please, whatever you do, don't do anything without telling me first.'

He nodded, his eyes moving about my room, taking in the lack of anything but books. I could see he wasn't listening. I tried again but he waved my words away.

'I just want to protect you, Jean-Luc.'

He looked sharply at me. 'Protect me? Like you did when I was young?'

'I will protect you. You can ask for my help.'

'I don't need it. I've got by without you until now.' I could see he intended to hurt. 'Why did you come and live here? Mum always said it was typical of you, but she wouldn't say why.'

I thought of the word typical and wondered what she meant. In a way, probably not the way she said it, she was crushingly right. 'My war came when I was young. I wanted to go to university, but the war changed that. So when I left your mother ...'

'And me.'

'I can't change that, Jean-Luc.' I stared at my bookshelves. 'I also came here because the hospital I was sent to in Paris to cure me of shell shock was here in the Fifth. Books and psychiatry. It was the one place I thought I'd feel safe.'

'She also used to criticise you for calling yourself Eddie. She said you'd forgotten yourself.'

I looked at him, he was getting some of the resentment he must have felt towards me out into no-man's-land, a live grenade we could throw back and forth at each other until it exploded in his face or mine. But I could also see something else in his worried features. He wanted me to give the right answers. I wasn't sure there were any. I poured us both a little more whisky.

'She was probably right. I forgot myself a long time ago. I didn't call myself Eddie. When I was a young cop, I used to moonlight working on the door in the jazz clubs in Montmartre to make some extra money. It could have been one of the happiest times I'd ever known if I'd let it. It was the American musicians who started calling me Eddie and it stuck. All the criminals and the other cops got to know me as Eddie and that's how it's stayed.'

I started to feel tired. I could see Jean-Luc's eyelids drop. I had no idea what the last few days had been like for him, but I knew how mine had gone. I waited until I heard his deep breaths of sleep before I spoke again.

'I had to leave. My war never left me and I couldn't stay. I couldn't love your mother and I couldn't stay and be unhappy and make you both unhappy too. I had to go and it was the hardest, worst decision of my life.'

He shifted in the armchair, fast asleep. And there are things I can't even say to you knowing you're asleep. Things about my own father and my mother. And my dead brother you've possibly never heard of. Reasons why I couldn't stay with you. And how I've never regretted that decision, harsh as that sounds, but I've never been able to live with it, either.

My own thoughts began to drift as sleep came.

The tapping started up again.

Sunday 7th June 1925

'You never think of Charles.'

'I'm not allowed to think of anything but Charles.'

'He was your brother.'

My mother turned away. I could hear the catch in her voice. And the resentment. It hadn't been far away at any point in the last four days – my parents' annual duty visit to Paris.

We stood on the platform at the Gare de Lyon, each one willing the train to be ready soon, the smouldering firework of their stay doused for another year. The iron made a tapping noise with the heat and I had to blot the sound out. Sylvie was a short distance away, holding tightly to Jean-Luc's hand. My son was staring wide-eyed at my parents and me.

'You've changed, Édouard,' my father told me.

'War does that. I'm sorry. Maybe I should have had the grace to die too.'

'You know we don't mean that.'

'I hate that war,' my mother said with venom. 'What it did to us.'

'To us?'

'You're constantly tired, Édouard.' My father tried to calm the waters. 'We worry about you. Are you sure you're happy being a policeman?'

I tried to be honest with him but he couldn't meet my gaze. 'It's not being a policeman that makes me unhappy, Papa.'

'I have something for you.' Out of his suitcase, he took a book and gave it to me. It was *Le Grand Meaulnes* by Alain-Fournier, killed in the early days of the war. 'It's about a young man searching for something he's lost. I think you should enjoy it.'

'He never found it again though, either, did he?'

I regretted it the moment I said it, and then the porter told them they could board their carriage and it was too late. I kissed them both lightly and watched the train pull out of the station, a numbness returning. Turning, I saw Sylvie and Jean-Luc walk away from me in the opposite direction, leaving me caught in the middle of all the people I was losing.

'Who was Charles?' Jean-Luc asked over dinner when we got home.

I just shook my head at him and didn't answer. Instead, I finished my meal in silence and got up to leave for Montmartre and the jazz club.

'That's right,' Sylvie hissed at me. 'Run away when there's something to be faced.'

The tension vanished the moment I walked through the double doors and I heard the musicians warming up. I breathed in the scent of the night and let my eyes close for a moment while I listened to the tune. I opened them to see Dominique getting ready at the mic. I smiled but she looked away and the evening began its slow descent.

As I did my rounds, I came across Fabienne in worried discussion with one of the singers, who gave her a piece of paper with a note written on it. Fabienne left before I joined them.

'Women's problems, Eddie,' Grace told me. 'Don't ask.'

Fran the barman winked at me from behind the peeling gilt

paint of the bar. He was pouring water through a funnel into a whisky bottle. The aroma it gave off failed to mask the cloying sweetness of cheap perfume that imbued the faded seat plush. I couldn't wait for the doors to open and the lights to dim.

It turned out to be one of those tense nights with endless flares of bad temper. The singer's microphone faded in and out and the audience grew restless. For once, I wanted the shift to end so I could do my proper job and be a policeman, happy or not. Towards the end of the evening, I walked in on Claude, the owner, in one of the back rooms. Dominique was with him. As I watched, he handed a pile of banknotes over to a couple of the Corsicans, who'd been rowdier than ever that night.

'What's happening?' I asked him.

He looked shaken. 'Please, Eddie, just leave it.'

The younger of the two Corsicans pulled out a knife and held it loosely, flicking the tip up and down in his fingers. 'Yes, Eddie, just leave it. And close the door behind you.'

'Put the knife away. I'm a cop. You really don't want to annoy me.'

He laughed. 'A cop? That just means we have to pay you a little more. Or do you want one of the whores?'

I lunged for him, but Dominique stood between us. 'Don't, Eddie. I'm begging you.'

'She's begging you, Eddie,' the young guy mimicked.

'So are you,' I told him.

The older guy looked me up and down. 'We know who you are. We know what you did to one of our friends. So we'll come to a deal. We won't pay you like we usually do with cops. But as long as you turn a blind eye to our business matters, we won't make your sweet little kid an orphan. How does that sound?'

I made a move, but Dominique held her hand lightly on my chest, her eyes desperate. It was enough. I stood still and watched the two men pick up the money and leave. The young one squeezed Dominique's arse and winked at me.

'Very nice.'

'What's going on here?' I asked Claude and Dominique once they'd gone. The anger was raw in my voice. 'I can sort this out.'

'You, Eddie?' Dominique said. 'You can't sort yourself out.' Dismissing me with an angry flick of her hand, she brushed past me and out of the door. I turned to Claude and was shocked at the look of irritation towards me on his face.

'Just go, Eddie. No one wants your help.'

I tried finding Dominique in the club, but she'd already left. I checked my watch and yawned. My shift at the station was due to start in less than half an hour. From behind the bar, Fran watched me.

'Tired, Eddie? Come with me, I've got something that might help with that.'

He led me to the store room where bottles were kept and closed the door behind us. From behind an air vent in the wall, he pulled out a small package. Through my exhaustion, I stared in bewilderment and then shock as he tipped some white powder onto the top of a box. He gestured me to take some.

'No, Fran, that's not me.'

'So what is, Eddie? Because I sure as hell don't know. And I don't think you do, either. Try it. It'll take one edge off and give you another.'

With little more to lose, I leaned over the powder and took the cocaine up into my nose for the first time. I felt nothing for the briefest of moments, a disappointment that nothing had changed, but then the buzz hit me like all the light bulbs in the city coming on at once and I saw life with a clarity I hadn't known in a long, long time. I leaned down and took in some more. I looked at Fran and grinned. He took some too and began talking at racehorse speed.

'Do it, Eddie. Go fuck the world. It deserves nothing better. And don't let any bastard stop you.'

Tuesday 18th June 1940

18

No men in grey were going to stop me that morning.

'I'm here to see Major Hochstetter,' I told the two on the door of the Lutétia. A different two from the previous day. 'He's summoned me.' He hadn't. 'I don't want to keep him waiting.' That, at least, was true.

It worked. Bluster and orders, the soul of the military and the key to riding roughshod over the ranks. It had helped that I was irritable. I'd slept mercifully little. The old dream that had been threatening to come back since the Germans had invaded had almost broken through my defences in the night. Thankfully, the horror of it had woken me up. And Jean-Luc had left by the time I'd got up. Guiltily, I'd placed the note to him from Sylvie between two books on my shelf. I had no answer to myself why I hadn't given it to him.

Inside, the busy efficiency of the foyer hid a chaotic bustle as a secretary accompanied me up a flight of stairs to the first floor and along a corridor. There were boxes and papers everywhere, and secretaries and soldiers who seemed to be hurrying here and there with something taken urgently at random from one pile or another. I recalled the road signs outside the Opéra and I thought again that the Germans were more than prepared for war. It was the peace that had taken them by surprise.

Hochstetter's affability did the same to me.

'Édouard, I was going to come and see you. I must apologise for my behaviour yesterday. At times I am guilty of being over-zealous and these are trying times for us all. I'd be honoured if you'd join me for breakfast.'

He really did know how to be disarming. It was another of the weapons in his armoury. I wasn't so well-equipped.

'What have you done with the three railway workers?'

'Always so eager. Very laudable.'

A junior officer came into the bedroom that had been turned into an office and asked Hochstetter to sign something. He scanned it quickly, his eyes moving keenly over the paper, and signed it before handing it carelessly back to the officer. As ever, he had that calm that implied more industry than the bustle of others. That was one of the things I found most unsettling about him.

'They have all been released,' he told me. 'It is quite simple, really.'

'No, it isn't. It's our job to question them, not yours. They're either suspects or witnesses in a murder investigation. It has nothing to do with the German army. You could have jeopardised my investigation.'

'You're quite right. Please accept my apologies. As the new order in Paris, it is our job to ensure matters run smoothly, and that includes leaving you to get on with your job. It is a lesson we are all learning.'

'I still don't understand why you needed to question them.'

'Forgive me, I was merely trying to assist.' He looked at me pointedly. 'I find we're often able to be more persuasive in getting the answers we seek than the local police are.'

I was saved from having to answer by a knock on the door. Two French waiters brought in the breakfast on two trolleys.

I hadn't seen so much food in one place for months. Without making eye contact, the waiters placed everything on the table and left. I recalled Jean-Luc's judgement of me. Each of us in our way was working with the Germans, whether we liked it or not.

'You like to own people,' I told him.

'It's simply largesse. Whether you choose to accept it or not is your decision.'

He took out a cigarette and tapped it on the end of a silver case before lighting it with a match. I'd have expected a gold lighter. He offered me one but I refused. I didn't panic at the sight as I had once, but after the gas attacks of the last war, the thought of voluntarily inhaling fumes was the most appalling pastime I could think of. The greater temptation was the crois-sants and coffee in front of me. I thought of the food rotting in the railway yard and felt a brief spike of anger.

'By the way,' he went on, 'one of the workers, Thierry Papin, was arrested last night after his release for breaking the curfew. As a sign of the cooperation between us, I have already ensured that he has been handed over by the German authorities to the French police. I am sure you will know how to reciprocate that.'

'I'm sure you'll find a way.'

'Quite. In fact, I have some other news for you that goes in some way towards repaying your debt. It concerns your friends in the Geheime Feldpolizei. I gather you paid them a visit yesterday. Unfortunately, I could have saved you a fair degree of discomfort as I have learned that the men who questioned you have nothing to do with the GFP. Instead, they're Gestapo agents. I'm very grateful to you for bringing it to my attention.'

'Gestapo? So why say they're GFP?'

'Because the Gestapo are not supposed to be here. As I

intimated yesterday, the Wehrmacht have some reservations about the behaviour of the SS in Poland. Hitler's intention is for Paris to become the second city in the Reich, so we have no wish to create unnecessary problems with the populace here. Consequently, we managed to persuade Hitler to order that no Gestapo units would accompany the army and that all police units would be under the command of the Wehrmacht. Unfortunately, Himmler wasn't happy with that, so Heydrich sent a small group of Gestapo agents dressed as Geheime Feldpolizei with the army. It appears that their purpose here is to pave the way for the Gestapo to establish a base in Paris. I have already sent a report to Berlin with a strong complaint and a recommendation that they be found and arrested and sent back to Germany.'

'You have even more in-fighting than we do. Let's just hope it doesn't do the same to you as it did to us.'

He stood up to let me know it was time for me to go. 'Well, enjoyable though our discussion is, Édouard, I'm afraid I'm going to have to bring it to an end. I am expecting a visitor. In the meantime, I would recommend that you don't approach the Gestapo the way you did the GFP. Although I'm learning that it takes little to set you off and a lot to stop you. I would recommend you don't let that become your Achilles heel.'

I closed the door on him in his makeshift office. 'Or yours.'

Crossing the road outside the hotel, on instinct I turned to look back. I saw Ronson walking up the steps and into the building.

'What did Major Hochstetter want?'

Le Bailly had been pouring himself one of his thick brews when I'd climbed to his eyrie above the marshalling yards. He poured one for me too. I recalled the smell of Hochstetter's coffee and almost regretted not having succumbed. We sat down in his two mismatched chairs, no doubt salvaged from the huts at some time.

'I don't know, in all honesty. He didn't really ask about the men killed at the yard or if I saw anything. He just wanted to know what I did, and then he told me what was expected of me and that I was to do my job as always without hindering the Germans in any way. Nothing I haven't heard a million times before from officers and management. You served in the last one, you know what I mean. That's why I was involved in the mutiny. They'd asked too much of us, and we all saw what was happening in Russia. We'd had enough.'

'Were you punished?'

He shook his head. Somehow it didn't surprise me. 'There's one thing you should know. I'm not just a union official. I'm a member of the Communist Party. It was that time that made me join.'

'I'm no Communist, but I would have been ready to mutiny by that time.'

'You didn't?'

'I was in a prison in Germany. I was captured at Verdun, otherwise I might well have joined in.'

'That war and the things we did and the things we witnessed brutalised us beyond repair. Made us willing to take actions we would never otherwise contemplate. When I saw the Germans coming into the yard on Friday morning, it brought it all back.' He was shaken at the memory. He took a gulp of coffee to hide it. 'Prison? You must have picked up some German.'

'Some. Did Hochstetter make anything of you being a Communist?'

'Not in so many words, but it was there. I reckon I'm all right for the time being because of the Nazi-Soviet Pact. I don't think the Germans will want to rock that boat. They'll leave me alone as long as it suits them. I know my workers and how to get them to work, the Boches are going to need that. And no one knows the Gare d'Austerlitz and the marshalling yards like I do.'

'And then?'

'Who knows? Right now, I have to reach a modus vivendi with the Nazis that works for us all.'

After leaving Le Bailly, I was early for the noon meet with Lucja, so I bought a newspaper at a kiosk and waited on Place des Vosges. The paper was the first one to come out since the occupation of the city and it told me how rosily things were going for the Germans. I flicked through it in disgust. French newspaper, German words. In the absence of any desire to tell us anything about the war, it devoted page after page to one of the people who had committed suicide on the day the Germans entered the city. One of France's most eminent neurosurgeons, Thierry de Martel, left a note saying he refused to leave Paris and injected himself with a fatal dose of phenobarbital. I might not have shared his politics, but it was a pointless loss.

I saw Lucja the moment she entered the square. Scanning the gardens and the porticoes, I couldn't see any German sightseers today. I got up and greeted her with two kisses.

'You learn quickly,' she commented as we sat down. She handed me the folder of letters. 'Janek studied these all through the night. They're innocent. Love letters, nothing more. No hidden messages or signs that he could find.'

'Do you think the way they're bound is significant?'

'I don't know. Fryderyk was a bookbinder. The little I saw of him, he was an obsessive character, and I don't think that was just because of what he'd been through. I think this was possibly just his way of keeping documents.'

I looked at the folder. I still didn't understand why Fryderyk would buy a safe for them but not keep his passport in it too. A result of his obsessive nature and his grief, maybe.

'When the Germans turned up in the city on Friday, we found four men, refugees, gassed in a railway truck.'

She looked as surprised as I was at what I was sharing with her. 'You think it was the Nazis? They would gas people in a heartbeat if it suited them.'

'No, I don't think it was them.' In all honesty, I hadn't seen them as the killers, but Weber's reaction to the name of Bydgoszcz came back to me yet again. 'It's just that the four men were Polish, and one of them at least was from Bydgoszcz.'

Lucja hung her head. 'We knew of some refugees who were looking for a way out of Paris. They told us they'd found some-one who'd get them out by train. We thought they'd escaped.'

'Do you know who was going to get them out?'

'They spoke of a bar called the Cheval Noir. Someone they met there.'

'The Cheval? That closed down years ago. Are you sure?'

'That's all I know, I'm sorry. Who do you think killed them?'

'I'm still in the dark. My feeling is that it was someone who'd agreed to get them out, then taken their money and killed them. Or someone else found them and robbed and killed them before the first person had the chance to get them away. Either way, by the time the bodies would be found, the train should have been long gone, but then the Germans arrived and the trains weren't running.'

'Why would they gas them instead of shooting them?'

'It's silent. It's also impersonal. When you shoot someone,

you see them die. If you throw a gas canister into a truck and close the door, you can tell yourself you didn't do it.'

She let out a long sigh. 'Or they panicked. I suppose I want to see the Germans as being responsible. One more crime of hatred. Killing Poles because they've acquired a taste for it.'

I took a sideways glance at her and saw the anger in her eyes again. I recalled the *grusspflicht* incident yesterday and, like her, wondered when simply having to salute the occupiers would be the least of our worries.

'How do I get hold of you the next time I need to see you?'

'One of us will come here every day at noon and at seven in the evening. We'll wait for ten minutes. If you or we don't show up, the other one will leave until the next opportunity.' She looked sideways at me. 'That's German seven and noon.'

I wrinkled my nose in disgust. 'I have a telephone at home you can call. I wouldn't trust the one at the police station.'

She smiled wryly. 'I wouldn't trust the one in your home, either. There's something I didn't tell you. Fryderyk was so frightened on the Friday he died because he'd seen one of the German officers who'd taken part in the massacre. He recognised him from the photographs he had.'

I closed my eyes and tried to imagine how Fryderyk must have felt seeing one of his wife's murderers. 'It keeps coming back to Bydgoszcz.'

'Do you know what the gaus are? They're the German administrative regions that have been imposed on Poland. My family is from Poznan, which is in what the Nazis call the Reichsgau Wartheland. The gauleiter there, Arthur Greiser, is a believer in racial cleansing. He is measuring people's features, their noses, their eyebrows, their mouths, to discover who isn't racially pure and then he's sending them away and no one is seeing them again. As far as we know, they're being deported to the most easterly areas of Poland, near where the Soviets are, and ethnic Germans from other countries are being brought in to take over their homes and their businesses. We don't know how many people have been sent away. Bydgoszcz is in the Reichsgau Danzig-Westpreussen, where this isn't happening so much. Thousands of people in the region have been murdered or deported, but my family believes that everyone there is getting off lightly compared to them. The problem is that we in Poland all know these things are happening, but we have no idea of the extent of them and nothing that will convince the world that it has to do something. The Americans need to be told before they'll enter the war, before they'll do anything. Even the Germans – ordinary Germans safe in their homes – they need to be told the evil the Nazis are doing in their name.' She flopped back, defeated by her own words.

'Do you think Fryderyk's evidence will do that?'

'I don't know. I hope so. Fryderyk was pushed over the edge by what happened to him, so it's sometimes hard to believe he had anything of value. Janek is convinced it was nothing, just the madness of his grief speaking.'

'Where did Fryderyk see this German he recognised?'

'He didn't say, but he had a job at the Hotel Majestic as a dishwasher. It might have been there.'

An old nineteenth-century palace a few minutes' walk from the Arc de Triomphe, the Majestic was where the German High Command had set up its headquarters. They certainly didn't believe in slumming it. I thought what a cruel twist it was that a refugee from a massacre in Poland should have been working in a hotel requisitioned by the Nazis. 'Do you know if the officer recognised Fryderyk?'

'He didn't say. But even if he hadn't been recognised, he would most likely have been detained. When the Abwehr took over the Hotel Lutétia, there were Polish refugees staying there who had fled arrest by the Nazis in Poland. They were all caught like fish in a net, all now imprisoned. There are round-ups every day in all the hotels. The Nazis keep returning for anyone they missed.'

'Do you know of any Poles working at the Majestic? I want to get in to see if Fryderyk might have left anything there to do with the killings in Bydgoszcz.'

'I know of a man called Borek who works as a concierge. He left Poland years ago and has lived in Paris since the late twenties. Because he's not here fleeing the Nazis, I don't know where his allegiances lie or if he can be trusted.'

'Can we go there now? Would he trust you enough to talk to me?'

She checked her watch. 'I can try and introduce you, but I don't have time to go into the hotel. I'm not sure it's safe for me, either.'

We left the square and sat in silence on the Metro, Lucja afraid of anyone overhearing her accent. When we emerged from the station a short walk from the Majestic, a German army lorry was standing outside the hotel's main entrance. Soldiers were shepherding over a dozen men and women from the door to the rear of the lorry. Next to me, I felt Lucja tense up.

A heavy-set man with a huge black beard reaching down to his shirt front was being escorted by two large gefreiters. At the tailgate, he reached forward and effortlessly helped lift a woman up and into the lorry.

'That's Borek,' Lucja told me, her voice constricted. As she spoke, I saw her exchange a glance with him before her gaze turned to the waiting lorry. The tailgate banged with a loud metallic clang every time someone climbed in. Lucja's face was white, a sheen of sweat on her forehead, and she began to shake uncontrollably. She put her hand hurriedly to her mouth. 'I can't stay.'

She turned and walked back towards the Metro. I could see her struggling not to break into a run. I looked back to see Borek waiting patiently to be put on the truck.

19

'I need to speak to this man. He's wanted to help with my enquiries. I'm a detective with the Paris police.'

Borek looked quizzically at me from inside the lorry. The German officer I spoke to, a slight man in his thirties with slick hair and prominent front teeth, simply shook his head at me. 'You have no jurisdiction here.'

'He's a French citizen. If you look at his papers, you'll see he's naturalised French.'

I kept my fingers crossed that that was the case. Taking his cue, Borek took his ID out of his concierge's uniform and showed it to the officer. Reading it upside-down, I was relieved I'd been right. The officer, who looked more like a sinister country solicitor than a soldier, reluctantly ordered the Polish mountain to be unloaded from the truck. I watched the other people have to stay seated, fear on their faces, and felt a stab of guilt that I could do nothing for them.

The soldiers slammed the tailgate shut and the officer got into his staff car. Borek stood alongside me as we watched the small convoy go. He turned to inspect me. I might be tall and strong, but I was dwarfed length and breadth by his bulk.

'What is it you want, friend? I have no trouble with the police.'

His accent was heavy, stronger than Lucja's, his voice a rumbling fog. He was like a bear who's eaten well: safe for the time being, but you wouldn't want to be near him when he got hungry.

'To talk. I just want to ask you about a man you used to work with. Fryderyk Gorecki.'

'Ah, Fryderyk. He has gone, left while he could. When the Germans came.'

I stared at him. 'Is there somewhere we can go? There's something I need to tell you.'

He led me around the corner to the hotel's rear entrance. There were no Germans around, so we stopped and I took a deep breath.

'Fryderyk's dead. He killed himself the day the Germans arrived.'

He looked at me in disbelief. 'He would never have left Jan.'

'Jan died with him.'

'But he doted on Jan. His wife died. Jan was all he had left. He never let him out of his sight. You never saw a man love his child so much.'

The huge man's eyes were glistening and I felt sorry for him. I was working out how to ask him my next question, but he carried on talking of his own accord, his voice deep and distant.

'He was very upset the day the Germans arrived. He'd got more and more agitated as they got nearer the city. More and more erratic. But the day they entered Paris, he was much worse. Shaking. The first Germans came into the hotel and he was nervous like we all were, but then he saw someone, I don't know who, and it terrified him. He wouldn't tell me what was wrong, he just picked up little Jan and left and he didn't come back. I thought he'd left Paris.'

I couldn't help feeling disappointed that Borek hadn't seen

who it was who'd alarmed Fryderyk. My instinct told me it was Weber, but I had no way of being certain.

'I want to get into the kitchens to see if Fryderyk left anything that would explain what happened. Did he leave anything in the hotel? Anything for you to look after? No matter how innocent it might seem.'

'Nothing. But we all have a cupboard where we store personal items. I don't think Fryderyk's has been touched. It's this way.'

He led me inside the hotel and we made our way along the service corridors to a door that led into a small staff room with a few cupboards, a scuffed table and half a dozen chairs.

'Fryderyk sometimes left Jan in here to sleep. He might have left something in his cupboard.'

I took a look at the sparse room. It wasn't going to take me long. I checked Fryderyk's cupboard first, but there was nothing but an apron and a picture book he must have used to keep Jan occupied. I also went through all the others, checking the linings of an old porter's coat and forgotten belongings, but again I found nothing. I turned to the table and chairs, crouching underneath and looking for anything stuck to the underside. No joy, so Borek took me through another door into a steam-filled and noisy kitchen. He showed me where Fryderyk used to wash dishes. Two sinks and a long drying rack for pots and pans and plates.

'Fryderyk used to sit Jan down here while he worked.'

I placed my hands on the sink and tried to imagine how Fryderyk must have felt doing this with his wife dead, his home gone and his business as a printer and bookbinder destroyed, all the while trying to keep everything together for his son. There was nowhere that Fryderyk would conceivably have considered to be a safe hiding place for whatever evidence he had. Looking at the bleakness of where he spent his days and nights, I had to consider one of two possibilities. One was that any record had died with him. The other was that he simply hadn't had any in the first place, that it was just the desperation of grief that had made him believe he had.

Borek led me out of the kitchen when we heard someone snapping their fingers.

'You,' an accented voice said in French. I turned to see a German officer looking at me. 'You, come here.'

Fighting the urge to check my gun under my jacket, I walked towards him. I could see Borek pale.

'Bring a wine list. Oberstleutnant Fischer has been waiting for it. Room 132.'

'Certainly, sir. It will be the first thing I do.'

I watched him march off and I slowly let out my breath. So now I looked like a waiter? Borek led me to the outside door and I asked him one more question.

'The woman who was with me outside. Do you know her?'

'No. I've seen her before, but I don't know who she is.'

20

'Hochstetter told me that Papin had been handed over to us.'

Dax looked surprised, not so much by the raised voice as by his door banging sharply against his office wall, scuffing off another piece of plaster. I was to blame for both.

'He has.'

'I've just been to the cells to question him, but I'm told he's not there. Hochstetter hasn't handed him over.'

'Papin's been released. The Germans brought him in this morning, and we let him go.'

'But he was suspected of burglary. He might be part of the gangs using the sheds for storing stolen goods.'

Dax flicked a piece of paper over his desk at me. 'No evidence to hold him on. Released without charge.'

I scanned the release form and cursed. Auban's signature was at the bottom. 'I thought he broke the curfew.'

'So you want to start charging people for breaking the Boches' curfew, Eddie?'

'I do when it's Papin.'

I left his door shivering in its frame and went to my own office. Barthe told me that Auban hadn't come in yet, or I'd have warmed his heels too. Instead, I recalled Hochstetter's advice not to go chasing after the Gestapo and picked the phone up.

I started with the plushest hotels in the city and began ringing around. By the fourth, I'd got the questions down to seven seconds before moving on to the next one on the list.

'Anyone called Müller or Schmidt staying there? Baby-blue piping on the uniform? Baby blond head on the body?'

None of them had anyone claiming to be the GFP staying with them, much less the Gestapo, although I imagined they still weren't admitting to that until Adolf gave them his blessing or Hochstetter had them sent home. My money was on Adolf.

I realised after half an hour it was going to be an impossible task, although I did pick up one interesting piece of information from the Hotel Bristol. It had been booked by the US embassy for their staff.

'There are a number of American journalists staying here too,' the receptionist told me.

'I bet you're glad you've got them instead.'

'I couldn't possibly say.'

I asked for a couple of names and put the phone down. My mood was a lot lighter than it had been half an hour earlier. I hid Fryderyk's folder of letters under some papers in my desk drawer and, checking that Auban still hadn't returned, I left Thirty-Six.

Ronson was in the downstairs bar when I got to the Bristol, drinking a cocktail with a couple of Americans. She gave me that smile that looked like she'd been caught stealing again.

'Eddie Giral, just the guy I wanted to see. Just not here.' She climbed down off her stool and took my arm to walk through the foyer. 'So you found me, then? I said you were a good cop. I want you to take me far away from here, I've got something I want to tell you.'

'Like what you were doing with Hochstetter?'

'Oh, Eddie, Eddie, that's the least of it.'

I drove her to the Jardin du Luxembourg and parked by the gates near the Medici Fountain. In the gardens, a couple strolled past us, as though the city had never been occupied. A man walked slowly by, carrying a briefcase and loosening his tie, on his way home from work. Everywhere I saw a strange and superficial normality returning to Paris, like a warped reflection of itself in a damaged mirror. It was hard to believe that the Germans had entered the city only four days ago.

Ronson seemed to read my mind. 'I've loved this city, but it's a shadow of itself. Know anywhere quiet we can go?'

I took her to the apiary. 'Very few people come here. The bees worry them.'

'It's amazing,' she said in wonder. 'I didn't know it existed.'

The small, shaded enclosure was deserted, the bees calm in their hives under the tiled roof of the open-sided shelter. Further rows of white-shuttered hives straggled the perimeter of the little square in front, closing it off to the outside world.

'I come here to read sometimes. It's peaceful. And the bees don't mind.'

'You're a strange man, Eddie.'

'So why were you seeing Hochstetter?'

'You been following me again?' She grinned. 'Nothing. Just an exchange of views. It's really not important. Not compared with what I'm about to tell you.'

We sat on a wooden bench beneath the trees, facing the shelter. Only a low humming let us know the bees were there. She looked at the hives before speaking again.

'What do you know of the German resistance?'

'I know they're not resisting as much as we'd all like them to.'

She laughed, a rich sound that came from her chest. 'No, they're too divided. At the last count, the RSHA, the Nazi security office, had three different networks in the Rote Kapelle alone, and those are just the ones they know of.'

'The Red Orchestra.'

'You know more German than you let on.'

'So why is Hitler still in power if there are so many of them?'

'Yeah, I guess that's the rub. The problem as I see it is that even though most of them hate Hitler's guts, between them they all disagree on what it is they do want if they did manage to get rid of him. You've got everyone from the liberals, who want a democracy back, to the conservatives, who like Hitler's policies, they just don't like his way of going about getting them. And then you've got the Schwarze Kapelle – the Black Orchestra – which the Nazis reckon goes deep into the foreign ministry, the aristocracy, the Wehrmacht, the Abwehr and who knows where else.'

'Are they all anti-Nazi?'

'In the Wehrmacht, you've got a bit of everything. The Luftwaffe's more pro-Nazi. The Abwehr's different. The head of it, Canaris, won't allow Nazis to be senior officers. The problem with it all is that you've got army officers and diplomats who might want Hitler out, but they still want to hang onto all the territories he's gained. That doesn't go down too well with everyone, especially the countries the Nazis have already occupied. And then you've got others who just want to tell the world what's going on in the Nazis' name, like atrocities in Germany and Poland.'

I looked away, my immediate thought on the dead men in the railway yard and Fryderyk Gorecki's possible evidence of atrocities in Poland, but I said nothing. I still didn't know how far I could trust her.

'And the other problem is that no foreign governments trust any of them anyway,' she carried on. 'Not when they have no idea what any of them wants to put in place of the Nazis. And the Brits won't go near any of them after they got their fingers burned at Venlo.'

'Venlo?'

'The Netherlands. Before war was declared. Some supposed German resistance supporters wanted to trade with the British secret service in exchange for help in deposing Hitler. Problem is they were Gestapo agents posing as resistance. They arrested two British army officers who are now in a KZ, a concentration camp, somewhere in Germany. Since then, the Brits don't want to know and the US is very sceptical about anyone claiming to be anti-Hitler. Which is playing right into the Nazis' hands.'

'Did you just bring me here to cheer me up?'

'Don't let it get you down. There are still some of us – governments and press – who want to work with these groups. We just have to find the right guys to help. Hitler has to do everything he can to keep the States *out* of the war. People like me have to do everything we can to bring us *into* the war to stop him. Which brings me to Weber.'

'Weber? You're not going to tell me he's German resistance.'

'Weber wants to join the good guys. He wants to defect. He has something he wants to trade and he wants me to get him out of France and over to the USA in exchange for what he knows. And he won't tell me what he knows unless I do just that.'

'Why would he want to defect? No one in their right mind would think the Germans are going to lose this war any day soon. It took them six weeks to get to Paris. Poland, Belgium, the Netherlands, Czechoslovakia, Norway, Denmark, all defeated. Only the British are left standing, and everyone is just waiting until they fall.'

'That's exactly his argument. It's happening too quickly.

Adolf's overstretching himself and Weber reckons it's all going to come tumbling down like a house of cards once the Soviets turn on Hitler or Hitler turns on them. Von Ribbentrop and Molotov signed the non-aggression pact so they could carve up Poland between them, but the point's going to come when one of them gets greedy and takes a bite out of the other. As to which one does it first, your guess is as good as mine. Either way, Weber wants out before that happens.'

'He's pro-Hitler. He was a member of the Nazi Party in the early days, and still a sympathiser. He's the picture of Nazi self-belief.'

Ronson snorted. 'Hochstetter tell you that? Weber says he saw things in Poland that changed his beliefs for good.'

I stared at the light slowly fading on the summer flowers. 'And you believe him?'

'Yes, I do. And that's why I need you to play ball, Eddie. I need Weber to keep his head down until I can get him out. And until that happens, I want you to leave him to sit nice and quiet in his swanky Rue du Faubourg Saint-Honoré apartment.'

'Faubourg Saint-Honoré? Nice to see him sacrificing his creature comforts for the cause.'

'Commandeered by the Wehrmacht. Belongs to a family called Weitzmann, who left in the exodus. So, what I don't need is for Hochstetter to be taking an interest in him. And for that, I need you to stop wanting to interview him about these four guys dead in the rail yard.'

'It's a murder investigation. I can't do that. I have to stop whoever it is from killing again.'

'What you have to do, Eddie, is get some perspective. They're four men. We're talking about millions of men, women and children all over Europe who might be saved if the Nazis are stopped.'

21

I watched Ronson leave the apiary and sat a while longer to consider her words. Everything she said made sense, and it left me strangely deflated. In France, we'd begged Roosevelt to enter the war against Hitler and a lot of people had felt real anger at American reluctance to get involved. If resistance in Germany and pressure from journalists like Ronson could make that happen, that had to be good for all of us.

The problem was I trusted Weber about as far as the distance I could hurl him back to Berlin.

'One good howitzer should do it,' I told the bees. They hummed back soothingly.

It also took an axe to my investigation into the murders of the four men in the railway yard. Did my discovery of the person who killed four men achieve anything more than that? One arrest in the middle of a world's destruction. Normally, that would have been enough, I had to admit. I was a cop, that was my job. But now, with half the continent busy slaughtering the other half, Ronson was right. I should be more concerned with what was going on outside my world.

Lucja had also told me what was happening in Poland. Brutality on a scale I couldn't believe. I wasn't entirely sure I could or even did believe it. It was surely too sinister, too cold to be true. I thought that the SS had probably shot civilians at random, but atrocities in every town and every village seemed too fantastical to take in. We all exaggerated about the last war, we still did. Maybe we were exaggerating about this one too. I remembered the stories of Germans crucifying prisoners on barn doors, of them digging up the dead to boil them down to make soap. And people believed them, they'd believe any falsehood to justify their own actions and further their own wishes. All of which made it almost impossible to know what to believe now.

I watched a lone bee return to its hive, a latecomer hurrying home before its own curfew, and thought of Fryderyk escaping the Germans and giving up. I understood his need to believe in something to survive, an obsession to cling to. I believed in my job, I believed that what I did was right. But if that were taken away from me, I knew that like Fryderyk, I'd crumble. His evidence – the evidence he said he had but no one had seen – was either as real as the sun setting on the city or as false as the time the Germans had imposed on the sunset. But it would have been real to him, and I had to consider that his taking his own life was because, ultimately, when the Germans arrived, he knew he had nothing tangible to show.

I had a sudden memory of a new captain from Burgundy, a rich kid no one liked, sticking his head above the trench in the last war. A sniper had taken his face off while we sat in weary silence, too jaded to warn him not to be an idiot. Given the amount of interest in Fryderyk, I worried that if I were to pursue his supposed evidence, I'd be doing the same as the captain. Raising my head above the parapet for a false hope. I had to decide if it was a risk worth taking. Especially now that my son had found me. I got up reluctantly to leave the park and looked at the hives, the bees out of harm's way for the evening.

'But then there's the safe,' I told them. 'And a collection of items a refugee chose to keep in a piece of furniture he couldn't afford.'

Half-doing as Ronson had told me, I forgot Weber for the time being and drove to the streets south of Gare d'Austerlitz. The Cheval Noir, the bar where Lucja said the refugees had found someone to help them, had infested this area before we'd finally shut it down. I used to like the old place; it was like a flea market for picking up bargain criminals.

At the arse-end of a rotten alleyway, there were no signs that it had reopened. Just paint flaking off broken window shutters and a scuffed and battered door. Ancient posters advertising long forgotten *bal musette* dances and circus acts hung blown and tattered on the ravaged brick walls. If the Cheval Noir had reopened, it wasn't serving the tea-dance crowd. I spotted an old guy sitting on a rickety wooden chair outside his front door. He was staring at me. His drooping mouth ruminated tirelessly over toothless gums.

'So the Cheval's opened up again?' I asked him.

He picked up his chair and carried it indoors. 'Fuck you, cop.'

'Is that a yes or a no?' I asked the closed door.

On the way home, I found a bistro in my neighbourhood that was open. The evolving feel of the city was something I was having to get used to by the hour. Elusive shadows of the real Paris emerged in the corner of my vision, but when I focused on them, they were just a compromise, an ersatz replacement to appease. I couldn't decide if they were a sign of resilience, capitulation or resignation.

The small restaurant had little to offer and the atmosphere was sombre but they still had more food than I did at home. In the end, I had a plate of stew that was more water than stew, while I recalled the piles of vegetables rotting in the railway yard. The owner told me the folk legend of how we got the word 'bistro'. I was too tired to stop him.

'Another time we were occupied. Russians in the Napoleonic War asking for their food to be delivered "bistro", which means quickly in Russian.'

I smiled and chewed my food in silence. Everyone in Paris had that story. It no longer mattered that it wasn't true. I wondered what legends would grow up about this latest occupation and whether it would be us telling them or the Germans.

Monsieur Henri answered that one for me much sooner than I wanted. He was peering out of his front door. I really wished he'd left in the exodus. He told me the latest piece of nonsense he'd heard.

'The Russians have bombed Berlin and the Pope's killed himself.'

I ignored him and trudged on upstairs to my flat. Wanting to hear something I could vaguely believe, even if I couldn't understand much of it, I sat down at my kitchen table and turned the radio on. I didn't want to have to stomach any more Nazi propaganda, so I turned it down low and searched across the dial for the BBC. I found it and took a sip of the whisky I'd poured myself. I understood very little, but it was comforting not to hear French voices telling us of the glory of the Third Reich.

As the sound washed over me and the malt rinsed through me, I got up and took the pile of items I'd taken from Fryderyk's safe to the table. It was the first chance I'd had to take a proper look at them. I might not even have done that had it not been for meeting Lucja and Fryderyk's claim to have had evidence of atrocities. As I sat down, I thought again of the lies we fed ourselves. The legend of the bistro and Monsieur Henri's outlandish rumours. I had nothing to say that Lucja's words and Fryderyk's supposed proof weren't just more of the same.

The folder of letters was still in my drawer at Thirty-Six, so I looked at the other folder, with its two photos bound meticulously inside. Fryderyk did seem to have been an obsessive character. I couldn't help feeling a stab of sadness at the sight of the three of them together. A family, gone. Jan was laughing, clutching something to his chest that I could barely make out in the dark exposure. But it was Ewa that intrigued me. Smiling quietly, she was caught in a moment of joy with her husband and son. She had fine features, a slender nose and inquisitive eyes. Her hair was drawn back in quite a distinctive way, held in place low on her back by the look of it and gathered abundantly around her face.

Putting it down, I picked up the first of the two Polish books. It looked like some sort of textbook. The one thing that sprung out at me was the author's name: Ewa Gorecka. I presumed that Gorecka must be a feminine form of Gorecki. Inside the book was a dedication to Fryderyk and Jan. I sighed and imagined Fryderyk's pride at Ewa's achievement. It was probably one of the few memories of his wife that he'd been able to take with him. I flicked through the pages, but nothing fell out.

I did the same with the second Polish book. It looked like a novel, but I had no idea what the title meant. Checking inside, I saw that it had been printed in Bydgoszcz and it hit me that it must have been one that Fryderyk had produced. I looked at the two books together. He'd kept them for sentimental value, worth more to him for the life he'd lost than a passport.

It was the Céline book that was discordant. That and the equally vile pamphlet inside. I had no idea why a victim of the Nazis would own a book in French that was as rabidly anti-Semitic and racialist as anything that Hitler and his cronies had dreamed up. I took longer to look through these than the Polish books as at least I would have understood anything out of place, but I found nothing. Nowhere in the book or the pamphlet was there a marking or a note or anything out of the ordinary. I placed them in a pile with the other items.

Staring at them, my mind wandered, but I was brought back when I suddenly heard French being spoken on the radio. I went to turn it up, but checked myself, instead pulling my chair nearer to the table. It was a French brigadier general, de Gaulle, about the only one who'd had any success against the Germans when our army fell and who'd been criticising our defence plans for years. No one had listened to him. He was calling on us in France to carry on the fight against the Germans and to resist the occupation. I wondered if people would listen to him now.

Feeling oddly flat rather than uplifted by the speech, I poured the rest of the whisky back in the bottle and went out into the night. I couldn't stay inside my flat. And if Jean-Luc were to come, he had a key to let himself in. I wasn't sure I was up to another night of explanations and recriminations.

Luigi pulled the curtain aside and sighed. 'I'm surprised you keep coming back here, Eddie.'

I walked past him and noticed all the various uniforms, the field grey of Adolf's army and the collarless shirts of our own home-grown miscreants. 'I like coming here, Luigi, it makes me feel good about myself. I'll have a whisky. The good stolen stuff you keep under the counter, not the watered-down muck you serve everyone else.'

I had a sudden vision of all the times I'd seen Fran watering down the whisky when I'd worked in the jazz club. Compared with Luigi, he was as honest as a babe in arms. And as full of shit. I hadn't set foot in the club in Montmartre for years, but I knew it was still going. I wondered how it would fare now with the Nazis in town.

'I don't know anything about any stolen stuff, Eddie.'

'Good job I do then, Luigi. It's in the cupboard to your right.'

I took my illicit drink to a table where I'd spotted two people I wanted to see.

'He's the goddamned finest officer in the whole of the German army.' Groves' voice was slurred with Luigi's black market brandy. Even in the gloom of what Luigi took for mood lighting, I could see his ruddy jowls, the shape of the years layered thickly over his jaw.

'That's up against some pretty stiff competition.'

'Ain't it just?'

The American had his arm around Weber's shoulders at the same table as on Saturday night. There were fewer clients tonight, just a hard core of sleaze with a smattering of low-grade criminals and middle-ranking German soldiers. In the corner, I spotted Pepe talking to Le Dingue. Neither of them had seen me yet.

'Do you know what he did?' Groves went on. 'He's so good, such a good officer, he was the first to go into that railway yard on the day they arrived in Paris. He wouldn't let his men go in first. Now that's a leader of men.'

My ears pricked up. I glanced at Weber; he was too drunk to be taking part in the conversation, leering instead at a time-served prostitute sitting at the bar.

'You were there?'

'Goddamn right I was. I'm a journalist, travelling with the Wehrmacht 87th Infantry Division. Covering the story from the soldiers' point of view.'

'What did you see?'

'Goddamned finest officer in the whole German army.'

He sank another draught of brandy. His head dropped forward and he jolted back into wakefulness. 'Goddamned finest officer.' He slumped forward again, dragging Weber down with him.

I stared at them in frustration. I wasn't going to get any sense out of the American, and I wanted to know what he saw that day. And I especially wanted to know what he meant by Weber going into the railway yard first. Looking blankly at the pair of them, I thought again of Bydgoszcz and Weber's reaction to the name and of Fryderyk's panic at seeing a German officer at the Majestic. A frightening thought that had been grubbing away at the back of my head for a day or two started to worm its way to the front. I knew I had to try and get hold of Groves when he was sober. I looked at him now, snoring low in Luigi's bar and wondered when that was likely to be.

Out of the corner of my eye I saw Pepe sidle past the counter on his way to the exit. His studious stare fixed ahead of him told me he'd seen me and was making his getaway. I stood up and cut him off when he thought he'd made it.

'Pepe, you pleased to see me?'

'Yeah, sure, Eddie.'

'The Cheval Noir? Who's running it now?'

'It's closed.'

'I won't ask again. Who's running it now?'

'I don't know, I swear. I just know it reopened on Sunday. They reckon you cops won't worry about it with the Germans here. The lot who operate around Austerlitz use it.'

'Know of any cons they're running?'

A German officer with cheap brandy eyes squeezed past us and clapped Pepe on the back, beaming drunkenly at him.

I watched him stagger off. 'New friend, Pepe?'

'Fuck you, Eddie, that's all I'm telling you.' Some of his cockiness was back. He gestured at the Germans in the bar.

'Yeah, a new friend. Loads of them. And they're the ones that hold sway now. Not you. So fuck you, Eddie.'

I leaned in to him. 'I wouldn't push it, Pepe.'

'Or what? What can you do now? And if you want to know about any cons, take a look at your own lot first. You know about the bent cop you've got, do you? Working with one of the gangs operating out of Austerlitz?'

'Old news, Pepe.'

'Like hell it is.'

I leaned back to hide my shock and let him go. It was anything but old news. I stood at the bar to collect my thoughts. I knew we weren't angels. We all had our weaknesses, we all turned a blind eye to the odd petty crime for the sake of a bigger collar, a lot of us cut corners, but for Pepe – who assumed we were all bigger criminals than he was – to single out a bent cop, disturbed me. More importantly, it meant that if it was a gang getting people out of the city, a cop was possibly involved in that. Or in killing them in a railway truck.

I turned from the bar to see a figure I recognised at a table. With his cap off, his head looked even more like a baby's, with that wispy blond hair that refused to lie flat. Müller, professedly of the GFP, actually of the Gestapo. He hadn't seen me. He caught my eye as he stood up, ready to leave, in a flash of blue piping, so I followed him outside to the small lane that led to Boulevard du Montparnasse. I called his name after him, but he didn't stop at first. I called twice more before he halted.

'That's the problem of using false names,' I told him when I pulled up alongside. 'You can never remember them when you need to.'

Under a sliver of light escaping from an upstairs window, his eyes were less expressive than Bouchard's reluctant guests. 'What do you want?'

'Direct, I like that. I want to know why the Gestapo are interested in Hauptmann Weber and an American journalist called Groves. And why you thought thumping me was going to help.'

The word 'Gestapo' scored a hit. His dead eyes lit up like a hearse on a dark night. 'I am an officer in the Geheime Feldpolizei.'

'And I'm Adolf's sartorial advisor. Why did you ask about Bydgoszcz?'

'Why are you asking about Bydgoszcz?'

I sighed and grabbed hold of his lapels. 'We can ask each other that all night, so I'm not asking nicely anymore. What is it about Bydgoszcz?'

He smiled. Taken in all, I think I preferred the funereal look. 'You are very brave. Not many people threaten the GFP.'

'I'm a Paris cop. I've been threatened by worse than you.'

'Oh, I'm not threatening you. I never threaten. I don't need to.'

I felt a heavy object pushed against the side of my head. I knew immediately what it was.

'I was wondering where you were.'

Turning, I saw Schmidt standing beside me. He'd crept up silently in the night and was holding a Luger to the side of my head. I stared him in the face. If Müller's eyes were dead, Schmidt's were two metres in the ground.

'Unless you call this a threat,' Müller added.

I felt a calm that had come to me a thousand times in the night. Twisting to face Schmidt, I caught hold of his wrist and pushed his hand up so the Luger was hard against the middle of my forehead.

'That's how you hold a Luger to my head. Right here, like this.' I leaned forward into him, pushing his arm back. I could feel the circle of the barrel indenting my flesh. For once, his face registered an emotion, one of surprise and uncertainty. 'I've got a lot more experience than you at this.'

His eyes flickered to Müller, unsure how to react. In that brief and bizarre moment, I held the power over the man with the gun to my head. To one side, I saw the baby head slowly shake, and Schmidt briefly looked me in the eyes before finally putting the gun down.

'You really don't know what we're capable of,' Müller told me, some of his composure back.

'That's the one way in which we're equal.'

They turned their backs on me and walked to the boulevard. I watched them go until the memory of the gun at my forehead faded.

Friday 19th June 1925

'You really don't know what we're capable of.'

My lungs were pulsating, my head clearer than a mission bell, the cocaine humming through my system. I saw everything, knew everything, felt everything.

'And you really don't want to know what I'm capable of,' I told him.

The Corsican who'd pulled a knife on me a couple of weeks earlier was holding Fabienne by the wrist. Her words begged me to leave it be, but her expression told me he was hurting her. He leered at me.

'Be the good little cop and do as you're told.'

I know I took a breath. That's all.

In the trenches, I once saw a star shell go off before it was supposed to. They were projectiles sent into the sky that then burst, igniting a magnesium flare that burned while it slowly fell to earth by parachute, lighting up no-man's-land for snipers to kill anyone trapped there. But that time, it burst while the handler was loading it. There was no explosion, it was almost silent, but it burned with a brightness that left me shocked and blinded for minutes after. The handler lay shattered and bloodied in the trench. It took four of us to scrape him up.

The Corsican wasn't dead, but he lay bloodied and twisted

and I was so blinded by the cocaine, I had no memory of his getting into that state. I was the magnesium and the drug the fuse.

'Jesus, Eddie, what are you doing?' Fabienne had her hand over her mouth, trying not to cry out.

I looked down at the man and had no recall. 'I don't know.'

Someone had gone to get Claude, who was holding onto the door, staring in horror at the man on the floor. The Corsican was breathing and had begun to move, whimpering at the pain in his arm. It was bent in places it shouldn't be. Claude was holding his head in his hands.

'Christ, Eddie, what have you done?'

'My job, Claude. Protecting the customers. Which is more than you're doing.' I had the bite of the cocaine back in my blood.

'Go home, Eddie. And don't bother coming back.'

I saw Dominique shake her head at me as I brushed past. I tried to say something to her but nothing came. Instead, I picked up my things and walked in silence through the streets from Montmartre to the police station. I got there in time for my shift, changing out of my club suit into my police one in the detectives' room. The cocaine was wearing off, so I slipped into the bathroom and snorted some more from the back of my hand. I waited a few moments for the thrill to hit and went back to the room I shared with the rest of the shift.

'Giral,' the night sergeant called me. 'Where've you been? I want you at the Gare d'Austerlitz. Reports of a burglar caught in the act, but he got away from the uniforms. He's taken refuge in the marshalling yard. They're out searching for him but they need more bodies. Go.'

I didn't trust myself to speak coherently, so I just nodded.

'And make sure someone else drives,' he called after me.

In the car on the way to the railway station, I held onto the door handle, wanting to get there and find this burglar. I needed to find him. The cop driving growled at me.

'Christ's sake, Giral, leave the door alone. You'll have it open.'

We drove over a cobbled stretch as I answered. My voice came out in garbled belches. 'Hurry up, he'll be gone.'

The driver laughed. 'Fuck, you're off your head.'

I looked around at the back seat but it was empty. 'Isn't there anyone else going?'

'What d'you say, Giral? I can't understand you.' He laughed some more. Even in my state, I could hear the mocking in his voice.

'Don't push it.'

He laughed again. 'Nah, still don't know what you're saying.'

I turned in my seat to face him. It took an age to focus on his face.

'I won't tell you again, Auban.'

Wednesday 19th June 1940

22

'I won't tell you again, Auban.'

'Hell, Giral, you were the one on at me to come and talk to them. Make your fucking mind up.'

'Just go.'

He held my look for his usual moment longer than was necessary. Unusually, I saw something in his eyes that showed he'd seen something in mine. For one fleeting second, he looked afraid.

The morning was unnaturally still in the railway yard, the sky clogged with soot, any sound of labour muffled in the thick air. A sledgehammer resting against his leg, Font looked impassively at us both over his moustache. Auban puffed out his chest and glared at me but turned away. He shot a look at Font before stomping off.

'No love lost between you two,' the railway worker commented.

'What did he want?'

'Asking about last Friday.'

I turned to watch Auban disappear from the yard and wondered why he'd suddenly started taking an interest. After Pepe's revelation last night, I still had the thought of a bent cop on my mind, and Auban still had all the numbers.

'So how come you know Auban?'

'I don't. He's just another cop asking questions.'

I watched his face as he answered, but saw nothing.

'So where's Papin?'

He shrugged, the gesture made extravagant by his scrawny height. 'Checking the sheds. Le Bailly told us to look through them all. See if you lot missed anything. Waste of time, you ask me. They're all in it together with the Boches, telling us it's to get the railways up and running to get food and fuel into Paris. Back to Berlin, more like. Swims with the tide, Le Bailly does, just like his party. He'll get his comeuppance, when the Nazis and the Reds fall out.'

For a rambling moan, it sounded pretty reasonable to me. I questioned him about anyone who might have helped the Poles try to escape using the railways, but he said he knew nothing.

'See anyone who shouldn't have been here?'

He grinned for the first time, spreading his moustache out almost to his ears. 'Only the Germans.'

I tracked Papin down in the sheds. He was leaning against a rickety wall, in the shade of a hut. His eyes were bloodshot, his skin grey.

'Celebrating,' he mumbled. 'I wasn't doing anything wrong. I was just celebrating after the Boches let me go, and I forgot about the curfew.'

I could smell the alcohol seeping out of his pores and on his breath. It wasn't just Monday night he'd been cheering himself up.

'You were caught burgling.'

He sneered and spat on the ground. 'You believe the Boches? I was out after curfew because I'd had a few too many, that's all. The last thing I'd be doing would be thieving after dark with the German army here.'

'So Auban let you go?'

'Not a clue who it was. Some cop told me I was free to go. You all look the same to me.'

His eyes were like slits for most of the conversation, so I couldn't make out his expression. What I could make out behind him in the gloom of the hut were lots of eyes. Peering in, I saw they belonged to teddy bears. Dozens of them, pulled out of boxes, probably during our search on Sunday. They looked incongruous as a backdrop to the hungover surliness of Papin. I gladly left him to suffer. He was right, all I had was Hochstetter's claim that he'd been out burgling.

Walking back through the marshalling yard, I heard the sharp stones crunch under someone's feet. I turned but saw no one amid the empty trucks, signals and huts. Back out in the narrow streets, I stopped in a doorway and waited patiently. Hearing footsteps pause indecisively, I stepped out to find myself face-to-face with Auban. A momentary startled look gave way to the cocky sneer he'd evidently been born with.

'What were you doing here?' I asked him.

'Interviewing the workers. It's what you wanted, isn't it?'

'It's what I wanted five days ago. Why are you here now?'

'Doing my job. It's so important for us to find out what happened to a bunch of Polish cowards running from the Boches.'

'Is this another order from Hochstetter? Like the one to hand French workers over to the Germans?'

Auban imitated my pronunciation of the major's name. 'So you know German, Giral, no one's impressed.'

Annoyed, I squared up to him. 'I don't like bent cops, Auban.'

'Bent cops, Giral? Jesus, you're really scraping the fucking barrel now.'

'You signed the form to let Papin go. Why? You turn up here in the railway yard for no proper reason. Why?'

'As I said, scraping the fucking barrel. I didn't sign any form. And I'm here doing my job that you insisted I do. Shit, I know less about what you're talking about than you do, Giral.'

My face burned red, the wall around my temper crumbling. 'I'm watching you, Auban.'

Auban shoved me away. 'You, Giral? You can't even watch over your own fucking family. Your own fucking kid. Don't forget, I know you, I know what you did.'

I felt the wall collapse and fall. My fingers formed a fist and I took in a long breath.

Auban lay motionless in the doorway. His face was bloodied and torn, his shirt front ripped. I stared at him. I couldn't recall what had happened. I prodded his chest with my hand, wincing at the pain in my fingers. His head rolled back and one eye opened. He looked up at me.

'I will make you pay for this, Giral. I will fucking kill you.' His voice was thick and rasping because of a cut on his lip. He pitched over onto his side and began to pull himself up.

Numb, I turned and hurried away, but after a couple of streets, I stopped and supported myself against a wall, shaking with anger and fear. I pulled air into my lungs in deep gulps. The box had been opened.

I used the Metro to calm myself down. I couldn't face Thirty-Six, so I instinctively took the line that would take me to the unsafe haven of my home. I sat in one of the carriages reserved for the French and stared at the shifting darkness between stations. A new city was emerging under the streets of the old one as more and more people began to use the underground instead of travelling above ground. We moved around in a smoky light in tunnels filled with fumes, white faces avoiding anyone's gaze, especially those of the German soldiers who came and sat next to pretty women, intimidating them, instead of sticking to the better carriages reserved for the occupiers. Ours was a city that wasn't at peace with itself. As the train pulled into the first station, four young German soldiers – fitter and stronger after years of sly preparation for war than our boys – were laughing among themselves on the platform before getting into the next carriage. If only you could harness resentment, the energy emanating from the people around me would have fuelled every car in Paris for a year.

Changing trains, I stood on the platform and felt the rush of air as a train approached. In the blurred reflection of the carriages slowing to a halt I saw the face of someone behind me. When I turned to look, no one was there. I felt uneasy, like in the trenches when you knew a sniper was watching for movement. I had no idea if it was real or just a sensation I felt after what I'd done to Auban. I closed my eyes in the carriage, but quickly tried to open them again. The dream that had scared me since the Germans had arrived was threatening to take hold and I couldn't force myself awake. My eyes were locked tightly shut, but instead of my mind jolting me to my senses to flee the terror, it had decided to give me a whole new dream, one that didn't have the stark horror of the nightmare that terrified me and that, oddly, wasn't as true to my experience in the trenches.

This time, I'd gone straight from the front line to the prison camp in Germany, where my father and mother were waiting for me. Neither of them spoke to me, they just half-looked at me in the same way that they had when I returned home from war in 1919 and my older brother hadn't. Charles, my older brother, who'd only enlisted after I had and who was killed at Verdun while I was captured. I felt I'd never seen my parents look directly at me since. I no longer knew the colour of their eyes. I knew they blamed me for his death. He wouldn't have gone into the army if I hadn't, and I wasn't with him to keep him safe. It was why I had to leave Perpignan. That and the war and the other losses that my self-preservation was fighting a rearguard action to shield me from were the reasons why I was no longer able to be at home anywhere, with anyone. One of the reasons I'd been unable to be a proper father to my own son, a proper husband to my wife.

Getting off the train at my station, I heard raised voices along the platform. Two young men were trying to get into the carriages reserved for Germans. One of them was Jean-Luc. Cursing, I hurried to where a group of Wehrmacht soldiers, an officer among them, were pushing and shoving them. In the scuffle, my son's friend made a break for it and ran down a tunnel. A group of soldiers broke off and pursued him, the other passengers hindering their chase. Jean-Luc lashed out with a foot and got a punch on the jaw from a feldwebel in return.

'I'm a cop,' I told the officer, showing him my ID. 'I've been following these two.' I avoided the look of frightened anger on my son's face.

'We are arresting this young man. He looks to be of military age.'

'He's much too young. I know his family. They're well known to the police.'

The officer appraised Jean-Luc. 'Is that right? It's hardly surprising.'

'Oh, he knows my family,' Jean-Luc growled. 'What a coward for a father I have.'

'You see?' I told the officer. 'You have my word he's too young for the army. I'll take him in, give him a night or two to cool off in a cell.'

I saw doubt on the German's face, but they were still trying to keep us sweet, so he gave in. 'I would suggest a word with the family.'

'I'll bear that in mind.'

As calmly as I could, I marched Jean-Luc along the platform to the exit. I didn't see what had happened to his friend, but the other passengers glared at me with a scorn that chilled me. An elderly man stood in front of me and hawked loudly before spitting a heavy gobbet of phlegm in my face. I fought down nausea, wiping my cheek with my sleeve. Barely containing my anger, I gripped Jean-Luc more tightly than I realised until he yelped in pain.

'Boche pig,' a woman whispered at me.

I shouldered my way past the old man, my son firmly in my grasp, and walked out of the station through a gauntlet of hatred.

At home, I threw him into my armchair. 'What the hell do you think you're playing at? You're going to get yourself arrested. For nothing.'

'One of us has to fight.'

'You've lost one war, Jean-Luc, don't lose another.'

He shrank into the chair, tucking his knees under his chin. I knew how he felt. The fight in us both from just a few moments ago had already gone, replaced by the same desperate listlessness I'd felt so many times over the years. I sat down next to him.

'Why do you carry on?' he asked. 'With all this, with the Germans here?'

I wasn't sure what I was supposed to say. 'I have to.' It was the only reason I could think of.

'Or what?'

'Or we become monsters.' I had a vision of Auban in the doorway and had to look away.

'You can just go.'

I looked at his eyes shrouded in gloom. 'I can't just go. Where would I go to?'

'You've got no reason to stay that I can see.'

'What is it that you want to do, Jean-Luc?'

'Something.' He sighed heavily. 'It doesn't matter either way. I'll be out of your hair soon.'

'What does that mean? You know you can stay here as long as you want.'

'No, I can't. I've got to do something. I've been finding other *poilus* and we're meeting up tonight. We're going to get out of the city and rejoin the army.'

I couldn't help hiding my surprise with annoyance. 'Just like that? You're going to get out of the city. And where are you going to find the army? They're on the run faster than you'll be able to catch them.'

'I'm meeting someone who's going to help get us out. At a bar called the Cheval Noir. Not all of us give up so easily.'

'Oh, Christ, no, Jean-Luc, not that. Please find another way.'

He sat up straighter. 'They're using the trains. They're running again and we can get out under the Boches' noses, helped by the Germans themselves without them knowing. And if anything happens, there are about thirty of us. We'll be able to make a stand.'

I stood up, angry with him. 'Please, Jean-Luc, I've told you what happened with the railway. Four men died on Friday. Killed because someone promised to get them out of the city by train. You have to swear you won't choose that way to get out of Paris.'

'I'm doing it. I'm seeing someone tonight. We could be gone by the weekend.'

'So you're not actually going tonight? You're just meeting someone? In that case, let me come with you. I might know these people, know if they're to be trusted or not.'

I saw a moment's hesitation on his face. It was a look I remembered from his childhood, when he said he didn't want my help with something but secretly did. It was where the conversation had been heading all along without either of us knowing. 'I won't let you stop me,' he insisted.

'I'm not going to stop you. I know you have to get out of Paris, Jean-Luc. It's not safe for you to stay here, but I want to make sure you get out safely. Please let me come with you.'

He stared at me for a moment. 'All right, but don't try to put me off.'

We arranged to meet near the Cheval Noir. I remembered the meeting time with Lucja on Place des Vosges. 'I have to see someone first. If I'm late, you wait for me, do you understand?'

He nodded reluctantly, the childhood look on his face. He wanted me there with him.

23

Auban wasn't at Thirty-Six when I got there. I wasn't unduly worried. What did worry me was that in the corner of my vision, sitting watching me, I could see a younger version of myself that I'd hidden away in a dark cell a long time ago. The more I tried to cage him, the more he tried to get out.

I was certain that Auban had to be Pepe's bent cop. I wanted him to be the bent cop. What I wasn't so sure about was how far it went beyond that. He'd been the first detective on the scene the day the bodies had been found, alerted by Font and Papin. I thought of his possible involvement in promising to get refugees out of the city, and from there, of being involved in their murders, and I was briefly glad that I'd battered him. The me in the corner of my vision smiled, a wicked smile I'd never caught my own self doing.

I was saved from that avenue of thought by two German soldiers who appeared at my door and ordered me to come with them.

'I'm busy.'

'We have orders to take you by force if necessary,' the more senior of the two told me. Neither of them had blue piping on their uniforms, which was the only positive I could find.

'I've told you. I'm not going with you.'

One of them hefted his machine gun and pointed it at me. 'Well, since you asked nicely.'

Downstairs, they showed me into the back of a Wehrmacht staff car. The junior soldier climbed into the passenger seat next to the driver. The other one got into the back with me. I asked him what this was about but he motioned me to remain silent as the driver set off across the river, cruising sedately across town. The Germans had established a 40 kph daytime speed limit, and as far as I could see, this guy was the only member of their army to stick to it. I was torn between relief and irritation. He pulled up outside the Hotel Lutétia, so neither emotion won. The louring hulk of the Cherche-Midi prison stood quiet on the opposite pavement. Normally used to house military prisoners, it had been emptied two days before the Germans had got here, its inmates sent to an internment camp in the Dordogne. I wondered how long it would be before the Germans started treating people to one of its two hundred solitary confinement cells again. I felt a shiver run through me.

The two soldiers showed me to the same room at the Hotel Lutétia as I'd been to the last time. It still had a makeshift air about it. The atmosphere was stifling despite an open window. A French waiter was clearing away a tray with an empty coffee cup and plate as I was shown in. My resolve wasn't going to be tested with a non-rationed meal this time.

Hochstetter crossed his legs and took a long drag on a cigarette. I could hear the leaves spit and crackle as the end glowed a deep red. For some reason, that annoyed me more than anything else.

'I won't be summoned,' I told him. 'If you want to speak to me, you come to Thirty-Six. Or you phone me. I take it you do have phones in Germany? Or are you too busy building motorways?'

'Why on earth would I give you time to think what to say when I can just as easily summon you?' He idly waved the match out and dropped it in a glass ashtray on the table. 'You went to see the Gestapo, Édouard. I expressly told you not to take matters into your own hands.'

'I didn't go to see them, they were just where I also happened to be, so I asked them what their interest in me was.'

He smiled. 'That is curiously truthful, yet also curiously different from the version I received.'

'Maybe your lot's intelligence isn't all it's cracked up to be.'

'I really wouldn't count on that, Édouard. I won't always be able to protect you, you know. In fact, I may not even wish to. You should bear that in mind. Anyway, to the reason why I invited you here. Although after your wilful refusal to cooperate regarding the Gestapo, I am almost inclined to send you on your way.'

I was struck again by how easily Hochstetter could change from one extreme attitude to another in the blink of an eye, from polite urbanity to threatened violence. It was what made him more dangerous than the Gestapo thugs and GFP automata. It was also, I realised with a shock, where I horribly and latently resembled him. There but for the grace of Adolf.

'I admire you, Édouard. Which is why I have something for you. I have found in Hauptmann Weber's files that he served in the Reichsgau Danzig-Westpreussen region of Poland.'

I remembered Lucja telling me the name. 'I'm not sure what that means.'

'The Reichsgau Danzig-Westpreussen includes the town of Bydgoszcz.' I hid the catch in my throat and listened to him carry on. 'I want to be certain that the same mistakes that were made in the invasion of Poland are not made in this country. Like you, I want to be sure that justice is done. And perhaps more importantly from my point of view, that it is *seen* to be done. We do not want to create antipathy towards us needlessly. This is not Poland. We see France almost as Germany's equal. Paris is destined to be the second city of the Reich. A rather luxurious and enjoyable second city, far away from the machinations and politics of Berlin. We would not want to see that jeopardised for the sake of one officer.'

'Where is this leading?'

'You want to find the murderer or murderers. I want to ensure that whatever the result of your investigation, it does not harm the incipient relationship between our two cultures.'

'So what exactly is it you want?'

'I want you to work with me, Édouard. If you continue as you are doing, I can promise you that you will get nowhere.'

'You can promise me?'

'You may see it as a threat if you wish.'

Before I had any need to counter, the same junior officer as the previous day hurried in and whispered something urgently to him. Hochstetter looked irritated by the interruption. So was I. He hadn't got to the point of why I was there. Within a heartbeat, the door opened again and an officer walked in, tapping his gloves against the perfect crease of his trousers. He had four nice neat studs on one collar and two jagged lines of a double-S on the other. He was the first I'd ever seen. I saw a diamond sewn to his sleeve with the initials SD in the middle. I knew that that stood for Sicherheitsdienst, the Nazi Party's security service. I also knew they were something to do with the Gestapo. I decided to behave.

'Obersturmbannführer Biehl,' Hochstetter greeted him, his voice cold.

I gathered from the change in Hochstetter's attitude that an obersturmbannführer was a higher form of being than a major. And because Biehl took a seat while Hochstetter stood up. I figured an unkempt Paris cop trumped them both, so I stayed where I was. Biehl's gaze slid over me without any sign of acknowledgement. He was tall and refined with flowing blond hair and a look of bored aristocracy.

'I have just flown in from Berlin, Major Hochstetter,' Biehl commented affably. 'Nice offices you have, I must say. We're in the Hotel du Louvre. Very central, damn good for eating and whoring, I imagine.'

Well, that's nice, I thought, do enjoy our city.

Hochstetter was more composed now. 'I take it you're here with regard to the illegal deployment of Gestapo officers in Paris.'

Biehl simply laughed. 'A misunderstanding. Many of us in the Führer's special employ felt that it was better for the good of the Reich for the Gestapo to have a presence in Paris.'

'You were expressly prohibited from accompanying the Wehrmacht in France.'

'My dear Hochstetter, you're making a mountain out of a molehill. I've just left Berlin and I can assure you that the Führer has no problem whatsoever with the Gestapo establishing an office in Paris. Quite the contrary, he welcomes it.'

Hochstetter pointed to me. 'This is Inspector Giral of the French police. He was assaulted by your agents.'

Biehl glanced at me and shrugged. 'Your point being? Major Hochstetter, you should remember that as I just said, the Führer himself accepts a Gestapo presence in Paris. I'm sure you wouldn't want to question his wishes.'

'You should, perhaps, apologise to Inspector Giral.'

'Don't be absurd.'

Through the open window, a bee flew in and settled on a small coffee stain left on the table. Lazily, Biehl slapped his leather gloves down on it, squashing it into the mahogany surface.

'You Germans really don't like bees, do you?'

24

It was gone noon and too late to see Lucja at Place des Vosges, so I took the Metro across the river to the Hotel Bristol. The person I wanted to talk to looked semi-sober for once, even after last night's drinking. He was ordering a Martini before lunch.

'I got nothing to say to you.'

'You said you would.' Groves looked nonplussed at that. 'Last night, at Luigi's, we arranged to meet so that you could tell me about Hauptmann Weber. Don't you remember?'

He stirred his drink before biting the olive off the stick and chewing on it. 'Bullshit. I know perfectly well everything I said last night.'

'You told me that Weber was the finest officer in the German army.' I pulled up a barstool and sat next to him.

'Listen, whatever-your-name-is, I'm a journalist embedded with Weber's unit. I'll tell the world he should be Pope, Mahatma and the Führer if it means I get a story out of him.'

'I want to ask you about the morning you arrived in Paris. At the railway yard.'

'Listen. I don't give a diddlysquat what American cops want of me, so don't think I'm going to start giving a shit about what some Frenchie wants. I'm embedded with the German army. If I want to keep my place there and keep getting stories out of them, the last thing I'm going to do is waste my time talking to a French cop. You got that?'

'You said he was the first one to go into the railway yard. What did you see?'

'What did I see? I saw him being the first one to go into the railway yard.'

'And what did you see when he did that?'

'Are you listening? I already told you I'm telling you nothing. And if you want to ask me about any Germans, why don't you ask me about your precious Major Hochstetter? He's not the whiter than white, I'm-too-good-to-be-a-Nazi, officer on a white steed you think he is.'

'So tell me that instead.'

He swivelled unsteadily on his stool to face me. 'Have you ever been to Berlin? The whole city works on informants. Everyone's telling tales on everyone else. Who's doing what, who with, how often. You name it, there's a snitch to tell it and a Nazi ear to tell it to. And Hochstetter is one of the biggest and best bastards at it.'

'He claims he's not a Nazi.'

'Makes no difference. A German guy I knew, a journalist, was giving him information to keep out of Sachsenhausen, the concentration camp near Berlin. Only he couldn't find enough to tell him, so he started making it up. Until he came down with appendicitis and was rushed to hospital, which is around the time Hochstetter realised this guy had been lying to him.'

'And he had a sick man sent to prison.'

Groves snorted, a bubble popping out of his nose. 'Hochstetter didn't send him to prison. Hochstetter sent him out the hospital window. Four floors down. It wasn't only his appendix that burst. You better hope you don't outlive your worth to him, my friend.'

I stared into his eyes, but they were so fogged, I had no idea if he was telling me the truth or not. I considered Hochstetter and thought he probably was. Groves turned back to face the bar.

'What about Ronson? How long have you known her?'

The change in direction took him by surprise. 'Few years. I knew her in Berlin. She's not a bad journalist, considering she's a woman.' He let out a low belch and drained his Martini, gesturing to the bartender for another one.

'Were you embedded with Weber's unit in Poland?'

He laughed sourly. 'Poland? No foreign reporters were embedded in Poland. No reporters were allowed anywhere near the Germans in Poland. Now, if you've got no more questions, you can go.'

I wasn't going to get anything more out of him, so I left him to his Martini lunch. I asked at reception if Ronson was there, but I could see that her key was in its pigeonhole.

'She's just left,' the receptionist told me. 'You can probably catch her outside.'

I did. With a man. And she didn't look pleased.

'Aren't you going to introduce me?' I asked her.

'I'm busy, Eddie.'

'There's no need for introductions on my account, Inspector Giral,' the man said, which surprised me almost as much as it did Ronson. 'Please join us.'

I looked at Ronson and shrugged. 'Well, you're going to have to introduce one of us.'

She still didn't look happy. 'Eddie, this is Jozef, although you can safely presume that that's not his real name.'

He was tall and elegant with a moustache clipped to millimetric perfection under a Modigliani nose and probing eyes. Laughing, he began walking, leading us away from the hotel.

'Don't say a certain hauptmann's name,' Ronson whispered to me as we fell into step behind him.

Jozef led us to a bench in the gardens in front of the Marigny theatre, tucked away under the trees. From where we sat, we had a good view of anyone who might approach us. I decided Jozef probably wasn't his real name, as Ronson had suggested, and that he probably also knew what he was doing. It remained to be seen how much of a comfort that was going to be.

'So how come you know who I am?' I asked him.

'Because you have contact with a group of people that includes someone you know as Lucja.'

His French was good, but I'd come to recognise Polish accents. I looked questioningly at Ronson, who explained in her own way. 'Jozef is from the Polish army. He's in Paris now, and I don't ask him too closely what exactly it is that he does here, and he doesn't tell me. And that should tell you everything you need to know.'

'You should also know that my position here is unknown to the German and the French authorities and that it's imperative that it stays that way.'

'For God's sake, I'm just a Paris cop. I don't know a thing about spies. Are you the ones following me?'

'Yes. As are the Gestapo and the Abwehr. Not in person, but through their informants, that's how they work. You're a very popular man, Eddie.'

'Not so much,' Ronson commented.

'I was going to arrange a meeting with you through Ronson,' Jozef went on. I could see that was news to her. 'She appears to have credible evidence of what the Nazis have been doing in Poland. We would like you to help her in making that evidence known to the outside world.'

'I spoke to you about this,' she reminded me.

'The testimony of one jaded Nazi?'

'The eyewitness account of one who knows more than anyone,' Jozef replied. 'One of the perpetrators. To a cynical world, that is worth a thousand victims' stories.'

'So you want me to go along with you. Keep my head down, so your source can keep his head down.'

'You got it in one, Eddie.'

'Personally,' Jozef said, 'I would quite happily execute Ronson's source for war crimes, whoever it may be, but I have to go along with it for a greater good. And I would ask you to do the same. It's essential that whatever information he has to trade becomes known to the world outside Europe.'

'Basically the USA,' Ronson added. 'I hate to say it, but we're the ones you need to convince.'

'The Nazi-Soviet Pact will fail,' Jozef continued. 'One day, one of them will turn on the other. They're two sets of thugs who can't help themselves. The day that happens, those of us caught in the middle will be the ones to suffer. It's not just the Nazis who are in Poland, the Soviets are as well, and believe me, we Poles don't see a great deal of difference between the two.'

'And that means getting into bed with the German resistance who are prepared to seek help to topple Hitler before any of that can happen. Which is why you've got to play your part too, Eddie.'

'My part? My part is being a cop.'

'Jesus, Eddie, we've been through all this. There's a greater good going on here.'

'There's one thing I should add,' Jozef said. 'You need to question the people you believe.'

'You don't say.'

'Eddie, behave. Jozef is one of the good guys.'

'We've become aware that there have been a number of anomalies in the actions of Lucja and her group, routine errands that have gone wrong. We're uncertain how far we can trust them. We know little of Lucja before Germany invaded our country. I would suggest you exercise caution in your dealings with her.' Jozef's words hit home, much as I didn't want to think it. 'There is one other point. You are trying to find the evidence that Fryderyk Gorecki supposedly had of Nazi crimes in Poland.'

'Who the hell is Fryderyk Gorecki?' Ronson asked.

'And how the hell do you know about him?' I added.

Jozef just gave me a wry stare. 'I represent the intelligence agency of the Polish government. All official actions go through us. You should know that at no point did Fryderyk Gorecki approach us with any information. We have no proof that he did, in fact, have any evidence or that if he did, it was genuine or credible. We only have the word of Lucja's group, and we're worried that that might be untrustworthy.'

'Dear God, I miss good old-fashioned criminals.'

'You're an old dog, Eddie,' Ronson said. 'Time to learn some new tricks.'

I glared at her while Jozef carried on. 'Fryderyk was an unstable and grieving man, Eddie. We have little faith in the quality of any information he might have had. The evidence of a German officer who served in Poland will carry far more weight than the fantasy of a man so unable to cope, he killed himself and his young son. I understand your concern, Eddie, but we think that Ronson's evidence is potentially more credible and that we should be focusing our efforts on obtaining that.' He stood up and prepared to leave. 'We would strongly appreciate it if you were to ignore any other avenue and allow that to happen.'

Nodding his head at Ronson, he hurried away from us and disappeared into the streets. His parting shot had been spoken with a steel every bit as menacing as Hochstetter's.

'I find I'm getting a better class of threat since the Germans have been in town,' I told Ronson.

'So who's Fryderyk Gorecki, Eddie? And when were you planning on telling me about him?'

I looked at her in surprise. 'You really don't know? Fryderyk Gorecki was the man whose flat you were trying to get into.' I told her as much as I wanted of the information about atrocities he supposedly had and about Lucja. She listened in silence. 'So why were you trying to get into his flat?'

'Because of Weber. I saw his reaction to the name of Bydgoszcz when Hochstetter mentioned a guy from there who'd committed suicide and I wanted to check it out. To make sure that Weber's telling me the truth. There's something murky in Weber's past and I need to check it won't damage his story. But I didn't know the name of whose flat it was.'

'Do you know Groves well?'

She looked surprised. 'Not very. I've come across him a few times in Berlin and Spain. He was embedded with Weber's unit on the march through France. He was a good journalist once, got to the stories others didn't. Until it all went sour.' She made a drinking gesture.

'Do you trust him? He's very cosy with Weber.'

'He's a journalist after the same stories I am. Of course I don't trust him.'

'What about Jozef? Do you trust him? You don't want him to know who Weber is.'

'I have to protect my source. If I tell him who it is, they'll forget me and go straight to him to get the information out of him any way they can. She turned to me and a grin broke out, illuminating her face. 'Anyway, I'm a journalist, Eddie. This has Pulitzer written all over it.'

25

I watched Ronson go and sat alone on the bench for a few moments, checking that neither she nor Jozef had doubled back to follow me. In calm silence, I digested everything that Jozef had said, and one thing stuck in my mind. In telling me not to believe that Fryderyk's evidence was worth anything, he'd assumed I had much greater faith in it than I really did. I realised that I hadn't particularly been pursuing any proof that Fryderyk might have had. I wasn't even sure I'd believed he'd had any at all. Instead, my own obsessions had turned his story into a private search for answers, and little more. It was the safe and the items in it, the intruders in his flat, the mention of Bydgoszcz, they'd been what had piqued my curiosity. And now, yet another anonymous and senior officer had tried to dissuade me from doing something by insisting it was all worthless.

'And that,' I told a scrawny pigeon pecking at scraps on the dusty ground, 'is all it's ever taken to really annoy me.'

Leaving the small square, I picked up my car from Thirty-Six and drove a circuitous route to Place des Vosges. I tried not to think of all the petrol I was using. At this rate, it was likely to run out sooner than the whisky did. Parking a few streets away, I illogically approached it more warily than before, even though I'd already known I was being followed, and watched the bench from under the arches. A gaggle of small children was playing around a group of four mothers. It looked incongruous in the new Paris, ghosts of past days reminding of us of what was lost.

As it turned seven o'clock, I sensed someone walking towards me from inside the shadowed arcades. I turned to see Lucja approaching. She smiled and greeted me again like an old friend, the tiredness in her eyes the only sign that betrayed how she was really feeling. It was a face I wanted to trust.

'Have you got anything for me?' she asked, after we sat down on a bench.

I stared at the uneven slabs in the square, finally taking the decision that had dogged me all the way here. 'I found some books in Fryderyk's flat. I hadn't told you about them.'

She gave a slight shrug. 'You were right not to. You have to be careful who you trust.'

Hiving off the doubts Jozef had sown, I described the three books and the two folders I'd found in the safe.

'We'd wondered the meaning of the safe,' she told me.

'I don't understand the significance of what he kept in it. They might just be for sentimental reasons, but one of the Polish books looks like a science textbook, by Ewa. The other seems to be a novel and was published in Bydgoszcz, I presume by Fryderyk's company. They and the letters together might have a significance.'

'Can I see them? Where are they now?'

'You'll have to come with me to my flat.'

I saw for a brief moment in her eyes that she was struggling with the same doubts as I was about who to believe. She finally nodded at me and we got up. We took a walk around the square, like a couple strolling in the evening, to make sure no one was watching, before taking one of the narrow lanes that led off it. Retrieving my car, we snaked through the backstreets of the

Right Bank before crossing the river on the Pont Royal. On the way, I told her that I'd have to leave her on her own for a while as I had to go out.

'You trust me alone in your flat?' It seemed to please her. It worried me.

After a couple of streets, I asked her if she could tell me where her group's orders came from.

'I can't tell you that. And I only know the next person in the chain.'

I described Jozef to her without going into too much detail of how I'd met him.

'No, I don't recognise him. But that doesn't mean anything. As I said, I only have dealings with one person outside our group. It's safer that way.' She was nervous and began to talk as my roundabout route took us past the Sorbonne. 'We will see what happens to your universities when term starts after the summer. The Nazis don't trust universities. In Poland, they've closed many of the schools. We're *untermensch*, apparently. We don't need to learn anything as it's wasted on us. And any teaching is in German only, not Polish. You have to pray the Nazis don't have a fraction of the surprises in store for you that they had for us.'

She went quiet and leaned the side of her head against the window. I drove in silence and parked a street away from my building. Checking again we weren't being watched, I led her inside and up the stairs. I looked at my watch. I had to meet Jean-Luc at the Cheval Noir an hour before curfew, so I'd have to leave almost immediately. The drive back had taken longer than I'd realised.

'Have you eaten?' I asked her as I showed her to the less-used armchair. 'There's not much, but you're welcome to anything you can find.'

I placed the two Polish books on the table in front of her. I also showed her where the French book and the pamphlet were on the shelf, just in case there was a meaning to them I hadn't seen.

'They were in the safe too.'

She picked each one up. 'You're right. A school textbook and a novel.' She shook her head at them. 'Initially, I can't see any significance.'

I left it until the last minute to leave her in my flat. The smallest doubt still picked away at the base of my skull, but you sometimes had to go with your instinct. Mine was not to believe the ones who kept telling me to trust them. Still, the uncertainty slowed me down. I was going to have to get a move on to be at the Cheval Noir in time before my son was to meet whoever it was he was seeing.

I ran down the stairs two at a time and emerged into the fading light of the day. Glancing around, I hurried to my car. Walking quickly, with my head down, I heard an engine whine behind me as it sped up. I turned to see a figure jump out in the growing dusk. A child's head on a man's body. Müller. He was still wearing the grey uniform of the GFP.

'No, not now,' I told him, ready to fight my way from them as two other arms wrapped around me from behind and I saw a smile on Müller's nightmare face.

Stamping down on the foot of the attacker behind me, I managed to shake loose his grip and shrug one of his arms off me. I twisted enough to see it was Schmidt, as I'd guessed. In front of me, Müller's smile dropped, along with his jaw when I caught it cleanly with my right fist. So far, it was the most satisfying moment of the war. I elbowed Schmidt behind me and readied for another go at Müller, but Schmidt recovered and landed a fist on an already burning kidney and my legs folded. I tried to butt my head back at him as he hauled me up, but his grip was tighter than before, his arms squeezing the air out of my lungs.

Müller rubbed his jaw and smirked at me. I hadn't broken it. It would have been an improvement. I felt a sudden pain in the side of my neck and saw him withdraw a syringe, the plunger buried deep inside the chamber. I struggled a moment longer and tried to swing a fist at him, but my arms were trapped.

In the back of a car, in the moments before my head began to float, I knew I'd seen something today that should have meant something to me. I grasped for it but it spun slowly away.

Friday 19th June 1925

I felt the drug fizz through my veins, seeking out the synapses and neurones and blasting a hole through my exhaustion. I'd sniffed some from my hand when I'd checked the gate into the marshalling yard while Auban was parking. Right now, I could have lit up Eiffel's tower for him and had energy to spare.

I looked around for Auban, but he was standing by the car. Walking back to him, struggling to keep my footing, I asked him what he was doing.

'The suspect's reported to be in there.' He pointed back the way I'd come. 'At the end, in a warehouse. Off you go.'

I had to remind myself why we were there. A burglar, I remembered. He'd been thieving in the flats nearby but had escaped from the cops. I wasn't sure why I was supposed to be searching for him in the railway yards, though.

'Aren't you coming?' I asked Auban.

'Nah, got to look after the car. Sergeant's orders. He said to send you.'

I looked back over my shoulder at the dark entrance. It was pitch black. My anger with Auban of a few minutes ago had evaporated with the powder in my nose. I could do anything.

'Sure.'

I turned and walked slowly back to the gate. Behind me, I

could hear Auban laughing. 'Off you go, Giral. Because I'm not going anywhere fucking near it. Not with you like this.'

I waved my hand calmly in the air and pushed the gate open. Dotted before me like a string of pearls on a jazz singer was a row of arc lights, each one casting a feeble pool of light at its base. I walked from one to the next, clinging to the brightness, steadying myself on each post as I got to it. The last light in the string lit up the side of a railway carriage, parked in a siding. As I got near, I saw it was in a long line stretching ahead of me into the darkness. Following the carriages, I heard a sound coming from inside one of them. I tried to get up onto the bottom step, but it was high off the ground and I struggled to gain a purchase.

A torch shone in my face, blinding me. Someone spoke. 'I'm a cop. What the fuck are you doing here?'

'I'm a cop. I'm looking for a burglar.'

'For Christ's sake. Show me your ID.'

I handed it over and the man shone his torch on it. With the glare gone, I could see him now, but he wasn't someone I recognised. He wasn't from my station. I asked to see his ID too. He showed it to me. He was an inspector. I tried to straighten up. He climbed down out of the carriage and turned back towards it. I saw him help another figure out, a woman. I recognised her and greeted her.

'Hi, Josette.'

She smiled and hurried off. She was one of the prostitutes who worked the area around the station. She quickly disappeared into the night.

The inspector came up to me and shone the torch into my face. 'Christ, Detective, you're off your head. What have you been taking?'

'Nothing, Inspector. What were you doing with Josette?'

He shone the torch down again and laughed ruefully. 'Perks of the job, kid. Well, I suppose we've both got something on each other, haven't we? So don't go telling anyone you saw me. I'm way off my patch.'

'I've got to find this burglar.'

'You're on your own, kid. I shouldn't be anywhere near here.' He was buttoning his trousers up when we both heard a sound from further up the line. A foot sliding on the loose stones of the ballast between the tracks. He looked at me and swore.

'I guess that means you're helping.'

He cursed again. 'Now what have you got me into?'

He drew his gun and told me to go around the other side of the carriage. I ducked underneath the couplings and followed the line of the coaches. The stones scraped again. It was coming from the other side, where the inspector was. Ducking back under the next coupling, I rejoined the side of the track I'd just left.

I heard the inspector call out to someone. 'Who are you?'

I heard another sound. An iron bar scraping along the ground, like someone had kicked it. Ahead of me in the gloom, a shadow appeared. I couldn't tell which way it was going. I suddenly realised I was unarmed. It took me an age to get my pistol out; I had to stop and look down while I fumbled in my holster for it. Looking up, I saw the figure had drawn nearer and I panicked, but I didn't have a firm hold on my gun and I dropped it. It fell to the ground with a loud clatter and the figure turned towards me. I heard a voice say something but I couldn't tell what it was.

Dropping to the ground, I scrabbled around for my pistol in the dark, cutting my hands on the sharp stones as I searched blindly.

I heard the iron bar again, scraping on the tracks.

The drug in my veins was wearing off and I felt a rising panic.

Crawling on my hands and knees, I was too numb with fear and cocaine to feel the stones cutting into me. Reaching forward, my fingers touched something cold and hard. I recoiled momentarily before I realised what it was. I reached out for it again, but couldn't find it in my terror, until suddenly my grip finally closed on the iron bar. I felt the weight of it in my hand and struggled to my knees.

I looked up in time to see the figure in front of me, less than a breath away. It was turning towards me, drawn by the sound I'd made, its shape growing in the darkness, unfurling in the night.

It made a sound of its own.

Thursday 20th June 1940

26

I was having the dream.

In a strange and unfamiliar room, surrounded by roses, the sound of tapping came to taunt me.

I was standing in a trench. I tried to open my eyes, but I couldn't. I was standing in a trench, in mud and blood and outrageous noise. A shell burst a short distance in front of me, the sound of shrapnel spattering to the thick syrup ground. I was struggling to open my eyes, but I didn't have the strength and I could see everything vividly. I wanted them to open before the next shell burst. And the one after that. Especially the one after that.

The second one burst. Nearer. I turned to the two friends standing either side of me and I wanted to tell them to go, to run, to get away, but no sound came out of my mouth. They looked at me and smiled. They were going to be all right. I turned to them again. Philippe, on my right, now had my father's face, looking at me with disappointment. On the other side, Louis had my brother's face, his eyes shut, blood seeping from his head. His eyes sprang open to look at me, startling me, and he was Louis again. I turned back and Philippe's face was there. I tried to scream at them but I couldn't. I was gripped in the mud, unable to move, unable to pull them away. They were like my father and brother. Philippe, older than me, Louis, the kid in our pack. All three of us from Perpignan, all three from the same rugby team. We'd enlisted together and survived together and now the third shell was coming through the air at us as we stood together. I faced forwards, looking at the German trench across no-man's-land and I saw it fly towards us. I heard its flight and I heard it detonate and I heard Philippe and Louis scream and now I could scream too, the sound breaking out of my mouth in waves of desperation that I was too late.

The shell burst. Overhead. Raining molten metal down on our trench and pounding into my two friends. I saw Philippe's head explode as a shard pierced his skull, his body thrown back, his hair and brains and bones left to rain down again and again on my face. I turned away to see Louis's chest burst open, the blood spraying me, washing the mud out of my uniform and leaving a stain that would never leave, and he dropped to the bottom of the trench, falling against my leg like a broken dog.

And I stood untouched in the middle. Not one piece of shrapnel from the shell had hit me. I had heard them and felt the heat as they passed me and the wood from the trench walls splinter and bite back at me, but no shrapnel from the shell that destroyed my two best friends hit me. A miracle, the doctors in Paris were to tell me after. A curse, I wanted to tell them but couldn't.

And afterwards. The seconds afterwards when I couldn't see through the blood and gore of my friends on my face and head but I could hear the tap-tap-tapping of the last pieces of mud raised by the blast fall back to earth around me and on me and I didn't know why I was still alive.

A tap-tap-tapping.

And a gunshot.

There had never been a gunshot in the dream before. There

hadn't been one on the day my friends had died next to me. But there was now. Just the one.

I tried to get up, but my body wouldn't let me. I raised my head, but it fell back to the bed under its own weight. I saw forms in the room. They were moving among the roses. And voices. Indistinct, muffled through the aftermath of the explosion of the gunshot.

A hand pulled at my jacket front and lifted my head and shoulders up. All I saw was grey. I thought it was Hochstetter come to save me. Instead, the figure pushed an object in front of my face until it filled my vision. It was just a shape that slowly took form until I recognised it. My gun. My Manufrance that had been taken from my car. He let me go and I fell back into unconsciousness.

I awoke, my head ringing with pain, the room swirling every time I opened my eyes. Slowly, I could keep them open for longer and the room slowed down its dance. It was a bedroom, one I didn't recognise. The tiny stains on the walls took on an outline and I saw they were flowers. Every wall was decorated in a wallpaper of small red and pink roses. Gradually, the details of the two phony GFP men in my street and the injection came back to me. I could take that, it was the wallpaper that hurt.

There was another bed next to mine. Sitting up slowly, I swung my legs onto the floor and held my head while I waited for it to catch up with the rest of me. It took its time. When I saw what was on the other bed, I wished it had taken even longer.

It was the body of a man. There was an untidy and glistening bouquet of red and pink where he once had a chest.

I stood up gingerly and looked down at him. It was Groves, now very firmly and finally embedded with the German army. I looked around the room and saw no one else in there. There wasn't too much in the way of furniture, either. From the cheap bedside tables and twin beds, it was obviously a hotel. I tried walking but nearly collapsed, my hand briefly landing on the American's leg as I doubled over.

Taking deep breaths, I waited until I was more confident on my own legs and slowly made it to the door, one hand to balance myself, the other pressing down on my head to stifle the ache searing behind my eyes. I pulled it open, gasping for air. I figured if it was a hotel, I could get down to reception and put a call through to Thirty-Six, but when I looked up and down the empty corridor, another memory returned to me. I backed inside and closed the door. Turning around and leaning against the panelled wood, I surveyed the room and the body lying on the bed.

My gun.

I recalled the figure in grey holding my Manufrance in front of my face. It had been just moments after the gunshot that had sounded the syncopation to my dream. I looked at Groves lying sallow on the bed as it only just dawned on me that I'd been set up. My gun used to kill Groves, me a ready suspect, there to take the blame for his murder. Other memories came back. The two Gestapo men waiting for me in the street.

'Jean-Luc,' I whispered.

He had been waiting for me at the Cheval Noir. I checked my watch. Seven in the morning. Unless it was really six and Müller or Schmidt had taken it on themselves to change the time. I somehow doubted they had Hochstetter's attention to detail. Jean-Luc would have given up hours ago. It was only then that I remembered Lucja, alone in my flat, the Gestapo prowling the area.

I heard a tapping.

Shaking the noise out of my head, I looked for my gun, even

though I knew it wouldn't be there. The drab sparseness of the room took mercifully little to search.

I heard the tapping again and suppressed a shiver. Turning, I saw a bee beating again and again against the window, deceived by the light. Holding on to a chair for support, I opened the window and let it out. I watched it disappear into the clear blue sky above the buildings, the first bright day we'd had free of soot in a week, and I envied it with a cold passion.

I heard another noise from outside, one I recognised. Looking out through the smeared panes, I saw two police cars coming quickly to a halt outside the hotel. Beyond them, a third accelerated towards the building. It stopped and Auban emerged from the front passenger seat.

I stepped back and stumbled to the door again. The landing was still empty. I heard nothing from downstairs, but I'd figured from my view out of the window that I was high up. That gave me a short start. There was no lift and the stairs were at the far end of the passageway. It would also be where Auban and the other cops would be coming up.

Holding onto the wall for support, I made it to the staircase and peered over the edge. I finally heard voices and saw a hand on the rail, still down at the bottom. Dragging myself hand-over-hand along the banister, I pulled myself up the stairs to the next floor. The voices behind me grew louder. Slowly, I climbed to the top floor. The voices were now on the landing two floors below. I'd run out of stairs. I looked down. No one had followed me yet. I reckoned that if they assumed anything, it'd be that I was still in the room with Groves.

There was just one door at the top of the stairs. I tried it but it was locked. I realised there was nothing for it but to make some noise. I'd never be able to work out how to pick it in my state. Holding onto the banister, I kicked at the door handle but was too weak to get any purchase. I tried again, better this time, but still not enough. I heard sounds below. They'd hear my next attempt but I had no choice. I kicked it a third time and felt the wood around the lock splinter. A shout sounded from downstairs.

'Fuck this.'

Taking as long a run-up as I could, I charged at the door, hitting it at the weakest point by the splintered wood. It gave but didn't open. Struggling for breath, I stumbled back to the wooden handrail and hurled my body at the door again. This time, I fell through, the door quivering on its hinges. Luckily, the hotel and all its fittings were older and flimsier than I felt.

Staggering across the flat roof, I made it to the low wall dividing the building from the one behind it. I rolled myself up onto the wall and fell over the other side, the blow knocking the breath out of me. From behind me, I heard the sound of shouting from inside the stairwell. I looked around and saw that four roofs met at this point, other roofs stretching off unevenly either side. I hoped it would confuse the cops pursuing me.

Pulling myself to my feet, I lurched to a service door on the other side. It was locked. Looking around, I found a pile of old bricks stacked against the wall, so I grabbed the top one and smashed it down on the lock. It came off first go and I fell through, almost tumbling down the stairs to the landing below. Next to the staircase, a fire reel was folded like a firecracker on the wall. I quickly unfurled the hose and dragged it back up the stairs. At the top, I hooked the hose around the door handle and led it back to the banister. As I did, I felt it jerk. Someone was pulling at the door from the other side. Wrenching the hose back, I managed to get it to the banister and lash it tightly, wedging the door shut as much as I could. It wouldn't hold forever, but it would buy me some time. The pursuer continued to tug at the door, banging on it and shouting at me to open up.

I hurried downstairs, not so much running as stumbling quickly. Halfway down, I heard sounds of the door coming under attack and I staggered faster. I was in a residential block and I was able to make it down to the entrance hall without anyone seeing me. Or my pursuers getting past my own little Maginot Line. At least mine worked.

Peering out through the wrought-iron and glass door, I saw no cops in the street. I was on the opposite side of the block to the hotel entrance, so they'd be unlikely to be anywhere near. Decisively, I pulled the door open and emerged into the sunlight, gulping in great breaths of morning air. The light blinded me.

Hugging the stone walls, I hurried away as quickly as I could. There were no cops around this side of the block and very few pedestrians. I looked around me to get my bearings so I could look for the nearest Metro station. I needed to get home.

I was in Pigalle, near my old stamping ground from my young days. They were coming back to haunt me. As I walked, I wondered what the tip-off to the police had been. An American journalist dead in a room. Or an American journalist and a mouthy French cop ready to take the blame.

I thought of the second option. 'I can assure you, I'm not.'

My apartment door was open. Instinctively, I reached inside my jacket and found my service pistol in its holster. I was surprised to find it still there.

Treading silently through the narrow hall and into the living room, I took one look and put my gun away. Whoever had opened my door was long gone, my apartment a wreck, my kitchen cupboards and drawers open, their contents strewn over the table, my books thrown on the floor.

My books thrown on the floor.

I searched through them. In my fug, the way they were piled on the floor reminded me of a news film I'd seen from Germany some years ago, where storm troopers were eagerly throwing books onto a fire in a city square while a crowd watched. I wondered when they'd start doing the same here. I had a few they'd see as ripe for burning.

The two Polish ones had gone. For a brief moment, I remembered Jozef's distrust of Lucja and the doubts resurfaced in my own mind. The Céline book was still there, the pamphlet still tucked inside it. If it wasn't a set-up of Lucja's, whoever had trashed my place must have thought that it was one of mine. That annoyed me almost as much as the thought of the tidying up I was going to have to do.

My head aching again, I went into the kitchen and scraped away the worst of the debris to find my coffee pot. At least they'd left me the good coffee. I made the strongest brew I could take and used it to wash down the painkiller powders I'd bought the first day I met Lucja.

I went back into the living room to find a man there. My reactions were slow, and it was a full moment before I realised it was Jean-Luc. He was gingerly wiping his face with a towel. I could see a cut on his forehead, the blood cleaned away, and a bruise swelling up on his left cheekbone. He was walking like he'd been punched in the stomach.

'They took my fucking shoes.' Looking down, I saw that his feet were raw and swollen. 'I had to walk home like this. They took what money I had and they took my shoes. My fucking shoes.' I reached out towards him, but he shrugged me away. 'And where was my father? Where he always fucking was, all my life. Nowhere.'

'I'm sorry, Jean-Luc.'

'You promised. You promised you'd be there. Look at me. I had nothing and they took even that.'

'I'll put it right, Jean-Luc.'

'You're too fucking late. I need you before things happen, not after. You weren't there to help me. You never have been. You're not a father, you're a waste. Look at you, you're still taking drugs. Mother told me all about that. You're a waste.'

I sat down heavily on my armchair. I was too tired, my head too confused, but I had to try and explain to him what had happened.

'Someone gave me the drugs.'

He looked at me in despair. 'You're unbelievable.'

'I mean, it wasn't me. I didn't mean to. I was forced.'

There was a heavy knock at the door.

'More drugs?' His voice was acid.

I looked at him in panic. 'Go into the bathroom and don't come out.'

'What's happening?'

'Just do as I say.'

I got up and almost manhandled him into the bathroom and closed the door. Whoever was outside banged on the door more forcefully.

I stood in front of it to gather my thoughts and slowly pulled it open.

27

'Murder in time of war. A strange affair, don't you think? Some might feel that there is too much else going on to concern ourselves with an isolated killing. Others, like you, would argue that if civilisation is not to crumble, we have to continue to punish murder even when thousands of young men are falling to enemy bullets every day.'

I stared at Hochstetter across his desk in the Lutétia and tried not to blink. When I'd opened my door at home, less than twenty minutes ago, I'd almost felt relief at seeing two German soldiers standing in front of me. I'd expected Auban, come to arrest me for Groves' murder. With Hochstetter's words, that relief was turning out to be as short-lived as one of his informants. It wasn't Auban arresting me for Groves, it was Hochstetter, come to claim my soul. For a brief moment, I wondered why he would have been involved with the Gestapo's set-up.

'Le Bailly said the other day that war brutalises us,' I told him. I was buying time while my synapses caught up with me. 'He's right, it does, but my job is to ensure that we don't become so brutalised that we're immune to murder and unable to distinguish what is acceptable and what is not.'

'Quite right, Édouard, and quite eloquently put, considering.

You are concerned with what is acceptable. So am I.' He took a cigarette out of his case and tapped the end before lighting it. He flicked the match to extinguish it and dropped it into an ashtray. 'But I wonder if you are still so eager to see justice done for a single death.'

What I was really eager for was a coffee and some more powders to calm my head and an acre of field to lie down in. 'I'm also concerned with the truth. War and occupation can't be a reason for truth not to prevail.'

'Truth in time of war? An even rarer concept than murder. But I suppose that both are causes that are dear to you. Especially now. Which brings me to the reason I brought you here. Our quid pro quo, if you like.'

'So glad we're not being vulgar.' Here it comes, I thought. My choice. Arrest for murder by my own police, or protection from Hochstetter in return for not falling out of the nearest window. For the time being, at least.

'Hauptmann Weber.'

'Weber?' My mouth had been on the verge of forming Groves' name. My heart suddenly racing, I surreptitiously wiped my clammy palms on my trousers.

'I should tell you that despite what I said previously about the protection Hauptmann Weber has because of his Party connections, his record in Poland is a serious blot against him. We made mistakes in Poland, but this is France; we are more interested in having the French on our side. And if that means making an example of an officer who already has a stain on his name, then the German High Command might see the possibilities of a more pragmatic solution. One that is more amenable to both sides.'

Mentally, I had to pull myself back from a precipice, but as one worm died, another that had burrowed its way into my head reawakened. 'What is it you're offering me Weber for? I'm only interested in him as a witness.'

'That is precisely what I'm suggesting. An example of him as a sign of cooperation between the German High Command and the French police. I have understood it correctly, haven't I, Édouard?' He smiled that Hochstetter smile that made you feel the need to count you still had all your fingers.

'What exactly is it you've brought me here for?'

In answer, he got up and asked me to accompany him. Still wary, I followed him into the suite next door. A soldier was standing in the ante-room, outside a closed door. He opened it to let us through into another bedroom converted into an office. Oddly, I noticed the peripherals first, the dark wooden desk where the bed should be, the trolley with the remains of a hearty breakfast, the German soldier standing guard to the side of the door. And at a small dining table on a straight-backed chair, Hauptmann Weber sitting staring at me with a look of loathing. I turned in surprise to Hochstetter.

'Hauptmann Weber has agreed to answer your questions. In my presence.'

I saw Weber's expression. I doubt that 'agreed' was the most accurate description. My own look would have been more ambiguous. From anticipated stick to unexpected carrot in the beat of an uneasy heart.

'I have been held here since last night,' Weber complained. 'I have to object to this treatment.'

I took a seat opposite him and moved a used coffee cup on the table away while I gathered my thoughts. Hochstetter sat down in another chair, equidistant between me and the hauptmann like a tennis umpire. I began by asking Weber to describe to me the events of the Friday morning. He looked first at Hochstetter and then at me and told me in a bored monotone how he and his unit had secured the railway lines south of Gare d'Austerlitz.

'Were you aware of the bodies in the truck before the police arrived? Or of the presence of gas?'

'No to both questions.' He turned to gaze out of the window and exhaled heavily.

'Were there any French workers in the railway yard when you got there? Would you recognise any of them?'

'Of course I wouldn't. There were some there, but they were of no threat or importance to me.'

'Could any of your men have been involved in the deaths of the four men?'

'They are combat troops. They have fought and killed Frenchmen from the Belgian border to Paris. Do you think it would matter to me if any of them killed four Poles? But to answer your question, no. They could not have been involved in the killings. I would have known. They are Wehrmacht soldiers, disciplined, obedient. They would have told me when ordered to.'

'Not forgetting that Paris had been declared an open city. The killing of civilians would be regarded as a crime.'

'I told you. My men did not kill any civilians, Polish or French.'

'Could you describe your actions on that morning?'

'I occupied Paris while Frenchmen ran in panic. What else do you want me to describe? I am an officer in the Wehrmacht and we are at war. I care nothing whatsoever for your four Poles and I do not know how or when they died.'

He looked at Hochstetter and spoke in German. I looked down at my hands and pretended not to understand. 'How can you allow a French policeman to question a German officer?'

Hochstetter interrupted him, also in German. 'I'm afraid,

Hauptmann Weber, that speaking in German won't work. I suggest you may just as well speak in French.'

Hiding my own surprise, I looked up to see Hochstetter nod at me and carry on talking to Weber, this time reverting to French. 'Hauptmann Weber, I am sure I don't need to tell you that we are in the process of absorbing France into the Third Reich, and that it is to play an important role in the future of our people. Consequently, we need to show respect to the laws and justice of France. We need to find the truth, Hauptmann Weber, and we cannot be seen to be condoning the over-zealous actions of German officers.'

Weber looked as dumbfounded at the major's stance as I was. 'Offering me up as a sacrificial lamb, in other words.'

'Quite the contrary. You are being given the opportunity to state what you witnessed that day, so that we can then all move on with the task we each have in hand. You are a Wehrmacht officer, not an SS officer. I have made sure that Inspector Giral is aware of the difference. And of the difference between the actions of the Wehrmacht and those of the SS in the invasion of Poland, I am sure your words will support me in that.'

'The American journalist, Groves, claimed you went into the railway yard before allowing your men to go in,' I said.

Weber snorted. 'Groves is a drunk. He doesn't see anything.'

I tried to gauge his expression and Hochstetter's as he answered. All I saw was irritation from Weber and impassive calm from the major. Neither gave any hint that they knew of Groves' death.

'Did you or your men search the sheds in the railway yard?'

'No, we were still securing the tracks and the surrounding area when the discovery of the body by the French workers was made. Otherwise, my next order would have been for some of my men to check the buildings in the vicinity.'

Hochstetter interrupted. 'You should be aware, Hauptmann Weber, of the consequences of any illegal action that any German soldier might take while in this country. We all have a duty.'

Seeing Weber stunned by Hochstetter's comment, I decided to chance it. 'Are you aware of a town called Bydgoszcz?'

Weber stiffened and appealed to Hochstetter again, but the major wouldn't be drawn. 'Yes, I am aware of Bydgoszcz. I am also aware that some civilians were killed in the town after they had fired on our troops. What you are not aware of is that actions of that kind in Poland were undertaken by the SS, not the Wehrmacht.'

With Hochstetter seeming to be on my side, I pushed my luck further. 'Were you involved in any actions against Polish civilians while you were in Poland?'

My luck ran out. Before Weber could reply, Hochstetter put both hands on the table. 'I don't think this is relevant to your investigation of the murders here in Paris, Édouard. Surely Hauptmann Weber is a witness, not a suspect, to these deaths. I don't see that events in Poland should bear any relation to your investigation.'

'I'm trying to establish motive, Major Hochstetter. Whether Hauptmann Weber's experience in Poland might have led to similar actions here in France.' I forced myself not to point out to him that he'd been the one to bring up Poland.

'In that case, I'm afraid I have to call the interview to an end. I feel that Hauptmann Weber has answered your questions satisfactorily. Any subsequent questioning falls outside the arrangement we had.' He stood up. 'May I say that both he and I are pleased to have acceded to the wishes of the French police and cooperated in every way we can with your investigation. You may go, Weber.'

The hauptmann got up and put his cap on. 'I am glad that German common sense and justice has prevailed.' He saluted and left the room.

'The leutnant here will see you out, Édouard,' Hochstetter told me.

I looked at him in surprise, not so much at his calling a halt to the questions but at allowing me to go so far before arbitrarily declaring the interview over.

The officer showed me out and I walked away from the hotel in frustration. The whole interview had been dictated at Hochstetter's pace, which seemed random at best. Knowing Hochstetter, it would have been anything but that.

The other question that came to mind was how he suddenly knew that I understood German.

28

I felt like a pebble on a beach back home in Perpignan. One that's taken thousands of years to wash up onto the shore only for some thoughtless day-tripper to send it skimming back into the sea. I was trying to work out Hochstetter's motives in the interview I'd just left. Letting me ask the questions about what happened at the Gare d'Austerlitz only to snatch it away from me when I got near. Leading me to ask about Poland in the first place, and then cutting the interview short when I did. I had no idea what his plan was, but I knew I'd come tumbling back in on the next wave.

I wasn't ready to brave Thirty-Six yet. I didn't know what awaited me there, an angry Dax or an arrest warrant for murder – and I was in no real hurry to find out. Instead, I stopped by my apartment. I wanted to explain myself properly to Jean-Luc now I was thinking more clearly, but he'd gone. I looked at the mess in despair. No one had tidied the place up while I'd been out, but at least there was no Auban waiting for me. That would have to be good enough.

Noon was approaching. I walked in bright sunshine towards Place des Vosges, avoiding going anywhere near police headquarters on Quai des Orfèvres. Halfway over Pont de la Tournelle, past Landowksi's modern statue of Sainte Geneviève that the Nazis no doubt would have hated as degenerate, I stopped to enjoy the view across the river and the sun on my face. I was learning to snatch small moments of calm when I could. Then a German armoured truck growled past and I was back in the world. A man on a bike rang his bell as he rode by. The more the cars disappeared from the streets, the more bikes I saw. I had a feeling they were going to become one of the new currencies of the city.

Another bell rang. A woman cycled past, a small girl clutching hold of a precarious seat mounted on the rear. As they passed me, the girl dropped something. I called after the mother to stop and went to pick it up. It was a teddy bear. I held it out to the child, but couldn't let it go. I recalled the bears in the box in the railway yard and a lone one lying in the street, the one I thought might have belonged to Fryderyk's young son.

'Are you going to hand it back?' the mother asked, irritated.

I apologised and gave it to the girl, watching them slowly cycle off, gathering speed on the rough cobbles.

Shaking the image out of my head, I quickened my pace and emerged onto Place des Vosges a few minutes after noon. Blocking all thoughts of Jozef and the doubts he'd sown out of my head, I sat on the bench I'd first sat on with Lucja until long past the allotted time, but she didn't turn up. Whether I liked it or not, Jozef's words about her trustworthiness came back to me. If Fryderyk had indeed had any evidence and it had been hidden in the books, Lucja now had it.

I wanted to know what had happened in my home last night, almost as much as I wanted to put off showing my face at Thirty-Six, so I walked through the Pletzel to the Marais, to the flat where Lucja and her group had taken me after Fryderyk and Jan's funeral. There was no concierge here and the scuffed and peeling downstairs door opened into a dingy inner courtyard that escaped any threat from the day's sun. A smell of stale food permeated the dank walls.

Upstairs, I knocked on the door and listened out for the sound of nervous scurrying, but I heard nothing. Knowing what I'd find, I picked the lock and entered the flat. It was tidy, the chairs tucked under the table, a pile of blankets neatly folded in one of the bedrooms. It was also empty. They hadn't even left the vodka. I could have done with it right now.

Heading reluctantly back to the river and Thirty-Six, I was still on the Right Bank when a commotion up ahead interrupted my thoughts. I'd been dragging my heels like a kid on their first day at school. Looking up, I saw a German patrol car stopping suddenly where Rue de Rivoli cut across the narrow street I was on. By the time I got to the crossroads, two soldiers with rifles had hauled over a young man about to cross the main road.

'Papers,' I heard one of them shout.

The Frenchman they were harassing was shaking with fear, his face pale. It was only as I drew near that I saw why. He was wearing army trousers, the sort Jean-Luc had been wearing the night he turned up in my stairwell. He had to be a *poilu* on the run. Instinctively, I looked around to make sure my son was nowhere near.

'French,' I shouted to the German soldiers, pulling out my ID. 'I'm a French cop.'

One of the Germans turned to look, his rifle aiming at me. An officer got out of the car. Looking like Hochstetter without the presence, he certainly hadn't attended the same charm school. He also had a Luger pointed in my direction.

'This is a German High Command affair,' he told me officiously. 'Leave now or I will arrest you.'

'He's French, a deserter, it's my job to arrest him, my jurisdiction.'

The *poilu* looked at me in shock. I willed him to go along with what I was doing, but his expression turned to one of disgust. One of the two soldiers with rifles held him loosely by the arm.

The officer sneered. 'He is an enemy soldier. This is German jurisdiction.'

The young kid took what he thought was his opportunity and shook off the soldier, turning to run into the narrow street I'd emerged from. His captor took a step forward and took aim, but I lunged for his rifle and pushed the barrel up into the air. His shot deafened me but vanished harmlessly into the sky.

The second soldier's shot didn't.

In alarm, I turned to see the *poilu* fall heavily in the road, a red blossom budding from the middle of his back. Before I could reach him, the German fired a second shot. I saw the young man's body judder as the bullet hit him.

'Why?' I shouted at the soldier, reaching for him.

His companion stood in front of me, the end of his rifle against my chest. I felt the hard metal dig in to my skin, the pain bruising my breastbone.

'Shoot him,' the officer ordered, turning away.

'Major Hochstetter,' I called out quickly. 'Of the Abwehr. Talk to him.'

'Ah, Édouard, perhaps now you can see who it is you are able to trust.'

Hochstetter sat next to me in his staff car as his driver drove me the short distance from Rue de Rivoli to Thirty-Six. Either his name or that of the Abwehr had worked its magic on the pompous officer, who'd phoned the Lutétia from a café. Amazing how far jobsworths will bend when it comes to worrying about their own neck for a change.

'There was no need for the young soldier to die. He panicked. People do unpredictable things when they panic.'

'Did you know him?'

'Does that matter?'

Hochstetter yawned, a genteel sigh into the back of his hand. 'This is war. Young men die. It really is of no concern.'

'And I'm supposed to trust you?'

'Trust is a finite quality, Édouard, we cannot extend it to just anyone. As you will see, the more you place your confidence in me, the better it is for you. We're here.' We pulled up outside Thirty-Six and Hochstetter gestured to my door. 'You may thank me another time.'

I waited until Hochstetter had gone and took a deep breath. I wasn't sure I was ready for whatever was waiting for me. I also needed to get home to make sure Jean-Luc was all right. Looking up, I saw Barthe staring out of the third-floor window at me, his face without expression, and the choice had been taken away from me. I wondered who I was going to have to convince first I was innocent of Groves' murder. And more to the point, who was going to believe me. I know I wouldn't, in their shoes. But then I knew things about me they didn't.

No one accosted me on the stairs, and there were only about half a dozen detectives in the main room when I got up there. Auban was in the far corner with some cronies. They stared at me as I crossed the floor. Auban's left eye was puffed up, his cheek and jaw bruised and a cut on the bridge of his nose. He looked at me with a hatred I'd forgotten.

So far no one had arrested me for Groves' murder. I figured I was winning.

Dax's door opened and he stood in the threshold, his face dark with anger.

'Giral, in here. We've been looking for you.'

271

29

'Where the hell have you been?'

I'd been in Dax's office for the time it took him to ask the same question three times and it was sinking in that maybe things weren't quite as bad as a window seat with Hochstetter.

'I've been interviewing Weber, the German officer, about the four men in the railway yard.'

'Oh, Jesus, Eddie, don't tell me you're seeing German involvement in that.'

'I'm not.' At least I hadn't been, but I kept that to myself. 'What did you want me for?' An unfortunate choice of words, but there you go.

'An American has been found murdered in a hotel in Pigalle. A journalist.'

I sat down cautiously. Even though the expected hammer blow hadn't come, my legs were still unsteady. I made it look like I was concentrating on Dax's words.

'What do we know?' Not much, I hoped.

'Anonymous phone call this morning. The caller said they heard a gunshot in the hotel and that a man had been killed. You weren't here, so I had to send Auban to check it out. There was a suspect at the scene, but he fled before our men could get to him.'

'Did they get a sighting?' I felt a trickle of sweat on my fore-head but didn't dare wipe it.

'Nothing. We don't even know if it was a man or a woman. But it's Pigalle and the victim's an American, so my guess is it's a prostitute or a pimp.'

For once I gave thanks we lived in an unenlightened age. 'Who took the phone call?'

'The desk downstairs. Why does that matter?'

'So is Auban in charge of the investigation?'

'No, Eddie, you are. And before you start complaining you've got too much work, I need you to do this. We don't want the added complication of an American citizen killed in Paris. A journalist at that. Not now. I want this to go away and you're the best man for that.'

'Not sure how to take that.' Although I was relieved at being the one to run the investigation.

'I don't care how you take it, Eddie, just get it done. The body's with Bouchard now. Get over there and see what he's got to say.' Before I could leave, he had one other question. 'And what happened to Auban? Someone's given him a pasting.'

'Classic mistake, Commissioner. He was questioning a sus-pect and the wrong one fell down the stairs.'

'Don't bullshit me, Eddie. I know what you're capable of.'

I left him and Thirty-Six. I also knew what I was capable of. The trouble was that it was proving to be the most efficient way of getting things done in the new order of things and I was growing to loathe and fear it. I crossed the bridge to the Right Bank, my step lighter than it had been less than half an hour ago. But then I remembered that the Gestapo was setting me up and that pretty much did for the cheery gait.

*

Bouchard was sitting down by a slab, reading what passed for a newspaper these days, when I got to the forensic institute. A form lay under a white shroud next to him, a coffee cup nestling up against it. Bouchard took a careful sip.

'Gone quiet,' he said. 'No one's killing each other now the Germans are here.'

'That's their job.' I thought again of the young *poilu* I saw being shot.

'Got your American here. I take it that's what you've come for.' He pointed to an enamel dish. 'Dug that out of his chest. A slug from a Manufrance. Vicious little buggers, those things.'

'Aren't they just. Any more than that?' I pulled the sheet back and saw Groves' familiar face, now waxen. He looked healthier than he did when he was alive.

Bouchard put his paper down and tapped the dish, making the bullet clatter around inside it. 'Single shot. Close range. Normally, I'd be able to say when I can tell you more, but nothing's normal these days.'

I had to hide my relief. 'Might I just as well take the bullet with me? For our records?'

'Why? We still need it here for examination. Although with hardly anyone in the forensic service, I've no idea when that's going to be.'

I'd reached for the bullet but pulled my hand back. 'That's why I asked.'

'Just leave it with me. I'll know soon enough.'

'Thanks.' That was as comforting as Hochstetter offering support.

'You knew the victim, didn't you? Auban said you did.'

I hesitated for a moment, deciding how much to say. I also wondered how Auban knew. 'He was a journalist, embedded with the Germans on their way here.'

Bouchard looked at Groves with me. 'War makes for some strange bedfellows, doesn't it?' I recalled the American lying dead in the hotel room next to me and looked at Bouchard sharply before catching myself. 'Reckon they did it, the Germans?'

'Dax thinks it's a prostitute or a pimp.'

'What do you think? You knew him, you must have some ideas.'

'I barely knew him, Doc. I'm keeping an open mind.'

'Really?'

'Yes, really.' I covered the body again to mask my irritation.

'Well, good luck with it. You're going to need it.'

'What do you mean?'

He looked surprised. 'Germans in town, no proper forensic service.'

I held one hand over the other to hide a sudden juddering of a nerve. 'Of course.'

'This war's affecting you, Eddie. You're not at all at ease.'

'Maybe you're right. I saw a *poilu* shot and killed by the Germans this morning. It's affected me more than I thought.'

'I understand.' He clapped me on the shoulder as I left. 'But don't worry about your bullet. I should be able to get something more on it for you at some point.'

Madame Benoit was distraught when I got to Rue Mouffetard.

I think I wanted to distract myself from the threat of accusation for Groves' murder. An unsanctioned investigation into the suicide of a refugee who may or may not have had evidence of German atrocities and whose story was being pursued by the flotsam and jetsam of occupation seemed like an innocent enough pastime in comparison. And with the books gone, I had to find another straw I could clutch at.

'The Germans have been here,' the concierge told me,

wringing an aged handkerchief in her hands. 'They made me give them all of Fryderyk's things. I'm afraid they might still be near.'

'Let me make you a pot of coffee.' Because I could do with one. 'And tell me what the Germans looked like.'

At my words, she stopped dead in the corridor. 'He was horrible. Like one of those Grand Guignol plays they all go on about.'

'Like someone stuck a boiled cabbage on a man's body and glued candy floss to it?' I sat her down in the small kitchen and put the pot on to heat. 'So they took everything?'

'I gave them the boxes you left. They asked if there were any more and threatened me and made me go up to Fryderyk's flat with them, but there's nothing left there.'

'Is there really nothing else of Fryderyk's here? Did he give you anything to look after? Even if it didn't seem important at the time.'

'Just the safe.' She picked at the hem of the handkerchief and looked away.

'Did anyone come to see him ever? You didn't see him give them anything?'

She shook her head confidently. 'No one ever came. He only had Jan.'

I was struck by the change in her reactions to my questions. 'Are you sure you didn't keep anything else of Fryderyk's? Or Jan's?'

I saw her floundering. I recognised it. I'd done enough of my own this morning.

'It really doesn't matter,' I told her. 'But you do need to tell me.'

She looked guilty. 'It's my grandson. My son-in-law was serving on the front and we don't have any news of what's happened to him. I just wanted something for my grandson to make him happy. And it was left in the street. The police didn't take it, so I thought it wasn't important. It was only a teddy bear.'

'Was it in the boxes you handed over?'

She shook her head. 'It's in the cupboard over there. I won't get into trouble, will I? I've got nothing I can give my grandson.' I thought for a moment she was going to burst into tears, but she suddenly looked startled instead. 'There's someone in the corridor. I know every sound in this building. I locked the front door after you came.'

The door into her kitchen opened and Schmidt came in, followed by Müller. The concierge gasped.

'That's him. The one with the cabbage head.'

The wind was momentarily taken out of Müller's sails.

'Old French saying,' I told him.

I tried to stand between the two Germans and Madame Benoit, but Schmidt was too quick and grabbed hold of her by the wrist. She winced in pain. I reached for him, but Müller already had his Luger pointed at my head. The concierge was crying in a low moan.

'We would like another word with you,' Müller told me. I could see Schmidt tightening his grip on Madame Benoit.

'I see why they asked Adolf not to invite you,' I said.

Müller smiled – I saw what Madame Benoit meant by Grand Guignol – and turned his gun from my head to the concierge's.

'Inspektor Schmidt here would pull the trigger on the old woman without a moment's emotion,' he said. 'I wouldn't. I'd really rather enjoy it.' He cocked his head to one side, his look inquisitive, like he was already imagining the moment. I had no doubt he'd do it.

'OK, OK. If you leave her here, I'll come with you.'

I saw his finger tense on the trigger.

'Oh, it is so, so tempting.'

With a sudden, startling movement, he pulled his gun away and gestured that I should follow him. I heard Madame Benoit exhale in fear.

'When you let go of her.'

Müller gave the order and Schmidt released her arm. She immediately grabbed hold of it tightly with her other hand and sobbed. I put my hand on her shoulder and told her I'd be back to see her.

'That is just so touching.' Müller smiled, false like a viper.

Outside, they sat me in the back of their car and drove me across the river and deep into the heart of the Right Bank before stopping. Not a soul passed us. In the front, Schmidt reached into the glove compartment and pulled out a gun. My Manufrance. He showed it to me.

'I see there's no need to tell you what this is,' Müller commented.

'No, I'm just surprised. I thought you lot were too thick to be this subtle. I expected electric cables and aching genitals at least.'

'That can be arranged.'

Schmidt's response wasn't as witty. He just slapped me open-handed in the face and held my gun to my head. I'd have the imprint of his fingers on my cheek for a week. I held his gaze for a moment and pushed my forehead against the pistol.

'You still haven't worked it out, have you?'

Pocketing the Manufrance, he opened the door and indicated I should get out. It was Müller that spoke, gesturing to the gun.

'We own you now. We can bury you in a French prison any time we want.'

They drove off and left me on the Rue du Faubourg Saint-

Honoré. It was just a short walk to the Bristol. I supposed I should thank my Gestapo playmates for something.

Inside the hotel, I asked the receptionist to call up to Ronson. She came down to where I was waiting in the lobby.

'I want to see Jozef,' I told her.

30

'I love this place,' Ronson said. 'I wish I'd discovered it in happier times.'

In the Jardin du Luxembourg apiary, the inhabitants were quietly humming to themselves in their hives. Ronson was buzzing next to me. We were waiting for Jozef to show up. She hummed a tune in time with the bees.

'OK, what is it that's got you so excited?'

'I spoke to Weber yesterday evening. He says he's willing to give me what he's got to trade.' Her eyes were shining. I could feel her excitement.

'How do you know you can trust him?'

'Because if he wants to get out of Paris, he has to trust me.'

'And how far would you trust him?'

She laughed. 'He's a former member of the Nazi Party. Of course I don't trust him, but I do believe he's got information that he wants to use to save his own skin.'

'And you think Hochstetter's got his eye on Weber?'

'Most definitely. Hochstetter's no fool, he knows there's something going on, he just doesn't know what. He'll be using his informants and anyone else he needs to use to find out what it is.'

'Why don't they just send Weber back to Berlin if they suspect him?'

'That's the last thing they'd do. If they suspect he's involved in something, they'll want him here where they can keep a close eye on him. Weber might not be acting alone in this. The Abwehr will be wanting to bide their time to flush out anyone else who's implicated. That's why I really need you to keep him out of your investigation. I need him to keep as low a profile as he can.'

I looked away. More bees were buzzing around the hive, coming home as evening drew near. A figure approached from across the patch of grass near the apiary.

'Jozef's here.'

We stood up and joined him in the dying shade of the trees opposite the beehives. He looked around warily. It struck me he wasn't sure he could trust me not to hand him over to the Germans. So much for military intelligence.

'What is it you want, Eddie?' His voice and manner were polite, but the coldness of the officer wasn't far below the surface.

'Lucja. She's gone missing.'

He looked annoyed. 'I asked you not to pursue this.'

'I'm not. I'm investigating the deaths of four Polish refugees. Lucja knows something about it.' She probably didn't.

'Does this involve the source that Ronson is trying to help?'

'No.' Which only goes to show I can lie as well as any spy.

He seemed to inspect me while taking a decision. 'We know that Lucja and her group left the apartment they were staying in. We've checked it and found no trace of them there.'

'So where have they gone?'

'We don't know. We don't tell cells such as hers where to go, but we expect them to keep us informed. We've heard nothing.'

'If they don't contact you, will you be able to find them?' I had to keep the importance of finding Lucja out of my voice. I needed to know what had happened in my apartment and who had the two Polish books.

'You appear to be devoting a lot of time to finding the killers of four refugees. That seems very conscientious given the events around you.'

'I'm a cop. No event changes that. My job's to find whoever killed these four men and make sure they don't kill again.'

'Please say you're not still after this guy's evidence, Eddie,' Ronson added.

'Will you be able to find them, Jozef?' I insisted. 'Because if you do, I want to know where they are. I will expect you to tell me.'

'I will tell you.' He made to leave. 'But don't make me regret trusting you.'

We watched him disappear through the diminishing sunlight towards the park gate.

'Or me,' Ronson added. 'Leave Weber and Poland to me.'

'How do you know Jozef? Or that he really is with Polish intelligence?'

'Jesus, Eddie, you've got to believe someone. We're not all out to get you. Except Hochstetter.' She flashed a grin at me. 'He's definitely out to get you.'

'He's out to get Weber. He had me taken to the Lutétia to interview him.'

'He did what? Jesus, Eddie. When was this?'

'This morning. I didn't even know Weber was going to be there. I was careful to question him as a witness, but Hochstetter veered the interview to seeing Weber as a suspect, and the moment I went along with that, he called the interview to a halt.'

'You think he wants Weber arrested for these killings in the railway yard? That wouldn't make any sense. If he suspects Weber of conspiracy, he'd want him out in the open where he can see him.'

'If Weber's arrested by us, it means he can't leave France with his evidence and he won't be sent back to Berlin. That way, he's out of the game and Hochstetter still gets to keep an eye on him. It's a safer bet.'

'Hochstetter play safe? That would be a first.' She looked at her watch. 'Curfew time's drawing near. This girl's going home. What are you doing?'

'I'm going to a bar that's just reopened called the Cheval Noir, which makes Luigi's place look like the Opera Garnier on gala night.'

She stopped. 'Jesus, that sounds great. Can I come with you?'

'No. It's police business.'

'Ah, Eddie, you just said the wrong thing to a journalist. Get your coat, we're going.'

I didn't argue further and decided to take her with me. It was getting near curfew, but I had my police ID. 'If the Germans stop us, I'll tell them I've arrested you for being fucking annoying.'

A rectangle of light appeared around the aged door sitting uneasily in its frame. The Cheval Noir didn't run to the luxury of a black curtain like Luigi's. A couple of toughs were standing outside, each in a check cloth cap and a collarless shirt. I'd arrested them both in my time.

'Evening, boys. Table for two. We're dining with Jeannot.'

Grudgingly, the older one, a long-serving gang member with a neck the size of a prop forward's thighs, opened the door to let us into a smoke-laden cavern of wonder. In the faded light, the walls were peeling and stained with nicotine. A dozen or so pale and hostile faces turned to face us. On the dance floor at the back of the dingy room, a bored accordion accompanied three couples shuffling around, the men engulfing the women, who did a strange recoil dance, constantly pushing hands away from places they weren't supposed to go.

'Some place,' Ronson whispered. 'Do they do cocktails?'

Jeannot was at a table playing cards with four others. Like every other male in the place, he wore a light tweed cap, tilted slightly towards the back of his head and over his left eye. Unlike them, he wore his shirt buttoned to the neck, the collar still on, but with no tie. The women wore tight sweaters and pencil-slim skirts to below the knee. The whole city was in uniform these days. One way or another.

I left Ronson leaning against the bar and pulled up a chair at Jeannot's table. His thin lips were pulled back over pointed yellow teeth, his dark eyes dead and nose sharp as a cur's. A large church candle like the ones stored in the sheds stood in the centre of the table, burnt a quarter of the way down.

'Very devout, Jeannot. And just what I came to see you about.'

'You're brave coming here, Eddie. I'll give you that.'

'Lighten up, Jeannot, I'm just here to ask a few questions. You see, I was going to ask you about all this thieving and storing all the stuff in the sheds we both know you've been doing, but honestly, I'm not too worried about that right now. That's between you and your conscience. What worries me are these killings. When we've got some nasty little thugs running around taking money from refugees in exchange for getting them to safety, and then killing them instead, I'm bound to think of you.'

'You need to be careful what you say, Eddie, I'm among friends here.'

'And fine upstanding friends they are too. Although I see them as more the sort to offer to help French soldiers, for example, and then rob them. You know, nasty but cowardly with it.'

He laughed, a rough sound like a knife on bone. 'Now who'd do a thing like that, Eddie?'

'You fucking would.'

It wasn't me who'd spoken. No matter how much I'd been thinking it. Over my shoulder, I found a young man with a black eye and bruised face straining to get at Jeannot. It was Jean-Luc. I closed my eyes for a moment. I hadn't seen him come in. One of the toughs from the door was pulling him back, but Jean-Luc broke free and landed a punch square on Jeannot's mongrel nose. It was immensely satisfying by proxy.

'Deal with him,' Jeannot told his cohorts, stemming the flow of blood.

'You took money from *poilus*, you piece of shit,' Jean-Luc shouted.

As my son drew back for a second go, another gang member punched him in the ribs. Resisting the need to flatten the thug, I grabbed Jean-Luc's shirt front instead.

'You're coming outside.' I gave him a warning look and held my hand over his mouth. 'Don't say a word. I'm arresting you for assault.'

'You saw that, Eddie,' Jeannot said from behind me. 'An unprovoked attack. I don't know what the country's coming to.'

I turned back to look at him. 'Don't push it, Jeannot, I will be back with more questions.'

I was pulled up short by the sight of one of the couples on the dance floor. Dressed like all the other gang members in tweed cap over the left eye and collarless shirt undone to the second button, a lanky figure pawing some poor woman was steadfastly trying to push his dense moustache into her face.

'Font.'

Still holding onto Jean-Luc, I made my way towards the railway worker, but Jeannot gave a signal and eight of the gang immediately crowded around me, hustling me towards the door. I held onto my son to keep him safe from them.

'Bye, Eddie,' Jeannot called, his yellow teeth bared in a rodent smile.

A couple of the heavies got in a couple of jabs to the ribs that had already taken a beating, but I got a couple of shots back, so I reckoned we were equal. At the bar, Ronson watched impassively as I was taken past her. She gave the slightest of nods and turned to look at the dance floor.

The toughs pushed me outside and closed the door on me. Looking at it and wondering what Ronson was playing at, I backed off with Jean-Luc into the shadows towards my car.

Jean-Luc tore my hand from his mouth. 'Still protecting the wrong people?'

'No, I'm trying to protect *you*. How many more times do I need to tell you?' I took him to my car and put him in the back seat, cuffing him to the window frame.

'The only person you've ever protected is yourself.'

'You'll never know how wrong you are, Jean-Luc.'

I left him and went to wait for Ronson, wondering why she was taking so long. After five minutes, the door opened and she walked calmly out.

''Night, boys,' she told the two doormen.

She walked slowly towards the end of the street. I stepped out so she could see me.

'If you'll just wait a few moments, Eddie.'

The door to the bar opened and I saw Font, picked out in the jaundiced light cast momentarily from inside. Emerging cautiously, he began to follow Ronson. As he passed me hidden in the shadows, I saw the look of hopeful lust cross his face and I almost felt sorry for him. Grabbing him from behind, I forced him towards my car.

'Partners,' Ronson said.

'I don't even want to know,' I told her.

Struggling in my grip, Font complained. 'What are you arresting me for?'

'I'm taking you in for questioning about the murders of the refugees.'

'You're crazy. That wasn't me. You've got it wrong.'

'Well, you'll have a night or two to give it some thought.'

Only he wouldn't.

I heard the din from behind me. The two doormen had evidently seen what was happening and called for reinforcements from inside. An army of cloth caps and no collars streamed out of the bar. Within seconds, we were surrounded. Most of them were brandishing knives or clubs. There were even a couple with the old-fashioned Apache knife, knuckleduster and revolver combo.

'Very nostalgic,' I told them.

'You have a friend of ours,' Jeannot said from the front of the circle.

'I do. And he's staying with me.' Holding onto Font with one hand, I drew my pistol with the other.

Jeannot smirked and gestured at the crowd around him. 'I guess they don't teach you about numbers at police school.'

They moved inwards, pressing us back. Out of the corner of my eye, I saw Ronson retreat towards the car. On the far side of it, some of the gang were closing in on the window where Jean-Luc was sitting. One of them raised the stick he was holding.

I leaned in to Font and whispered in his ear. 'Don't stray far, Marcel, because I'll be coming for you.'

Still with my gun unholstered, I shoved Font back towards Jeannot and signalled to Ronson to get into the car. We were outnumbered, but they still wouldn't charge a gun if they didn't have to. Font stood next to Jeannot and I got into the passenger seat, forcing Ronson to move onto the driver's side.

'I think it might be a good idea for you to drive,' I told her.

31

'You're my father. We've never shared a glass of wine.'

I looked in the mirror. 'You are kidding.'

We'd dropped Ronson off at the Bristol and were heading back to the Left Bank. She'd nodded at Jean-Luc.

'What are you going to do with this young guy?'

'I'll think of something.'

As I crossed the Pont Neuf, hoping to avoid German patrols, Jean-Luc sat in the back seat, looking at the reflection of my eyes. I had to turn back to face the road. Driving through blackout city streets with just two slits for headlamps was like trying to see your way through a conversation with Hochstetter. I drove to Montparnasse. If Jean-Luc wanted to build a bridge, no matter how odd it sounded, I wasn't going to stop him.

'You've got a young gentleman friend,' Luigi commented slyly.

I withered him with a look, another skill I was rediscovering.

Two Wehrmacht officers stood next to us at the counter while Luigi poured our wine. I heard Jean-Luc muttering something and turned to see one of the Germans stare at him, a quizzical look on his face.

'Fuck off back to Berlin,' Jean-Luc said to him. Fortunately, the German didn't understand the words, although it wouldn't be long before he got the sentiment. He gave a half-smile to show his misunderstanding. 'Stop fucking smiling at me, Boche.'

My son squared up to the soldier, who was starting to get the drift, but I pulled Jean-Luc back by the collar and stood between them as the other officer stood next to his companion in support.

'He's had bad news,' I explained to them in German. I made sure no one around could hear me, except Luigi, but there was nothing I could do about that. 'His father.'

The first officer, my height but slightly built and with fine brown hair he was constantly pushing back from his forehead, inspected my face. He seemed to calm. 'He has my sympathies. I lost my father in the last war. I never knew him.'

The German smiled at Jean-Luc and I felt a flare of hatred towards him burst in me. That brief moment of humanity from the people who had broken us made the shame of defeat more ignominious. Feverishly, I stamped down the lid on myself and forced a smile in return. I sensed my son tense for a response, but I tightened my grip on his collar.

'Just keep quiet, Jean-Luc.'

I nodded at the two Germans and led my son to a table in the far corner of the room. I shoved him down into one of the chairs and sat next to him, blocking him from getting up again.

'Looking after your German friends again?' Jean-Luc asked me.

'Looking after you, but my patience is wearing thin. This is why you wanted to come, isn't it? Nothing to do with sharing a glass of wine with me. You want to provoke a fight with a German.'

'Do you blame me? One of us has to stand up to these people. We can't all live our lives as cowards.'

'Don't be so fucking stupid, Jean-Luc. This is not the way to do it. You're just going to get yourself arrested or killed for no reason. Show some sense.'

I felt a tap on my shoulder and turned, expecting to find the two officers had followed us.

It was worse.

'See where your French justice gets you?'

It was Weber and he was drunk. With luck, his liver would give out before my temper did. I stood up. I was just that bit tall enough to intimidate him.

'That was German justice.'

'Either way, you got nowhere. I have been exonerated.' He struggled over the word. 'You are nothing. Of no use.'

'You really think so? Looked to me like Hochstetter was happy to see you take the blame for whatever it is you've been up to. I think he intends for us to meet again about this.'

His eyes focused in and out on me, the wine in his glass sloshing over his uniform. 'You cannot touch me. You should learn that. No German would betray a fellow officer.'

'Hochstetter? You might need to think again about that one. He'll sell you for whatever purpose suits him. That's when you'll see where French justice gets you.'

He belched loudly in my face and backed away, his movements exaggerated in an attempt not to stumble. I watched him go and sat down. Jean-Luc looked at me in silence for a few moments.

'So I'm not to antagonise the Germans?'

'No, that's my job.'

We looked at each other for a second and laughed. Not a deep laugh or a long one, but a moment shared and the first time I'd heard him sound anything other than on the edge of anger or despair. The sound of it dissolved into the dark corners of a room filled with occupiers and villains.

'So who was he?'

'It's complicated.' I explained a little more about the four Polish refugees found gassed in the railway truck. I was surprised that I needed to talk to him about it. Especially after years of sharing nothing with anyone, about my work or about anything else. 'I think he was responsible for killing civilians in Poland.'

'What's that got to do with the murders in Paris?'

I explained about Fryderyk Gorecki committing suicide on the day he'd seen someone at the Hotel Majestic that had terrified him. 'Fryderyk was from a town called Bydgoszcz, in Poland. His wife was killed there, along with other teachers, by the Nazis. I think Weber was involved in those killings. Some of the men killed at the railway yard were also from Bydgoszcz. Weber was at the yard the day the first group of victims were found. I don't have any evidence, but I believe that there is a possibility that he could have killed them to cover his tracks for what he did in Poland.'

I had to pause to take in what I'd said. I'd never really allowed the thought of Weber being the killer of the four refugees to take root, and the idea that I'd just expressed it shocked me.

'Why use gas? Why not just shoot them?'

I thought it through as the words tumbled out of me. 'The Germans don't want to be seen to be acting the same way in France as in Poland. Weber would know that the Wehrmacht wouldn't tolerate his shooting the Poles in cold blood, so he used gas to confuse the issue and to hide it from his own men.'

Jean-Luc peered past me like he was trying to hunt Weber out in the room. The edge of anger had returned. It scared me as much as my own did.

'This is where I've failed,' he said in a low voice. I don't think he was even talking to me. 'I've allowed animals like this to get through to Paris and get away with slaughter. And they'll slaughter more unless I do something about it.'

'Leave him to me, Jean-Luc. Please. Don't be too eager to kill. It makes us no better than this man.'

Friday 19th June 1925

I'd killed him.

I rocked back and forth on the ground. From somewhere, I heard a keening sound, a low moan that burrowed into my brain. It was some moments before I realised it was coming from me. I was sitting now. Small, sharp stones had stuck to the side of my face when I'd been lying down, curled up between the rails. They were digging into my flesh. Hurriedly, I brushed them off, wincing at the sting of the tiny cuts they left. I raised my head slowly, the comedown from the drug sending a jagged pain shooting through my head at each movement.

The dead man was lying less than a metre from me.

I'd killed him.

The thin light cast by the lamps told me what I already knew. It was the inspector. Blood ran in thin rivulets through his hair and down his cheeks to pool in a small dark puddle below him. I closed my eyes and cursed at the thought of what would happen to me.

I realised with horror that I was still holding the iron bar. The one I'd picked up in my panic at the approaching figure and swung wildly in the dark. Touching the end, I felt it was sticky and I saw blood and strands of hair on my fingers in the lamplight.

'Oh Christ, no.' I dropped the bar with a clang that rang through the yard and I held my head in my hands.

Beyond the inspector, I saw a second mound. It was another body. It, too, lay motionless. My head sank again.

I heard another moan. Not from me this time. Looking up, I swore I saw the inspector's body shift position ever so slightly. I listened and watched, but saw nothing more. My head tricking me into believing what I wanted to believe.

But then I heard it again.

The inspector's hand moved. I saw he was trying to force himself up onto his elbows. I looked briefly at the iron bar and got to my feet.

'What the hell happened?' he asked.

I knelt down by him and held his arms, pulling him to a sitting position. I saw him try to focus on me. He asked the question again.

'You were hit.'

He suddenly threw up, a stream of bile smelling of alcohol and stale meat that spattered across the stones, splashing my trousers. 'Who are you?'

'A cop. Like you. We were looking for a burglar.'

He looked around uncertainly. 'We're in the railway yard? I remember that.'

'You remember Josette? The prostitute you were with?'

He groaned again, a deep sound in the night. 'What the hell happened?'

I pointed to the body lying nearby.

'That's the burglar. He's dead.'

'Help me up.'

I lifted the inspector slowly to his feet. He was unsteady, his face showing his disorientation. He slowly looked around. When he was ready, I helped him the short distance to the body. I turned the man over to find a gunshot had taken away half his face. I'd seen worse in the trenches and felt strangely detached. The inspector cursed. I don't know if it was at me or at the sight of the dead man.

'You killed him,' the inspector told me.

I gasped in shock. 'No, you did.'

He looked sharply at me. His eyes were still glazed. 'You're lying. I don't remember. I didn't even fire my gun.'

'You did. I couldn't get to you in time to stop you.'

I sensed him assessing it all. 'See who he is. If it's your burglar, we'll say it was in self-defence.'

Gingerly, I felt inside the man's jacket pocket and pulled his papers out. The inspector found his torch on the ground and shone it at the document.

'He's a railway worker,' the inspector said. 'He's not your burglar. You've killed an innocent man.'

'I told you, I didn't kill him. It was you.' I saw a moment's opportunity to deflect suspicion that it was me who hit the inspector with the bar. 'And you did do it in self-defence. He came at you and you shot him. I saw it all. I thought he'd killed you.'

A glimmer of doubt crossed his face and he put his hand to the wound on his head. His eyes flickered, the concussion hitting him. 'I don't remember. We'll soon see who did it. Whose gun has been fired?'

I pulled my Browning pistol from my holster and counted the bullets in the magazine. It was full.

'You could have replaced the bullet while I was out cold,' he argued.

'Smell it. It hasn't been fired.'

In the dark, we looked around for his old MAS revolver. It was lying where he'd fallen. I held the torch while he broke open the cylinder. There were only five bullets, one chamber was empty. The smell told us both that the gun had recently been fired.

'*You* killed him,' I said.

'We don't know that.'

'It was your gun. You killed him.'

The inspector put his revolver away in his jacket and buttoned it up. 'OK, kid, this is your word against mine. And I'm an inspector and you're so high, you don't even know what day it is. No one's going to believe you.'

'And it was your gun that killed him. And you were here because you were with a prostitute when you were supposed to be on duty.'

'OK, kid, we both stand to lose things if this gets out.'

'How's it not going to get out? There's a man lying dead.'

I saw his expression in the jaundiced light. 'And we're the only ones that know about it. As things stand, we're both as guilty as each other.'

I was about to object but thought better of it. As the drugs in my head cleared, I realised he was right. If it did come out that I'd taken cocaine when the man had been killed, no one would believe me. I was also so relieved that I hadn't killed the inspector – and that he'd believed it was the dead man who'd hit him – that I was ready to accept anything he said.

'There's only one thing we can do,' he went on. 'Make sure this never happened.'

'How do we do that?'

He gestured me away from where the carriages stood. 'I grew up in this neighbourhood. I know it.' He pointed down at the ground in front of us. In the gloom, I made out a manhole cover. 'This is where it ends. Washed away through the sewers out of both our lives.'

'We can't.'

'Got a better idea? Or do you fancy a date with the guillotine?'

I closed my eyes and swore because I knew he was right. Between us, we pulled the dead man over to the manhole and lifted the lid. He made a low splash somewhere beneath our feet, muted by the metres of earth we'd buried him under, carried away by the city's waste. It was a sound I knew I'd never forget.

'This binds us, kid,' he told me. 'But don't forget one thing. I'm senior. I'll always be believed, not you. And I'm sure there are plenty of cops in your station who know about your nose habit. I'm not the one who stands to lose here.'

'You were the one that killed him.'

'That's for you to prove if you dare, and if you're stupid enough to think you'll get off in any way. You just helped dispose of a body. Now we shake on it and we go our separate ways. What's your name, kid?'

'Why do you need to know?'

'For when our paths cross again. Maybe we have to help each other again one day.'

Reluctantly, I told him. 'It's Giral. What's yours?'

He turned to leave. For a moment, I thought he wasn't going to tell me.

'It's Dax, kid, remember that.'

Friday 21st June 1940

32

I was awoken by a sound. It was merciful, as in my sleep the arm-chair I was in was just beginning to mould itself into a trench, the two arms into Philippe and Louis, the soft cushion into thick mud, sucking me down into the pit. Below my feet, I heard the splash of water. Another faded memory come back to life.

I heard the sound again. Someone was moving about in my kitchen. I looked around in surprise at the books and papers strewn on the floor in front of me. I had no recollection of coming to sit in my armchair last night. There was an empty glass on the table in front of me, an aroma of whisky trapped inside. I got up and went into the kitchen.

'Jean-Luc?'

I found a familiar figure, but it wasn't my son. She had tidied some of the mess up and was cooking something on the gas stove. I could smell coffee. She looked back at me over her shoulder and spoke.

'For a cop, your apartment's pretty damn easy to break into. Have some breakfast, you look like you could do with it.'

'What are you doing here?'

Ronson turned and grinned, a skillet with tomatoes and eggs in her hand. 'Making breakfast. I brought you a present, by the way. Hope you like it.'

She divided the food from the skillet onto two plates and nodded at a bottle of whisky standing on the counter. It was a good one, but with what we had on offer in Paris, anything would have been good. Next to it was my service pistol and the Luger and bullets.

'I found the Luger and bullets on your coffee table. I thought I'd better bring them through here so you didn't have an accident.'

Absently, I replaced the rounds in the magazine after removing the dud bullet and putting it in my jacket pocket. I didn't remember even taking the Luger out last night. I took the gun through to the bathroom and hid it behind the tile. As I turned, Ronson was standing in the doorway, watching.

'Bang,' she said, her eyebrows arched. 'Hell, Eddie, I thought I was untidy.'

I looked at the mess in the living room left by whoever had ransacked the place. 'I call it early Gestapo.'

'You're one strange guy. Come and eat.'

Before following her, I checked Jean-Luc's room but it was empty. The bed was made to a soldier's precision. My son, the conscientious *poilu*.

We sat at the kitchen table and ate.

'You cook almost as well as a Frenchman,' I told her. The first bite of egg melted in my mouth. I hadn't eaten one for a month.

'Do you a deal, Eddie. You come with me today and I'll help you tidy this place up tonight. Trust me, it's big. There are two guys you really need to see.'

'Who?'

'Come with me and you'll find out.'

I had more than enough to do but I was learning that Ronson's nose for events was worth the detour. We took the Metro to a garage on the Right Bank, where a large shape stood under a canvas tarpaulin. Ronson pulled it off to reveal a shining black Renault Viva Grand Sport.

'Mine. I've been saving some gasoline for a rainy day. Got half a dozen cans in the trunk. This looks like a rainy day to me.'

'You must earn more than a cop does.'

'I told you, I'm a pretty good journalist.'

The car was fitted with WH plates. 'These are reserved for German cars. How did you get them?'

'Hochstetter. He likes me. He tells me things, I tell him things. The things he tells me aren't worth shit, the things I tell him I make up. But it kind of works.'

'He must like you a lot. I only got SP plates out of him.'

She manoeuvred the big car out through the narrow lane and turned north-east, heading out of the city. Thanks to the WH licence plates, two German checkpoints waved us through.

'The Germans are going to limit French ownership of cars, you know,' she told me. 'You're pretty lucky to get SP plates. And even they won't do you any good on Sundays from now on. Only German cars allowed on the roads in Paris on a Sunday.'

Outside the city, Ronson opened full throttle and neither of us spoke for some time as the car ate up the kilometres taking us away from Paris. Were it not for Jean-Luc I would have welcomed never going back.

'What exactly do you do, Ronson?'

'I told you, I'm a journalist.' She said she was from somewhere outside New York and that she'd lived in Paris for some years before going to Berlin. 'To catch the rise of Hitler. Everyone wanted to read about it back then. After that, I reported on the civil war in Spain before moving back to Berlin after that war had ended and this one had begun. It's an ill wind, as they say. What about you?'

I thought before answering. 'I'm from Perpignan, in the south. I moved to Paris when I came out of the army after the last war ended.' That was all I told her. I didn't tell her how much I couldn't face working in the family bookshop after I came back from the war or about what had happened to me in the war or about why I'd first gone to Paris. I never told anyone that.

'Why a cop?'

I looked out of the window at the grass flowing in the breeze like a boat's wake. 'To try and put things right.'

'You're one of the strangest men I've ever met, Eddie. So what's the thing with the Luger?'

'It's nothing. Just a gun I took from a German in the last war who was trying to kill me.'

Leaving the forest at Senlis behind us, we began seeing more German military vehicles on the road and Ronson slowed down to a speed that wouldn't attract attention until we came to a sign saying we were entering Compiègne.

'This is the site of the Armistice,' I told her. 'In 1918.'

She shook her head. 'This is *going* to be the site of the Armistice.'

Before I could ask her what she meant, we were stopped at a checkpoint. Ronson spoke to a Wehrmacht officer in good German, explaining that she was part of the press corps and that I was a senior policeman from Paris. He checked our ID more thoroughly than the Germans in Paris did before finally allowing us through. He told us to park before reaching the Armistice clearing.

'You're about to witness history, Eddie,' Ronson told me, parking the car on the edge of the town by some trees. She made me leave my service pistol hidden under my seat. 'You won't get far with it today of all days.'

'But I'm a cop.'

'Not today, Eddie. It's way too dangerous. You'll see why.'

As we approached the clearing on foot, we steadily saw more German soldiers, most in what looked like dress uniform, and a feldwebel directed us to an enclosure where a small number of people were waiting for something.

'Journalists,' Ronson explained in a whisper.

In front of us, row after row of faceless troops stood in helmeted silence. They were more frightening than the ones we'd faced in the last war. I could feel my legs begin to shake and I had to root the soles of my feet to the ground to stop them. A band was playing musical arrogance. More soldiers marched into the clearing from our left, around the small lawns in the centre.

It was only then that I realised that the railway carriage in which the Armistice had been signed at the end of the last war had been taken out of the building where it was normally on display and placed in the middle of the clearing.

'The exact same spot as 1918,' Ronson told me.

I saw too, beyond it, that the memorial to the French fallen in the war had been covered by a swastika. I remembered my friends and I clenched my fists and had to stop myself from running over to tear it down. Two more soldiers ran a baby swastika up a flagpole in the centre of the lawns, facing the railway carriage. I could also see the statue of Marshal Foch, which hadn't been covered up, looking across to the carriage, as though someone had taken the decision to place it under his gaze.

Within a minute, I saw who.

I gasped and tried to hide it.

I closed my eyes and held my face up to the sun, the warmth a reminder the world still turned. I opened them again and looked down through the calm shadows cast by the tightly packed pine and elm trees, their reach falling short of the bright, dusty path leading straight. They fell short of the figure, one of a small uniformed number, on the path. His face was set in a cold solemn stare, the peak of his cap revealing glimpses of frozen eyes, his mask in barren contrast to the spring of his step.

'Hitler,' one of the journalists whispered.

As Hitler strolled, he occasionally placed his left hand on his belt buckle and raised his right arm in stiff salute to his soldiers. I felt my teeth tighten each time he did it. He stopped a short distance from where I was standing and turned to offer the same salute to the generals and admirals accompanying him. Beyond them, senior officers scuttled along the shaded grass verge, some of them hurdling a small post, to keep up with Hitler's entourage. Next to me, Ronson let out a discreet laugh. I couldn't. I knew why she hadn't let me keep my gun.

In silence, we watched as Hitler stood in front of the statue to Marshal Foch and stared up at his face, taunting him, before he turned to walk back to the carriage. He appeared to ask a German officer if this was the right way in and climbed up the short steps. He can invade half Europe, but he can't work out how to get into a railway carriage without asking.

'Be a pity if he fell and broke his neck,' I murmured. Ronson shushed me.

A short while after Hitler and his entourage entered the carriage, she nudged my arm and pointed in the direction where the German leader had come from. 'The French delegation. Hitler's making them sign the Armistice here, where Germany surrendered in 1918. The humiliation is complete.'

I watched our own senior officers march past the ranks of soldiers, escorted by German officers. I recognised General Huntziger at the head of our side, between two Germans. They were escorted to the carriage and went in. Ronson looked at me and gave a wry smile. Unsure of what was going to happen next, we stood and waited. Ronson spoke to a journalist next to her, another American I think, when I saw them both stiffen at something happening in the clearing. Hitler was leaving the carriage. The French delegation and most of the Germans didn't follow.

'They'll be staying back, telling the French exactly what demands you're all going to have to put up with from now on,' Ronson said.

Hitler walked past the troops while a band struck up the German anthem. He was heading for the memorial draped in the swastika, I imagine to hide our triumph in 1918 from him. As he approached, some German soldiers broke out from behind the ranks in his wake like children at a circus procession and took gleeful snapshots of him.

'That's a picture I'd take too. Hitler's retreating arse.'

Ronson tapped me on the arm and put her finger to her mouth. She signalled that we should leave. We backed away from the press corps. It was a relief. I couldn't have faced seeing Hitler stand in front of the memorial to our fallen.

I turned on Ronson once we'd left the clearing. 'Did you really think that that would be of interest to me?'

She stopped and looked at me before leading me on again. 'No, but this will.'

33

We walked the short distance through the town back to Ronson's car. There was no one about when we got there. As I climbed in, I noticed that two of the petrol cans had been moved to the floor behind the front seats. I quickly checked under my seat and found my gun still there. I pulled it out and put the holster back on under my jacket.

Ronson drove off, heading south-east out of Compiègne instead of back in the direction of Paris.

'Where are we going now? I need to be back in Paris.'

'I need you to see this, Eddie.' She kept looking in the rear-view mirror. It was the first time I'd seen her nervous.

We only drove a short distance into the forest before pulling off the road onto a track that led behind a grove of trees. She cut the engine and birdsong instantly filled the vacuum left by the heavy rumble of the engine. She listened intently for a few moments before getting out of the car.

'So who's in the boot?' I asked.

'Now, that's why you're a cop, Eddie,' she replied, grinning, the old Ronson back.

With one last look around, she opened the boot. The first thing I saw was a German soldier curled up in the narrow space amid the remaining four petrol cans. I thought for a moment he was dead and Ronson had got us involved in some sort of execution, but the figure slowly unfolded and stretched and hauled himself out until he was sitting on the edge of the boot. He rubbed his back and neck.

It was Weber.

He ignored me for a few moments and then asked Ronson what I was doing there. 'This is not what we agreed. I will only speak to you, not the policeman.'

Ronson explained to me that Weber had been an observer at the clearing but had left when the world was watching Hitler. 'We arranged it yesterday. I just didn't tell him about inviting you along.'

She turned back to the German and told him that I could be trusted. 'It's in your interest that he knows your story. Otherwise I can't help you.'

Weber looked up at me and sighed angrily. 'All right.'

He stood up and stretched and we walked a short way further into the thick of the forest. I kept my hand on my gun in its holster all the while. When we'd gone a hundred metres or so, Weber stopped by a fallen tree and leaned against it. Ronson sat down at the other end. I stayed standing. An animal snuffled through the undergrowth away to our right and I scanned the trees. We were alone.

Ronson looked up at Weber. 'You said you'd bring the information you had to trade.'

Weber looked at her and breathed out heavily, folding his arms tightly across his chest, but I had a question of my own to start with.

'Why are you so eager to hand over this information? Germany doesn't look like losing this war.'

Weber sighed and looked at me. 'I joined the Nazi Party in 1933. I believed in the dream of the strong Germany that they sold us and in the need to right the wrongs that had been done to us after the last war. Many Germans still do believe in it because they haven't seen how it translates outside our borders. What we are called on to do in the name of National Socialism out of sight of the German people. I was an adjutant at a conference between Hitler and the senior officers last summer. I believe in the superiority of Germany, but Hitler said that the war against Poland was to be a war of extermination and that we were to kill without pity or mercy all men, women or children of the Polish race or language. And we have done. You in France have been spared this, you cannot understand it. As the war has gone on and as I've seen what the Party is ordering us to do, I have come to realise that I was wrong. That Hitler and the Nazis are wrong. And I'm not alone in this. There are others like me who were once Nazi supporters who have now turned against the Party.'

'You've learned your lines at least.'

'And you have evidence of what happened in Poland?' Ronson asked him.

'Poland? No, this is nothing to do with Poland.'

Ronson looked as dumbstruck and furious as I felt. I walked over and grabbed hold of Weber by the front of his vapid grey uniform. 'You've lied to us all along.'

'What do you mean nothing to do with Poland?' Ronson almost shouted.

Weber calmly looked at me. 'I suggest you let go of me. I never said my information was about Poland. Those are your imaginings.'

Ronson turned away in exasperation. 'For Christ's sake.'

I tightened my grip. 'So why does Bydgoszcz mean something to you?'

'It means nothing to me. Again, that's simply your imagination.'

Ronson got up and came to stand close to us. 'So you brought us here for nothing?'

'I brought you here with evidence of a plot to assassinate five hundred American citizens. But if you'd rather I didn't share it with you, we can walk away now.'

My grip loosened in my surprise and Weber took the opportunity to brush my hand away. Ronson stood open-mouthed in front of him. The German's look of calm self-assurance was quickly back in place.

'Why didn't you tell me this before?' she asked him.

'I had to know I could trust you. I'm still not sure I can. What I have is a *Sonderaktionsbuch*, a list drawn up by the SD of over five hundred influential US politicians, journalists and writers for assassination. The Nazis are targeting anyone in Washington and New York, and American journalists in Europe, who are arguing for the USA to come into the war to stop Hitler.'

'That would be more likely to bring the States in,' Ronson objected.

'These would be clandestine operations. Accidents, poison, random murders framing innocent locals. The Nazis would be too far removed to be implicated.'

Ronson backed away and paced the small clearing, her expression going from shock to excitement. I was too busy seeing images of Groves in the hotel room and Schmidt taunting me with my Manufrance to feel her joy.

'Jesus. This is huge. And it's on paper? An official document? When that gets out, the US is going to have to stop sitting on its hands.' She could barely contain her enthusiasm.

'How come you got hold of it?' I asked him.

'Enough questions, Eddie,' Ronson said. She went up close to Weber. 'OK, I'm in. Let me see it.'

'No. Not until I've been assured safe passage out of France. Then you can have the list.'

'What?'

A blackbird sang out across the slow silence between us as Ronson and I thought of Weber's words. The German leaned against the pine, bored, idly picking with a thumbnail at the dried bark. The breeze had fallen, no leaves rustling, no branches creaking, the shadows unmoving against the sunlight. Until all three of us were pulled short by a sound. Metal on metal. A tailgate banging open. Orders shouted in German. A dog barked. I looked to where the noise was coming from, but saw nothing.

'Soldiers,' Ronson whispered urgently.

'You set us up,' I accused Weber, but he looked just as startled.

'No, I don't know what's happening.'

There were more noises of people moving through the trees. Other dogs joined in the chase. Somewhere, someone shouted an order.

Instantly, the three of us ran the short distance to Ronson's Renault. The crashing through the trees behind us grew louder. With the sound of pursuit getting closer, none of us worried about keeping quiet. We heard a dog racing through the undergrowth, let off the leash by its handler. Weber stopped metres from the car and drew his gun. Taking aim, he fired off one shot that blew the German shepherd back off its feet. A shot was returned, fired blindly in hope, that zinged through the trees near our heads. I couldn't see any of our pursuers. Weber fired off another shot. It passed close enough to my head for me to hear the strange zipping noise I remembered from the last war. I looked at him, but he'd turned away already and was running to Ronson's car.

Ronson had the engine started and I followed Weber in through the passenger door. She'd lifted the front seat, and he and I tumbled into the back well. She threw it into reverse before the door had closed, the engine whining as she skidded back onto the road. Putting the car in forward gear, she put her foot to the floor and slid down the road away from the forest. I looked through the rear window, but no one was in sight behind us. We turned a corner and Ronson fought to keep the car under control, accelerating all the time, its six-cylinder engine opening out along a straight stretch of road, taking us far away from danger.

'Hell, that was good,' she shouted.

I climbed into the passenger seat and looked at her face, glowing with excitement. 'You say I'm strange.'

Weber sat in the back in silence. We let him out at a cross-roads on the way to Compiègne.

'It's better to leave me here,' he said. 'I can walk back to the town. It will arouse less suspicion.'

Ronson drove off and I turned to see the German walk towards Compiègne, his back upright, his stride confident. I tried to think of a list of five hundred Americans to be assassinated but I couldn't. Instead, I thought of Fryderyk, Ewa and Jan, of innocent civilians dying in Poland and of four men in a railway yard in Paris. And I thought of the bullet that passed close by my head and I watched Weber walking calmly to Compiègne.

'Bang,' I murmured.

34

'You don't find it an odd coincidence that the Germans turned up?'

We were driving through back roads and country lanes away from Compiègne and towards Paris. I felt a surprising sense of relief to be heading back.

'Adolf's in town. The place is crawling with military.'

'Out here? In force like that?'

'What are you saying?'

'You arrange to meet Weber in a clearing in a wood, and a truckload of German soldiers with dogs suddenly turns up.'

'You think it was a tip-off?'

'I think it was a set-up. Hochstetter, Biehl, Weber even. But someone knew you were going to be there. And how come we got away so easily?'

'Jesus, Eddie, get some perspective. They shot at us. And who cares anyway? You heard what Weber said. This could end the war. All you have to do is let him give me the *Sonderaktionsbuch* and I'll make sure he gets out of France and over to New York. We need any way we can find to stop the Nazis. If we don't, a handful of refugees in a railway yard's going to be child's play in comparison. We've got a chance to try and stop that.'

We drove in tense silence past a row of German lorries coming the other way.

'*Sonderaktionsbuch*. A special actions book.'

'Your German's pretty good.'

'Hochstetter seems to think so.' Since Hochstetter's comment, I'd been trying to remember all the people who knew I understood German. Ronson was on the list. 'It's not just the refugees here, it's what the Nazis did in Poland. You thought that was what Weber had to trade. That's going to go unknown.'

'You still want to believe in the evidence of this Polish guy that committed suicide, don't you?'

'Jozef, the Polish cell and even you have tried to convince me Fryderyk's evidence is worthless at best. But both you and the Polish cell tried to search his flat, the Germans took his belongings and someone trashed my flat looking for something. Wouldn't you believe it?'

I turned to look out of the window. And the one vision I kept seeing was an impoverished refugee wheeling a safe he couldn't afford through the streets of Paris and up four flights of stairs. For what? For everyone to tell me it was worthless. Ronson was right. I did want to believe in Fryderyk and whatever it was he thought he had.

'Jesus, you're still looking for it. There's a bigger picture here, Eddie, you need to see it. This changes everything.'

'I am seeing it. If Fryderyk did have something, we need to tell the world, we need to take a gamble on it. It's no more than you're doing with Weber. You haven't seen any evidence to back up anything he's saying, but you're moving heaven, earth and me to get to it. If Fryderyk's evidence exists, we should be doing just as much as you're doing for Weber.'

'Too many ifs, Eddie. We get Weber's information out, we

stop whatever happened in Poland from happening again. You have to let him go for a greater good.'

'And if Weber is responsible for killing people in Poland? And the four refugees in the railway yard? Aren't the Nazis winning if I allow him to go free?'

'Eddie, would you be so eager to bring Weber to justice if the Nazis were going down the same road here they did in Poland? Who stands to gain by punishing one guilty man compared with millions of innocents?'

I felt strangely flat. In the dappled sunlight playing catch through the trees, I considered the Nazis' list of people they wanted to kill for disagreeing with them and I thought of the fading mirage of Fryderyk's evidence and I knew that she was right. In her place, I'd go with Weber's evidence. 'Would Groves be on this list?'

'My guess is he would have been in the past, but I'd be surprised if he were now. He was influential once. In the early days, he wrote plenty of articles opposing Adolf, but he's been anyone's gun for hire since his career and his drinking went on the rocks. Why?'

'He's dead. He was killed yesterday morning.' I explained most of what had happened in the hotel room. I didn't tell her he was killed with my gun.

She deflated in a moment, the excitement gone. 'Jesus, Eddie, I hadn't seen him but I didn't think anything of it. Hell, I hope I'm not important enough for this *Sonderaktionsbuch*.'

'If I was going to kill journalists, you'd be right there at the top of my list.'

'You're too kind.' She burst into laughter a second before I did, a gallows moment shared. 'So who do you reckon did it?' She rubbed her eyes with the heel of her hand. 'If it is because of the list, I'd normally say it was the SD or the Gestapo, but they're not in Paris. The Wehrmacht made Hitler agree not to let them out to play.'

'They are in Paris. They're here disguised as GFP.' I told her about my run-in with the two agents and Biehl turning up from Berlin. 'What's the thing with the Abwehr and the SD? Hochstetter and Biehl?'

'The Abwehr are military intelligence with the regular army. The SD, the Sicherheitsdienst, are more or less the same, only for the Nazi Party. They hate each other even more than you and Weber do.' She went silent for a moment. 'This puts a whole new complexion on things, though. I knew Biehl was in town, but I didn't realise that was why. Scary bastard. Old aristocratic family, unusual for his sort to become a Nazi, but not unheard of. The upper classes don't like Hitler because they think he's an upstart, but there are still plenty like Biehl who are pragmatic enough to see him as a way of restoring Germany's former glory. Hochstetter too. Good family, all the right connections, willing to go along with the Nazis while it suits him. Probably not a Nazi, but a patriotic German. There can be a lot of overlap when they want there to be.' She looked shaken for once. 'One ray of sunlight, though. It means that Weber's information is what he says it is.'

'You'd think so, wouldn't you?'

We drove into the outskirts of Paris, through suburbs of silenced windows and people in meagre clothes staring with cold disdain at Ronson's car. It was the first full Friday of the German occupation and the city had the feel of a gutted fish left to rot as the market closed. The carcass was there but the eyes were unseeing, the vital organs ripped out, the smell of decay hinted at.

'I don't know where this is, but it sure as hell isn't Paris,' Ronson commented as we drove round Place de la Bastille. The square was empty but for German troops counting the hours until they were off duty to savour the night of the city that was no longer there because of them.

She dropped me off outside my flat. 'Don't forget we got a date this evening to clean the place up,' she reminded me. 'I brought the whisky, you bring the feather dusters.'

Watching her leave, I decided to check on my flat before returning to Thirty-Six. I still had no idea how Jean-Luc spent his days and sometimes wondered if he came back in after I'd left for work. I climbed the stairs to find him standing amid the bookish rubble of my living room.

'When were you going to tell me?'

His question took me by surprise. I looked at the mess around us. 'You've already seen this.'

'Not that.' He held up a piece of paper. 'This. When were you going to tell me about this?'

In his hand I saw the note that Sylvie had left for him at their flat. I involuntarily glanced at the bookshelves. It would have been dislodged from its hiding place when my night visitors had taken to redecorating my home. I'd forgotten about it. At least that's what I told myself.

'I was going to tell you, Jean-Luc.'

'You knew how I could find Mum, but you lied.'

'I didn't lie. With everything that's been happening, I just forgot.' His look told me how much he believed that. 'And you couldn't have found her. How would you have got past the Germans and crossed the front line to get there? Besides that, you still don't know where she is. She could be anywhere in Perpignan.'

He simply shook his head at me. 'She'll be with Grandma and Grandpa.'

'My parents?'

'They've always helped us. When Mum couldn't afford things, they'd send us money. We used to see them some summer holidays. They came to Paris to see us twice.'

I sat down heavily in my armchair and stared sightlessly at the whisky tumbler on the low table. I'd been punched and beaten without end since the Germans had arrived, but nothing hurt as much as this blow from my son and parents. They hadn't come to see me in Paris in this time. After years of reproaches for my leaving my wife and son, my parents had never spoken again about it. I had no idea they were still in contact with them. I should have.

I looked up to see Jean-Luc's expression. It was beyond scorn. His voice was cold when he spoke. 'I'm not even angry with you anymore. I've had enough. Seeing you now, I'm glad I grew up without you.'

He turned and went into the kitchen. I got up to follow him. I briefly glanced at my phone and partly assuaged my guilt. I only had a phone because I was a cop. Like most people in the country, my parents didn't, so there would have been no way for Jean-Luc to contact them, even if he had known his mother was with them. Even if I'd told him.

I found him standing by the sink. My son shook his head at me one last time. His voice was calm. 'I'll be gone tonight.'

'You don't need to.' I had no way of telling him I didn't want him to leave.

'I have to. There are nearly thirty of us. *Poilus*. We've slowly been finding each other. We're getting out of the city to find the army, carry on fighting the Boches.'

'How are you getting out? You know it's not safe.'

We sat down on either side of the kitchen table. 'Give me some credit. I learned my lesson with the crooks at the Cheval

Noir. We're dealing with someone at the railway. They know how it all works.'

I looked coldly at him. I could feel the hurt I felt coming out. 'The Gare d'Austerlitz? Christ, Jean-Luc, how many times do you need to be told? It's not safe. I told you what happened to the four refugees.'

'But you said that it was the Boche officer that was responsible for that.'

'I said it was a possibility. It's probably more likely to be someone at the railway. I don't know, Jean-Luc, but it's not safe. Find another way.'

'No, I'm going. I'm not staying here to be a lapdog to the Boches. I'll take my chances.'

I slammed my fist down on the table. 'Christ, I can see you were brought up by your mother.'

He stood up, a look of disgust on his face, and made to leave. I tried to get up to stop him, but he pushed me back into my chair and brushed past.

'I'm sorry, Jean-Luc, I didn't mean that.'

I heard him in his room and then footsteps across the living room. I expected to see him come back into the kitchen, but instead I heard the front door slam and the sound of him running down the stairs.

'You fucking idiot,' I told myself, jumping up to follow him.

He was younger and quicker and by the time I'd got downstairs, he was gone from sight. I figured he'd head for the Metro, so I ran towards the Saint Michel station. A train was pulling out as I got to the platform but I couldn't see him on it, and I had to kick my heels until the next one. I wasn't certain where he'd go, but I decided my best bet was the Gare d'Austerlitz. He'd either be there, or I could at least find out something about a train leaving that night.

When I got to the yards, I started searching through the warren of huts, but I realised that was pointless, so I climbed up to Le Bailly's watchtower. The union official wasn't there and I was free to scan the yards from his vantage point, but I saw no movement in the sheds, just the usual slow parody of work that the occupation had engendered. Down on the ground, Le Bailly stalked over and climbed the stairs to the hut.

'What are you doing here?'

'Are there any trains leaving tonight?'

My question stopped him. 'I haven't had any orders. The Boches don't tell us until the last minute when they want a train to go. There is one waiting to take equipment to the front.' He pointed to the north side of the yard. 'But it could go today or tomorrow. I don't know yet.'

'Who would know if it was going to be leaving tonight?'

'The Germans. Then they'd tell management and management would tell me. Is this to do with the refugees?'

'Have you seen any *poilus* here today? Could they be hidden in the huts?'

'*Poilus?* What's going on?'

I turned to face him. My expression startled him. 'Can you get your workers to search the sheds now? I need to find a group of *poilus* who might be hiding in there.'

'I can't. The huts aren't really part of the railway. I can only order them to work within the marshalling yard itself.'

'You ordered Font and Papin to search them the other day.'

'I didn't. That's why I never knew anything about the gas. If any of them had ever told me there was white star in the huts, I'd have called the police in years ago.'

I shut my eyes. 'Font. He's been lying all along. And Christ knows where he's got to?'

Le Bailly looked surprised. 'He's here, working.' He pointed out of the window. 'There he is, by the workshops.'

I climbed down the stairs and crossed the tracks towards Font. The sleepers were slippery underfoot and I had to watch my step. He looked up as I approached and I saw a look of panic on his face. Holding a huge spanner, he ran away from me, into an engine shed. Gingerly, I entered the building and saw him ahead of me. He'd cornered himself in a workshop. Another worker was welding metal and I shouted at him to get out. The door clanged shut behind him and I approached Font. He hefted the spanner, ready to lash out at me with it.

I unholstered my gun. 'Not a good idea. Get rid of the spanner.'

He threw it to one side. I pushed him back against the wall and gripped him by the throat.

'What do you know about the train running tonight?'

'I don't know what you're talking about.'

I felt his spittle on my face filtered through his moustache. Angered, I put my gun away and reached out for the oxyacetylene torch that the welder had left behind. The flame was still sharp and I held it near Font's face.

'I won't ask more than once. What do you know about the train taking *poilus* out of here tonight?'

'You're insane.'

'No, this is insane.'

I held the torch next to the side of his face, burning through a metal pipe on the wall. The sparks flew off into his moustache and onto my face and his. I felt small pinpricks of pain on my cheek. The smell of burning hair was acrid in the sweltering workshop. He struggled but I held him firm with my other hand.

'Who else is involved in this with you? Was it you that killed the refugees?'

'I've got nothing to do with that.' He strained to get away from the heat, his eyes bulging in terror.

'Who else is involved in promising to get the *poilus* out to-night? Is it Jeannot or anyone at the Cheval?'

'No, they're not running trains. They're just robbing people trying to escape.'

'So who is it then? Papin? Le Bailly?'

Tears ran down his cheeks. 'I don't know what you mean. Please. It's nothing to do with me. I just store the stolen stuff in the sheds. I don't know anything about the trains.'

'Where are the *poilus* supposed to be meeting you?'

'I don't know anything about that. You've got to believe me.' His voice faltered on each word with his sobbing. 'I've got nothing to do with the refugees or anyone. I just store the stuff in the sheds, I swear.'

'What about Auban?'

'He's the bastard that handed us over to the Boches, that's all I know.'

I studied his face, the tears flowing freely, mucus dribbling from his nose. Stepping back, I let go of his throat. He crumpled to a crouching position against the wall and covered his face with his hands. His cries settled into a low moan and I could do nothing but stare at him. I saw the torch in my hand and turned it off before throwing it to the ground. Hurrying outside, I leaned against the rough brick wall and retched, the bile rasping in my throat, bitter in my mouth. I tried to let tears come but I couldn't. I still had to find my son.

35

'I can't, Eddie, we haven't got the manpower.'

I held my hands up in frustration at Dax's words. 'You've got to. There's another train running tonight and I've got information that about thirty *poilus* are going to try to get out. They're in danger. It's the same set-up as the refugees. I know it.'

'How have you got this information?'

'I can't say, but it's reliable.'

'Then I can't do anything. I'm sorry, Eddie, but I need more than a vague promise about having information before I can order hundreds of police that we don't have to the railway yard to stop a train that might or might not be running. Come back with more for me to go on and I'll consider it. Anyway, you've got other investigations. What's the news on the American journalist?'

My anger was a breath away from spilling over. 'He's still dead.'

'Don't push me. What have you turned up?'

'You were right. It was a robbery that went wrong.'

'What about the bullet? You need to get an answer out of Bouchard. I don't see any progress on this. I need more, Eddie.'

'More? And if I find German involvement in this murder?'

Dax looked like a magnesium flare about to explode. 'Then you unfind it.'

'In that case, it was the Germans.'

'Get out, Eddie.'

I left his room, wondering why there was never an oxy-acetylene torch to hand when you needed one. The memory immediately made me shake, but then the recall of my son slamming the front door brought me back. I sat in my room and tried to think of another way to solve this. In vain, I rang my flat again but there was no reply.

'Have you had an interesting day, Édouard?'

I closed my eyes and groaned. I involuntarily recalled seeing Hitler strutting through the trees at Compiègne, being shot at in the woods, discovering my son was in danger and threatening a suspect with a naked flame.

'Not really. And I don't have the time for social calls right now.'

Hochstetter ignored me and sat down at my desk.

'I'm here regarding this American journalist, Groves.'

'That's nice, you've come to lay a wreath.'

'Let's hope it's not yours. No, I would like to know how your investigation into his murder is progressing. Actually, that's not true. I've come to tell you how I expect your investigation to be progressing.'

'I appreciate the help, Major, but you really shouldn't have.'

He held a slim finger up. 'Do not make the mistake of acting against my wishes. In your investigation into Groves' murder, you will not see any connection between Groves and Hauptmann Weber where there isn't one. I hope that is clear.'

'Except that Groves was embedded with Weber's unit and they used to get stinking drunk together.'

'You misunderstand. I said you will not see any connection.' He gave me one of those looks that could freeze your eyelids shut. 'You have pursued Weber to the point where you must see he has nothing to answer for. It would now be in your best interests not to see any wrongdoing on his part in this case. Have I made myself clear?'

'Perfectly. And I'd just like to say how effective your efforts in deterring me are.'

'Sarcasm, Édouard, an ugly trait. Don't forget that my job here is to help you. Don't let me regret that.'

'Certainly not by an open window.'

He looked nonplussed for a moment and then laughed, a short, sharp military bark. 'Ah, Groves and his stories. Nothing like a journalist with an active imagination, don't you think?'

All the while he'd been talking, an awful solution slowly presented itself to me. A way out of my predicament. A gamble I had no choice but to take.

'I have some information for you, Major.'

I hoped the moment I said it that I wouldn't regret it.

'The window wasn't open.'

He lit a cigarette agonisingly slowly. I was treated to the whole ritual, from tapping it on the silver case to searching for an ashtray in which to drop the dead match. How they made it to Paris in six weeks, I'll never know.

'Why are you telling me this, Édouard? I appreciate your co-operation, but I'm uncertain why you would inform on French soldiers attempting to escape.'

I'd told Hochstetter about the thirty *poilus* trying to get out of Paris by train that night. Thirty voices clamoured in my head at once, none of them complimentary. 'Because I think it's another set-up. I think they're the next victims of whoever killed the Poles on Friday morning.'

He studied me through wraiths of smoke. 'So you would hand French soldiers over to the Wehrmacht to prevent their murder. I would say that's probably one of the bravest decisions you will take.'

You have no idea how brave, I thought. 'You're the lesser of two evils. And believe me, I never thought I'd say that.'

'I'll try not to take offence at your words, Édouard. Although I don't understand why you would give this to me, not your own police.'

'Manpower. We don't have enough men to do it with any assurance of success. And because Dax won't sanction it without further evidence.'

'We are more similar than we seem, Édouard. Good men in bad times.'

'And bad men in good times.'

He looked puzzled at that but let it go. 'I will arrange matters. But I will expect you to be there.' He stood up to leave. 'One thing, and don't think that this has escaped my attention. I thought you suspected Hauptmann Weber's guilt in the deaths of the Polish refugees.'

'I like to keep my options open.' I didn't flounder for a heartbeat.

'Indeed. So do I.' Neither did he.

He left my room and I waited a second or two before rubbing my face in horror. He was right. I'd put French soldiers, including my own son, in one sort of danger to avoid putting them in another. I only hoped that the evil I was to bring upon them was less than the one I suspected. And that the evil I suspected was as real as the one I had just created.

'So you sit here and regret it, or you do something about it,' I told myself. I'd only been to the horse races at Longchamps once, dragged there by other cops in my early days, and it had bored me senseless. But I did learn about reducing the odds.

The first one was Mayer, downstairs in the evidence room.

He nodded in growing disbelief as I set out what it was I wanted him to do.

'That's one hell of a risk,' he said. 'Why do you want me to do it?'

I had to trust him. 'My son is one of the *poilus*.'

'I didn't know you had a son.'

'I can't order you to do this,' I told him, 'I can only ask it. You can refuse if you want.'

'Eddie, I wouldn't miss it for the world.'

My second and only other possibility of reducing the odds was going to be a lot less amenable. Or probable. A good job I hated horse racing as I would have made a lousy gambler.

I slipped out of Thirty-Six and planted myself in front of the Hotel du Louvre. The Nazis really didn't believe in forgoing their creature comforts on their Parisian jaunt. Looking up at the Second Empire building, it felt to me like a symbol of Paris under our new occupiers: a place of astonishing beauty inhabited by evil. I steeled myself and walked in through the front entrance.

I thought of asking at reception for Biehl but I recalled Ronson calling him a scary bastard, so I tried for Müller instead, despite his looking like Nosferatu in a nursery. The receptionist told me he wasn't allowed to call up to their rooms, so I asked him to send a note up instead. I might not have been as polite as I should have.

'So which one of us is Doctor Caligari?' Müller asked when he and Schmidt came down in the lift. He had that smile on his face, like he'd spent the afternoon stealing sweets from orphans. He'd given up on the uniform.

'The insane manipulator getting the sad, thick bastard to hurt people? You tell me.'

I looked pointedly at Schmidt after I'd said it. He scanned

the hotel foyer and decided it wasn't the place to give me a slap. I'd probably been counting on that.

'Why have you come here?' Müller insisted.

'I'd like my gun back, please. You see, I'm a detective in the French police and I'm formally requesting you return my Manufrance to me. In the interests of good relations.'

Müller stared at me for a second and burst out laughing. It was much worse than his smile. 'I do so admire your stupidity. Why don't you accompany us upstairs and we'll hand it over to you?'

'No, send Cesare here upstairs to fetch it for us.'

The Doctor Caligari reference was lost on Müller, but Schmidt got the joke. He stood up close to me and shoved his Luger into my ribs. As a bookseller's son, I should have known not to judge a book by its cover.

'No, Inspector Giral, perhaps you should come upstairs with us.'

Schmidt jabbed at me with the gun and herded me towards the lift, where they took my service pistol off me.

'That's two of my guns you've got now. I am counting.'

Schmidt punched me full in the face and they led me to an opulent bedroom, littered with documents, maps and guns. My Manufrance wasn't among them. Schmidt slapped me down into a gilt chair and kept his Luger pointed at me. Müller bent down and pushed his face into mine.

'Now why are you really here?'

'You got me, Doc. I've always wanted to be questioned in an antique chair.'

Schmidt hit me. I was braced for it, and he used his left hand because the gun was in his right, but it still rocked my head from side to side. It also reminded me of the tiny burns I'd picked up doing some questioning of my own on Font. What goes around, comes around.

'Unfortunately, we don't have any electric cables to hand,' Müller said, 'otherwise we could have fulfilled your genital wish.'

'It was only ever a suggestion. Whisky and a helping hand to the lift will do just as nicely.'

Schmidt hit me again. I settled in for a rough evening. Which was just as well as he hit me two more times, opening up the cut over my left eye again. Soon, I couldn't see out of it for the blood dripping into it.

'I will ask you again. Why are you here? And don't insult me by asking for your gun again.'

'How should I insult you?' Two more slaps. I was trying to remember why I'd come here. I saw another thump coming and called out an answer. 'I know you're Gestapo and that Hochstetter is trying to get you sent home. That means I don't have to take any orders from you or fear you. I came to tell you that. And to get my gun back.'

Müller looked at Schmidt and laughed. 'He really is this stupid.' He signalled his beast to hit me a few more times. 'Now you're here, perhaps we can learn some more from you.'

I shook my head and took a few more hits. Schmidt had changed to the body now, which was a relief. Because I was seated, he couldn't get so much of a run-up. The relief from that wore off after the third punch to the ribs.

'OK, OK, stop.' They waited to hear what it was I had to say. My words came out in retching gasps, each lungful of air another burn. 'French soldiers. Escaping the city. Tonight.'

'Is your son going to be among them?'

It was a different voice. I looked up and saw Biehl leaning over me. I hadn't heard him come into the room. He looked entirely sanguine at the state I was in.

'My son?'

'I know you have a son. Will he be among the French soldiers trying to escape tonight?'

'My son died on the Meuse.'

I began to cry, every sob driving a knife through my lungs. My tears weren't entirely false. I saw a moment of doubt cross his face. His information wasn't as complete as he'd thought. That asked the question of who he'd got it from.

'You will stay here and come with us to the railway yard when the time comes.' He spoke to Müller. 'Allow him to clean himself up.'

After I'd washed my face and bathed my wounds, they left me in the bedroom. I watched the door close behind them and heard the key turn in the lock. Through the pain, I thought of what I'd done.

And smiled.

36

The first flare rocked the night sky, taking everyone unawares. Including me. And I was expecting it.

Hanging in the air under its tiny parachute, the flickering red magnesium lit up the whole of the marshalling yard in an infernal glow, the blood light casting the shadows into a darker hell. But for the flare, everything at my feet would have remained in blackout.

I was in Le Bailly's tower. Below me, I saw a faint crimson reflection on the tracks that ran south to north. Beyond them, further to the east, the makeshift huts lay cluttered in relative darkness. To the left were the workshops and the terminus, their forms blurred in the flickering light. To my right, the tracks disappeared south into the shadows of streets and buildings.

Behind me was the man with the gun watching over me.

'That should make the RAF happy.' I forgot myself for once and said it in German, but he was too shocked to notice. 'Still, we should be safe up here.'

When they'd brought me to the Gare d'Austerlitz from their hotel, Biehl and his symphony of horrors had parked me in Le Bailly's tower with just the one Gestapo heavy to keep an eye on me. If the RAF were to happen along right now, we'd have been like ping-pong balls on water spouts at a funfair, just waiting to be shot off our perch.

As the flare fell dying to earth, I took in the scene below me. I caught sight of Hochstetter at the northern end of the sidings, the soldiers he'd mobilised dispersed the length and breadth of the yards. I hadn't spotted where Biehl and his chums had got to. I saw no one else, least of all any *poilus*. There were no workers in sight. The Gestapo had told Le Bailly to go home when they'd commandeered his little hut, and he'd hurried off gratefully into the night. Something else I didn't see was the string of trucks waiting for departure that Le Bailly had shown me earlier. I worried my ploy was going to be too late.

My less than stoic guard jumped at the fresh sound of gunfire. Except it wasn't gunfire.

'That should do the trick,' I mouthed to the blackened window. 'Thanks, Mayer.' I smiled quietly, the skin around my broken lip cracking painfully.

In my mind's eye, I could picture him, flitting through the darkness to my right, to the south of the yard, letting off the fireworks and military flares we'd found on Sunday's search. Just as I'd asked him to do earlier that evening. In our planning, we hadn't dared use the sheds for cover for fear of drawing the Germans towards any *poilus* hiding in them. And the hospital to the west was impossible because of the risk of gunfire straying into the buildings. The only option we had was the dark route of the tracks heading south, where there was plenty of cover from the buildings. I'd told Mayer to disappear into the narrow streets the moment it got too risky. He should lose any pursuers easily in the night, but a jolt of guilt at the risk I'd asked him to take hit me.

Another flare lit up the sky.

'Move,' the heavy ordered. He evidently didn't want to hang around in the hut for too long under the lights.

He followed me down the shaky stairs, his gun hovering somewhere behind me in the night. At the bottom, he shoved me with his left hand towards the warehouses to the north, near where I'd seen Hochstetter. Mayer let off some more fireworks to the south, the noise reverberating like a battle in its confusion. I heard the first gunshots from the Germans firing off in unsure response. It should have reminded me of the trenches, but I was too on edge, hoping my plan would work. Such as it was. Biehl keeping me hostage at the hotel had been a bit of a setback to the planning stages.

The yard was still lit as the guard marched me on dainty feet across the treacherous tracks and I quickly scanned around me, looking for Hochstetter or any Wehrmacht officer. I had a sudden vision of stumbling across Weber in the mess of shooting guns and realised I'd probably be his fairground attraction if his chance arose. I was almost grateful when the flare went out again. In its last moments, I'd seen where Biehl was – cast in giant shadow against a brick wall of the warehouses. It wasn't far from where I'd seen Hochstetter earlier.

More gunshots were fired, some of them getting tooth-grindingly close, as the Germans shot randomly into the dark. I recognised chaos in the shouts of the soldiers and officers and smiled again at myself despite the pain of my aching face and the fear of chance bullets. Mayer let off a few shots of his own for authenticity. I silently thanked him for his initiative.

Amid all the shouting, a third flare went up, this time from further away to my right. Mayer was retreating. I knew he wouldn't be able to send up many more before he had to get away from danger. The longer it went on, the less the confusion would be as the Germans twigged what was happening.

In the glow, I saw Hochstetter. He was taking command, evidently realising it was a diversion and ordering the soldiers not to pursue the source of the flares. More importantly, he saw me. He crossed the tracks to where I was standing. I could see Biehl a short distance to my left.

'You didn't say they would be armed,' Hochstetter shouted above the din. 'Any deserters will be regarded as enemy soldiers and shot.'

'We're no longer at war.'

'The armistice hasn't been signed. We are still at war. I have given the order for any French soldiers resisting to be shot.'

He turned away and ordered some of the soldiers to search the huts. I cursed. I'd been caught between two evils and made my choice. On the one hand, I'd pictured Jean-Luc's possible death at the hands of the killer who'd murdered the four Polish refugees last Friday. On the other, I was sentencing him to certain arrest by the Germans. Dead or imprisoned. There had been no contest. I also kept the hope in my head that I could possibly bargain with Hochstetter for my son after his arrest. Sell the soul that Hochstetter sought in return for Jean-Luc's safety.

In the meantime, I'd also enlisted Mayer's help as an outside chance that I'd get away with it altogether. Jean-Luc's life and freedom amid the confusion. A desperate throw of the dice to save a life and its liberty.

In the final glow as the parachute fell to earth, Biehl was highlighted once again. So was the look on Hochstetter's face. In the dark, he stormed over to the SD officer. I heard their voices raised.

'This is a Wehrmacht operation,' Hochstetter shouted. 'You have no authority to be here.'

'This is an SD operation. We uncovered this plan.'

'You didn't uncover any plan that the Wehrmacht wasn't aware of.'

I felt rather than saw my guard drift over to where the two officers were arguing. He'd evidently forgotten about me. Mayer, bless his heart, let off some more fireworks and gunshots, and I sensed the soldiers around me getting edgier, the sound of hobnails clattering on wood and steel more intense. Someone nearby fired off a machine gun into the darkness, the noise momentarily deafening me.

I did my own drifting. I'd seen from the tower that the goods trucks that Le Bailly had told me were being readied for the front had gone, so I made my way towards where the trucks had been last Friday, when the Poles had been killed. I ducked to keep below the bullets. A few metres before coming to the spot, a flash of gunfire revealed Weber to me. He hadn't seen me, but was caught on open ground between the warehouses and the huts.

'Never a gun when you need one,' I told myself. Biehl had taken mine away from me. I was two weapons down to his lot and not happy.

I'd managed to skirt Weber when Mayer sent up another flare, this time not so fortuitous. Trapped in the glow were about a dozen *poilus*, their eyes shining in the crosshairs. Behind me, I heard shouting and turned to see Germans hurrying with their weapons towards the young French soldiers. Looking back, I saw Jean-Luc picked out in crimson silhouette against the huts. He saw me. With German soldiers behind me, pointing their weapons at him and his companions.

'Over there,' I shouted in German, trying to divert the soldiers away from the *poilus*. 'Behind the trucks.'

I tried to lead them away. Some followed, but as the light died, I heard others shouting that they'd found the *poilus* and calling for support. I cursed and hid in the darkness between two goods trucks standing idle, listening to the Germans I'd tricked run past me in confusion. When I peered out, Jean-Luc was nowhere in sight, the other young men vanished back into the tiny alleys.

Feeling my way in the night, it hit me that the trucks I was among were in the same place where the ones on Friday night had been. The realisation chilled me. For that brief moment, finding them in exactly the same spot, I felt I'd made the right choice in bringing Hochstetter in, to protect my son from whoever had killed the Poles. I hoped I had.

I heard a noise from inside one of the trucks and pulled a crowbar out of the lock to slide the door open. I held on to the heavy iron tool. It wasn't a gun but it would do. Climbing up, I could just make out some figures moving. I called to them to ask who they were, but no one replied. A match lit in the truck and I saw five young men. They looked terrified.

'French?' I asked them. They nodded. 'You're not safe here. Go back into the huts and lose yourselves.'

'We can't. A cop told us to come in here.'

'I'm a cop and I'm telling you to get out.'

The sound of gunfire was more sporadic now that Mayer had done his work and in the lull, I heard a sound from outside. I jumped back down and hurried to the end, where I could make out a figure on the other side of the gap between the trucks. He asked who I was. It was Auban's voice.

'What are you doing here?' I asked him.

'Christ, Giral, you choose your moments, don't you?'

My eyes were more accustomed to the dark now no flares had gone up for some minutes and I saw a movement from Auban. Instinctively ducking back out of sight, I felt the wind of the bullet pass me the same moment I heard the shot.

The huts were a short sprint across open ground and I ran for them. A second shot sounded, but Auban was firing wildly in the dark and I reached the shelter of the makeshift buildings before he could shoot again. My heart pounding, I felt my way into the maze, my feet sounding heavy on the years of broken bottles and debris underfoot. Stopping at the corner of a hut to listen, I heard a sound to my right. If it was Auban, he'd entered the huts somewhere to the south of me. Turning my head this way and that to pick up any noise, I heard the same crunch of glass underfoot.

'You're unarmed, aren't you, Eddie?' I heard him call softly through the darkness. He couldn't keep the triumph out of his voice. 'Otherwise you'd have fired back.'

Bolder now, he roamed through the uneven pattern of sheds, his footsteps coming nearer. I heard him to my right. Backing around the corner of the hut, I listened more intently but he'd gone quiet. Somewhere in the dark, I heard the movement of feet. Quiet like thieves stealing in the night, not soldiers hunting their prey. I realised it might have been the *poilus* I'd sent into here for their safety, only now I'd put them in danger from Auban. Silently, I hefted the crowbar.

Auban must have heard the sound too and he shot blindly towards its source. I was terrified I'd led the young men to their death, but no cry or noise echoed back in the night. In that brief moment, the muzzle blast from his gun gave him away. He was almost next to me, on the other side of the corner I was hiding behind, facing away from me.

Remembering the vision of his position that I'd had, I swung the crowbar roundhouse and felt it smash into his arm and side, knocking the gun out of his hand. Trusting to luck, I lashed out again and felt it hit home. He grunted and fell heavily to the ground. I waited a moment before nudging where I thought he'd be with my foot. He didn't move and I kicked him harder, but there was no sound or response. I reached down to search for the gun with my fingers but I couldn't find it, and I had to move when I heard other sounds drawing near. From the edge of the huts, I ran back across the open ground to the trucks. Sure enough, the *poilus* had gone from inside.

To my horror, Mayer let off one final flare from the southern edge of the yard. It burst in the distance, so the light was weak, but in its glow I was picked out against the wood and metal of the wagon. Hochstetter was illuminated opposite me. He was flanked by more soldiers than I could readily count in the dying light.

'Most enlightening,' he commented.

Behind him, I saw what I assumed were the young men who'd been in the truck, lying motionless on the ground. The night sky and the tracks were tinged red. Beyond them, herding close together under the guns of Hochstetter's soldiers stood more *poilus*, their faces lowered. Other soldiers joined them, shepherding yet more *poilus* in front of them. The sounds of skirmish steadily calmed.

Quickly searching among the French soldiers standing in a huddle, I looked for Jean-Luc. He wasn't there. I looked back at the young men lying as though asleep on the ground and closed my eyes in a prayer I'd never believed in.

Thursday 2nd July 1925

His eyes were shut. He was still. I turned away and let my breath out slowly.

Between my police shift and my job at the jazz club, I rarely saw my son awake. He seldom came to me when he was. Hearing him exhale gently, I left his room and called a goodbye to Sylvie. She didn't reply.

At the jazz club, Claude was cool with me. I did my job, was polite to the customers and still got on with the musicians. Like the club itself, all was well on the surface. Underneath was another song. I stood at the back and watched Dominique perform. Her voice mesmerised and saddened me as it always did. Her singing was like the character in the book my father had given me, searching for something that had perhaps never existed.

In the lull at the bar while Dominique sang, I saw Fran in the rooms that the public never got to see. There was none of the faded gilt and chipped chandeliers of the salon. Just chairs too broken for use and years of grime trapped in the corners. The sound of Dominique's voice filtered and distorted through the walls like the building was lamenting its purpose. Fran was handing a twist of paper to a customer, an ageing roué with an arthritic stare who commonly pestered the performers. Averting his gaze from me, the elderly man handed over his money and scurried out of the room.

'Anything you want, Eddie?'

I shook my head and left Fran to his business. I was a cop and he knew I couldn't touch him. Not now. Another one who in some way owned me.

Back in the salon, Dominique had finished her set and was nowhere in sight. Joe and his band took up a new beat, with drums and cornets, livelier than her unrequited melancholy. The room shook, and everyone in it, high on the sound or buzzing thanks to Fran.

I caught up with her outside, catching some air in the alley behind the dressing rooms. It was still fresher than the smoke-intoxicated club. She'd unzipped her dress at the back to cool down. I stood in silence for a minute.

'Thank you,' I finally said. She'd been the one to get Claude to take me back.

'No need, Eddie. You all right?'

'I'm all right.'

She gave a sad half-smile and went back inside for her next set on stage, reaching behind her back for her zip. I waited alone outside and looked up at a ribbon of stars glittering through a tight corset of darkened buildings. I could have wished the moment to last forever.

I heard the commotion the moment I went inside. Another of Fran's less licit customers was firmly gripping Dominique's shoulder with one hand while reaching behind her with the other. She hissed at him to let her go.

'I'll do your dress up. Come on.' His voice was slurred.

Coming from behind Dominique, I pulled the man's hand from her back and gently pushed him away. Dominique turned and saw me, her face immediately showing panic.

'Why don't we get you back to your table in time to hear Dominique sing again?' I asked him. 'I'm sure she'd be happy to dedicate a song to you if you'll just let her.'

He looked confused, but saw the appeal of that. Without any cajoling from me, he released her shoulder. 'A love song?'

'I'm sure it will be.'

I led him to the door leading from the corridor to the main room. Once there, he made his own way back to his table, where his friends were calling him over. Dominique caught up with me at the door.

'That's the Eddie I like.'

She turned to head backstage. You and me both, I thought.

While she sang, I listened from the corridor. The door opened again and two of the Corsicans came through, the older companion of the one I'd beaten and a younger one, his replacement. They were with Joe. I saw in his eyes a plea not to do anything.

'Everything all right here?' I asked.

The older one came up and patted my face. 'We're all fine, Eddie, you know that. Now, maybe you'd like to leave us alone to do business.'

'Are you all right, Joe?'

'It's fine, Eddie, I promise.'

With a lingering look, I left them. Joe, I knew, was paying them not to break his fingers, a hindrance to a musician. Claude had forbidden me from doing anything about it.

'You did the Corsicans a favour,' he told me when he took me back. 'The young guy you put in hospital was trying to take over from the old guy. If you hadn't stopped him, they would have. Now, just leave it at that. Look away when you have to and be grateful they haven't taken it any further.'

I closed the door on Joe and the two Corsicans now and let slip a curse.

I looked away, too, at the police station. Auban was at a desk, his feet up, swapping a betting story with another cop. Avoiding him, I changed my suit and looked at the papers on my desk.

'Hey, Giral,' Auban called over to me. 'I got a great tip for Longchamps if you're interested. After all, you'll believe anything anyone tells you.'

'What does that mean?'

He got up and winked at me, an exaggerated gesture that set his companion off sniggering. 'You mean you don't know? You've got to be the only one.'

Before I could answer, the sergeant called me over for a job. Luckily, it was without Auban for company. Relieved, I went to the toilet first. Locking the door, I took out a twist of paper and opened it. Not one I'd bought from Fran. I was careful to keep this away from the jazz club. Closing my eyes in anticipation, I leaned forward and sniffed up the powder, waiting for the power to surge.

The job took up most of my shift, and two more sniffs of cocaine, and I was still shaking by the time I got home. Bleary-eyed, Sylvie came out into the living room.

'Stop the noise, Édouard, Jean-Luc is asleep.'

'Wake him up, then. His father's home. He shouldn't be sleeping at a time like this.'

'It's the middle of the night. Please.'

Sylvie put her hands up to placate me, and I backed away from her, a momentary panic running through me. I heard a loud voice and realised it was mine. Jean-Luc began to call for his mother from his room.

'He never calls for me,' I told her. 'You've made him hate me.'

'No, Édouard, you did that. I don't want you to destroy yourself, but if you will, I can't have you ruin your son's life too.'

For one brief moment, I could have felt remorse, even climbed up from my depths, but I suddenly smelt smoke and saw the shells approaching that had killed my friends. I descended further into a trench of my own making. 'You want to know what destroying a life looks like, Sylvie?'

She held her hands up. 'Calm down, Édouard.'

I heard the first of the explosions in my head and I could almost smell the chlorine, feel the destruction of myself from the inside. 'Do you want to know what destroying a life looks like? You really want to know?'

The second shock wave went off and I saw the look of concern on her face. I didn't know what she had to be worried about.

'Please keep calm, Édouard.'

She recoiled from me and the third and final crack of sound and despair was on its way. It was the smell of burning. Flesh burning, eating into my head. I closed my eyes for a moment and opened them again. She was holding her face in her hand and crying. I looked up to see my arm raised above my head.

'Stay calm, this isn't you.'

'Please.'

I had no idea who spoke the last word.

Saturday 22nd June 1940

37

It was a smell I'd almost forgotten. Fresh coffee and fresher bed linen.

'Now, what was that all about, Édouard?'

Hochstetter's voice startled me. I sat up. I was lying fully clothed on a soft bed in a sumptuous hotel room. I remembered. Hochstetter had had me marched away from the railway yard last night and taken to the Lutétia. As prison cells went, it was a lot more amenable than the Cherche-Midi down the road. I felt a shock of guilt that I'd found sleep after hours of arguing to a closed door to be let out.

'No breakfast?' I complained.

He was seated in an armchair by the foot of the bed. The smell of his coffee was like a finger of aroma tickling the tip of my nose. Taking a sip, he looked idly at the window.

'You will push me too far one day. How did our friends in the Gestapo know about the attempt to escape the city?'

I faked a morning yawn to gather my thoughts, trying to recall the course of events the previous night. 'I imagine they must have informants too.'

'You were with them, Édouard. Don't try my patience.'

'I was with them because they'd picked me up again. When they were on their way to the Gare d'Austerlitz.' His look told me he didn't buy it, but I had other worries. I tried to put my police officer voice on. 'I want to know what happened to the French soldiers you arrested last night.'

He sat back and did his cigarette ritual. I had to fight an urge to get off the bed and throw the lot out of the window. 'They are safely in custody. As someone intent on maintaining justice, I'm sure you will welcome that.'

'As someone intent on maintaining justice, I want to see them. They should come under French law.'

He shook his head. 'They are prisoners of war. The armistice is not yet signed. That means they come under military law. German military law.'

'And the soldiers that were killed?' I had to stop my voice from shaking.

Hochstetter had had me pulled away before I'd had a chance to look through either the *poilus* lying on the ground or huddled under guard. I'd tried to count them. Between the two groups, there weren't the thirty or so that Jean-Luc had said there were. I didn't know if that was because some of them got away or if there hadn't been that many in the first place. I had no idea if Jean-Luc was among them.

'Killed? There were no soldiers killed.'

'I saw French soldiers on the ground.'

'I'm afraid you're mistaken, Édouard. In all the confusion, I think you mistook dead French soldiers for ones who had surrendered. Now, if that is all, I have a lot of business to attend to.'

I didn't dare ask if any *poilus* got away. He would have been unlikely to answer, anyway. Instead, I asked a question to know if I'd done the right thing. 'Did you find anyone who might have been involved in the initial killings?'

He looked bored. 'That is not my job.'

'Or your worry. You were never interested in stopping any more killings. Just rounding up French soldiers.'

'You're quite right on both counts. And much more naïve than I would have thought. I do wonder if there's a reason for that. But no matter.' He reached for something on a low table out of my sight. 'I have your gun.'

I thought for a moment it was the Manufrance, but I was surprised to see him holding my service pistol. The last time I'd seen it, the Gestapo were nursing it.

'How did you get it back?'

'I have a way of acquiring items that go missing. And now, it's probably time you left.'

'You're letting me go?'

'You were free to go at any time. I simply brought you here for your own safety. I'm afraid the Gestapo are none too happy with you. And I'd put your holster on in here if I were you, unless you want one of the soldiers in the hotel to misinterpret a Frenchman with a gun in Abwehr headquarters.'

Standing up, I put the holster on under his gaze. I quickly checked the gun. It was loaded.

'You're very trusting,' I told him.

He stood up. 'Not at all. I simply know how much rope to give you.'

I left the Lutétia unwashed and unshaven and took the Metro home. Jean-Luc wasn't there. The mess still was, the whisky glass dirty and forgotten on my table.

Needing to find out what had happened to my son, I returned to the railway yards. In the sunlight, there was nothing to suggest anything of what had happened the previous night. The trucks were still in the same place. A star was roughly chalked in white on one of them. Climbing inside, I found no trace of any of the *poilus*. And no sign of any gas canisters hidden ready to use. I had nothing to show I'd done the right thing. I just had my belief that the killer was using the same ruse to steal and kill again. And the need to do something right by my son for once. But the Germans rounding up the *poilus* before the killer had shown their hand had robbed me of the certainty that I was right. I had to suppress the idea that the plan had been genuine. That I'd been the one to rob my son of the chance of escaping. And the other young men, possibly even Jean-Luc too, of much more.

Out of the stuffy air in the trucks, I examined the ground where I'd seen the soldiers lying. Amid the oil and grease, I saw patches of what could only have been blood, drying to a dark stain in the sun. I wanted to believe that the blurred marks weren't enough to indicate what I dreaded, but experience told me they were. I could only stare and hope. Not just for my own son, but for all the other *poilus* I'd put in danger of one evil over another.

Le Bailly was making more of his foul coffee when I climbed to the top of his eyrie. It looked too much like the stains on the track for me to drink.

'Have you seen any *poilus* this morning? Anyone who shouldn't be here?' I asked him.

He shook his head and swept his hand over the view outside. It was unusually quiet. 'After last night, no one wants to come in. If there were any *poilus* here, I'd see them. I haven't seen any Germans either. I got here a couple of hours ago and found this. Nothing. The trucks for the front are still here, in different sidings. I told you, it's not a good way to get anyone out of the city.'

I stood next to him and gazed at the idle yards. I knew I needed to talk, but there was no one to tell me I'd made the right decision. 'I don't think that was the intention. I think the killer simply meant to take the money, kill the *poilus*, and take no risks of getting them out of the city past the Germans. That's why I did what I did.'

He looked pale and put his cup down. 'You can't really believe that.'

I stared sightlessly at the scene below. 'Have Font and Papin been in this morning?'

He shook his head. 'You really think they could be involved, don't you? Maybe it wouldn't surprise me. But no, I haven't seen them today.'

I pointed at the phone on his desk. 'If you do see anyone, be sure to call me.'

Overwhelmed with guilt, I drove away. I had another job – I had to check Mayer was safe. That was another fate on my conscience. Checking my watch, I thought of Hochstetter and the time. For a brief moment, I considered giving up now and changing the hour like he'd told me, but the time I saw stopped me. It was noon, theirs, not mine, but for once it didn't matter.

On impulse I decided to try. I hadn't seen Lucja since leaving her alone in my flat on Wednesday night and I hadn't been to Place des Vosges since discovering her apartment empty on Thursday, but I thought I should give her at least one more chance.

She was there. I almost couldn't believe it. Seated on the bench, wearing a summer hat to shelter from the sun. It obscured her face. Hidden under the arches, I watched her for a few minutes while scanning the rest of the square. There were no German soldiers today. The rundown gardens seemed to have lost their charm for the occupier.

Cautiously, I approached her. She saw me and did her usual trick of coming to meet me and giving me a kiss on both cheeks.

She seemed to sense my reserve and gave me a puzzled look before leading me to sit down.

'I didn't expect to find you,' I told her.

'I wasn't sure you'd come either. I was here both times yesterday and you didn't show up. What happened to you?' She traced a cut on my cheek with her finger.

I studied her face and wanted to believe in her the way I wanted to believe in Fryderyk's evidence. I was tired of not trusting anyone. 'It was a long day. I saw a man take a walk in the woods in the morning and I watched my son either arrested or killed by the Germans in the evening. And it was my fault. I tried to save him and I have no idea if I did the right thing.'

She looked shocked. 'I didn't know you had a son.'

I studied her as she said it, still wondering how Biehl knew about Jean-Luc. Needing to trust someone, I told her a little of Jean-Luc's plan to get away from Paris by train and what I'd done to try and stop it.

'It was the right thing to do,' she decided. 'You had no other choice.'

'But I don't know what's happened to him, and the Germans aren't telling me anything.'

'You might have to tell this Hochstetter you have a son. Even if it gives him a hold over you, it might be your only way to find out if he's safe.'

The thought had already gone through my mind, the decision a dilemma I was putting off as long as I had hope I could find Jean-Luc myself. I shook it out of my head. 'How did you get away? On Wednesday?'

She looked mystified. 'Get away? I just left. I waited but you didn't come back, so I took the two Polish books with me and left.'

'My flat was ransacked. I thought you'd been there when it

happened.' I registered her words. 'You still have Fryderyk's books?'

'I took them with me. Your flat was perfectly fine when I left. It obviously happened after I'd gone,' She looked concerned. 'Our flat too. Not ransacked, but we're certain it was compromised. We noticed unusual movements in the streets, so we left early on Thursday morning.'

'I know. I went there. Where did you go?'

'Please don't ask me. We will have to arrange to meet somewhere else, and at different times. It's becoming too dangerous for our small group. We have to get out of Paris, perhaps rejoin the Polish government in London.'

'Have you found out if Fryderyk hid anything?'

'Nothing. I've gone through both books page by page to look for any marks or code and I can't find anything. It's hopeless. If Fryderyk did have anything of value, I think we have to accept that it's gone.' She looked as tired and beaten as I felt.

I told her something of Weber and the information he had. 'The problem for me is that Weber possibly murdered innocent civilians in Poland, maybe even in Bydgoszcz, and he might have had a hand in the deaths of the Polish men in the railway yard. For his information to get out, he has to go unpunished for that.'

'Then he has to go unpunished.' Lucja's decisive words surprised me. 'For the time being. Punishing him for his crimes in Poland or here is a drop in the ocean. If we can't tell the world what happened in my country, we can at least tell them about this list of Americans. If the Nazis aren't stopped, many more Poles and many more people all over Europe will die. By letting Weber go now, you can try to stop it. You have to. And if Weber leaves, doesn't that remove the danger of further killings here in Paris?'

'If he's responsible for them. I want to believe Weber's behind them, but I can't be certain. And when Hochstetter seems to be pushing me towards seeing his guilt, it makes me question everything. My worry is that someone is using me as a tethered goat to lead them to the real truth.'

'Or hide it.'

I stared at the ground at our feet. 'Or hide something else entirely.'

38

'We've lost our family home, I haven't heard from my parents and I'm stuck in this basement. It felt good to be fighting back.'

I'd been relieved to find Mayer safe and sound in the storage room the moment I got to Thirty-Six.

'I'm sorry. I shouldn't have asked so much of you.'

He waved it away. 'Did you find your son?'

'No.'

Mayer waited until another cop left the room and called me through to the back room, where he closed the door. His face took on a more serious expression.

'I'm not going to like this, am I?'

'Probably not.'

From a high shelf, he pulled down a cardboard box and opened it, taking out a gun. I recognised it immediately as my Manufrance. I stared at it in astonishment.

'How did you get this?'

'Auban. He left it here last night with instructions not to tell anyone or do anything with it until he came back. I recognised it as yours.'

I picked it up and examined it. The magazine had one round missing. I knew where that had gone.

'Auban? How did he get hold of it?'

'He wouldn't say.' He closed the box and put it back on the shelf, leaving the gun with me. 'But since I'd trust Auban as far as I could throw him, I thought you might want it back. Want to tell me how come you lost it?'

'Not really. And I certainly don't know why Auban would have it.' That bit, at least, was true. Having to stop my hands from shaking, I put the gun in my waistband. Without knowing, Mayer had just got me out of jail on a murder charge and I couldn't thank him without giving myself away. 'I owe you one. For last night, I mean.'

'Have you seen Dax yet? He was looking for you.'

He found me. I tried sneaking into my room, but the commissioner leaned in the moment I got there.

'Have you seen Auban this morning, Eddie? No one knows where he is.'

'Well, you know Auban.'

'Tell him I want to see him.'

'I'll be sure to do that. Frankly, I'm more worried about the *poilus* at the Gare d'Austerlitz.'

'It's in hand, Eddie. Prefect Langeron has made an official request to the Germans for the names and whereabouts of any French soldiers taken prisoner or killed.'

'I want to know,' I called after him.

'And I want to know where Auban is.'

To be fair, I was worried about Auban too. Worried about why the Gestapo would have relinquished the gun, the hold they had over me, and worried why they'd give them both to Auban. Staring sightlessly through the window, I replayed everything that had happened last night. Two things stuck in my mind: Biehl knowing I had a son and Auban at the railway yard when no other cops had been sent there.

'It's not Hochstetter you were working with,' I whispered. 'It's Biehl.'

I felt the Manufrance dig into my waist. I'd assumed that Groves' murder had been to do with Weber's hit list of Americans. The Gestapo or the SD were the ones executing the targets and, in Groves' case, they'd set me up as an insurance policy. It meant they had power over me, a police detective in an occupied country. Which didn't explain why they'd then give the evidence to Auban and so lose that power.

Unless Biehl, with Auban's help, had other reasons for setting me up. Perhaps the plan had simply been to remove me by getting me charged with the murder. Which would then mean that Groves' killing was possibly nothing to do with Weber's list in the first place.

And that brought me back to the doubts I'd had all along about the credibility of the evidence Weber was trying to sell to Ronson in exchange for safe passage. Ronson herself had said that Groves would probably not be on the list because of his loss of influence and cosying up to the Germans, so if he was killed, there was a fair chance it was for an entirely different purpose. And Ronson had also argued that Groves' murder corroborated Weber's story, but if it was some scheme by Biehl and Auban, that cast further doubt in my mind on Weber's claims. I also just didn't buy Weber, I had to admit. Either way, now seemed as good a time as any to rattle someone's luxury apartment.

First, though, I replaced the Manufrance in my car and dropped by my own flat. I checked all the rooms, but Jean-Luc still wasn't there and I saw no signs that he had been. The mess from Wednesday night was still intact. So was Ronson's whisky. I left them both that way. I also had to pick up something that I thought might come in useful for my next extracurricular appointment. That was at a building on the Right Bank, on

357

Faubourg Saint Honoré. An elaborate wedding cake of an apartment block a short walk from the Élysée Palace. I told the new tenant just that when he opened the door.

'The Élysée's empty too,' I added. 'You going to be requisitioning that as well?'

'What the hell are you doing here?' Weber asked me. He was wearing his army trousers, but with just a plain white shirt over the top, the top three buttons undone and no collar. Another gangster in uniform, just a lot more successful than Jeannot's lot. 'You idiot, how do you know you weren't followed?'

'I don't. In fact, I'd lay good odds I was. Which makes it interesting. Who's going to be first to come knocking on your door because I have?'

I walked through the sumptuous hall into an even more splendid salon, littered with Louis XV furniture and Lalique chandeliers. Dust-framed gaps on the walls betrayed where the most expensive artworks had been taken, most likely by the real owners of the flat as they fled the city. Looking at the exalted signatures on the paintings left behind made me wonder just who the expensive ones must have been by. Mind you, the place would have been greatly improved by a book or two on a shelf somewhere.

'You know, it's funny,' I told him. 'I came to this flat in a past life when it belonged to the Weitzmanns. I was investigating a burglary they'd had. Before the war, we used to arrest people for stealing from apartments, and now here you lot are, taking the whole apartment and getting away with it.'

I sat down at a vast dining table on a chair the size of a tyrant's throne. Weber paced for a moment or two before sitting opposite me. He was the first to break the silence.

'What is it you want? We said all we had to say yesterday. Now it's up to Ronson to fulfil her side of the bargain.'

'Ronson's a lot more trusting than I am. I'd want to see this list you say you have before I'd agree to get you out of Paris. Just so I know it's real.'

He sighed heavily. 'It is real, believe me. And she will. I've agreed to give it to Ronson before she gets me out of the city.'

'Who's in this with you? Biehl? Hochstetter? Someone else in the Schwarze Kapelle I don't know about? Because I don't think you're working alone.'

'You're right. It's me, Heydrich and Goebbels. And Goering's just invited Himmler along for the ride. Of course I'm alone in this. You think selling your country is something you share easily?'

'Why not just go to London if you're so keen to get away? Then you wouldn't have to go through all this rigmarole.'

Weber laughed, an acidic sound. 'It isn't far away enough. It is only a matter of time before London falls, and if I'm there when it does, the Nazis and the Gestapo will find me. I need to get to America, and I need to get there with assurances of immunity. That is the price and the reason why I have to sell my information to Ronson.'

'Immunity for what? What you did in Poland?'

'It is always Poland with you. All right, I will tell you. In Poland I saw civilians being systematically slaughtered. It is far worse than any rumours you have heard. The Wehrmacht had units of SS and Gestapo attached to them whose job was to single out individuals and carry out mass executions.' He was red, rattled. 'I cannot believe in that. And I do not believe you came here for this.'

'No. I really came to see you about something else. You see, even if I don't trust you, I get the importance of this list you say you have, but I'm a cop. I also see the importance of the need for justice for the Poles who have died in my city. And more than that, I see the need to make sure that no more murders are allowed to happen.'

'You are a fool. I have told you. I had nothing to do with your little murders here in Paris. I care nothing for these victims of yours, but I had nothing to do with their deaths.' His voice had risen a notch, the usual calm gone.

In the silence that followed, I studied him. 'You see, Hauptmann Weber, I've been seeking redemption for fifteen years now. I know what it looks like. The problem is I just don't see it in you. This is what it looks like.'

I took out the Luger and placed it on the table. Then I placed half a dozen shells next to the empty magazine. Putting all of them in one hand, I picked one out. To Weber, it would have looked as though I'd chosen it at random, but I'd felt for the telltale indentation and inserted the dud bullet in the magazine before pointing the gun at my own head.

He laughed nervously. 'You're insane. Russian roulette with a pistol?'

'One of these shells is a dud.'

I pulled the trigger and watched him recoil in horror. The gun gave the dry click I'd grown used to over the years. I took it out and jumbled it in my hand with the others.

'That is redemption,' I told him. I picked out a shell. Again, I felt for the bullet with the small depression and loaded the gun before placing it in front of him. 'Now you.'

He looked at it for a moment, his expression uncertain, before slowly picking it up. His glance flickered from the Luger to me. I saw the smile I'd expected. Instead of pointing the gun at his own head, he pointed it at me.

'You want redemption?'

He squeezed the trigger and got the same dry click. I smiled at him and took the gun away, emptying the dud from it. In his consternation, he let me.

'You see. You are capable of killing in cold blood. And you're capable of deceit. You don't look at all like anyone who would be willing to give up everything you have because you feel guilt or shame at what you were made to do in Poland.'

His coldness was quickly returning, the calculation back in his eyes. 'I'm not giving up everything. I'm getting a new life. Look at the owners of this flat, these Jews. They left, they changed their life, but they didn't give up a single thing. Look at the wealth they took with them. What they left behind, they regarded as worthless. That is purely what I am doing. Shedding what has become worthless.' He sensed my own anger rising and seemed to feed off it. 'All right. If you really want to know, I killed civilians in Poland. The Wehrmacht did not *just* tolerate SS and Gestapo, some of us participated. I stood in a field in Bydgoszcz and in other towns and I fired on men and women in open ditches. Men and women that we had taken from their homes and their work and I shot them as they stood with their hands on their heads. Are you satisfied? Yes, I've killed Polish civilians, but I did not kill *your* Polish civilians. I am not *your* criminal.'

I looked into his eyes and saw no emotion there. I had to struggle to keep my own in check. I exhaled deeply before speaking again. 'If you're capable of killing civilians in a field, you're capable of killing them in a railway yard.'

'That is true. I am perfectly capable. But if I admit to killing civilians in Poland, why would I deny killing them in France?'

'You said it yourself. To make sure Ronson gets you out of Paris before the killing catches up with you.'

All the while he'd been distracted by our conversation, I'd reloaded the Luger.

'Another game. And this time, we'll play by your rules.'

I calmly pointed the gun at his forehead.

39

I was never a good gambler.

'So now we'll see who's got your best interests at heart. I know who my money's on.'

As I'd struggled with whether to pull the trigger or not, we heard the door to Weber's apartment open and footsteps cross the hall. Several of them. But instead of the Hochstetter I'd been expecting, Biehl was the one to walk into the room. Müller and Schmidt and two other henchmen trailed in his wake, only now they'd all given up the GFP pretence and were wearing plain clothes of dark suits and ties, which was just another uniform. Biehl was in his grey SD outfit, which spooked Weber. It was startling how afraid they all were of the Nazi Party security service. Perhaps I should learn to be that afraid too. Trouble is, I had Hochstetter to keep me scared at night. Biehl looked at me like he'd just blown me out of his nose.

'Sorry, is it me you're after or Weber here?' I asked him. 'Just wanting to clarify.'

To my surprise, Biehl smiled. Only it wasn't at me. He greeted Weber warmly by his first name. 'Karl, so good to see you. I haven't seen you since Berlin. We really must catch up now I'm in Paris.'

'Well, isn't this lovely?'

The SD man gave me a look that would have made a blind man blanch. 'Please excuse me. We're here as we have some questions for the inspector. Like why the Abwehr knew to be at the Gare d'Austerlitz last night.'

'You know, it's very flattering that you covet our country so much, but couldn't you have sorted out your own quarrels at home without bringing us into it? It would have saved us all so much bother.'

The building had one of the earliest and most ornate lifts in Paris, and therefore one of the slowest, which made for an awkward ride down, hemmed in between Biehl, Müller and Schmidt. The two extras were made to take the stairs. Weber was left to enjoy his marble halls.

'Just so we're clear,' I insisted. 'Is it me you're harassing or Weber you're protecting?'

We were in a crowded lift. Schmidt couldn't hit me. They'd taken my service pistol, though, but not the Luger, which I'd managed to hide in the back of my waistband before they'd come in. And Weber hadn't given it away to them, which surprised me. We got outside to find Hochstetter waiting by his car, with a dozen Wehrmacht soldiers around him.

'So that's where you were,' I told him.

Hochstetter ignored me and spoke to Biehl.

'I am here to take Inspector Giral into Abwehr custody.'

'Is that right, Major Hochstetter? In case you weren't aware, I outrank you.'

'I'm fully aware of that, Obersturmbannführer Biehl. I am also aware that Paris is under military command. As yet, the SD and the Gestapo have no jurisdiction here. Until that time, my authority outranks yours.'

You had to hand it to Biehl. His aristocratic upbringing meant he was unused to being denied anything, but it also meant he took denial with a class and an urbane menace I didn't usually come across in my line of work.

'Very well, Major Hochstetter. I have no doubt we will talk again when that situation changes.'

Hochstetter asked for my pistol to be returned and watched them leave.

'Why am I under Wehrmacht custody?' I asked him.

'You are not. I merely wanted to get you away from the clutches of the SD and the Gestapo. I see by your face that you are already well aware that they are the perfect combination of zealotry, ignorance and unfettered malevolence.' Hochstetter checked the magazine in my gun and calmly pointed it at my chest. 'I have warned you, Édouard, do not make me angry. We had an agreement. Leave Hauptmann Weber to me. I will tell you how and when you may pursue him. Otherwise, I will withdraw my cooperation.'

I looked down at the gun and back up at him. My expression was calm. 'Is it me you're following, or Weber?'

'Both.' His eyes betrayed both surprise and disappointment at my lack of concern. Lowering his arm with an unsure frown, he turned the pistol around and gave it to me handle first.

'I want to know what happened to the French soldiers.'

'In due course, Édouard. Now go home, you need to cool down.'

I did exactly as I was told. Almost.

In his arrogance, Hochstetter's driver pulled out in front of a cyclist, who forgot herself and rang her bell angrily. The sound of it echoed in my ears as the vision vanished in the streets. Staring, I left my hand on the car door, unable to move. The sudden image came to me of the young girl on the bike who'd dropped her teddy bear and of Madame Benoit's kitchen cupboard.

Underlying everything, Weber's words about his actions

in Poland and in Bydgoszcz were still fizzing around in my head like a loose firecracker. In a heartbeat, I'd gone from merely wanting to believe Fryderyk had evidence of what had happened to hoping that maybe he did have something that we'd all missed. If I'd believed that Fryderyk had really had any evidence, I'd expected it to be hidden in the contents of the safe, but perhaps I had to look beyond that. For the first time, I wondered if Fryderyk had sold us a double-bluff, the safe and its contents a distraction.

'She's gone shopping for food,' the concierge's husband told me when I got to Fryderyk's building.

'She'll be gone some time, then.'

He grunted. He was standing in the corridor in blue work trousers and a white singlet over his coarsely haired shoulders. 'I'm minding the store because I don't know what's happening with my job. I'm at the Renault factory in Billancourt. The Boches haven't told us whether we've still got work or not. If we do, it'll probably be building tanks for the bastards.'

I sympathised with him. 'I've come for Jan's bear. It's in the kitchen cupboard.'

He looked surprised. 'My wife will be upset.'

He fetched it for me and I drove my silent passenger back to my flat rather than Thirty-Six. Monsieur Henri was outside his front door.

'The British chopped off French soldiers' hands at Dunkirk to stop them getting on their boats,' he told me earnestly.

'And I saw Hitler taking a walk in the woods yesterday.'

'Piffle.' He snorted and retreated into his flat.

'No one wants the truth,' I muttered, climbing the stairs with Jan's bear hidden under my jacket.

Locking the front door, I went to the kitchen and took a sharp knife out of the drawer.

'Sorry, Jan.'

I slit the bear along the seams and pulled the two sides apart.

I put the remains of Jan's bear down on the kitchen table and looked at what I'd found. Numb, I opened my old bottle of whisky and poured a small shot into a glass and drank it. Sitting down, I looked at what lay on the table in front of me. At what Jan's bear had revealed.

Nothing.

Just the stuffing.

No papers, no photographs, no film.

I searched through the carcass again, pulling the wadding apart between my fingers, but I found nothing. I'd gone through every part of the toy, even the glass eyes, but Fryderyk hadn't used it to hide anything. Angry and unwilling to give up, I said sorry to Jan for the tenth time and carried on shredding the stuffing, tearing it into ever smaller parts, the fluff snowing down on me, covering my hair and face, until there was nothing left to destroy.

'Well, did you or didn't you have any evidence, Fryderyk?'

I looked down at the debris in front of me, my anger instantly calming. Slowly, I swept all of the parts up and put them into the kitchen drawer, out of sight. I sat in silence for several moments before suddenly standing up and brushing all the wadding off me, needing to get away.

Before leaving home again, I remembered to hide the Luger in its place in the bathroom, its magazine filled with live bullets. My three guns were where they belonged, but little was right with the world. I checked the flat before leaving. I was getting used to the chaos. I even liked the dirty glass gathering dust on the coffee table.

Subdued, I drove across the river to the Bristol and parked, a luxury I'd never have attempted in normal times. Ronson was at a table in the bar talking to some other American journalists, three men and a woman. She came and sat with me, choosing a table as far away as possible from her competition.

'Jesus, Eddie, you have more cuts and bruises every time I see you.'

'There's a war on.'

'I see why you're a cop. You heard the other news? There isn't a war on. The armistice has been signed. You guys have officially surrendered to the Germans.'

I recalled Hitler in Compiègne and how he must have left his generals to go over the fine details of the humiliation that he'd started in the railway carriage. I took a deep drink of the whisky that Ronson had ordered for me.

'Anyway, where were you last night?' she asked me. She saw my look of puzzlement. 'You were supposed to come and pick me up so we could tidy your apartment, drink that whisky.'

I pointed to my face. 'This happened.' I told her something of the events at the railway yard. I didn't tell her about Jean-Luc. 'The Germans aren't letting us know where our soldiers are or their names or how many of them were killed.'

'And you want me to dig around and shame them into re-leasing that information or I'll send the story to the States?'

'You should be a journalist, you're quite good at this.' I drank another draught of whisky to hide my concern for my son.

'Consider it done, Eddie. I'll get onto Hochstetter.'

'Don't say I told you about this. I'm in his bad books. I went to see Weber and Biehl showed up while I was there. So did Hochstetter.'

Ronson stared at me, her face darkening. 'Are you fucking crazy? What are you playing at?' Her erstwhile companions looked across and she lowered her voice. 'We're this close,

Eddie. *This* close to showing the world what the Nazis are getting up to. This close to the end of Hitler's Reich. And you jeopardise it by chasing after Weber for a handful of Poles and evidence that might not exist. Tell me you're not fucking crazy.'

'I don't know what I am. I know Weber's evidence has to get out.' She looked triumphant but I cut her short. 'But I also know I'm this close to finding who killed the Poles and stopping them from killing them again. That's my job.'

'You're quite something, Eddie, you know that?' She drained her glass. 'Jesus, you're annoying. But I can never stay mad at you long. Come on, let's go clean your apartment before curfew starts.'

'How could it possibly get any better? House cleaning on a Saturday night under German occupation.'

'It'll be fun.' She punched me on the arm. It was about the one part of me that wasn't bruised.

We drove in separate cars, Ronson in her flashy Renault with WH plates in case she was out after curfew. Monsieur Henri wasn't on the landing when we climbed the stairs to my flat. I told Ronson what she'd missed.

'Pity. Must be fun hearing his stories every day.'

I opened my door to find a light coming from the living room. I hurried inside.

'Jean-Luc?'

It wasn't Jean-Luc. It was Lucja. She was injured, bleeding from a wound on her arm.

Auban was with her.

40

'She needs water, Auban.'

Lucja was sitting in my armchair. She was holding a piece of cloth around her left forearm. Blood was steadily seeping through the material and dripping onto the cushion. Her lips were parched but her forehead and cheeks were wet with sweat. Her face was grey. She seemed to be flickering in and out of consciousness. Standing next to her, holding a gun, Auban looked at her.

'She'll keep. What is it with you and Poles, Giral? Like fucking them, do you?' He leered at Lucja. 'I can't say I blame you. She looks pretty ripe for it, doesn't she? But she's still a Pole.'

'You animal,' Ronson said.

Auban pointed the gun at her and back at me. 'Shit, you really do like foreign chicks, don't you, Giral? Something wrong with Frenchwomen?'

'What did you do to her?' I demanded.

'Me? Nothing. She just seems to have got herself shot.'

'The Germans.' We all turned on hearing Lucja's weak voice. 'They found us.'

'What is it you want, Auban?'

'Next time you try killing someone, Giral, make sure they're dead. But then we all know you never really had it in you. I was just keeping an eye on you, that's all. Watching your flat this evening when this lovely lady showed up. Told her I'd help her up the stairs. And I did.'

'Who told you to keep an eye on me? Biehl?'

'Well done. You finally got there. So who is she, Giral? I can see she's a Pole, but who is she? I reckon Biehl would be pretty interested in knowing that too. So why don't I call him and ask him to come on over?'

'The books have gone.' Lucja spoke again, her voice more distant.

'She's been saying that for the last hour. What does she mean? Something else I reckon Biehl would want to know.'

'Why Biehl, Auban?'

'Because like me, he wants you gone, Giral. And me in your place. Someone friendly who'll know the right thing to do.'

'So why doesn't he just kill me and have done? Instead of this set-up with Groves?'

Lucja groaned about the books again but Auban ignored her. 'Because Biehl sees you as Hochstetter's man. Not even the Gestapo would want to have to answer those questions if they just killed you. Their way's much more satisfactory. I can just see you in Fresnes surrounded by all the criminals you've put there. It was so sweet, it landed in our lap. Hochstetter's mechanic gave me your gun when they returned your car. They thought it was normal police practice and just handed it over to me.'

'I take it Biehl was responsible for this as well.' I gestured at the mess in my flat.

'Yup, I told them you had nothing worth finding.'

Lucja groaned with pain. Her eyes were glazed, all focus gone.

'For Christ's sake, Auban, she needs water. If she dies, you've got nothing to show Biehl.'

He looked at Lucja and at Ronson. 'You, go and get her some water.' Ronson made for the kitchen, but Auban stopped her. 'Think I'm stupid?' He pointed with the gun at the dirty glass on the coffee table. 'Too many knives in the kitchen. Use the glass there and go into the bathroom.'

Ronson glanced at me before doing as she was told. Auban tried to keep an eye on her, but I moved forward and he turned his attention back to me, threatening me with the pistol. I heard Ronson turn the tap and the glass being filled. She came back, the drink held out in her left hand. Tripping slightly as she approached Lucja's chair, some of the water spilled over. Auban instinctively put his gun hand up and it faced away from Lucja. Ronson quickly raised her right hand from her side. In it, she was holding the Luger. She held it to Auban's head.

'Put the gun down,' she told him.

Before he had time to think what to do, I reached forward and took his pistol from his grasp. Ronson grinned. 'So that's what the Luger's for.'

I pointed Auban's gun at him and I told him to sit down on the other armchair, his hands underneath him. I pulled my own service pistol out and put Auban's on the table by Lucja. Auban looked at one to the other of us and laughed.

'Come on, Giral, you know you haven't got the spine to kill. You're a joke. We've laughed at you for years. That railway worker in '25, we all know you didn't do it, but you were so fucked up, you thought you were to blame.'

'Shut up, Auban.'

'Or what? You couldn't kill then, you can't kill now. You're weak. You knew it couldn't have been you that killed the guy, but you went along with it instead of standing up for yourself. And you've been taking it up the arse ever since.'

'I'm warning you.'

The gun in my hand was shaking, my finger squeezing tighter on the trigger. The explosion of the gunshot was magnified in the room deafening me. I looked at my hand in shock. My gun hadn't been fired. I looked at Lucja, still holding Auban's gun. She'd picked it up and pointed it at his head, squeezing the trigger in one fluid movement. It ruined the upholstery on my spare chair. It didn't do Auban much good, either.

Her eyes tired but more alert than she'd made out, Lucja spoke in a low voice. 'Pray these people never take over your country. Pray the Nazis do not behave in your country like they have done in mine.'

'Holy shit,' Ronson said, looking at the mess that was Auban.

'She still needs water,' I said.

Ronson put the Luger down and gently eased some of the water from the glass between Lucja's lips. Lucja coughed, spluttering up a little of it. I knelt down and felt her cheeks. They were burning.

'I'm all right. I'm not as bad as I made out.'

'She's still bad,' Ronson said. 'She needs treatment straightaway. I know where we can go.'

'What about Auban?'

Ronson glanced over at him. 'Jozef. His lot will come and clean up. They do a pretty good laundry collection service. I'll call them when we get to where we're going.'

'Can they be trusted?'

'Believe me, Eddie, they'll sort this out. Hell, they might even tidy the place.'

I looked at Lucja, raw and restless on her chair, and I turned to Auban. His was a different type of raw, seeping now onto my floorboards. I looked away. A tired and frightened refugee had killed a fellow cop in front of me and I didn't know how I felt about it.

'Come on, Eddie, we've got to move.' Ronson clucked at me. 'We've got half an hour until curfew. We'll take my car. WH plates.'

She drove us steadily through the darkening streets and enfolding blackout as far as Neuilly-sur-Seine, on the north-eastern fringe of the city. It wasn't somewhere I knew well. It wasn't the Paris of gangs and killings for petty reasons that I dealt with but one of shading trees and clean grass, orderly avenues and light-coloured buildings. Lucja was talking more normally now, but her breathing was ragged with the pain. Ronson turned the car into a gateway and pulled up in a courtyard.

'The American Hospital. I'll go on in.'

She returned with a doctor and a nurse before I'd managed to get Lucja out of the car and we carried her into the building. Two men who were leaning against the wall ran over and helped carry her along a corridor to a room. After she'd gone in, Ronson and I sat outside and waited. The two men who'd helped came back along the corridor towards us. They were an odd-looking pair, both wearing ill-fitting and mismatched clothes that looked like they'd been found in the bottom of a forgotten wardrobe. They approached us and spoke to Ronson in English. I only caught bits of what they were saying. One of them said something that made Ronson's jaw drop open in astonishment. She turned to me and translated what they'd told her.

'They're British soldiers. Ambulance crew with the British Expeditionary Force. They got cut off from their unit before they could get to Dunkirk, so they drove south instead, one step ahead of the Germans all the time. In the end they made it to Paris and found their way to this place and now they're stuck. They've been sheltering here ever since, working as nurses and general dogsbodies until they work out how to get out of here.'

One of them said something to her about an ambulance and she laughed.

'And their ambulance, a British Army ambulance, is parked in one of the outhouses here. They want to get out of the city and head north, to the coast, and get a boat back to Britain. I told them that that route is impossible. The Germans are all the way between here and the north and all along the coast. They'll never make it. I said their best bet is to head south, down through France and Spain as far as Lisbon. There are still boats going from there.'

'Isn't Spain risky?'

'It's neutral for now, and refugees are still getting through, but yeah. Franco's not quite in bed with Hitler, but they're kindred spirits, so the drawbridge might go up at any time.'

I looked at the two men and shrugged. They smiled ruefully at me. We heard footsteps and saw the doctor walking towards us. This time he realised I was there and spoke French.

'We'll keep an eye on her overnight. The gunshot wound was superficial, but she's weak and there may be an infection, although she's not in any danger. The fever should go down in the next day or so.'

I asked if I could see her again before I left and he showed me the way to her room. She was asleep, stacked up on pillows under fine white sheets. The nurse who'd come to the car was sitting with her.

She looked calmer than in any moment since I'd known her. The tension in her face had fallen away. I replayed the moment she shot Auban and her words afterwards and I could only imagine what she must have seen that would make her kill him so calmly. I knew I could never judge her. I had been so close to squeezing the trigger myself.

'You saved me,' I whispered to her.

41

'I had to square it with Jozef that the information I had wasn't about Poland.'

'Right.'

'So they'll probably trash your apartment even more.'

'Right.'

'You're not listening to me, Eddie.'

She was driving us back into the city from the American Hospital.

'Can you drop me off on the Right Bank? There's something I need to do.'

'What about the curfew?'

'I'm a cop, I've got ID.'

She let me out at the address I gave her and drove off. 'Try not to fall in the river, Eddie, you're away in your own world.'

Dax was surprised to see me. I'd climbed the stairs to his flat deep in thought after everything Auban had said. He fetched a bottle of brandy and two glasses and we sat at his kitchen table.

'You live alone?'

'My wife left me. A long time ago. Is this about Auban?'

'No, I don't know anything about Auban. It's about the guy we killed in 1925.'

He looked panicked. 'For Christ's sake, Eddie, that's ancient history. We have a mutually assured guarantee. Maybe it was me that killed him, but you were off your head on drugs. We got away with it. Why are you bringing it up now?'

'Because it isn't ancient history. Because of that one time, I go along with everything you want. I argue with you, but when push comes to shove, you know I haven't got a leg to stand on.'

'Neither of us does, Eddie. That's how this works. We keep each other in check.'

'That's not how this works. You've always had the upper hand. Until now.' I leaned forward and stared into his face. 'I know you're bent.'

'What the hell are you on about?'

'What I want to know is if that extends to the promise to get people out of the city. Are you involved in the deaths of the four Poles and of the *poilus* last night?'

'You don't know the trouble you're creating for yourself, Eddie. We'll talk about this on Monday.'

'When you argued with Hochstetter about the railway workers being handed over to the Germans, I thought you were doing your job. But then, Papin was released without charge.'

'Auban signed the release form.'

'No, he didn't. You signed it in his name. Auban wasn't even in Thirty-Six when Papin was released. You've been protecting him, and probably Font too. And I want to know if that extends to helping them with the refugee racket.'

Dax poured us another brandy each, his expression thoughtful. 'I grew up near the Gare d'Austerlitz. I was in a gang before I became a cop, and that's what saved me. I've done some wrong things, God knows, you'll know that better than anyone. But I'm not bent. I ran with their fathers, Font and Papin's. I don't protect them, I look out for them.'

'What's the difference?'

'The difference is I'm not on the take and I'm not involved in any murders of refugees or plans to con *poilus*. And neither are Font and Papin. They're low-level thieves and fences, like I was when I was a kid, but they're not involved in this. If they were, believe me, I'd be the first to give them a good beating and haul them in.' He gave me a pointed look. 'If anyone understands turning a blind eye, it's you.'

I took a deep draught of his brandy. 'And I'll continue to turn a blind eye, but only when it suits me. You're still protecting criminals and I now have that on you. We're equal. You no longer hold sway over me.'

'You're changing, Eddie. You're becoming the cop I heard stories about back in the day.'

I got up to leave. 'If we're going to have a hope of surviving any of this, we're going to have to find worse versions of ourselves. I don't like it any more than you're going to.'

I crossed the river on foot, the Metro long since closed for the night, but there were no German patrols in sight to stop me. In many ways, they were here, but they weren't here. The question was going to be knowing how to play the game understanding that those were the rules now.

I opened my flat door to find the light on. When Ronson had told me at the hospital that Jozef would be dealing with Auban's body and my apartment, I'd told her they'd need a key.

She'd looked at me sympathetically. 'Believe me, Eddie, they won't need a key.'

It was immaculate. You'd never have known a man had been killed in the living room just a few hours earlier. I checked the armchairs and the wall behind and I found nothing. The cushions felt softer than they had in years. They were certainly cleaner. Jozef and his team had even put all the books back on the shelf. I'd consider having someone killed here every spring if this was the service.

Quickly, I checked the books. The Céline one was there, the pamphlet still inside the front cover. Oddly, the thought of Poles who'd had to flee their country finding it while they'd cleaned up made me feel grubby, even though it wasn't mine. I thought of the two Polish books that Lucja had taken on Wednesday, Ewa's textbook and the novel printed by Fryderyk's company, both now gone. The Luger was on the low table. I checked the magazine was full and took it through to the bathroom, returning it to its hiding place.

I realised by the sounds coming from the kitchen that some-one was still working in there. I went through to tell them they could go.

'Jean-Luc.'

My son was at the stove, making an omelette with the eggs that Ronson had left on Friday morning. I watched him but he wouldn't face me. I was shocked at how much like his mother he looked just then, and I felt the same loss and love that I felt the day I left them both when he was a child. He was my son. He could have been the one thing that was precious to me if only I'd known how to cope with the one thing that wasn't – myself. I reached for him, but he recoiled.

'I'm sorry, Jean-Luc.'

I tried again to embrace him, but he pushed me away. I saw for the first time that his trousers were badly ripped, evidence of what had happened last night, and I found it strangely sadder than his coldness towards me. I wanted him to say something, if only to curse me, but his mouth was closed in the obstinate line I hadn't seen for fifteen years.

'I was trying to help,' I told him. 'I thought I was doing the right thing.'

'How did the Germans know we were there?' His voice crackled like the oil spitting in the pan.

I sat down heavily and looked at him. 'I told them.'

He looked at me in disbelief. 'You told them? Because of you, French soldiers got killed. I saw five lying dead, because of you. Most of the others were taken prisoner, because of you. God knows what'll happen to them. Are you proud of that, Father?'

The first time he called me 'Father' and it was intended to hurt. I watched him make the omelette, each flip of the eggs a gesture of rage.

'I asked for your help and you didn't give it,' he went on. 'I tried to tell you what I was going to do and you betrayed me. Me and other *poilus* trying to do our duty. What is it? Are you ashamed because you've sold out? I'm glad now that you disowned me all those years ago. I disown you.'

'I didn't disown you, Jean-Luc.' I didn't know what more I could say about that. 'I was trying to save you.'

He turned his back on me to watch the omelette. I could smell it burning. I stared at his shoulders and thought of what I could tell him. That I'd been terrified that if I hadn't told the Germans about his plan to escape, I'd possibly be investigating his murder right now. That even though I was certain of that, the doubt still assailed me that I'd done the right thing. That I'd tried to prevent a greater evil the only way I could see how, by committing a lesser evil. And that I would always question whether my decision saved his life and that of others, or it had most of them captured or killed. It was one more choice in my life I would have to live with.

I would also have to live with knowing that his stubbornness in insisting on paying someone to get him out of the city had helped get his friends taken prisoner. And killed. And that if there was one thing I could never make him live with, it was that.

'I had nowhere else to go tonight,' he said, 'otherwise you would never have seen me again.'

'What are you going to do? Will you try and get to your mother in Perpignan?'

He ate the omelette standing up, evidently reluctant to share a table with me.

'I want to get to Britain. I heard Brigadier General de Gaulle talking on the radio tonight and he made sense. We have to carry on the fight against the Nazis, not give in like Pétain. And others. I won't stand and watch while they kill more refugees with chlorine gas. And I won't let you stop me.'

I couldn't disagree with him. 'I won't stop you, Jean-Luc. Paris is no good for you. But, please, just promise me you won't put yourself in the hands of someone you don't know to get out of the city.'

He stabbed at the food on his plate. 'I'm going to head for Brittany and get a boat over to Britain. Join the Free French. I don't want to be like everyone else under the Nazis. Everyone lives with a clenched fist in their pocket but does nothing about it. But I'm going to. I didn't stop the Germans when they broke through our lines. I'm going to stop them now.'

I remembered Ronson's words to the two British ambulance men. 'The coast is too dangerous. Especially the north. It's the first place the Germans will secure to prevent the British from attacking. I've heard that boats are still leaving from Lisbon.'

'Lisbon? How do I get to Lisbon?' He sat down finally and looked at me. 'What will you do?'

I had nothing I could say to him, even though I knew what I had to do. I had to stay here and make sure we didn't become monsters. Even if it meant becoming one myself.

'It's time we slept.'

I wished him goodnight and watched him go to the spare bedroom. A long mac I hadn't seen before was on the kitchen chair and I went to get it for him. It was heavy. I hefted the right-hand pocket and took a pistol out. An army one, an officer's, not one a *poilu* would have. I left it where it was and closed my bedroom door behind me.

I slept. In my bed. Without nightmares. Even though my son hated me, I was safe because he was with me.

Sunday 5th July 1925

I looked in Jean-Luc's eyes and I saw the reflection of a monster. I was no longer safe with him.

'Come on,' Sylvie called to him as she opened the front door.

They were going to the park for Jean-Luc to play. I watched them go and stared at the closed door for what seemed an age. Neither of them had turned to say goodbye. Silently, I roamed the flat, picking up clothes and books. There was little to show. My old army kitbag was by the door. Finally, I took down an old tin box I kept at the back of the wardrobe and placed it in the bag before closing it.

Going into Jean-Luc's room, I breathed in the clean air of a child and looked at his bed. I kissed the fingers on my right hand and let them rest on his pillow one last time before turning away. In the hallway, I left my keys on the table and closed the door behind me.

In my new home on the Left Bank, I sat in twilight in one of the two armchairs and sipped my whisky thoughtfully. This would not be a place for white powder. I'd rented the place on the spur of the moment the day before and now I was sitting here alone for the first time. The contents of the kitbag lay on the other chair and in the smaller bedroom I'd promised myself Jean-Luc would sleep in one day. I closed my eyes in shame when I thought of him. And of Sylvie. I knew now that I loved her.

I hadn't hit her on Thursday night. I'd had one of my dark descents and raised my hand, more in fear than in anger, but I hadn't touched her. One last trace of good in me. But I knew that because of my fears, I was a danger, first and foremost to myself, and because of that, to Sylvie and Jean-Luc. Not physically perhaps but in every other way. I looked around my empty new flat at the loneliest, most desperate decision I'd ever taken and I knew I'd chosen the only path I could.

To distract myself, I picked up the old tin box. Inside, I found something I hadn't looked at since the war. I recoiled instantly. A Luger. There was a shell in the breech. Hesitating, I took it out and examined it, recalling the dullness of the sheen and the small indentation in the metal. In a trance, I reloaded it. I had no idea if it worked or not. I hadn't tried firing the gun since the day I'd taken it off the German officer who was trying to kill me.

Suddenly wanting to get away from it, I went into the kitchen to fetch a glass of water. The pipes hadn't been used for some time and they gurgled before releasing a jet of water that burst out of the tap and over my sleeves and front. Staring at the sink, I heard the echo of a splash and recalled for the hundredth time the sound the water had made two weeks ago, when we'd dumped the man's body in the sewer. I relived it like I'd relived it every day since.

Again, I saw Dax, the inspector, in the blackness in front of me and the iron bar in my hand. In my panic, I'd hit him over the head with it. I'd realised immediately after that it was him. I thought I'd killed him. He'd fallen to the ground with a thump and I'd bent unsteadily over him, the drugs still confusing me. That was when I'd found his revolver. He'd drawn it when we were searching for the suspect.

As I'd tried to understand what I'd done, the other man, the one we'd discovered afterwards was a railway worker, had come towards me in the dark.

'What are you doing?' he'd asked.

'I'm a cop.'

He'd looked down at the inspector lying on the ground. 'You killed him. I saw you.'

'I thought he was a suspect.' My thoughts were still blurred.

'I know him. He's from round here. He's a cop too. What have you done?'

I'd looked at the man for the first time. He was older than me, too old perhaps to have served in the war, his face scored with deep lines. In the bitter light, I'd seen his accusing look. I'd looked back at Dax and tried to think what to do.

'I saw you,' the man had repeated. 'You killed him.'

I'd exhaled, the feel of the cocaine still in my nose. My situation had hit me fully between the eyes.

'Yes, I did, didn't I?'

Standing up straight, I'd turned the gun on the man and fired and watched him fall. The look of surprise on his face had reminded me of the German officer whose Luger I'd taken that day in the trenches. I'd felt the same lack of emotion.

I recalled now dropping the revolver next to Dax. I'd found my own pistol and replaced it in its holster before sitting down. I remembered looking at the two bodies and wondering what I was going to do, all the while rocking back and forth. And then the inspector had come round and we'd argued about the dead man and who'd shot him.

Dax had bullied me into taking my share of the blame. I'd fooled him into believing he had blame to share.

Draining the glass of water I'd poured myself, I went back into the living room and sat down. Holding the gun in front of my face and lifting it to my forehead, I felt the cold of the metal against my skin.

I closed my eyes for the first time and squeezed the trigger in my dark new home.

Sunday 23rd June 1940

Opéra

The gun was gone.

Jean-Luc's coat was no longer over the back of the chair, the gun gone with it. So was he. I wondered like I always did if it was for the last time. I checked his room. His ripped trousers were balled up and thrown to the bedroom floor. Unused to the order in my flat, I moved things back to where I wanted them and untidied the kitchen. I found the remains of Jan's bear in the drawer and quickly closed it again. I had a moment's regret for Madame Benoit and her grandson, another child missing a father.

It was early. Another fractured night's sleep, an image rather than a dream trying to surface in my memory. Even so, I'd missed Jean-Luc leaving. A door quietly closing in my dream had proved to be my son stealing away at dawn before I could stop him.

Someone knocked on the door now. My immediate reaction was that it was to do with Auban. The call that hadn't come for Groves was now coming for Auban, but I opened the door to find two German soldiers on the landing. They were almost a welcome alternative.

'Inspector Giral?' one of them said. 'Please come with us. Do not bring your police firearm.'

Hochstetter's car was waiting for me at the pavement, its roof down in anticipation of the early morning sunlight that never found its way into the depths of my street. The man himself was in the back, hunched against the damp chill of the Seine. A feldwebel sat in the driver seat, an officer next to him. A second staff car, also open-topped, was parked behind it. Obersturmbannführer Biehl was sitting in the back seat.

'How remiss of me,' Hochstetter said. 'I forgot to send you a formal invitation again.'

'Two cars? I'm flattered.'

'Don't be, Édouard, they're not for you.'

I looked around at Biehl. He didn't wave. 'Is the ober-thingy observing?'

'You could say that.'

I didn't answer. Jean-Luc was walking along the other side of the narrow street, just metres away from me. As he passed, the bottom of his mac flapped open briefly and I saw with horror that he was wearing the khaki army trousers he'd been wearing the night he'd arrived, the bloodstains scrubbed but still visible. He saw me and I gave the slightest of shakes of the head. He was smart, he carried on his way. His glance would have looked to anyone like the most natural of curiosity at seeing two German cars in a narrow street. I remembered the young *poilu* who'd been shot and hoped against hope that Hochstetter and his cohort would be too busy to notice my son's uniform trousers. I tried to distract Hochstetter.

'Where are you taking me?'

'The wolf is leaving its gorge again.'

'I am busy, you know. Cryptic Abwehr officers at six o'clock on a Sunday morning do little for my mood.'

He tapped his hand lightly against the top of the door and the car set off, finding its way to Boulevard Saint-Germain and instant floods of sunshine bursting the banks of the tall buildings. Hochstetter uncurled himself from his bundled-up position and closed his eyes to the sun. I didn't dare turn to see if Jean-Luc had got past them all right.

'A splendid morning, don't you think? Perfect for a little sightseeing trip. Although I notice you have yet to change your watch to Berlin time. I do expect you to rectify that at some point on today's outing.'

We crossed the river and turned onto Rue de Rivoli, a strange pulsing echo bouncing back to the car as we drove past the gaps in the arcades. Because of the hour and the German-vehicles-only rule on Sundays, we had the city to ourselves. Hochstetter wasn't giving any instructions and we weren't heading for the Lutétia, so the driver obviously knew where he was supposed to be taking us. I found it oddly depressing that a lot of the Germans had already learned their way around the city. We finally pulled up on Place de l'Opéra, to the side of the opera house, and the driver cut the engine. A hush fell over us after the sound died away and I looked around. More German military cars were parked in the square.

'What are we doing here?'

'You will see, Édouard.'

Another open-topped car drove up from the rear of the opera house and slowed in front of the ornate building. As it did, a soldier who was perched on the edge of the rear seat jumped down and ran forward to open the car door. The vehicle was packed and all the occupants seemed to be queuing to get out, each one swathed in an army coat. There was still a chill in the air at this time of the morning. I wished I'd had a warmer jacket on. As the swarm emerging from the car opened out to reveal the individual members, I couldn't help letting out a gasp.

'I thought you might want an opportunity to see your hero again,' Hochstetter commented.

More senior German officers converged on the group from the car as a further four sedans pulled up in the square and they all crowded around the central figure of Adolf Hitler before hurrying up the steps and into the building. Other officers and NCOs shoved at each other to get closer.

'I know you were in Compiègne on Friday,' Hochstetter added.

'Why the wolf and the gorge?'

'Because the Führer's headquarters in Belgium is known as the Wolf's Gorge. He has left the safety of the gorge to visit his latest spoils of war. He has suddenly decided at the very last minute that he wants to see Paris. An impromptu sightseeing tour.'

I turned my gaze back to the opera house. Hitler's group was inside and there was nothing to be seen.

'Why have you brought me here?'

'I told you, so you could renew your acquaintance with the Führer. From afar, of course. And because I want to keep you close, Édouard, in case you have some notion of trying to uphold the law. I would never allow that on a day such as this. If you look around you, you might see someone else you know.' He gestured at a car on the other side of the square, facing the opera house. I could see Weber in the driver's seat. I didn't tell Hochstetter, but beyond Weber's car, I also saw a smaller car, with Müller and Schmidt in the front seats. 'Security. The Armistice doesn't come into effect until Tuesday, so there's always the possibility that some hothead might try to snatch some glory by making an assassination attempt on the Führer.'

I felt an intake of breath from the other occupants of the car and I turned to see Hitler hurrying down the steps out of the opera house. He strode determinedly across the pavement amid a bevy of shining officers and scattering NCOs in dull forage caps. His eyes didn't move once from the course he was taking, his soldiers clearing his path so he didn't have to stop or look or consider anyone or anything of the streets and people he now owned. Quickly, he climbed into the front seat of his car. The roof remained down. He was evidently more confident about his popularity in Paris than Hochstetter was.

On the other side of the road, a man and a woman with a dog on a lead went past, wheeling a little cart. They turned to look at the group but didn't react. I wondered if they'd recognised who was in the car.

Hochstetter ordered his driver to wait until Weber's car had passed and to follow it. I turned in my seat to see other cars take their place in line, while yet more turned down different roads. They must have known the route Hitler would be taking. We followed Weber at a short distance behind the convoy.

'We are following Hauptmann Weber,' Hochstetter commented, 'to ensure that everything goes smoothly today.'

I watched in silence as the party ahead of us stopped at the Madeleine and everyone scrambled out of the car and into the church, almost immediately scurrying back out again.

'Not to Adolf's taste?' I wondered out loud.

Hochstetter gave a half-smile but I saw the officer in the front seat bristling. In movement again, Hitler's party drove round Place de la Concorde, Hitler standing up in his seat to get a better view. Two uniformed cops saluted in surprise and a skinny priest in long black robes hurried by, his head resolutely down. I suddenly realised that there were no journalists, like there had been in Compiègne, no foreign press corps or film cameras or radio. Just an official German crew taking footage. I commented on it to Hochstetter.

'We wouldn't want a skewed version of this event to reach the world, would we?'

'Heaven forbid.'

I had to confess that there was a part of me that was horribly fascinated by what I was witnessing. We suddenly jolted to a halt at the start of the Champs-Élysées, throwing us forward then back in our seats. I quickly looked ahead to see if someone was doing us all a favour, but Hitler was only too well. He'd evidently ordered his driver to stop and was standing up in his seat once more, gazing around.

We started off again, driving past a closed cinema. It was advertising an American film that no one would be going to see anymore since they'd all left in the exodus: *Going Places*. A little further on, Hitler's car was already passing another boarded-up cinema advertising another Hollywood movie: *You Can't Take It With You.*

'Am I the only one to see the irony?' I asked.

Hochstetter shook his head in mild amusement, but the officer in front turned to glare at me. We reached the top in time to see the huge Benz sedan carrying Hitler stop on Place de l'Étoile and the tour party pile out yet again. Hitler, his hands clasped behind his back, was reading the inscriptions on the arch, but in our car, I was the only one looking the other way. One street over from where we'd pulled up, Jean-Luc sat astride a motorbike. That worried me enough. The glimpse I caught of the gun partially hidden under his coat terrified me. I looked back from him to Hitler standing underneath the Arc de Triomphe, partly clad in scaffolding, and I began to shake. I recalled my son's words about being a soldier who hadn't en-gaged the enemy and my mind raced, scared at every possibility for his presence that came to me.

Jean-Luc saw me, his face impassive. I had to keep all

expression off my own, although my fellow travellers were rapt in the sight of their Führer, even Hochstetter, despite his air of bored worldliness. Casting my glance around while trying to work out what I should do, I registered that there were no other cars near us. Weber's vehicle was on the other side of the square, just visible to one side of the arch. Biehl's car was a short distance behind ours. I had no idea where the two Gestapo men were. Looking back, I saw Jean-Luc turning the throttle on the bike.

Not knowing exactly what I was going to do, but with the three Germans distracted by the sight of a small man with an odd moustache standing underneath an arch, I stood up quickly and jumped out of the side of the car. Landing on the balls of my feet, I was up and running moments before Hochstetter noticed what I was doing. I ran towards Jean-Luc, but he was already picking up speed. He saw me and suddenly looked un-decided. He veered away from his course and turned away from the square. I could have stopped and danced with joy.

Looking back over my shoulder, I saw Hochstetter staring at me, an expression of distilled anger breaking his urbane calm. The officer in the front seat made to get out and give chase, but Hochstetter put his hand up to stop him. He wouldn't want to draw any attention to what was going on while Hitler was in town. I'd been counting on that.

I carried on running and was quickly swallowed up by the side streets off the square. I couldn't find Jean-Luc. Behind me, I heard a car engine gunning. I ran down another street, Rue Lord Byron, and had the sudden absurd idea that he'd approve. I almost laughed in the adrenaline rush. I heard the car that was giving chase overshoot the road and slam the brakes on, then the high-pitched whine as it reversed at speed. It would be on me in a few moments, and I had no idea where Jean-Luc had gone. I looked around for a doorway I could disappear into. Finding nowhere, I took a left, where a doorway beckoned, but before I could reach it, I heard the car pull up alongside me. I stopped, realising it was no good.

I looked over. It wasn't Hochstetter's. The passenger door was thrown open.

'Get in,' a voice called to me.

Arc de Triomphe

'America's finally come to the rescue,' I commented.

'You call that a thank you?'

Ronson picked up speed straightaway and turned deeper into the streets off the Champs-Élysées, anxiously looking in her mirror all the time.

'I think you're driving the wrong way. Hope there are no cops around.'

She turned to look at me and then back at the road. 'You're a piece of work, Eddie, you know that?'

The sound of her words faded as I had a fleeting moment of realisation. The Place de l'Étoile. The star from which all roads emanated. I'd have to come back to that thought. If we ever survived Ronson's driving. Stopping suddenly outside the Chamber of Commerce, she turned the car to face the entrance into the garden at the rear of the building. Inching slowly up against the gate, she forced the doors apart by breaking the central lock and drove through the gap.

'That'll do the paintwork good,' I told her.

'It's Gestapo or paintwork. I know which one I'm taking.'

Inside, we both jumped out and pushed the gates closed behind us. I held my breath and leaned forward against the wall, bowed at the waist. I saw Ronson listen out for any movement the other side. We soon heard a car prowl slowly past. It had evidently lost me and was cruising the streets to pick me up again. It didn't stop.

'Hochstetter,' I finally said, getting my breath back.

Ronson shook her head. 'He didn't move. It was two guys in plain clothes who were after you. They looked like Gestapo.'

'Well, that's a relief. I'd hate to upset the major.'

Ronson looked at me and let out a roar of laughter, quickly covering her mouth with her hands. I looked down and began to laugh too, the sound coming out in gasps as my breath returned in waves of sharp pain down the length of my throat. We let the Gestapo and the laughter pass and Ronson carefully opened the gates and looked up and down the street before we got back into the car and drove slowly out.

'Drive the right way this time.' I had to strain to listen as I was crouching, hidden in the well behind the passenger seat. 'Where are we going?'

'I've arranged to meet Weber at some point on Adolf's Parisian holiday. He telephoned me in the wee small hours to tell me that Hitler was going to be in town. Adolf's decided that now Paris is one of his toys, he wants to play with it, so last night he told them the places he wanted to visit. The Germans have spent half the night dragging curators out of their beds to hand over the keys so they can let him in. The problem for us is, it's spooked Weber, said I had to get him out now or never. He's afraid Hochstetter's on to him.'

'How do you know the route?'

'Weber told me. He's been assigned to the security detail, so he knows the itinerary. We've got meeting points all along the route. I've got to keep trailing Weber and he's going to make his move when he thinks he can and meet me at the first possible rendezvous. He's got the *Sonderaktionsbuch* on him. I'm going to get him out of the city and down as far as Lisbon and he's going to give me the list.'

'And you don't find that strange? He thinks Hochstetter's on to him but they still trust him with Hitler's itinerary.'

I saw Ronson turn to face me and look quickly back at the road ahead. 'What are you trying to say, Eddie?'

'You're being set up.'

I was tumbled about in the rear well as Ronson took a corner sharply, the gears crunching. 'Jesus, Eddie, not now.'

'The *Sonderaktionsbuch* is a fake. Weber was supposedly in disgrace but he still had access to it. Don't you find that odd?'

'He found it, Eddie, he found it. In Berlin. He didn't have access to it, he just found it, for Christ's sake. Why would it be a set-up?' A second sheer turn crashed me into the hard metal of the side wall. 'The SD killed Groves. That proves it's real.'

'You heard Auban last night. Groves was killed by Biehl with Auban's help to get me out of the way. It was nothing to do with Weber's list. And Auban planted my gun in the evidence room yesterday.'

'What do you mean he planted your gun?'

'It was the one used to kill Groves.'

'Tell me, Eddie, we are on the same side, aren't we? So you're telling me Weber's made this up just so he can get out of Europe?'

'I don't even think he wants that. There's something more going on here. Weber's a Nazi, a believer. I can't see why he would think Germany's going to lose. It's too glib. He comes across this information in Berlin by chance, when he's supposed to be under a cloud, and he waits until he's in Paris to bargain with it. I don't get it.'

'Do you know what it's like in Berlin, Eddie? Sure, they're dancing in the streets at all the victories they're racking up, but there are rumours. Stories of what exactly went on in Poland are getting back to Berlin and no one knows what to believe. I spoke to a family in Berlin whose son committed suicide the day he returned to the city. He told them he was ashamed to be German and then he shot himself in the zoo gardens with his army Luger. The Nazis made them say he was murdered by a Jew. There's a story to be told, Eddie, and it could save so many more lives.'

'I know there's a story to be told.'

She was silent for a moment before answering. 'You're still after this Polish guy's evidence, aren't you? That's why you don't want to believe in Weber's.'

I was quiet. Partly because I knew she was right. Looking up, I could see the tops of buildings floating past outside the window. I felt the car slow down and stop. Ronson spoke again.

'We're going to have to talk about this after. We're coming to the next place on Hitler's wish list. The Palais de Chaillot.' Her tone changed to one of wonder. 'This is so strange. Adolf Hitler's driving round the tourist sights of Paris in an open-topped car, and there's barely anyone around. No one knows he's here.' I heard the car door open and Ronson got out. 'Stay there.'

Stretching up to look out of the window, I saw Hitler walking on to the terrace before disappearing down the few steps to the belvedere overlooking the Seine and the Eiffel Tower beyond. When the Germans had entered Paris, the lifts to the top of the tower had been sabotaged, so they'd had to hike all the way up to plant a giant swastika. Within days, the summer winds had torn it to rags, so they'd had to go up again and leave a much smaller one. It was so small, you couldn't see it from the ground. It was like old man Eiffel was getting his own back.

Looking around, I was horrified to see Jean-Luc slowly riding past without seeing me. I called his name but the window was shut. I got out of the car and walked after him, fighting the urge to run. He pulled further away from me. There were some French civilians around now, early risers not quite believing what they were seeing, but we were greatly outnumbered by the Germans fawning over their Führer. I saw Jean-Luc get off his bike and lean against the wall on the other side of the terrace from me. The raincoat he wore was much too big for him and fell almost to his feet. The mercy was it hid his army trousers. I tried to get nearer but there weren't so many people out of uniform that I could have lost myself in the crowd, and I was on the wrong side of the square from Jean-Luc, mainly because Hochstetter was between me and him. And he was looking at me, his face barely containing his anger. I think I preferred the calm amusement. I saw him look around, but he couldn't come and get me as he daren't make a scene. That was all that was saving me right now.

I looked at where Hitler was standing. He'd changed his coat from the heavy one he was wearing earlier to a fetching muddy brown mac as the sun rose and the day got warmer. A photographer and a film cameraman were setting up in front of him as he prepared his pose with his latest toy.

Looking back towards Jean-Luc, I saw he hadn't moved, but I could no longer see Hochstetter. I was about to head for where my son was standing, when a hand grabbed my arm and pulled me back.

'Are you mad, Eddie?' Ronson whispered. 'I told you to stay in the car.' Despite her anger, the journalist in her was enthralled by the events around her. She pointed to the two uniformed clones either side of Hitler. 'Speer and Breker. An architect and a sculptor. They've got plans for Paris.'

'We don't have our own?' It's funny how the small things annoy you the most.

As we spoke, we noticed the low tide of people turn back towards us. Hitler was on the move again and we were swept along in the entourage ahead of him, clearing his way. I kept watch on Jean-Luc, but he stood back against the wall as Hitler and his inner circle passed him by. I exchanged a glance with him. He looked straight at me but gave away no flicker of expression.

Ronson caught hold of me more urgently. 'Come on, Eddie, we've got to go.'

I looked around and spotted Hochstetter making his way laboriously against the surge of sycophants to get to me. Ronson pulled me away and we walked quickly back to her car before the major had got anywhere near us. I climbed in the passenger seat, and Ronson started the engine up. Hitler was already in his car and heading away from the palace. Turning, I saw Jean-Luc get on his motorbike and kick it into life, falling in line to the rear of Hitler's caravan. I knew I had to explain.

'You see the young guy on the motorbike?'

'That's the kid you arrested at the Cheval Noir the other night. What's going on, Eddie?'

'We have to protect him. He's my son.'

Ronson nearly swerved. 'Your son? I didn't know you had a son.'

'It's a long story. The short one is that I think he's going to try and kill Hitler.'

'Jesus Christ, Eddie, are there any more at home like you?' She thumped the steering wheel. 'He won't get within a hundred yards of Hitler. And all he's going to do is complicate matters.'

'He's my son.'

'Ain't he just.'

Les Invalides

'This is it.'

We were crossing the river from Palais de Chaillot for Les Invalides, Ronson had told me. 'The next stop on Hitler's glory trail. I think he wants to make sure Napoleon's dead.'

Weber had thrown a cigarette packet out of his car window and Ronson had shifted in her seat. Once on the Left Bank, she drove along Quai d'Orsay, but when we reached Les Invalides, she headed straight past. I craned around but I couldn't see Jean-Luc.

'Where are we going?'

'Jardin du Luxembourg. Weber's given the signal. The cigarette packet. The gardens were the rendezvous if he was able to make a move after the Palais de Chaillot.'

I looked around desperately for my son. 'We can't. I have to follow Jean-Luc. He's going to get himself killed.'

'Sorry, Eddie, this isn't a family outing. I'm meeting Weber.'

She was driving painfully slowly away from where Jean-Luc would be. Hitler's entourage had done everything in double-time, but now we were away from it, we had to slow down to the normal speed limit to avoid suspicion.

'You've got to let me out. I'm going back to look for my son.'

I held on to the door handle, forcing myself not to open it there and then.

Ronson looked in the mirror. 'No can do, Eddie, we've got company.'

I looked back to see a small black car shadowing us. It was Müller and Schmidt. Ronson swore and put her foot down, weaving from side to side to stop them from catching up. At the Pont Royal, she slewed the wheel hard to the left, nearly sending us skidding into the walls of the bridge as the car struggled to get a purchase on the cobbles. Coming out of the slide, she gunned the engine and the car lurched forward over the river to the opposite bank. When we'd turned off Quai d'Orsay, I caught a glimpse of Weber veering right into the narrow streets of the Left Bank. Ronson passed the Louvre and slowed down.

'Well, that's that. It must be Weber they're after.'

There was clear road behind us. No one chasing. But every turn was taking me further away from saving Jean-Luc. We zigzagged through the streets of Les Halles back to the river. There was no one following us and Ronson had brought the speed down to one that wouldn't invite a German checkpoint to pull us over.

'Still think Weber's evidence is fake? If this is a set-up, how come the Gestapo are after him?'

'Because they're not in on it. The Abwehr and the Gestapo never tell each other what they're doing.'

'The Abwehr? Are you telling me Hochstetter's involved in this? Resistance? You're one crazy cop, Eddie.'

We crossed to the Left Bank again and parked in a short street on the east side of the Jardin du Luxembourg.

'I've got to get back to Les Invalides,' I told her.

'Hitler's next stop is the Panthéon. That's nearer than Les

404

Invalides, but he won't get there yet. Come with me to see Weber and I'll take you straight after. I promise.'

Shaking my head, I made to leave, but suddenly saw Müller and Schmidt in their car, slowly cruising along the avenue towards us. They hadn't seen us so we ducked into the gardens and lost ourselves in the trees, heading for the ornamental pond. To our right we saw German guards on duty in striped sentry-boxes outside the palace. We carried on past. They weren't interested in us. I was being drawn yet further away. And I felt even more helpless without my gun.

We passed a young guy sitting on a bench. He looked the same age as Jean-Luc. For a brief moment, I wondered if he was also a deserter trying to get out of Paris, when I saw his trousers. They were army khakis. Recalling the young *poilu* shot in the street, I walked as near to him as I could and spoke hurriedly.

'You need to get off the streets and change your trousers. The Germans are arresting anyone they think is a French soldier.'

He simply stared at me. I recognised the same tired, haunted look I saw in my son's eyes. I insisted, but Ronson hurried me along. I turned once to look at the young man, but he hadn't moved. I felt again the horror of seeing Jean-Luc wearing his army trousers under his oversized coat.

Ronson wasn't to be deterred. Scanning the park all the time, she spoke to me. 'None of this means Weber's evidence is fake, Eddie. If anything, it makes it more real.'

'The one part of Weber's story I believe is his shock at what he saw in Poland. Not the cruelty, but the way Hitler is taking Germany down a dead-end path. This list is to get US support and bring down Hitler before things can get any worse. And before the Soviets and the Nazis turn on each other.'

She paused for a moment to look at me. 'Either way, we win.

The US enters the war and Hitler's stopped. Why worry if the *Sonderaktionsbuch* is fake if it gets the right result?'

I had no answer to that. We stole past the regimented rows of trees to our left. Normally a place of peace and shade from the sun, their ramrod-straight trunks and stiffly overflowing leaves now had the feel of an enemy army waiting in serried ranks to attack. Safer amid the overgrown paths, Ronson spoke again.

'But if it is fake, why not just hand the list over instead of this? Arrange a meet and give the US authorities the information?'

'Because after what you said happened to the British in the Netherlands, the Americans wouldn't buy it. That's why it had to look like the information was stolen and Weber was desperate to get away before he got caught.'

'I still don't see the problem, Eddie. Whatever it takes to bring Hitler down is worth it. Look around you. This is only going to get worse.'

The apiary was deserted when we got there, the bees calm in their hives under the tiled roof of the shelter. It was an ominous peace. Even in the shade of the trees, the heat was becoming oppressive. I was glad now I hadn't had time to put on a heavier jacket. Another car drove past beyond the gates, a rumble thrumming below the silence, and disappeared into the surrounding streets.

'If it is a fake,' Ronson said thoughtfully, 'and if Weber does have an accomplice, my money would be on Biehl. He's fanatical and ambitious, but not a fanatical and ambitious Nazi. He's the classic aristocratic German who wants all the gains Hitler's made, just without Hitler.'

'If it's a fake, it discredits any evidence coming out of Poland about the atrocities to ordinary people. It'll be another Venlo, making the Americans and the British sceptical about any sort of evidence that emerges. It will hide atrocities, not prove them.'

'Your Polish guy again. Sure you don't just want Weber for your own investigation here in Paris?'

I breathed in the scent of the aromatic plants. 'No. I know he didn't kill the refugees in the railway yard.'

I saw the look of shock on Ronson's face, but before she could reply, we both heard an iron gate squeal on its hinges and fell silent.

'It's Weber,' she said in a low voice.

We watched him come through the trees and cross to us at a quick walk. He was carrying a canvas satchel. He took his cap off and wiped his brow with the back of his hand before replacing it.

'I had to make the meeting now,' he explained to Ronson. 'The Führer keeps changing the route and I didn't want to get caught out before we could meet. He's at Les Invalides at the moment, visiting Napoleon's tomb. I couldn't have borne being there to see that. The only tomb I want to see now is Hitler's.'

'Nice speech,' I told him.

'You've got the *Sonderaktionsbuch*,' Ronson said in awe, gesturing at the satchel. Weber nodded, but held it more tightly to his chest.

'What do we do next?' the German asked her.

I'd been wondering that.

As it was, someone else decided for us.

It was Jean-Luc, emerging from behind the little shelter with the beehives in. He must have approached it across the lawn and through the trees, out of sight. I hid a gasp. As the day had grown warmer, he'd taken the raincoat off, his army trousers now clear to see. He had the gun in his hand. It was pointed at Weber. It had never been Hitler.

'Jean-Luc,' I pleaded. 'Go. Please.'

The gun wavered slightly but he kept it aimed at the German.

'I am a soldier. I haven't fought like you did and I haven't killed a German, but I am a soldier.'

'No, Jean-Luc, you don't understand. Not like this.'

He was near to tears, struggling to bring the gun under control in his shaking hand. 'I have to kill a German or I've failed in my duty. You must understand that. It's to help you. He's the man you told me about. The murderer of civilians. He deserves to die.'

The bees in their hives buzzed louder. As the humans danced around the little space, so the bees began to sound agitated.

'Jesus Christ, Eddie,' Ronson cursed.

I stood between Jean-Luc and Weber. 'No, Jean-Luc. This isn't the answer.'

'Stop protecting him.'

'I'm protecting you.'

In the confusion, Weber had pulled his own gun and was now pointing it at me. If I moved, he'd have a clear sight on my son. Jean-Luc edged around to try and get the German in his sights, so I followed him, my eyes darting back and forth between the two, making sure I was always between them.

'For Christ's sake,' Ronson hissed. 'We've got to get away.'

Above the hives, the bees began to gather in an angry mist.

A harsher sound rasped out of the shade to drown out the tense chorus in the apiary.

Someone had struck a match.

Panthéon

'Interesting scene we have here,' Hochstetter announced, emerging from the same side of the shelter as Jean-Luc had come.

Two Wehrmacht soldiers followed him, each one carrying a rifle. I glanced away to see another two appear at the gate, the officer and the feldwebel who had been accompanying us all morning. They stayed there, training their guns on our little tableau. Hochstetter finished lighting his cigarette and threw the match to the ground, unholstering his Luger in the same fluid movement. He looked from one of us to another.

'Now I know you, you and you,' he said, pointing his gun in turn at Ronson, Weber and me. 'But I don't know who *you* are.' He aimed the Luger more firmly in the direction of Jean-Luc.

I was caught. If I moved, I'd leave Weber with a clear bead on my son. If I didn't, Hochstetter had an unobstructed view of him. If I said anything, Hochstetter would know he was my son, which would put him in even greater danger and me at the bottom of the bargaining pile. If I said nothing, I had no doubt Hochstetter would shoot him without a moment's hesitation. It was only the German's curiosity that was keeping Jean-Luc alive. I threw as quick a glance as I could at my son, willing him to say nothing. In front of me, the noise from the hives was growing louder and the small moving clouds above them were becoming denser and more fluid.

Hochstetter spoke again. 'Would you care to enlighten me, young man? Although I see by your dress that you are an enemy soldier, so I would advise you to make it convincing.'

Jean-Luc looked to me for an answer, while my mind raced through the options I had. Anything I said or did would either lead to Jean-Luc being shot or to Hochstetter increasing his leverage over me. But the longer my son looked to me, the more Hochstetter would start to work it out.

From the trees, two more figures stepped into the arena, their pistols in their hands. Müller and Schmidt stopped a few metres apart. I saw a group of bees slowly detach from the swarm and drift towards Schmidt. Müller spoke.

'Major Hochstetter. Hauptmann Weber is of interest to the Gestapo. It is our intention to arrest him.'

Hochstetter had that expression of amused malevolence I'd come to recognise. 'I am sorry, but he is an officer in the Wehrmacht. I am afraid I'm not going to allow you to do that.'

'And we are afraid you have no choice in the matter, Major. We are the Gestapo. You have no jurisdiction.'

Before Hochstetter could answer, the group was stunned by the sound of a gunshot, deafening in the enclosed apiary. Instinctively, everyone recoiled, shrinking away and ducking their heads, but in my need to keep an eye on all those with a gun, I'd happened to be looking at Schmidt at just the right moment, so I was prepared for it. Dropping the Luger that he'd fired, he was shaking his hand in pain. A bee had stung him, and he'd pulled the trigger in reflex.

Able to react quicker than the others, I shouted at Jean-Luc to run. Turning back, I saw Ronson pull Weber away.

Hochstetter made no attempt to stop them, focused as he was on the two Gestapo men.

My way to where Jean-Luc had escaped was blocked, so I took the gate and made for the west side of the gardens, leaving the paths and running hard through the tall bushes. No gunshots or footsteps followed and I kept going until I found a gate and could get out of the gardens and allow the streets around them to swallow me up.

Leaning against a wall to catch my breath, I looked around but could hear nothing. Watching all the while, I started moving again, making my way to where Ronson had parked her car. Nearing the junction, where six roads came together, I saw Jean-Luc crouching in a doorway nearby. Without the coat, his army trousers seemed to me to shine like a beacon, obscuring any other feature, depersonalising him.

Walking forward, I heard an engine and saw Hochstetter's car cruising along the next street to the left, which led into the road where my son was hiding. As I tried to back away out of sight, Jean-Luc saw me and slowly emerged from his hiding place. I tried to wave him back, but he didn't understand what I was doing and kept on coming. Hochstetter would be on him in a matter of seconds.

I darted forward, out into the street and into the path of the staff car. It came to a halt centimetres from me and Hochstetter stood up in the back, the smile on his face once more. The officer in the front seat got out and walked towards me.

'Not so clever now, are you, policeman?' he said to me.

I couldn't see Jean-Luc, I just had to hope he'd guessed what was happening and stepped back into the doorway. I walked forward, towards the door that Hochstetter had pushed open for me.

'French bees have more balls than French soldiers,' the officer muttered to me as he slammed the door shut. He had an angry bee sting on the back of his neck, which cheered me slightly.

Hochstetter spoke sharply to him and turned to me, the urbane mask back in place. 'There is no need for crude vituperation, is there, Édouard?'

He tapped the door and the driver set off. We came out to where Jean-Luc had been hiding. He was nowhere in sight and I forced myself to look straight ahead. We drove up and down a couple of streets searching for Ronson and Weber, but Hochstetter looked at his watch and told the feldwebel to make his way to the next destination. His decision surprised me.

'The Panthéon. Another of the sights the Führer wishes to see. We really shouldn't keep him waiting.' He'd continued to speak in German after talking to his driver. When I gave no reaction, he laughed and switched back to French. 'Ah, Édouard, will I ever catch you out? Who was the young man in the gardens?'

He still hadn't caught me out. 'Hothead, I suppose. Protesting at Hitler's visit. Why do you still need me here?'

'I think what just happened in the gardens would answer that. And perhaps one or two others in our circus might decide to come by here too. I really wouldn't want you to miss it.'

We'd only been outside the Panthéon for a few moments when we saw Hitler emerge with his entourage. They were still moving at the same breakneck speed as when we last saw him. He had a tremendous scowl on his face and stopped to say something to the people around him, animated in displeasure.

'Somewhere else Adolf's not happy with.' I couldn't help myself.

The officer in the front seat turned, but Hochstetter held a hand up and he faced forward again. From the back, I could see his neck reddening, not just from the bee sting.

'Very droll, Édouard.' Hochstetter was the only one I couldn't rattle.

A car pulled up next to us and an officer got out. He had a small cut on his chin from where he must have nicked himself shaving in the morning's rush to roll the carpet out for Hitler. He said something to Hochstetter, who flared in a brief moment of fury before quickly ordering the feldwebel to drive back to the Jardin du Luxembourg. He took a moment to compose himself before turning to me to speak, but the anger I'd been unable to arouse was still apparent in his voice.

'With their customary excess of zeal, our friends in the Gestapo appear to have found our co-conspirators.' As we left, he looked at Hitler and the Panthéon thoughtfully. 'Another place of death. It appears that the two Gestapo officials have been seen by the Medici fountain in the gardens with two men and a woman, one of the men a Wehrmacht officer. I feel we are in somewhat of a hurry.'

I looked away from him to hide my panic. Somewhat of a hurry didn't come close. The car raced the short distance to the park but passed the entrance that Ronson and I had used such a little time earlier and went on to where the Medici fountain was, on the other side of the tall railings.

'You have to go back,' I called to the driver in German. 'There's no gate here, you have to go back to the entrance back there.'

Through the dense bushes and trees on the other side, I could see the high stone rear wall of the fountain. Someone was moving along the footpath at the other end. I gripped the seat in frustration. The driver quickly reversed to the gate and the four of us clambered out, none of them as quickly as I did.

I ran to the footpath as Hochstetter caught up with me. Together we raced towards the fountains. There were figures moving in the bushes that ran the length of the slender pool from the path to the carved wall of the fountain. No water was flowing and the place was silent but for the breeze picking at the leaves in the trees and the sound of feet crunching through the earth somewhere to the rear of the carved stonework.

We both saw the Gestapo men at the same time.

'I order you to halt,' Hochstetter called to them, but they ignored him.

They were both pointing their guns at someone hidden from our view behind the fountain. We ran towards them, the path by the side of the fountains seeming endless.

Hochstetter shouted again, 'Put down your weapons.'

He barked the order a second time, but his voice was drowned by the sound of gunshots.

We reached the end of the fountain. Two figures lay motionless on the ground. A third stood in shock between them and looked to me in fear as Müller and Schmidt took aim.

Sacré-Coeur

The handcuffs chafed my wrists.

Hochstetter stood next to me, leaning on the iron railing above the last short flight of steps leading into the Sacré-Coeur and dragging slowly on a cigarette. He was staring out over the city. The officer and the feldwebel were standing nearby, out of earshot. I tried to adjust the cuffs anchoring me to the railing. They were all that was stopping me from crumpling to the ground.

'The Führer has decided not to stage a triumphal parade through Paris,' Hochstetter told me. 'He wishes to spare the feelings of the people of the city.'

'Good of him. Could he also stop the marching bands going up and down the Champs-Élysées twice a day while he's at it?' I stared numbly into space. I was talking to keep myself together.

'Your voiced thoughts will get you into so much trouble one day, Édouard.'

I shook my handcuffs. 'I'm not now?' I wasn't sure I much cared.

Hitler had come and gone from the basilica. We saw him leave just a few moments ago. He'd stood near where we were now and looked out over the city. He hadn't gone in, an officer who'd been present had told Hochstetter. Apparently, he'd stood on the terrace and looked up at the building and said just one word: 'appalling'.

He had no idea how appalling. For the first time ever, I had to agree with something Hitler said. He was right. The Sacré-Coeur was appalling. It was a symbol of oppression and reprisal and humiliation, imposed on the city after the failure of the Communard uprising. It was discordant with the wishes of the people, built of a bright white stone and resembling a gaudy wedding cake that jarred with everything else about Paris, the result of one set of values riding roughshod over another. So it was ironic that Hitler should be the one to judge it.

'Who was the young man?' Hochstetter asked me.

I tried to answer but the words wouldn't come. I was almost grateful to the years of holding back the memories of the last war and the decisions I'd taken. They helped me now blot out the scene at the Medici fountain. The two figures lying dead on the ground. The third standing shocked and unharmed to one side of them. Still I didn't speak. I didn't trust myself to.

Hochstetter flicked his cigarette away and stood up straight. 'Ah, the Gestapo. One has to admire their childlike zeal and determination. They had Hauptmann Weber set firmly in their sights and they got to him, regardless of what others were trying to tell them. We are an efficient race, Édouard, but we are efficient individually. We each get our own job done but we don't appear to be too able to coordinate those jobs between ourselves.'

'You still beat us.' I couldn't keep the bitterness out of my voice.

He laughed at that. 'Your divisions have been even greater than ours for decades. But now the Gestapo have taken matters upon themselves and executed Hauptmann Weber. His plan to sell his soul to Ronson to save what was left of it has come to nothing. Fortunately, the papers he had on him are now in our possession.'

'You don't seem too concerned about Weber's death.'

'I have little regard for anyone who ceases to be of use to me. You would do well to remember that, Édouard. However, I will say that it is fortunate that we were able to spare Ronson's life, don't you think?'

A rivulet of sweat ran down my forehead into my eye. I had to bend down to my handcuffed hands to wipe it. I breathed in slowly as I did. I stood up straight again and focused on the buildings in the distance.

'Yes, it was fortunate.'

I relived the moment I rounded the corner at the Medici fountain with Hochstetter.

Ronson stood numb with fear. Weber lay dead at her feet to her left. Beyond him lay a third figure. The summer earth was stained an autumn copper. My eyes were drawn irrevocably to the army trousers, the blood stains on them deep and fresh.

'I guess you had a lucky escape, Eddie,' Ronson said to me, unable to keep the quiver out of her voice.

By force of numbers, Hochstetter forced Müller and Schmidt to hand her over to his own men. She turned to me as they led her away.

'I'm sorry.'

'Very fortunate,' I repeated to Hochstetter. 'What will happen to her?'

'Ronson? Even the Gestapo have the sense not to kill a neutral journalist. She will be deported as a non-desirable. She will possibly spend some time being questioned in Berlin, but she will be released and sent home to the United States.'

He looked directly at me. 'Who was the young man that the Gestapo executed?'

I made myself look him in the eyes to answer. 'I don't know.'

I turned away and stared out at the city at our feet. At the bottom of the first flight of steps below us stood the two cars in the convoy that Hochstetter had made me join less than three hours ago. Three hours in which the world had changed. Biehl was still sitting in the second car. For the first time, I saw the glint of metal around his wrists. I looked at my own handcuffs and felt nothing for him.

'What will happen to Biehl?' I asked.

'Obersturmbannführer Biehl. We have been observing him for some time. All the time that Hauptmann Weber was attempting to trade his supposed evidence with Ronson, it was Biehl who was pulling the strings. Between them, Biehl and Weber dreamed up a scheme to negotiate with the Americans to enlist their aid in bringing our government down.'

'But Biehl's in the SD. He's a Nazi.'

'Weber spoke many lies, but one thing that is true is that a small core of Nazi Party members have become rather disillusioned with Hitler. They see a danger in overstretching ourselves and in this devil's pact with the Soviet Union. They want him overthrown, but they want to keep the Nazi system of government in place.'

'Do you?'

'Another of your dangerous questions, Édouard. You are right, I am not a Nazi Party supporter, but I am German. I want a strong Germany with a powerful hold if we are to stop the Soviets from taking over Europe and if we are to avoid a return to the humiliation of Versailles. We have come too far to forgo all that we've won.'

'So Weber's list was fake?'

'Undeniably. The only way Biehl and his co-conspirators saw to achieve their aims was to concoct this fictitious list of Americans to be killed to garner support from the USA in deposing Hitler. Weber and Biehl colluded to convince Ronson of its credibility. That is why they killed Groves. While we're on the subject of fictitious evidence, your search for proof of supposed atrocities in Poland is equally a fool's errand.'

'Are you saying there weren't atrocities?'

'Of course there were. We know there were. In war, there are atrocities. By Germans, by Soviets, by French, by British. But the idea of a pre-ordained plan for extermination is so much fantasy, the imaginings of a crazed mind. There is no list or book or plan. Go home and get on with being a policeman.'

'Weber spoke of the systematic killing of civilians.'

'Weber told you what you wanted to hear. He knew you were chasing some rainbow of evidence from this unstable Pole who killed himself and his child. Weber simply used your own fantasies to sell his story to you.'

Hochstetter signalled to the officer in the front of Biehl's car and it slowly pulled out and drove away. Biehl sat motionless in the back.

'What will happen to him?'

'He'll have a choice. Suicide or execution. The question is what will happen to you. I must confess, I am in some confusion as to the part you played in all this.'

'I'm just a policeman. I was simply doing my job, investigating the murders.'

He lit another cigarette, picking the pieces of tobacco from between his lips. 'Yes, I believe you probably were. That tenacity I so admire in you. Unfortunately, the Gestapo's execution of Weber means that you will be unable to bring the murderer of these Polish refugees to justice.'

I held tightly onto the railings, the metal of the handcuffs cutting into my wrists. Hochstetter's triumph was too much to bear. 'War brutalises us.'

I looked up to see him staring intensely at me before the smile reappeared. 'For your own safety, perhaps you have to allow yourself to be brutalised for as long as it suits the people around you. Until then, I imagine it would be more prudent to leave matters as they are.' He paused before his final words. I saw an edge of resignation in his eyes. 'We will all live to fight another day.'

He reached towards me. I thought he was going to unlock my handcuffs, but instead he took my watch off my wrist. Checking the time, he put it an hour forward and carefully replaced it, fastening the buckle one notch too tight. It pinched my flesh.

'Now we are in harmony, Édouard. Please ensure it remains that way.'

Only then did he unlock the handcuffs. The blood flowed back into my hands, sending pinpricks of pain through my fingers. I rubbed them to try and improve the circulation.

'This has been an interesting morning, Édouard, but I'm afraid it must come to an end now. I am sure you can find your own way back into the city.'

I watched him summon the officer and the feldwebel and they went down the steps to their waiting car. After the car had vanished down the hill, I collapsed heavily against the iron railings warmed by the sun and held my eyes squeezed tightly shut. Finally, I picked myself up and walked down the steps, heading for the Metro station at the foot of Montmartre.

Le Bourget

The air was chill underground. I leaned the back of my head against the Metro carriage and closed my eyes to the truth and the emotions that I had blotted out while Hochstetter had held me in manacles. But now it filled my thoughts. No matter how much I fought inside my own head, my mind returned to the Jardin du Luxembourg. To the image at the Medici fountain. It was one I knew would find its way into my dreams in the nights to come in my desolate apartment.

My thoughts were disturbed by the sound of laughter. I opened my eyes to see two German soldiers flirting with two young French women. I stared at them for a moment, but had to look away before one of them noticed me. I knew I wouldn't be able to contain my rage.

Instead, I channelled my thoughts into thinking of all that Hochstetter had told me. I wished I could talk to Ronson and tell her everything that I now understood. I knew she'd tell me that nothing worth having was easy to get. And she'd be right. Because that's exactly what Hochstetter had done. He'd presented it as though he were sacrificing Weber to smooth the path of the occupation in Paris. Make it look like they were being fair and honest. Only he was never really offering me Weber. He'd placed him firmly in my sights while telling me how difficult it would be for me to question him, each time giving me a bit more information, then standing in my way, then revealing a little more. The harder he'd made it for me to interview Weber and the more he'd put suspicion on him, the more credible Weber had become as someone wanting to buy his way out. The higher the stakes and the harder the tasks, the more real the prize, which is what had appealed to Ronson.

And this mirrored precisely what Hochstetter had just done with Biehl. I knew Groves' death was nothing to do with the *Sonderaktionsbuch*, but rather Biehl's ploy to get rid of me to put Auban in my place. Hochstetter arguing otherwise had been his first mistake. It told me that Biehl had not conspired with Weber. Hochstetter had.

He'd known that I'd been in Compiègne on Friday because Weber had told him. I had no proof, but I was sure the soldiers turning up in the woods but failing to capture us had been another of Hochstetter's ploys to convince Ronson of Weber's cause. My being there was an added bonus. And every time Weber looked like he was going to crash and burn, Hochstetter had been the one who was there to pull the chestnuts out of the fire. In the gardens this morning, he hadn't stopped Weber and Ronson from getting away. And he'd taken the strange decision not to pursue them, but to go to the Panthéon instead, I'm sure to give them time to go through with the supposed handover. When Biehl had come to Weber's flat, it had been to look for me after the events at the railway yard. Hochstetter, I'm certain, was there to protect Weber. He'd been the one to pull me from Weber's flat. The one to threaten me any time I strayed off the score he'd composed for me. The conductor in the Schwarze Kapelle, directing the movements for the black orchestra.

Biehl turning up in Paris had been a complication. Hochstetter had had to fend the SD off while carrying on with the charade, but in the end, it had worked in his favour as it had added yet more credibility to his cause. By his own admission, Hochstetter wasn't a Nazi. Everything that he'd just told me of Biehl's motives were his own. He was the one to want to bring Hitler down while keeping all the gains. The one prepared to take the high risks to get what he wanted. And now with Weber dead, he'd been able to make the SD man the scapegoat to cover his own tracks. I sighed heavily, another slice of justice that would go unserved.

As my train pulled into the station, I recalled his final remark and the look in his eyes. There was resignation at the failure of his plan but also pragmatism. 'We will all live to fight another day.' I was sure he would. And that would be my fight.

Up in the fresh air, I retrieved Ronson's car from its deserted street and drove it back to my flat to wait. It was the grandest vehicle my building had ever seen. I wondered what I was going to do with it.

At the top of a staircase mercifully free of Monsieur Henri, I opened the door and breathed the scent of nothing. It no longer had the feel of my flat. Jozef and his team had turned it into a sterile cage. Releasing a roar of anger, I kicked over the low table, the one where I would store the Luger bullets while I went through the ritual of failing to kill myself. I felt the dud bullet in my pocket, but I wasn't finished yet. I pulled what few ornaments I had off the shelves and hurled them at the wall opposite, their shards zipping past me in rebound. I saw my chair, my lonely chair, and I kicked and kicked at it again and again until I collapsed into it and felt it pull me into its embrace.

My breath came in waves and I sat and calmed myself, looking at the debris on the floor. Standing up, I righted the table and put it carefully back into place. I felt a remorse at hurting the only home I'd known and I thought of Ronson. In the few days I had known her, she had been as near to a friend as I had come since the last war. I wondered if I'd see her again for as long as we lived under Nazi rule. I thought again of her belief in Weber's fake evidence and I wished I'd gone along with it. Even fake evidence of Nazi atrocities was more than we had now and it might have led to some good.

Lying on the floor in front of me was the Céline book. It was the only book I'd thrown at the wall in my anger, but now I couldn't help feeling a sense of shame at mistreating the one possession of Fryderyk's that had survived. It lay now, its spine ripped, the front cover hanging loose like a broken arm. The pamphlet lay nearby, its pages open.

Picking them both up, I replaced the pamphlet inside the book and closed the damaged front cover over it. Placing it on the table, I couldn't help remembering the moment I found it among the contents of Fryderyk's safe just nine days earlier. Why Fryderyk would have a safe and why he'd keep these specific items in it still nagged at me. Closing my eyes, I recreated in my mind the way I'd first seen them. The three books topped and tailed by the two thin card folders, the one on top containing letters bound together, the one at the bottom with photographs. Fryderyk had been a printer and a bookbinder. There had to be a reason for these three books. The one written by Ewa and the one printed by Fryderyk would have held sentimental value, but the Céline book was the cuckoo in the nest. I put myself into Fryderyk's mind as much as I could. If there was one item of all those in the safe that would be expendable, it was the book now in front of me.

Remembering what I'd done to Jan's bear and apologising to Fryderyk, I pulled the front and back covers completely off the book. They came away in one piece. Separating the endpapers,

I found nothing hidden underneath either, but as I pulled them away, I felt the cover itself give. Tearing the paper away, I slid out the card forming the front cover and saw that it was made up of two pieces of finer card bound together like the two folders. Or like a book. A book inside a book. Immediately I looked at the pamphlet on the table and back at the package in my hands.

'*You're* the pamphlet.'

I opened out the plain covers to find a first page in solid script, printed in German, and my hands began to shake. Instead of *Sonderaktionsbuch*, it read *Sonderfahndungsbuch Polen* in heavy Germanic script. Not the list of US targets that Weber had promised, but a Special Prosecution Book for Poland. I could only roughly make out the formal legal language of the opening page, but it looked like the preamble to the point of the document, the rationale for what was to come.

Not fully understanding, I went to the end of the pamphlet and found an internal SS memo, describing the purpose of the *Sonderfahndungsbuch* and issuing instructions. My hands felt foul holding the paper, a sensation that deepened the more of the document I read. I was reading a list with the names of over sixty thousand people drawn up before the war by the Nazi Party and the *Volksdeutsche*. All the people in the book were to be arrested and either executed or interned after the successful annexation of the country. As I read on, I expected to find the names of senior figures. Instead, it referred to ordinary people in what the document called *Intelligenzaktion*. Academics, artists, writers, doctors, lawyers, sportspeople. All targets. All to be executed.

I put the pamphlet down and shook with horror. I thought of Ewa. She wasn't killed in a random act, but chosen for execution because she was a teacher and because she had written a school textbook. Lucja was right. The rumours were bad enough. The truth was horrific.

Turning back to the document itself, I realised it was only a small part of what the original must be like, as one page ended mid-sentence and the next began with a list of names. I realised the letter was 'G'. Fryderyk hadn't had room to put everything here, so he'd just included the most relevant parts. And these were the parts of his evidence that he'd held back from the French authorities, fearful of letting it all out of his sight, or hoping to find other more amenable recipients.

Scanning through the pages, I found he'd kept the most personal and painful part. In the middle of a list of names that meant nothing to me, and probably also to the people who'd used it to execute their victims, I saw Ewa's name, followed by an address and the word 'Bydgoszcz'. Fryderyk's name came below hers. I ran my fingers over their names. Fryderyk had used the totemic power of books and the Céline tract to show what the Nazis were doing in Poland. One last touch of defiance.

'I wish I'd known you in life, Fryderyk,' I whispered.

Quickly, I undid the back cover and found a slightly different package. The card folder was in the form of an envelope. I shook it and three pieces of paper fell out. Turning the first one over, I saw it was a handwritten note in Polish, which I couldn't understand.

The other two pieces of paper were photographs.

The first showed a line of people from behind, their hands clasped on top of their heads. They were walking along a storm ditch by the side of a road. One of the women had a distinctive hairstyle, tied low on her back. I closed my eyes for a moment and opened them to look at the second picture.

The first person I saw was Ewa. The line of people had turned to face the front. To one side, a squad of German soldiers pointed rifles at them, a puff of smoke emerging from one of them. The man next to Ewa was folding, crumpling to the ground. Ewa looked straight ahead, at the expressionless soldiers in front of her. Weber was standing in their midst, his pistol raised.

I don't know how long I stared at the photograph. Probably only a matter of seconds, but I thought of Hochstetter claiming that the idea of a plan to exterminate civilians was the fantasy of a crazed mind. He was right, only not in the way he meant. I looked at the photo of Ewa and I couldn't feel triumphant. I touched her face in it.

'I'm so sorry.'

I didn't hear a key in the door, just a voice.

'Father?'

Holding the documents in my hands, I looked up to see Jean-Luc walking into the room.

I'd been expecting him.

Placing everything carefully on the table, I stood up and went to him. For the first time since he was a child, I embraced him, squeezing him as tightly as I'd ever wanted anything. The tears that had never come to me since the morning I stood between my two friends as they were obliterated in the trench finally came and I wept.

'What is it?' he asked.

I let him go and looked at him. I couldn't speak.

I pictured again the scene at the Medici fountain. In their hurried search in the park, the Gestapo had arrested the young man I'd spoken to earlier instead of Jean-Luc. They hadn't had a good enough view of my son in the apiary, and they'd been unable to see beyond the army trousers. All they'd seen was the uniform, not the individual. The next time I saw the young man was after they'd marched him away and lined him up alongside

Ronson and Weber and shot him, mistaking him for my son. I hadn't dared show any sign to the Gestapo or to Hochstetter of the relief that I felt. And I didn't dare show Jean-Luc now any sign of my guilt at the relief I'd felt that another young man had died in his place. I knew I could never tell him the truth of what happened in the Jardin du Luxembourg.

He looked crestfallen, dissonant with my own joy. 'I failed. I didn't kill that German officer.'

'Don't be so eager to kill, Jean-Luc. He's dead. The Gestapo shot him.'

'It should have been me.'

I held him. He was unaware of the meaning of his words.

'Come on, we need to go.'

We took Ronson's car and I drove carefully through the city to Neuilly-sur-Seine. There were no German soldiers in its leafy avenues and it was easy to believe for a moment that the city hadn't been occupied. I parked inside the grounds of the American Hospital and we walked through to the gardens at the rear to find Lucja sitting on a straight-backed chair placed under the trees. The two British soldiers were sitting next to her. When she saw us, she smiled and got up. Her forearm was swathed in a clean bandage and held in place with a sling.

'I thought you'd still be in bed,' I told her.

'I'm getting good care. But I need to get out of here.'

The doctor emerged from a door and, in a mix of French and English, told us that the infection had lowered dramatically and that the fever had gone. 'We have Dawson and Jenkins to thank for her care.'

I looked at each of them in turn and I wondered at how distant the war seemed and at how it was precisely because of the war that I was in this peaceful place with these people with whom I felt an ease that I rarely experienced. Out of the corner of my eye, I saw Lucja looking at me. She called me closer and spoke to me.

'Are you going to arrest me? I killed someone. What I did was wrong.' We sat in silence for a moment. A bee busied itself among the scented flowers.

'Sometimes justice can only be served by killing.'

She shook her head sadly. 'You don't believe that, Eddie.'

'I didn't.'

I watched Jean-Luc laughing with the two British soldiers under the shade of a plane tree. I didn't know he spoke English. The world had changed for all of us.

'It's all been for nothing,' Lucja said in a low voice. 'We still have nothing that will make the world believe what is going on in my country.'

'Yes, we do.'

Holding the Céline book out to her, I took the covers apart and shook out the papers hidden in the front and rear pockets before handing them to her. The first thing she saw were the two photographs. She almost dropped them in loathing, her hands shaking. I pointed to the woman facing the guns.

'That's Ewa Gorecki.'

'And Fryderyk had these photographs?'

She looked at the documents stitched together as a pamphlet.

'The *Sonderfahndungsbuch Polen*,' she whispered. She stared at the thick, unforgiving letters of the title.

'It's not the whole document. It's what Fryderyk kept back from the French authorities, but it gives an exact idea of what the original document is, and a list of some of the names.'

Lucja shook with a rage I couldn't imagine. 'These weren't chance atrocities of war. The heat of conquest. This was a cold, systematic plan to destroy lives.'

I read again the mention of a list of sixty thousand people drawn up for execution. 'Who are the *Volksdeutsche*?'

'Ethnic Germans in Poland.' She looked at the document again. 'We had neighbours and members of my faculty who were *Volksdeutsche*. They might have been involved in this. People we knew turned on us and condemned us to death without our knowing.'

I thought of Auban and others like him. 'I think we're going to see more of that before the Nazis are through.' I pointed at the letter with the two photographs. 'There's this note in Polish. I don't know what it means.'

She unfolded the handwritten note and scanned it quickly. Her voice faltered as she translated the gist of the letter. 'It was written by Fryderyk. It tells of how a resistance fighter who knew him had found the photos on an SS officer that they'd killed in an ambush. He was carrying a briefcase with the entire document and the photos. The man recognised Ewa and took the photos to Fryderyk, who was in hiding, waiting to get out of Poland. The resistance fighter entrusted the document and the photos to him.' She put the note down for a moment. 'Poor Fryderyk, what he went through. It says here too that the pages with names beginning with the letters "G" to "K" and the rationale and the two photos were all he had left, the rest of the document and another photo had been kept by the French authorities.'

'If he'd given these to the authorities, they'd all be missing now.'

I showed her the page where Ewa's name appeared above Fryderyk's. Without a word, she took the pages from me and flicked back through them before stopping. She pointed to a name. Zofia Galka.

'Do you know her?' I asked.

'That's my real name. I was on the list for extermination. The name above, Tomasz Galka, that is my husband. He was also a lecturer. On the day the Germans came, he was led past me in the corridor and we didn't dare acknowledge each other. Or say goodbye. The last time I saw him he was being herded onto the back of a German lorry.'

I closed my eyes and recalled her terror at the lorry that Borek was being forced into outside the Majestic.

'Why didn't Fryderyk just tell us?' she asked.

'He didn't trust anyone. Our authorities had failed him and he didn't know who to trust among the Poles. He was disturbed by everything he'd seen and by his fear of the Germans invading all over again. He didn't know what the right thing to do was, so he did the only thing he thought he could do.'

'Killing himself and his son?'

I considered Fryderyk again. I knew what fear and its aftermath could do to your mind. What it had done to mine. 'Maybe it was that dilemma that made him choose the way he did.'

I put the parts of the book back together and handed it to her.

'What am I supposed to do with it?'

'Take it to London. Show it to your government in exile and let them do with it what they will.'

'How do I get to London?'

I explained that Ronson's car was parked out in the front courtyard of the hospital. 'It has six cans of petrol and it's got WH licence plates. That means that to all intents and purposes it's a German car. You're very unlikely to be stopped. Ronson said that boats were still leaving Lisbon for London. Your best chance is to travel down to Spain and then on to Lisbon.'

She held up her arm in its sling. 'I can't drive.'

'You won't. You'll be going with my son.'

'Your son?'

I introduced her to Jean-Luc for the first time. 'He was in the army but got separated from his unit. He's trapped, just as you are. You both need to get away from Paris. You both want to get to London, you to join your government, Jean-Luc to enlist with the Free French. Together, you drive as far down through France as is safe and you get to Lisbon. If you have to abandon the car if it gets too dangerous, at least you'll have got out of Paris and got part of the way out of the country.'

I could see Jean-Luc staring at me, deep in thought, and then nod his head once. Jenkins and Dawson started saying something after it had been translated for them, and Lucja explained to me what they'd said.

'They want to come. They want to get back to their own country.'

'It's too dangerous. Two of you travelling won't arouse suspicion. Four of you will. And they don't speak French.'

Lucja held her arm up. 'The wound on my arm hasn't healed yet. It'll still need attention so it doesn't go septic again. They can do that.'

The two Britons looked at me expectantly.

'It's a good idea, Father,' Jean-Luc said. 'Four of us working together. We should all go.'

I looked at Jean-Luc and tried not to think of losing him again so soon.

'Yes.'

Lucja and Jean-Luc had nothing but the clothes they were wearing. The doctor and a nurse disappeared for a few minutes and came back with a change of trousers for Jean-Luc and some other clothing and food from the hospital kitchen. Jenkins and Dawson were away just two minutes grabbing a small canvas kitbag each. They were ready to go before I was ready for them to leave.

They left quickly, Jean-Luc driving, Lucja in the passenger seat and the two British men in the back. Jean-Luc tried to say something before he left, but he just looked at me.

'Go,' I told him.

I turned away as they drove through the gates, unable to watch. In my pocket, I felt the Luger bullet. Taking it out, I looked at it thoughtfully, tempted to hurl it into the bushes. Instead, I put it back in my pocket. Who knew what need I'd have of it in the days to come.

Above me, the sound of a plane throbbed through the calm. I looked up to see a German military aircraft lazily circling the city. I knew instinctively it was Hitler, leaving Le Bourget, taking one last look at his conquest before heading back to his wolf's gorge.

I remembered my son's comment about living with a clenched fist in our pocket and I curled my hand into an imaginary gun in mine and recalled Ronson.

'Bang,' I whispered.

I looked down to the ground again and walked alone out of the hospital gates. In silent streets beyond their protection, I slipped my watch off and pushed the hour back.

'This is my time.'

Postscript

'How did you know?'

An oil lamp threw flickering shadows of us both onto the inside of the blackout curtains. They rose and fell with the flame, threatening to devour. High above the marshalling yard, all sounds were muted by the night. Le Bailly was calm as he put his thick coffee down on the table between us.

'I could never understand why Hochstetter arrested you,' I told him. 'I couldn't see why he needed to question you. Until I learned more about how he worked. He wasn't questioning you, he was recruiting you. That's when things began to fall into place. Hochstetter knew I spoke German. You knew about my time as a prisoner of war. I figured you had to be the one who told him.'

'I had no choice. You've seen the position I'm in. It was either become an informant for him or prison. I told you, I couldn't face the thought of that. I'd die first.'

'Hochstetter's forceful,' I conceded. 'He has ways of making you cooperate. In your case to keep you as a Communist safe.'

'He wanted me to keep the workers in line and ensure things ran smoothly. But then he started demanding information. Who came here, what went on in the huts, who did what. He

434

wanted to know more and more. I'm sorry I told him about you, but you must see I had no choice.'

'Yes, I do. But that's not really the problem here, is it? You being a Communist.' High in the sky, the drone of planes thrummed to the bone, no doubt the RAF looking for a target. 'The problem is that Hochstetter found out that you'd killed the four Polish refugees. And that's the hold he had over you.'

He didn't deny it. He simply stared at me through the tendrils of steam rising from his coffee. 'That's the protection I have. From you.'

I recalled Hochstetter's veiled threat on the steps of Sacré-Coeur about leaving matters as they were. 'True. Hochstetter's made it clear you have that, and that I can't do anything. Not for now. What you don't have is protection from yourself.'

He looked calmer. 'So how did you know? You know you can't arrest me, so you might as well tell me.'

'You did the same as Hochstetter. You kept pushing me in the direction of suspecting others. First towards Papin and Font, then towards the Germans when I gave you the possibility of it being them. You also changed your story about who got to the yards first. You said at first that the Germans were already here when you came to work, but later you mentioned seeing them turn up.'

'You can't always remember everything.' He drank his coffee slowly. His sangfroid was beginning to get under my skin.

'But what really gave you away was that you knew the gas used was white star. We hadn't ever said what it was. We thought at first it was chlorine. Only someone who'd handled the canisters could have known what type of gas was used.'

He looked at me and nodded his head slowly. 'If it means anything, I panicked. I did mean to help them, but when the

Boches turned up, I had no choice. It was too late to get them away. There was nothing I could do.'

My cool vanished as his grew. 'There was always something you could have done that wasn't killing four innocent men.'

He shook his head, a dismissive gesture. 'I was trying to help. They came to me and told me they'd been robbed by the gang at the Cheval Noir. They were desperate and I took pity on them, even though I knew it was risky. But then the Germans came and I didn't know what to do.'

'Why don't I believe you?'

'It was the first and last time I ever tried getting people away.'

'The last? What about Friday night? You had one planned for then, a trap for the *poilus*. And my son.'

He finally looked shocked at the mention of my son. 'No, I had nothing planned.'

'I saw a white star chalked on the truck. That was the one you were going to use to put the *poilus* in. A sign so you could find it in the blackout. But the Germans coming here ruined your plan.'

He snorted. 'The trucks are covered in signs. We use them all the time. That means nothing. You can believe what you want to believe.'

'You're not going to tell me?'

I needed him to confess, to know I'd done the right thing. But I could see in the stubborn set of his jaw that I'd get nothing more out of him.

His confidence returning, he took a long drink of his foul coffee. 'This is interesting, but I have work to do. I have to keep the trains running.'

'I haven't finished.'

I placed my service pistol in front of me, my insurance policy. Silently, I pulled the Luger out of my pocket and lined the six shells up on the table. He watched, rapt, fear slowly dawning on him.

'You said you'd sooner die than face prison. This is a game I play to assuage my guilt.'

I held out the six shells for him to choose one.

I had no idea which one was the dud.

Author's Note

This book is a work of fiction but it has its basis in fact. The *Sonderfahndungsbuch Polen* did exist. Containing around 61,000 names, the Special Prosecution Book Poland identified the groups of Polish civilians who were to be executed or interned in concentration camps after the German invasion of Poland. Citing lengthy lists of undesirable individuals, including academics, political activists, teachers, actors, nobility, priests, doctors, lawyers, retired army officers and sportspeople, the document had been drawn up before the war by the *Zentralstelle IIP Polen*, or Central Unit IIP Poland of the Gestapo, which was created by Reinhard Heydrich to coordinate Operation Tannenberg and *Intelligenzaktion*, the names the Nazis used for the extermination of Polish civilians. As with the country's Jewish population, the mass killings were carried out by SS *Einsatzgruppen* and *Volksdeutscher Selbstschutz* units, the latter being a paramilitary organisation of ethnic Germans in Poland, with some help from Wehrmacht units.

Massacres really did take place in and around the town of Bydgoszcz, their victims including teachers from local schools, and it is estimated that around 10,500 people were murdered there in the first year of the Nazi invasion. Many of them were buried in mass graves in a valley outside the town, today marked by a memorial.

The *Sonderaktionsbuch* of influential US figures and the plot, real or otherwise, that Weber speaks of is an invention for this book. As far as I know, there was no plot or plan of this kind. What is based on fact is when Weber describes attending a conference where Hitler spoke of killing without pity or mercy all men, women or children of the Polish race or language. This is known as the 'Obersalzberg Speech' and was made to Wehrmacht commanders on 22 August 1939, a week before the invasion of Poland. A copy of it was used as evidence in the Nuremberg trials.

As in the book, there is no record of a prosecution list being compiled for France, but a similar document was produced for Britain in the event of a German occupation. Originally known as the *Sonderfahndungsliste G.B.*, it became known after the war as 'The Black Book' and contained nearly 3,000 names of prominent people in Britain who were to be arrested, although the book is notable for its errors and inconsistencies, including people who had already died, others who had left Britain and a number of omissions of outspoken critics of the Nazis.

As with many invasions before and since the fall of Paris, the victors who had been so effective in waging war found an inability to establish an efficient peace. The first weeks of the occupation were marked by confusion and constant changes in the governing of the city. This extended to the positions of German individuals and offices responsible for the everyday running of Paris and its institutions. It also led to unusual alliances and truces. One of these was evident in the treatment of French Communists in the first year of occupation. The Nazi-Soviet Pact, allied with this confusion, meant that while many Communists were arrested and harassed, others enjoyed an uneasy tolerance and even some degree of immunity. Ultimately, the effect of this was to bring members of the Communist party out into the open and into the gaze of the occupiers, which eventually became their downfall when Hitler turned on the Soviet Union the following year.

Part of this confusion was the arrival of the Gestapo in Paris. As in the book, they were prohibited by Hitler from accompanying the army, at the Wehrmacht's insistence, so Himmler and Heydrich concocted the plot of sending some twenty of them disguised as Geheime Feldpolizei, which acted as a bridgehead to establish a headquarters in the city. During the occupation, the name Gestapo came to be used indiscriminately by the French to describe the SD (SS intelligence service), the Sipo (state security police) and the Gestapo itself, a sub-department of the Sipo.

The key players in the story are entirely fictional, although with a view to placing it within its historical context, some real characters have been mentioned or appear as minor characters in the narrative. One of these is Roger Langeron, the Paris Prefect of Police, who did indeed tour the city's police stations at least twice on the day the Germans entered the city. The promises made by the senior German officers that Langeron relays to the police at Thirty-Six in this story are based on his real conversations with the invaders on that morning and the assurances they made him.

Another real character is Doctor Thierry de Martel, a celebrated neurosurgeon, who committed suicide rather than see the German occupation of the city. When newspapers began to appear in the kiosks again during the following week, they gave extensive coverage to his death to the exclusion of many other stories, most probably because of their inability to print much else given Nazi censorship. Regarding the matter of the suicides that Eddie witnesses, it is known that there were at least fifteen people in the city who killed themselves on the first day of the occupation. In a city that had lost over two-thirds of its population owing to so many Parisians having fled in the weeks leading up the occupation, this is an astonishing figure that would have had an effect on the police trying to keep order on that day.

Finally, strange as it may seem, there is still uncertainty regarding the date Hitler visited Paris, and it is likely he only spent a few hours in the city on the one occasion he went there. The two most commonly-quoted dates are Sunday 23 June and Friday 28 June. At least three of his entourage on that day, including Hitler's favourite sculptor Arno Breker and architect Hermann Giesler, cite the visit as having taken place on 23 June. Architect Albert Speer and Hitler's adjutant Nicolaus von Below claim the date was 28 June. Everything I've read leads me to believe that Sunday 23 June is more likely to be the correct date, and it is the one that I have chosen to use in this book.

What is known is that it was a whistle-stop tour of the main sights of the city. While he was in the city, it is claimed that Hitler didn't meet any French officials or the press, he didn't go into any French home, he didn't speak to any French person, his visit simply surprised a few people out and about that morning who weren't even sure it was actually him. It wasn't widely known even among the Germans in Paris that Hitler was coming to Paris. Most German officials only knew almost at the last minute, and they had to get keys to the various sites by getting the French curators out of bed at six o'clock in the morning. As the tour was so early in the day, and was over by nine o'clock, only a few French people witnessed Hitler's visit, and the international press corps got up later in the day to discover he'd been there and they'd missed him. It was said at the time with some irony that he wasn't even in the city long enough to go to the toilet!

And for a second and final 'finally', the rumours to which Eddie is subjected by his neighbour, Monsieur Henri, are all genuine rumours that were making the rounds in the early days of the occupation, which only goes to show that little changes.

Acknowledgements

Perhaps the first debt of gratitude I have is to Paris and the people of Paris whose stories inspired Eddie and this series. When you write novels set in this era, history has a habit of tugging at your sleeve – from the bullet holes in the police station where Eddie works to every street corner with a plaque commemorating a fallen Resistance fighter – but the moment that stopped me in my tracks was the small panel on a primary school in the Pletzel with the names and ages of the children from the school who never returned from Auschwitz. That one vision taught me that despite the apparent flippancy of Eddie's reactions to occupation and despite this being a work of fiction, my duty was to try to tell his story and that of Paris with honesty and respect. So, to Paris, thank you, with all my admiration and affection.

Three museums provided me with a great deal of insight and inspiration, and I would wholeheartedly recommend a visit to anyone interested in this period: Musée de la Libération de Paris - Musée du Général Leclerc - Musée Jean Moulin, on Avenue du Colonel Henri Rol-Tanguy in the 14th; Musée de la Résistance National, in Champigny-sur-Marne (currently moving to a new home); and Musée de la Préfecture de Police, on Rue de la Montagne Ste Genevieve in the 5th. Of the non-fiction books that have helped me in my research for the book, specifically this period of the very early days of the Occupation, I would highlight *The Last Days of Paris* by Alexander Werth; *The Fall of Paris: June 1940* by Herbert Lottman; *Diary of the Dark Years 1940-1944* by Jean Guéhenno; *Occupation: The Ordeal of France 1940-1944* by Ian Ousby; *Nazi Paris: The History of an Occupation 1940-1944* by Allan Mitchell; and *France: The Dark Years 1940-1944* by Julian Jackson.

It's a tremendous privilege to be published by Orion and I'd like to thank my publisher for believing in Eddie and in me, most especially Emad Akhtar and Lucy Frederick, who are not just brilliant editors and lovely people, but two of the best teachers I've ever had. If you've enjoyed Eddie and his story, so much of that is thanks to their wonderful insight and mentoring – the other bits are all my fault. Thank you too to the amazing team at Orion, who have all bowled me over with their extraordinary talent and professionalism. I'd also like to thank freelance copy editor Jon Appleton for all his hard work spotting the things I missed. And thank you also to Craig Lye for championing Eddie right from the start.

I know I probably harp on about this, but you also need a really good agent, and I'm lucky enough to have the best in Ella Kahn. A big thank you as always to Ella for her endless well of wonderfulness, not to mention her hard work, amazing skill and even more amazing belief in me.

And, finally, my thanks as ever to my wife Liz for all her love, support and patience. Large parts of this book have seen the light thanks to Liz knowing just the right time to suggest tea and when wine was called for. Thank you with everything I have.

Credits

Chris Lloyd and Orion Fiction would like to thank everyone at Orion who worked on the publication of *The Unwanted Dead* in the UK.

Editorial
Emad Akhtar
Lucy Frederick

Copy editor
Jon Appleton

Proof reader
Linda Joyce

Audio
Paul Stark
Amber Bates

Contracts
Anne Goddard
Paul Bulos
Jake Alderson

Design
Debbie Holmes
Joanna Ridley
Nick May

Editorial Management
Charlie Panayiotou
Jane Hughes
Alice Davis

Operations
Jo Jacobs
Sharon Willis
Lisa Pryde
Lucy Brem

Production
Ruth Sharvell

Finance
Jasdip Nandra
Afeera Ahmed
Elizabeth Beaumont
Sue Baker

Marketing
Lucy Cameron

Publicity
Alainna Hadjigeorgiou

Operations
Jo Jacobs
Sharon Willis
Lisa Pryde
Lucy Brem

Rights
Susan Howe
Krystyna Kujawinska
Jessica Purdue
Richard King
Louise Henderson

Sales
Jennifer Wilson
Esther Waters
Victoria Laws
Rachael Hum
Ellie Kyrke-Smith
Frances Doyle
Georgina Cutler